About the Author

Gerald Seymour spent fifteen years as an international television news reporter with ITN, covering Vietnam and the Middle East, and specialising in the subject of terrorism across the world. Seymour was on the streets of Londonderry on the afternoon of Bloody Sunday, and was a witness to the massacre of Israeli athletes at the Munich Olympics.

Gerald Seymour exploded onto the literary scene with the massive bestseller *Harry's Game*. He has been a full-time writer since 1975, and six of his novels have been filmed for television in the UK and US. *A Damned Serious Business* is his thirty-fourth novel.

Also by Gerald Seymour

Harry's Game
The Glory Boys
Kingfisher
Red Fox
The Contract
Archangel
In Honour Bound
Field of Blood
A Song in the Morning
At Close Quarters
Home Run
Condition Black
The Journeyman Tailor
The Fighting Man
The Heart of Danger
Killing Ground
The Waiting Time
A Line in the Sand
Holding the Zero
The Untouchable
Traitor's Kiss
The Unknown Soldier
Rat Run
The Walking Dead
Timebomb
The Collaborator
The Dealer and the Dead
A Deniable Death
The Outsiders
The Corporal's Wife
Vagabond
No Mortal Thing
Jericho's War

A DAMNED SERIOUS BUSINESS

Gerald Seymour

HODDER

First published in Great Britain in 2018 by Hodder & Stoughton
An Hachette UK company

This paperback edition published in 2018

1

A CIP catalogue record for this title is available from the British Library

B format ISBN 978 1 473 66351 0
eBook ISBN 978 1 473 66350 3

Typeset in Plantin Light by Hewer Text UK Ltd, Edinburgh
Printed and bound in Great Britain by Clays Ltd, Elcograf S.p.A.

Hodder & Stoughton policy is to use papers that are natural, renewable
and recyclable products and made from wood grown in sustainable
forests. The logging and manufacturing processes are expected to
conform to the environmental regulations of the country of origin.

Hodder & Stoughton Ltd
Carmelite House
50 Victoria Embankment
London EC4Y 0DZ

www.hodder.co.uk

For Gillian

PROLOGUE

He waited for his target to emerge.

Not a problem for Boot. He was blessed, the few who knew him well told him, with near limitless patience. He had no tic movements, did not lick his lips to moisten them, scratch at an imagined mole on his cheek, ruffle his hair. He was sitting in the back of a saloon car that had comfortable upholstery, and he shared the seat with an officer of the Swedish sister service. They, and the escort provided for them, had been enjoying coffee on a street leading into the square, Kornhamnstorg. Boot had been listening to the officer telling him of a son who had graduated to the ceremonial guard at the Royal Palace on the far side of the Old City, and he had been showing polite interest, when the message had come through. They'd bolted, the story unfinished.

Parking spaces for their car, and the escort vehicle, had been blocked off with plastic bollards. The driver had slid them into place. Boot had no complaint about the preparations, and they had an adequate view of the front entrance to the bank. A derelict was sitting on the pavement beside the entrance, cross-legged and clutching a plastic cup. He was well wrapped against a sharp wind coming off the water and gusting across the square wall. He wore two grubby anoraks and a pair of thick gloves and had a blanket over his knees. A few minutes earlier he had eased his wrist across his mouth, whispering into the microphone concealed in his watch to alert them to the target's arrival.

Boot showed no sign of tension or stress, nor of excitement or anticipation. But the blood coursed in his veins and his breathing was marginally quicker. He had studied the surveillance photographs provided by the Swedes, so had a picture in his head of his target. But there was always a frisson of emotion when the picture came to life.

The bank was situated on an attractive square. The autumn wind had scoured the pavements, and the central statue gleamed. The Swedish officer told him that the life-size bronze of a man crouching with a crossbow was Engelbrekt Engelbrektsson who had led a peasants' uprising six centuries before. Boot's lip curled. He had no time or sympathy for political agitators.

Sipping from a water bottle, Boot reflected that the unexpected always provided the tastiest dishes. He had learned that in a life-time in espionage. Had he spoken, he might have said, 'The best are those you don't plan for, they just come lolloping round the corner and drop into your lap.' This one, codenamed *Hatpin,* had materialised without warning. Boot could not have said, sitting in the car and holding his peace, where he would be led, and how much advantage could be extracted from the Russian boy. The Swede beside him chewed on his unlit pipe. The driver, small and *gamine,* lit a Gauloise and coughed smoke from between coral-coloured lips, enough of it to obscure the No Smoking sign on the dash. The man beside her and in front of Boot, clinked the mana-cles he had extracted from his pocket. Boot had been told that on the two previous occasions *Hatpin* had gone to the bank he had emerged within twenty minutes. The engine idled.

The tramp raised his head, alert to the need to attract more donors, have more *krona* coins dropped into his beaker. They were ready. A woman with a loaded buggy entered the bank. The Swedish officer nudged Boot's elbow. They were satisfied that there was no tail on *Hatpin.* The lift would be fast and without drama. The driver's smoke played around Boot's nose, and a bead of sweat might have gathered at the top of his spine, below his collar. Boot had flown to Stockholm the previous evening, had booked into an Old City hotel, with a tariff above the normal Service allowance, but the Maid, who ran his affairs at VBX, had stated – 'cross my heart and hope to die' – that nothing cheaper had available rooms: a good woman, the Maid, and part of a loyal team that supported Boot. But until he had the target beside him, and had put forward the proposition, he would not know whether the optimism was justified.

It was a debt repaid. The Swedish service had owed a favour to Vauxhall Bridge Cross, and might also have wanted their British colleagues to take ownership of a matter that could hurt their Russian neighbour. The list of complaints had multiplied – military threats through incursions by submarines into territorial waters; fighter bombers encroaching on air space, increased spy activities; a plethora of state-sponsored hacking into Swedish utility sites; and money laundering of organised crime gangs, based in St Petersburg, via Swedish banks. As the officer had said when meeting Boot at the airport, 'We think we're giving you the chance to hurt them. God willing, it will be a well-directed kick in the testicles.' The washing and rinsing of money had been the trigger for their action. *Hatpin* had an account recently opened at this branch of a prominent Stockholm bank. Monies were transferred electronically but he seemed drawn there to talk with an investment consultant each month. He had been picked up, the signal had been sent to London. The auguries were good. Had to be good, or Boot – with the seniority he carried as a Cold War officer, and relevant again as relations had chilled and he had assumed new, weightier, responsibilities – wouldn't have been allocated this chance.

The Swede grinned, said quietly into Boot's ear, 'Friend, I want to ask you something very personal. You excuse me. I hope it is not impertinence. What is "Boot", what name is that? We look it up, we cannot find anything of such a name. Even, I went to one of our star interpreters, the response was a shrug but no answer. Why are you called after what is a heavy shoe? Forgive me. Is it Mister Boot, or is it Boot and something, and . . .'

Boot did not have to explain. The tramp had reacted, a torn and dirty sleeve passed close to his stubbled face, his wrist close to his mouth. Boot saw the target.

Two steps out. A pause. A scan that took in the pavement from the Italian *trattoria* to his left, across the statue of the agitator, and up to the alleyway to his right, over the parked cars and across the bridge. Wide eyes displaying all the guilt of a cat that had been at the cooking, nervous, and seeing nothing.

Boot did not travel on a whim, or an off-chance. That the matter of *Hatpin* had landed on his desk, filtered by the Maid, indicated the prospect of a return for the investment of his time. He had behind him a career that was decent rather than exceptional. There had not been a moment when others on his floor of VBX would have said, 'No doubt about it, this was Boot's finest hour.' But *Hatpin* might be, just might be, the catch of his lifetime.

The target seemed satisfied, turned left, stepped over the tramp's trailing blanket and started to walk away. The car was on the move, the fag was stubbed out, the manacles clanked, and the Swede's breath hissed on the pipe stem. Boot sat tall, the space between them was empty and ready.

Boot would not be involved in violence, might sanction it, but would not soil his own hands. But the fact remained – loud, clear – he had access to big resources and the danger confronting him was also 'loud, clear'. Results were expected, and he was the man in whom the Big Boss placed his confidence.

The target was identified in the Swedish reports as Nikki.

Insignificant, hardly cutting the impressive figure on which Boot's reputation as an agent handler flourished. No colour in his face, the pallor of a young man who worked behind curtains or blinds or in basements. A thin fluff of hair across his cheeks. The only brightness on his skin from the acne rash plaguing it. A concave chest and narrow, rounded shoulders on which his clothing hung loosely. The anorak was cheap, the jeans faded, and the trainers loosely laced. He headed away from the statue of the martyred freedom fighter towards the quaysides where the ferries to the islands sailed from. It was difficult to reconcile this pathetic figure with someone reponsible for stealing currency valued at £412,000, give or take a few pence, from a bank in the depths of some wretched Stalinist-built outpost east of the Urals. Someone who had hacked into and leached from supposedly protected accounts, removing the loot to the imagined safe haven of an account with a prominent Swedish bank on the square of

Kornhamnstorg. A youth of that description, that clothing, that wealth, could only be a success at a chosen occupation: hacker in a criminal gang – and vulnerable. A considerable talent in Boot's armoury was the ability to exploit 'a vulnerable'.

The target walked at a brisk speed and did not look back. The back-up car overtook them, and passed the boy. Doors opened and two men and a woman seemed to block the pavement. Boot's car was almost level with him. The boy was held, too shocked to struggle or shout. The Swedish officer was out, had hold of the boy's collar. The crown of his head was shielded and he was pitched inside. For a moment the boy's head was across Boot's lap, then it jerked upright, and the officer was inside again. Manacles were fastened on the boy's thin wrists, and they accelerated away.

The boy started to talk, babbling in his own language. Would have thought the brutal suddenness of his capture to be the work of the *Federal'naya sluzhba bezopasnosti* and considered himself beyond their reach in safe, sophisticated Stockholm. As the words, cringing, came in a torrent he began to shiver. Boot slapped his face. Lightly but sufficient to silence him. From his years of experience, Boot believed that the first words were the only ones that counted. He spoke quietly, his voice barely above a whisper. The driver coughed as she lit another cigarette. The reports said that the boy spoke English when dealing in the bank, and he was fluent.

'Very good to meet you, Nikki. We think this is going to be the start of a most fruitful relationship. You've a flight to catch, back to St Petersburg, and the aircraft won't wait. Look upon us as friends. Let's be clear where we all stand, Nikki. No misunderstandings. You chose to hack and steal from a bank in your own jurisdiction. I would call that *greedy*, Nikki, and I would also call that *stupid*, and I would say that greed and stupidity add up to a considerable mistake. Nikki, the consequences of such a "mistake" should not be ignored. The consequences might be a call to FSB, right into the big block on Liteyny Square – and I would do the call myself – and you would be facing a very difficult interrogation, a very difficult few years – correction, many years – in a hard-régime labour colony. They'd beat you to pulp, then send you to the camps. You understand all that, Nikki. Fine to hack overseas banks, credit unions, all that sort of stuff, and they're all cheering you on, but hack one of your own and people will get powerfully angry. All right, so far?'

The Swede had hold of the boy and his chest convulsed and his eyes watered and Boot wondered if he were about to wet his trousers. He smiled. He had once heard the Maid tell Daff, in the outer office, that Boot's smile was one that the hangman would have reserved for a client when asking him to behave reasonably on the walk from the cell to the gallows. A thin-lipped smile, gimlet-eyed. The amount filched from the bank had been in the Russian media, and matched the size of the account here. A pretty fair limit.

'Or we can do business together. Be friends, colleagues. You will find that we are always truly grateful to friends, to colleagues who cooperate to their best ability. We might even – as a reward for good behaviour – invite you to London. Us being friends, colleagues, Nikki, comes at a price . . . you tell us all we want to know, everything of the world in which you live. Your choice, Nikki. Or do I make the call to Liteyny Square? I have the number. You might not get as far as the camps, Nikki. They might have killed you before that. Your choice.'

And afterwards? A few ground rules laid down, dates for future meetings, details of what was required of *Hatpin*: names, addresses, where the hackers were going for new trapdoors and assaults, and relationships in the area of state-sponsored work.

A nod to the Swede, a flick of his fingers and the driver slowed, easing towards the kerb. Boot did not shake *Hatpin's* hand, did not offer any gesture of trust, and the smile this time only flickered. The car stopped. The manacles were removed. The Swede was out on to the pavement. He reached inside and caught Nikki's anorak, dragged him sideways and pitched him clear of the door. A stumble, a stagger, a regaining of balance, and a woman nearly tipped over as she carried shopping bags past him, and he was gone. A short striding run. What any feral creature would have done if cornered, facing capture, and then knowing release. Boot watched him disappear into an alleyway that led into the Old City and away from the wide street where the ferry terminals were. He had done carrot and stick and, as was always the case, the threat of pain would achieve his aim.

The Swede had his lighter fired up and over the pipe's bowl. 'Did it go well?'

Boot shrugged. 'Time will tell, always does. I think he's quite a catch, that's my opinion, for what it's worth. We'll milk him, drain him dry. He'll take us towards "attribution". I have a good feeling. I believe we'll get value from him. If it should be towards "strike back" then I'm happy as a pig in shite . . . But we won't run before we've learned to walk . . . we'll know soon enough.'

'I felt almost sorry for him.'

Boot grimaced. 'Never wise in my experience to cough up sympathy. Treat him at arm's length, little Nikki, owe him nothing.'

I

The first wave had been a probing attack, looking for weakness. They had seen that off, pushed them back.

The early force of the sun was now behind them and full into the faces of the second wave – the serious assault. Surrounding Merc was his small army: ten boys and two girls crouched or kneeling in the shelter of the sandbagged walls, blasting through the firing slits. The repetitive thud of the machine-gun hammered in his ears.

The start line of the 'bad boys' was around 150 yards to the west of their hill. Some came at a sprint and were tall; some were bent low and almost crawled. Amongst the noise of the shots and the explosions from grenades and shoulder-launched missiles were the clear cries of the boys moving towards them. One dropped, and on they came; another fell and they pressed closer. There might have been fifty of them. At least three or four would be wearing vests padded with explosives. The aim of the others would be to provide enough covering fire to allow them to get up to the sandbags, then roll off them down into the main bunker or the communication trenches to detonate the dynamite sticks. If one of them achieved that and went on his way, express service, to Paradise, then Merc and his army would be stunned, wounded. If they were lucky, they'd have their throats slit then and there, and if they were not, then they'd be captured and face a fate not worth considering. They were in among the wire and twice anti-personnel mines were triggered and body parts spewed up, but they kept on and the gap closed and sometimes he could see the faces and screaming open mouths, and a few times he was able to make out dead and lustreless eyes.

He would be known to them. His reputation had put a bounty on his head of at least $150,000. For that pay-out they would take their time in his despatch and it would make one of the better videos. But if they were overrun, none of them would survive. No Convention counted here. They would all fight and would, at the end, drag the pin from the grenade that they all carried strapped to their chests – and the women would be a big prize.

But his fate, and his value, was not uppermost in Merc's mind.

Holding the position mattered to him. He was a Gun for Hire, called Merc as an abbreviation of taking money for his chosen trade, for being a mercenary. Not much money, but it went into an account in a bank in a small town in leafy England. One of his boys had the big machine-gun and one of the girls organised the belt, kept it not too tense, not too slack, and fed it. Merc had an AK, and had only to reach a hand out behind him, like a runner receiving a relay baton, and would feel a fresh magazine slapped into his palm. The boy who did the loading had taken an incoming in his thigh in the first probe of the day, when the light was a dulled grey, and there was no possibility of evacuation. None of Merc's little army could be spared to lug a wounded man back down the hill, so the boy had stayed and he was useful, reloading ammunition into magazines.

Corpses were spreadeagled on the wire – coiled razor – near to the position, while the living flapped arms and legs and tried to break free of the entanglement, and howled or cried, and failed.

The other girl would have thought it demeaned her as a fighter merely to feed a belt. She was Cinar and had a good arm for hurling grenades. Merc watched over her and should not have treated her differently to any of the others under his command, but he did and if their eyes met she would glare at him and break the contact.

They came closer. There were small pockets of dead ground under the wire and among the mines, and when the attackers reached them they could catch breath, renew their faith, and come again. There was a big man to the right of Merc's vision and he had a strong voice and carried a rifle in one hand and had an RPG launcher slung from a chest strap. It was not usual for Merc to miss. He always did single shots and never had the catch on automatic for a spray job. But the big man was charmed. He had a straggling dark beard and wore charcoal-coloured overalls, and the strength of his voice seemed to drag others forward. If the big man cleared the parapet and got into the trench or appeared at the sunken entrance of the bunker, then Merc and his people were lost. The ground they held was Hill 425 on the military maps that the command used in Irbil. It was the culmination of a finger of territory held with difficulty by Merc's paymasters, the Kurds, and was more of a symbol than a place of strategic importance. Merc would not give it up. Could have done. Could have called up on the radio, could have said that they were exhausted, had done their share.

The big man's voice boomed out, and in a few moments they would come again and try the last forty- or fifty-yard sprint. Some would throw themselves at the wire and others would come and leap on them, boots stamping into the small of a back or on the neck and use the bodies as stepping stones. He had fired three times at the big man and each time had missed the kill. The last time his bullet had danced away, diverted after striking a cast-iron pole to which the wire was fastened.

Could have called up on the radio, not made a request, but given a statement. 'Enough, enough, coming back.' Either the place would be abandoned or fresh militia would relieve them. Might have given the Command an opportunity to rotate, or to decide that Hill 425 was not worth the pain and the steady dribble of casualties. Had not done it. Had used the radio instead to call for air support and had been told that priorities would be assessed. Had known that 'priorities' meant the push south of the city of Mosul farther up the front line. His force, so small and insignificant, were all idiots. The biggest fool was himself. Idiots led by a fool. None of them had the stomach to turn their backs on the position and creep out under cover of darkness, abandon it. In the last month, nine had been killed defending it, and fourteen had been injured. The colonel in charge of the sector had declined to add to their numbers, and no air strikes had been made available. A little private war. Same on the other side, and their dead, bloated from the sun of several days, stank and rotted. More had joined them that morning. They had no stomach, any of them, least of all the girls who fed the belt and chucked grenades, to ease out from the trenches and let others take their place, or permit the men from down the hill to raise their black flag over the bunker. A depraved, mad obstinacy. Merc could have done with air strikes, could have done with close artillery support, but did not register as a priority.

He waited. They all did. They heard the shouting that threatened them, that appealed to a God that would reward martyrdom. The intensity of the shooting had slackened. They might have another minute before the next surge towards their position. The sunlight was clear behind them and the ground was well lit and brightness played on the curled mess of the wire and reflected off the blades of the razors. Easier to fight than to wait.

Some called him Merc because he was paid to fight. Others gave him that name because of a great love in his life. Stowed inside the bunker, beside the radio and along with the cases of ammunition and grenades and smoke canisters, was his Bergen rucksack. Under the stinking socks and soiled underpants was a wad of well-thumbed magazines. They reflected his dream. Mercedes Benz cars. When the front line was quiet, not often, he would sit with them, would talk to his army about the qualities of the brand, and which one he would buy. When? Sometime. When was sometime? A shrug. Beautiful cars, polished and scented, with leather upholstery, and priced in American dollars, or in euros, or in pounds. A dream.

The shouting grew. He murmured that the boys and the two girls should hold steady, *wait*, not fire before they had targets, and *wait* some more. Merc had no rank that counted on Hill 425. He was not addressed with the subservience of juniors. His word was followed and his instructions carried out because each of them, the boys and the girls who fought alongside him, recognised that his word was backed by nothing more and nothing less than their welfare. They knew that, should they decide to pull back, he would not come with them. They stayed, all of them, and waited for the next attack. The boy who had the thigh wound had worked hard as the combat slackened and had made a good pile of filled magazines, and the grenade sacks were bulging. They believed in him, and that was a burden that Merc carried. His hands shook and he clenched his fists on the stock of his AK, and the others would have seen only the whites of his knuckles and nothing of the tremors.

The voices grew in pitch. He waited, and knew that the surge would come soon – and knew it would be a long time until 'some-time', when he could walk into the big Mercedes showroom near his bank with a fold of high-denomination notes in his hip pocket and do a test drive and . . . He was able to keep his voice soft, just loud enough only for his boys and the two girls to hear him. Their trust brought him, many nights, to a point of near collapse: never shown. He looked around and lit on Cinar and should not have cared for her safety any more than for that of the other girl and the boys – or more than he cared for his own survival . . . would not make it easy for the bad boys hidden in the holes below the wire to claim a sack of dollars as reward.

And they came. No more thought of anything beyond rounds in the magazine and where was his bag with the grenades, and what part of his little fortress was the target of the big man; and no artillery to support them, and not a chance of an air-strike because they were not a priority. Movement and shouting, and the spatter of the incoming rounds and grenades arcing in the air, towards them and away from them, and hard fighting. They came without fear towards the trenches. He could not have said whether there would ever be 'sometime', and all for a small hill, a pimple on a landscape otherwise flat and featureless, only valued by those who wanted it and those who would not give it up. Maybe he would live and maybe he would not. The firing, the shouting and the explosions deafened him, and they came closer. The voice behind him stuttered with fear. Merc had reached out for a new magazine.

'Can we hold them, Merc? Can we?'

He smiled, the smile that made people trust him. The cold magazine casing was in his hand, then his fingers were gripped by the wounded man's. He could see the movements, wriggling figures edging closer. Merc dropped his voice.

'Well, we have to, don't we? Can we? Yes, probably.'

Bob called it a 'brains trust', Harry said it was a 'barnstorm' session, Leanne had it as 'clear water' thinking time, and Dunc had put it in his diary as a 'punch-bag' opportunity with 'nothing off the agenda'.

Screaming into their faces, making each of them squirm, was 'state-sponsored'. Chasing that tail was 'provenance': stacking up evidence, putting it on paper, shoving it under the noses of the 'Customers' for whom they worked. Their mobile phones were locked in a lead-lined safe in the lobby three floors below, a blind was drawn on the room's only window, a coffee machine bubbled. The title they worked under, once an eccentric called Boot had put them in place, was 'S-S/RussiaFed-CyberAttack/2018'. Traffic noise from a street in London's district of Pimlico seeped into the room. Customers, Boot had said, needed the truth, unvarnished, ungilded, and shoved up their nostrils. They had been together now for six months, meeting first once a fortnight, now more often; they were a high agenda topic and their reports went direct to the desks of the Director Generals at the security and intelligence agencies, and to Cabinet committees with the necessary clearance. They reported – each in their own way – on a new warfare, one of increased intensity. One that was not being won.

From the Security Service was Bob, early twenties and with an outstanding academic degree. He said, 'It's today's combat zone. The attack forces are all around us but the great and beautiful general citizen mass, busy making money to pay my salary, put their heads into sand, cannot cope with the complexity of the invasion. No tanks on our lawns, no fighter aircraft buzzing our airspace, no commandos coming ashore anywhere between Skegness and Clacton. A government-authorised raid with sophisticated malware precludes the need for nuclear weapons to be deployed by an enemy régime, and can do as much damage. Our problem: *they* are better in pretty much every degree at getting through our firewalls than we are of stopping them dead with our defences. As we make our "airgaps" wider so *they* ever more surely hop over the voids. The dangers are clear for us to see – but not the response we should be making, which is opaque, fogged. Someone said that the only light at the end of the tunnel was that on the train coming towards us, and fast. It is danger and we are sleep-walking towards it, and we cannot offer protection.'

Boot was dropped outside Vauxhall railway station. It was a dank November morning, and the light wind barely moved the heaps of dead leaves that had gathered in the gutters. A spit of rain was carried in the air, and the forecast was for more of it later in the morning.

He waved cheerfully to his driver and had a lively spring in his step as he set off across the wide road, ignoring the pedestrian crossing because it was too far down the pavement. His route towards the main gates took him into the heart of the traffic flow. Cars and vans and a double-decker bus wove around him. A few blared their horns and he acknowledged them with courtesy, but indifference. It was standard procedure that any officer arriving by a chauffeur-driven car at VBX used the station as a destination, not the guarded and barricaded entry into the building. Old friends were at the gate and he kept his smile fixed as he rummaged for his pass. He was amongst the mass of employees, many still in their Lycra from cycling to work, and some in athletic kit from jogging, and half of the girls looked a quarter asleep. The old friends were Arthur and Roy and they wore navy blue uniforms under bullet-proof vests and cradled Heckler and Koch machine pistols, loaded and cocked but with the safety applied, and had gas and pepper spray canisters on the webbing, and Tasers. A degree of familiarity was permissible, and his mood was good enough for him to wink at them and he was rewarded. Roy tapped a fore-finger on his armament's body in acknowledgement, and Arthur

ducked his head, but only fractionally. He showed his card and
headed past them.

It had been their third meeting. He had been booked on the last
flight out of Stockholm and the session was coming to an end.
Nothing much seemed about to be spilled. The Swede had gone
for a leak. *Hatpin* had leaned forward as if recognising that he was
alone with the real power, the one who called the shots. He had a
street name in an industrial park near St Petersburg airport, and
the description of a two-storey warehouse and office space from
which an organised crime group ran its affairs, and some identities. Good material but not earth moving. Nikki had leaned
forward as if assuming the Swedes would have microphones, and
had taken Boot's hand, gently but with a persistent tug, and had
taken him to the window, away from the furniture and the phone
and the power socket where the bugs would have been, and had
whispered a gaggle of words in his ear. A meeting. A gathering of
the principal hack-people that the group paid, a discussion of a
target and a drawing up of individual responsibilities, and there
would be an officer from FSB in attendance. The best in the field,
quality people. Something big, mouth-watering. Boot had asked
when the last similar meeting had been held, and been told that
there had not been one in Nikki's time. When would it be, the
meeting? Three days. Three nights. His mind had raced. He had
thought of the think-tank meeting that morning, stuck in a routine
and not going outside the bubble. He thought of the seminar he
was due to attend at lunchtime, and thought of the problem of
moving men and putting the kit in their hands, and doing the
recruitment, sorting the logistics, and of winning authorisation,
and of . . .

'That's interesting, Nikki. Quite interesting. Might be able to
play around with that. I believe I'd be prepared to demonstrate
some sincere gratitude if we could see this one through . . .' He
had been asked what the value of that gratitude would be and for
a moment his lips had pursed as if that were just one more difficulty piling high in his wheelbarrow. Boot had said quietly, 'Could
manage that, Nikki. Give me a gas station, a café, supermarket

car-park where on Thursday, before the meeting starts, my people would meet with you.' And had been given the supermarket and had written the name of the street on his hand, and a time. Had he been alone he would have punched the air. Instead he had murmured, 'I am a man of my word, Nikki, and it will happen, what you ask for.'

A quick coffee and the boy had been kicked out into the night. The Swede had asked him how useful the session had been and Boot had given his slight, self-effacing grin – another trademark. 'Might be something I can play around with, and might not.' In his mind was an hourglass, the sand running through it.

As he walked across the atrium and towards the bank of elevators, he imagined what Arthur and Roy might have wisecracked to each other.

Arthur: 'What's up with old Boot? Reckon he got his leg over last night?'

Roy: 'No chance. More like he's back from Waterloo and the Duke pinned a medal on him. Loyalty and long service.'

'Wrong, Roy, because he's got his wellies with him when he's been there, and hasn't.'

'Fair one, Arthur. Then it's a show he's doing, a good one from the look of him.'

Boot always said that those two veterans of the front gate had a better idea of the principal operations that the Service launched, who was down in the world, and who was climbing the ladder, and who was bedding who, than anyone else on the payroll. He took the lift to the fourth flour, and the corridor was blocked by new office tables and chairs, wrapped in protective plastic sheeting. Appropriate because Russia Desk was an expanding world and back up, almost, to Cold War levels – not before time. He was attached to the Desk, but loosely; not subject to all its disciplines but able to call upon its resources. A major meeting was called, not an everyday affair, which meant trouble and pain, and barely time to scratch an armpit. Daff, his fixer girl, was already in, and the Maid who ran his office. They'd looked up and seemed to quiz him and, with the door closed behind him, and his thick coat and the trilby on the hook, he said that it had been productive.

'Before, I rated it as good. When we finished I thought it was better than good.'

The Maid had a map opened across her desk. It covered the top end of the Baltic and was divided by a frontier line. Boot was seldom short of certainty and jabbed with his finger at a place, a few kilometres south of the coastline where the territories were divided by a river, and jabbed again. He dropped his bag. Later, when work eased, the Maid would take care of the contents, clean what needed to be cleaned, press what was crumpled, and return the bag, freshly filled, to the locked cupboard that held what he needed – clothing, money, passports – for any short-notice excursion – and there would surely be one in a few days' time if a plan could be formulated and sanctioned. So little time . . .

Boot had called in from the airport as he'd crossed the scrum of the early morning concourse, and said what he wanted, and was told where they were, what was arranged, where they chased, and at what time the Big Boss had rearranged his diary, and – a giggle – the French had been cancelled from the slot. He'd nodded and gone into his small room, with the view of the river, and rain dribbing on the darkened, strengthened glass. He slung his jacket on the back of the chair and felt – quite suddenly – a wave of exhaustion. The office was bare except for his chair and desk, and a small table on which, in a bone china ashtray, was a set of antique false teeth, dentures that had once been the height of technology. The only decoration on the wall was a framed print, the Duke's head protruding from a boot, a popular cartoon view of the great man at the time of his triumph. Not much deflected Boot from his principal recreation: visits to the battlefield in Belgium and the chance to walk where the great man had walked. What he planned would be, as the Duke had said of the battle, 'a damned serious business'.

The eldest of them, on the third floor of the 'safe house' in Pimlico, and an easy walk across the bridge from the south side of the

Thames and the VBX building, was Harry. His long hair nestled on his shoulders and layered over his collar; he wore a sweater that had been knitted by his mother. Late twenties, regarded as an authority in matters of cyber intelligence, chosen by Boot, given a cryptic brief, then sent to work. He had the floor, did not expect to tell any of them what they did not know already, but still felt the need for repetition of the obvious and heavily travelled routes.

He said, 'There is here, all around us, critical infrastructure. Start with utilities. Go to any of the major providers of electricity, gas, water. Are they being probed, phished? Yes. Can the power grid be shut down? Yes. Can airliners be disabled so they are unable to fly above communities that can't light their homes, heat them or cook in them, and can't flush their toilets unless they happen to have a rain-water butt? Yes. Does this happen? Yes, every day. An American city loses power and blacks out tens of thousands of households and storms are blamed or overloads or some hapless technician. They are never going to admit that a foreign government, unfriendly with its intentions, just wanted to test the skills and abilities of its foot soldiers, the script kiddies. A Scandinavian attack leaves thousands shivering in the dark and the authorities blame a gust of wind knocking over a tree that falls on a particular cable strung between pylons. Bullshit. *They* did it, and sent a message, loud and clear, despatched it First Class, Next Day Delivery. Why are *they* pushing against the inadequate counter-measures of our supermarket chains, infiltrating the machines that dictate what product goes where, and when? Why? *They* can screw the delivery systems, disable the software, and in three days our people go hungry. Food is as much a part of critical infrastructure as water, and the rest of what we take for granted. Most terrifying is that each year we put greater reliance on the web, hand over new functions to it. But we have not yet learned how to keep it safe from predators. *They* run us ragged, we are losing.'

Working her encrypted phone, Daff prised out names. Russian language, of course. Knowledge of the terrain, a necessity. Familiarity with the requirements and culture of matters covert, essential. Deniability, taken for granted. On a separate sheet of paper in front of her, under a hovering pencil, were the initials G F H, but they were left to lie as she searched out the men who would be the foot soldiers. She could call in favours.

She'd tried the Lithuanian agencies, and the Latvians, and the Ukrainians in Kursk, and Bulgarian intelligence. The favours might be granted because many of those countries' officers had flirted with her over the years and might have assumed that with one more drink, one more confidence and indiscretion and joke and laughter, she would head for the elevator doors of her hotel and they might follow and be rewarded. She had admirers because she was a well-kept, curvaceous mid-thirties, had good bottle-blonde hair in a fly-whisk pony-tail, bronzed skin on her cheeks and neck, and stood straight. For the last seven years Daff – Daphne inside the building but not within the walls of Boot's fiefdom – had been his fixer within matters of the 'Field'. Office administration stayed, well guarded, in the Maid's hands.

The break for her was from the Poles, and an out-station in Gdansk which had responsibility for matters, the sensitive ones, originating inside the Russian-militarised enclave of Kaliningrad. She was given names, and contact points. Putting a cart before a horse might have been an accusation levelled at her that morning. She would have countered with a blunt negative if anyone had dared put that assumption, and with the added weight of an obscenity. Boot had his pecker up, and when it was there he could drain milk from the udders of a barren she-goat, certainly from the Big Boss three floors above. Running before she could walk? In no way. Underneath those initials, G F H, she wrote a name: *Martin*. The Poles were not fulsome in his praise. If he had been from the top drawer they would not have shared his identity; he was classified as 'adequate'. They'd be shipping her, electronically, a redacted file on him and two others. The most she could hope for, but the major catch would be the man whose initials she had written down. It was good to feel the eddy and excitement of the chase in the cramped office space where Boot held court; and so rare to sense it.

He loitered at her shoulder. Her question: 'Getting there?'
His answer: 'I think so.'

Leanne had chosen clothes that were drab, poorly fitting and black. No make-up, no jewellery, no polish on her fingernails. Her hair was cut short. She was employed in the private sector, headed the cyber-threat response unit of a heavily funded accountancy firm. She earned more per year, probably, than the combined salaries of the three men with her in the Pimlico room. Her voice was North Wales, her ability legendary in a small circuit of those who needed to know, and she was twenty-four.

Leanne said, 'Let's stop fucking around the issue, give it straight to the customer. *They* are Black Hat. Maybe today it is organised crime Black Hat. Maybe tomorrow it is state-sponsored Black Hat. It is interchangeable. The same people in Russia – Moscow or St Petersburg, or any crap little city in the arse end of nowhere – do the business in both camps. Very expert, and often they know their way round our conduits better than we do. The criminal attacks are about loot, cash. *They* can strip out the assets from our bank accounts, from our credit cards. *They* have enormous resources. This is not like holding up a bank, having a couple of getaway drivers, and a tame banker for laundering. Planning, research, psychologists to help recruit the right material, are across international frontiers, are more careful and more covert than the blundering Chinese, and *they* pose a massive hazard. Imagine big housing estates in any northern city of the UK. Benefit day is coming up, except that the bank branches that supply the Social Security payments have crashed. The money is needed so the mob can get drunk, shoot up, feed themselves, but there is no money – it's gone, anywhere between Vladivostock and Irkutsk. The result would be civil disobedience. Violence on the streets, a society there that has no financial reserves, inability to get credit, pockets empty. There's no requirement for tanks and strike planes and nerve gas. Collapse is less than a week away. Russia, if the leadership gets angry enough, can close us down, make us go dark. What can we do about it? It is apocalypse time, and the threat is being yanked up. Organised crime in the Russian state is allowed because the intelligence agencies permit it – joined at the hip, a Siamese job. Sorry and all that, not a bag of laughs. We need to inflict some drama, instead we're dull as ditches. Something has to change.'

The phone rang. He was up a ladder, painting a ceiling. He came down the steps. They shook as his weight transferred and the tin swayed enough to spill paint on to his trainers He picked up the phone. A distant voice. A woman's. Speaking Russian. Was he Martin? Who wanted to know? A friend: he had been recommended . . . a joke. He laughed. Was he recommended as a painter, a decorator, or for . . .? He was not required to go any further. His name had come, he was told, from Polish friends, in Gdansk. He shivered, and his hand shook, and more paint flicked from the bristles of the brush he was still holding. He said that he now lived in the Estonian coastal town of Haapsalu and that what he had done for the Poles was more than fifteen years ago, and he was a middle-aged man now. He realised quickly enough that the woman at the end of this international call was ignoring his rejection of a summons to go to work, took no notice of it – steamed ahead . . .

For him, and for the other two, it had all begun in this town, Haapsalu, where there was a big railway station – no trains running to it now – and the Czars of Imperial Russia had come from their court in St Petersburg believing that the mud of the beaches and swamps would preserve their health. They had made Haapsalu fashionable. And many years later the same town, reached by an inlet sheltered by pine forests and heavily reeded banks had become fashionable again for a more clandestine trade. Fast boats came here in the dead of night, having supposedly evaded the radar of the occupying Soviet military, had landed spies, saboteurs, those who believed the shit given them by plausible ringmasters. The craft that carried them were from Germany's wartime navy, but the British controlled the ferrying of these men – patriots or traitors? – and their mission was to fight a guerrilla war against the new communist régime, and carry out espionage in between sniping Red Army troops. The town, famous for the spa and for the fishermen's brightly painted little wooden homes, and a collapsing mediaeval castle, had become a Cold War front line. It was where Martin's grandfather had been reared, and where he had died, shot down in the reed beds within five minutes of wading ashore. And it was where his daughter had been born. Martin was now on the wrong side of Haapsalu, the part tourists did not care to visit. He asked his caller who she represented. She said her clients were a security firm based in the Brazilian city of São Paolo.

What trust could he put in her? A clear, crisp answer – the daily rate, when it would start, what would be required of him, and the sum of 5000 euros, as an advance, would be sent within half an hour to any account he named. Life was not easy for him. The Polish money was long exhausted. He lived hand to mouth. He pulled his wallet out of his jacket. He gave his bank details, and was told he should check his account within three hours.

Martin, an Estonian citizen and fluent in Russian, a former asset of occasional Polish-funded operations, was recruited.

Fresh off the early train from the west country was Dunc. New at Cheltenham but well thought of in the doughnut building that housed the boffins, analysts, translators and interpreters – the cyber family of GCHQ – and part of a campaign to give youth its head. A week short of his twenty-third birthday and with a First Class degree from Cambridge. His first job and it was likely that the Government Communications Head Quarters would be his only employers. He took a deep breath and launched, had no particular idea what was wanted from him, so latched on to what he thought to be the central matter of Russia's hack industry, and rolled his tongue on the word.

'"Attribution". It's what we talk about at our place. To whom do we attribute an attack? Endless, repetitive and almost boring, but the only subject in town. Where are *they*? Where to find them? We are attacked night and day – every night and every day – by Russia. Attacks for theft, for reconnaissance, for espionage, neverending. *They* are all over us, and we are running to stand still. To hit them you have to have a target. Can't find it . . . Can have a district, a suburb, a neighbourhood. Cannot say it is this block of cheap housing, this floor, this room off the lift-shaft lobby on the right-hand side and between the bathroom and the kitchen, where the kid sits with his laptop. We don't have that ability. Or maybe he is routed through his mother's desk top. He is costing us billions of sterling equivalent each year, but we don't have a face on him. Whether it is state-sponsored or Organised Crime, it is criminality. Can we go to Moscow and the Ministry of Justice and demand action? Can, but we won't get it. You know all this. And the word *krysha*, which I translate as the "roof". The "roof" is protection. The criminal is sheltered by the intelligence agency, and the agency kingpins take a cut, a generous one. They are in bed together. Assume we identify an individual hacktivist, trace a line to his computer, make a target of it. We fry it, burn it, we wipe it, maybe we even get inside and sit and watch. He can get a new one. He can go down to the shopping mall and buy one for four hundred American dollars. Cheap stuff is good enough. We have no possibility of retribution, creating a viable threat of retaliation. *They* are immune to punishment. They must wake up each day and laugh themselves stupid at us. You can't strike back if you don't know who to hit. But you know that, don't you?'

'We do,' Bob said.

'A good summary,' Harry chimed.

'This man, this Boot, who tasked us originally – my impression – has no idea of the science of computers, probably challenged changing a light bulb.' Leanne's voice had the melody of a chapel choir, might have been chanting psalms. 'I said he was to imagine worms going up pipes for the spread of malware, but worms with sharp teeth for destruction, and with shopping bags for taking away goodies. That seemed to strike a chord with Boot. We've talked in generalities, the language of a kindergarten, and that's probably right for him, and for where he'll pass our paper. God alone knows the relevance of this confessional – we're neither winning nor punishing. Why would he need to know that? Or the

Directors? I reckon we fulfil no useful purpose, not unless something radical is on the table, which it isn't. Something has to
change.'

Nikki was the passenger, front seat, and they crawled in early
morning traffic.

His sister drove. They owned, between them, a VW Polo,
Thirteen years old and 150,000 on the clock. It rattled crazily and
the steering was poor, and when the snow came next month the
tyre traction would be rubbish. Nikki could have bought Kat a
Maserati or a Ferrari or a high-performance Porsche, but that
would have drawn attention to himself, and attention carried the
smell of danger. Ridiculous to think, driving from the airport
where the delayed flight out of Stockholm had finally landed,
heading for the factory estate in the Kupchino district, because he
sat in a seat covered by a dirty towel, his feet on a crushed carpet
of pizza boxes, that he avoided danger.

She knew nothing. She was Yekaterina, and in the music school
where she had studied before dismissal she had been Katcha.
Now the name she answered to was Kat. They had passed the
Park of the Internationalists. Tower blocks were shrouded in mist
to their left, fumes spewed from the traffic, and she edged towards
the building where he worked. She did not know about the money
he had taken from the bank accounts in the city of Krasnodar. Did
not know that the story of a friend in Stockholm was a tale of
convenience. Certainly did not know that the last three times he
had been to the Swedish capital he had met with an officer of a
foreign intelligence agency. She would have noted his restlessness,
his impatience with the traffic, and that he hissed through his teeth
and spittle was on his lips, but did not imagine that his freedom of
action and thought was now controlled by a distant and threatening force.

He loved his sister. The only girl he loved was the sister who
was a year and a half older than himself. She would drop him off
and then double back to get to the block where her piano teacher
lived. His work was a priority for him and for her. She would

starve without the money he was paid by the GangMaster, and the piano lessons would have been a distant dream. He loved her and she was the only family he acknowledged. He sat tensed in the seat, smoked hard and flicked ash from the window, letting in the chill air. Their father was dead, poisoned by vodka, and their mother loathed him and it was mutual. His sister, alone, mattered to him. But he had told her nothing. She would go to the woman, a greedy bitch and without sufficient talent to be a teacher, and try to enrich her talent with the piano, because she had been dismissed twenty-one months before from the Rimsky-Korsakov State Conservatory. Denied the reputation of the Conservatory she would never receive the recognition required to play in public. Perhaps that evening he would tell her, or perhaps the next day. Tell her he had sold himself, that he was in danger.

She took the car into the warren of small factories, warehouses and vehicle repair yards. At the end of an unmade road was the two-storey complex where the GangMaster did business. If they knew where he had been, whom he had met, what he had said, he would have been beaten and kicked until he was near death and then they might have chopped off limbs with a chain saw, or might have used electrodes on him, or might have fed him to a chipper, or thrown him, alive, into a furnace that supplied central heating to a public office complex. They lurched forward. She was hunched over the wheel, weaving between the potholes, flush with rain-water.

He hated them. Hated most things and most people. Hated the man he worked for, and his supposed colleagues – the other Black Hats – and hated the political police who had closed the Conservatory doors behind his sister, and hated the man who had come three times to Stockholm and who had fed him with candy and threatened him with a club. Loved only his sister. Might tell her that night, or might put it off until the morning. Might tell her about the assignation in the supermarket car–park . . . not knowing who he would meet, nor what would be asked of him, nor the consequences – knew that he had told them of a meeting of impor-tance in the building where he worked and it was due to start within a few hours of the rendezvous.

She stopped the car. They were far from the sight of any main artery. Lanes ran inside an outer wall of apartment blocks, eight floors high, and one led them towards a cluster of two-storey buildings, some with their own perimeter fences and guarded gates, and some open. They were sandwiched between Plovdivskaya ul, and Dunayskiy pr, and it was a backwater to which nobody would have come without purpose. This building was surrounded by a chain-link fence that was topped with coiled barbed wire. A dog – might have been a mix of mastiff breeding – was on a running wire and had worn a muddied trail short of the main fence. He sometimes threw it the remnant of a sandwich but had a good enough aim to ensure that the bait fell short and the dog could not reach the food, only slaver for it. There were delivery trucks beyond the gate, and parked up on a rutted waste area were half a dozen cars but there was no sign to tell a stranger why this complex warranted the protection of the wire, the high gates, and the two men who shared a booth that sheltered them from the weather. Nikki reached across, kissed his sister's cheek, but his lips were dry and chapped. He smeared his tongue across them, then tried to kiss her again, but she turned her head away. He thought she probably despised him. She might have regarded him as a parasite; he did not have the talent to play the piano, nor the fervour she brought to her protest work and which had cost her the place in a praised music school. He believed in little, and the keys that brought light to his eyes, calm to his mind, were those on his laptop.

He climbed out. He did not look back but heard her swing the Polo in a tight circle, the frosted ground crunching under the tyres. He went to the gate. They knew him. He did not know their names, but their appearance was the same: steroid-built shoulders, shaven heads and huge ham fists. They would do the beating and the kicking, start up the chipper, or drag on the firing cord to get the chain saw going. He was supposed to produce an ID card for the men to inspect, but it was back in the apartment that he shared with Kat. He pushed on the gate. He heard the little Polo fade down the track. One of the guards held it shut. He felt a moment of blinding obstinacy . . . no pleading about them seeing him every day and he'd left it behind that morning and . . . Nikki sat down. He sat in the mud and the slush from the frost, and others were behind him now and he stayed put. There was no room for the short queue to step over him or to get round him. He stayed silent. The gate was opened. He stood, wiped his sleeve on his wet backside and walked through.

In the past he would have thought of himself as a 'free spirit', an 'adventurer'. He travelled through trapdoors and put Trojan Horses in place, and let the viruses run free. Hacked savings accounts and penetrated the great corporations of the western world where technology blueprints were stored, and travelled inside foreign government ministries. Good times, but gone. He was no longer free. He had given the Englishman the location and timing and explanation of the meeting's importance, and had expected to see him blink, swallow hard, grin as if something special had been offered him. The reward had been the blank and seeming disinterest in the face . . . a lie. A lie because he had the rendezvous in the supermarket car-park. He entered the building, nodded to the girl at the desk, was recognised and given a small wave.

He might, that day, fillet accounts in a Credit Union in Brussels, or he might go back to a target of the afternoon before he had flown to Sweden and go inside a Ministry of Defence contracts unit in Santiago, but was not certain where that city was, or even which continent. But he was no longer free. He pressed the elevator button, felt the power in the machine, wondered who they would send, but felt no guilt, never had done – hated them all.

He would go to Chile . . . icons lit his screen . . . it was a state-authorised hack and the aim was to learn the terms the Americans offered to the local army for the purchase of armoured cars. Russia's government was in competition for the contract and would undercut on a sales pitch. He settled in his chair and neither of the boys across the room acknowledged him, nor did he greet them. An office in that ministry on the far side of the world was the work place for the men and women responsible for defining the purchase order; he had their names and the hours they were at their desk. This vulnerability was exploited, and their firewalls were no more capable of stopping his progress than a condom blocked transmitted disease. Very soon it would be the nominated 'zero day' when the necessary and identified e-mail train was exfiltrated, and it would go to the men from FSB who hovered close to the building, and who came on Thursdays to collect the required material. The keyboard on the laptop he used was worn, the symbols barely visible, and his fingers moved across them and his eyes were fixed on the screen. Nikki's world.

The wriggling snake he controlled went deeper, explored, sifted and rejected and twisted in a different direction. The memory of a meeting in a hotel room, and the treachery of what he had done, slipped from his mind.

They left the building in Pimlico, separately. In the preparation of their document, three pages of supposed wisdom, between nit-picking over language each had queried what their work might be used for. Bob, Harry, Leanne and Dunc had all failed to put together a decent reason for their effort. But Leanne had further confused them as, the last of the biscuits scoffed, she had taken a call from their employer, Boot. 'See you all again tomorrow . . . He didn't seem to me to be the sort of man who'd gratuitously fritter our time. There'll be a reason, decent or not, but we won't be told it.' She'd laughed, the first time in the day any of them had.

A grenade came diagonally over Merc's head. He could not see the man who had thrown it. It went high, dark against the pale blue sky. The mist had cleared but the smoke clouds from the explosions still lay on the wire. It flew, like a clumsy pigeon, and reached the top of its arc, hesitated, and then its momentum slackened; it rolled, wavered, came down lazily. It might have a six-second fuse, from the time a finger had ripped out the pin, an arm had extended, then the suck of breath and the swing, and the thing was launched.

He shouted. Merc saw that the trajectory would take it down

the trench from him to land close to the machine-gun and near the boy with the wound who filled magazines. They would expect the grenade to explode and hope that the defenders around Merc were, for a few moments, stunned, incapable; that they would charge and try to break through the wire and would hurl themselves into the trench line . . . and if they were there then it was curtains. It hit the top of the parapet, where the line of sandbags was hammered down to give proof against the power of a high-velocity round, and it wobbled, seemed to roll, and Merc could not know whether it would fall into the trench, before coming to rest. He watched it.

Nobody owned Merc. He was not subject to company discipline and was not moved around a chequer board at their convenience. Could have been said that he barely owned himself. He was a junkie for it, an addict. The syringe was the whine of the bullets and the crack of the firing and the thunder blast of the missile launcher, and with them came the screams and the shrieks and the cries – of fear and courage and pain – and there was the camaraderie of the kids he was with, and it was about the adrenaline that pulsed in him, and trust given him . . . Those with only a transitory view of Merc might have reckoned that he carried responsibilities easily. The boys and girls with him had a duty to have rifles at their shoulders and use them well because it was their land, their countryside, that was at risk.

Merc had been reared by his grandparents in a narrow, shabby street off the Oxford Road in the Thames Valley town of Reading, and those elderly people were not threatened by this distant enemy. He was there because it was beyond his powers to walk away. The money was interesting, but not important, and the dream in his life was that he would go 'sometime' but he did not know when. What he did know was that the grenade had trickled to a stop, wobbled and then moved, swinging its weight towards the trench, before loitering for a last time. Then it dropped.

Time seemed to freeze. He wanted to shout the warning again, but for once his voice was stifled, in lock-down deep in his throat. The grenade bounced, might have travelled six inches, then

nestled on the dirt. There had been no rain, not for days, so there
was no mud for it to slide into, to minimise its blast. It was close
to the feet of the machine-gunner, beside those of the girl who fed
the belt. Ten paces from Merc, five paces from Cinar, and within
an arm stretch of the wounded boy. Merc twisted his head away
and closed his eyes, and heaved his body against the wall of sandbags. The hot air blasted against his body, and the shock wave,
and the wet.

He heard nothing. The cloud enveloping him was dust, stone
particles and thick, but clearing, and the wet dribbled on his face
and when his arm brushed it, blood stained dark on his tunic and
fresh red appeared on the back of his hand and it tickled as it
wriggled down his vest and on to his stomach, but he had no
wounds, felt no pain, and the strength was not draining from him.
The girl who fed the belt was crouched and her body heaved as if
she was trying to scream, but Merc did not hear her, and there
was blood across the shoulder of the boy with the machine-gun.
Merc understood.

The magazines, filled and empty, were littered near the dismembered body. Merc felt shame. He had not witnessed it. At the
moment when the wounded boy had crawled the few paces
required, looked down at the thing then, consciously, had dropped
on to it, hidden it, one breath or two – not more – Merc had been
bent low and had protected himself and had expected to feel the
lacerations of the shrapnel. *Greater love hath no man . . .* What
many of the private military contractors obsessed with. To give a
life for another – would they do that? For whom? For their best
mate, or for a kid from a village up a mountain who had only flip-
flops on his feet? Much of the boy's stomach had left his body and
a leg was severed, and the head was unrecognisable.

Merc steeled himself. Unless he took control, they would be
gone in two or three minutes. He started to aim, shoot. He bawled
at the machine-gunner to keep firing, and aiming, and at the girl
to hold the belt at the necessary angle and feed – and yelled for
Cinar to get among the magazines and to keep filling them, and
keep passing them – and saw the savagery in her face as if loading

bullets into AK magazines was not her work, but she did. Merc knew the name of the boy who had given his life, but little more, and he had been with them only four days and was their most recent reinforcement and should have been at the rear and receiving treatment except that they had no spare hands to carry him back. The black-clothed bodies were rising among the wire.

Had to do it. Had to turn his eyes from the wire and the movement and the targets, and look down at his feet and past the gouts of blood and the pieces of salmon-pink flesh and drag the radio/phone from the ledge in the sandbagged recess, and hammer it on and shout his codename, and get into a command post, and call for air support, and give it to them straight, no varnish, yell it at them.

'Almost gone. Almost overrun. Must have air. Got to. Or four two five will be lost. Get the air here.' Merc's request would be evaluated. The communication was cut.

More grenades came, but none fell into the trench, and shrapnel whined over them and there was the song of ricocheting shots, but loudest were the shouts of the enemy. Sometimes the sun flickered on the knives that they carried. Eyes peered anxiously at him. If Merc failed them, then they were dead, and the Hill was lost, and it had all been for nothing. He fired, and fired again, and slung an empty magazine behind him and loaded another, and spat at Cinar that he needed replacements and she should be faster, and her anger was molten. He looked for the 'air', and did not see the fast jets or the Apaches. Sounds were seeping back into his head, but he did not hear the engines. And they came at him again, and seemed to have identified him as their principal target, because he was the Gun for Hire, the rock on which they foundered.

It was about survival, who wanted it most – him or them. Merc aimed and fired, aimed again and fired again, and had hits, but more came, and the big man was half naked and his black clothing was ripped and his skin was laced with bloody cuts, but still he came.

2

The skies stayed clear. No strike aircraft and no helicopter gunships. No clouds. An emptiness.

Around Merc, the line held. They had pushed back three surges in the last hour, but at a cost. Two more casualties lay prone in the trench. Neither would have had the strength to load magazines: one was quiet and had dulled acceptance in his eyes and his breath had a soft and bubbled spittle between his lips; the other had lapsed into unconsciousness and carried a head wound. Merc and his little army could not treat them, reinforcements troops or medics would not make the hazardous journey up a communications trench – and he had called again for air support. He wondered why the guy at the other end of the radio link assumed Merc gave a damn for the priorities of the push south of Mosul, or for a situation developing four kilometres to the west where the main defence line was buckling: if 'air' became available, down the line would have first call after Mosul. More of the enemy were coming up from their rear. Merc had seen the dust trails of the pick-up trucks that ferried them, the vehicles all sprouting black flags. Merc had his binoculars on them and wondered who had come from south-east London, and who from the suburbs of Birmingham, and if a few might be from Chechnya, the worst for cruelty. An air-strike or a fixed wing jet screaming along the length of the convoy would have devastated them, but no planes came, no gunships.

The others looked at him and to him, searching for a sign of his confidence. All of them were frightened and some showed it. Even Cinar was biting her lip, but turning away if Merc's glance settled on her. The pick-ups had gone, and the new men moved forward.

When they came to the wire they would start to crawl and begin calling to their God. When the battle was over it would barely count – victory or defeat or stalemate – not even a minor statistic. As if Hill 425 no longer mattered.

They could give up and pull back, and try to take the wounded with them – or leave them with grenade rings hooked to their fingers – and get to the rear end of the slight salient they had defended, and there would be a shrug from the Kurd major and he'd call up again on his command net. Back in the main bunker, where the fans pushed around freshened air and the computers chattered quietly, they might be relieved not to have the mercenary yelling for bombing support. That was where the Special Forces were, the Hereford crowd. They were rarely permitted to be 'boots on the ground' – they were supposed to train, offer guidance, but from the rear. Merc had a good relationship with them, he reckoned, but not good enough to make eyes wet if Hill 425 was lost. They regarded him as 'peculiar' or 'unhinged'. They were taking big money and he was not, and they were safe and back from the firing line, and he was at the sharp end. They were tactically aware and he wasn't.

Merc's band of brothers and sisters were the only ones on their side of the fight who cared for the Hill . . . along with the enemy. So, he and his dwindling force, with ammunition stocks not desperate but low, with exhaustion growing and nerves fraying, waited for the next charge up the hill, into the wire, across the open ground after the obstructions, and on to the parapets of sandbags. It would happen, a bookie's certainty, because they had brought up reinforcements, and he thought they would come again as soon as the new meat had reached the start line. Merc took a chance and moved down the length of trench, made sure that both the casualties had additional morphine, slapped shoulders and hugged the boys, tweaked the cheek of the girl who fed the belt, and then he went along to the southern end of the trench and did the same job. He didn't touch Cinar, but was close to her back as she peered over open sights, and he whispered to her that

her head was too high and made a target. The shouting was
growing in front of him and the boys from the pick-ups jogged
forward over open ground but Merc did not have a Dragunov
sniper rifle with the big optics and could not have dropped one of
them. Another sound mingled with the enthusiasm of fresh
fighters – the sobs of the ones already on the wire, hooked fast and
with bad wounds . . . No water, no comfort, and no prospect of
imminent martyrdom, the virgins in Paradise put on hold.

As a Gun for Hire, Merc had fought in some of the choicer
corners of the region over the last decade. No medals issued, no
citations offered, but his record would have been on file and there
were a few who had cast an eye on it who would offer him respect.
Not that respect, now, would make any difference. He had been
in bad places. Had done the 'arse pucker' route from Baghdad
International and down to the Green Zone, twelve klicks on
Route Irish with a reputation – justified – of being the most
dangerous highway in the world. Had done the convoys in
Afghanistan, riding shotgun in among the loaded trucks that
sluggishly brought food and building materials and gasoline to
the outlying fortresses occupied by the Coalition guys and the
spooks. He had been in Yemen where close-quarters combat was
normal and twice he and the other guys on the payroll had fixed
bayonets because the bullet count was so low. Now he was resi-
dent, temporary, in the Kurdish city of Erbil, had found a new
war and a new cause. He thought of jacking it, and would do
'sometime', and go to the Mercedes dealer in the Thames Valley
– but not that afternoon. The rest of them looked at him, believed
he had special powers: just an ordinary guy whose fix was the
sweet scent of cordite and gun oil.

The military experience, as against a private military contractor's, of Gideon Francis Hawkins stretched across twenty-three
months of service with the Pioneers, 2005 to 2007. It had been
about digging latrines and fortifying command bunkers and
strengthening perimeter defences in Basra and in Helmand. It had
been too regimented for him, the discipline seemed to choke him,
and he'd quit, and had gone to one of those outfits that supplied

bodyguards and protection and had signed up. As an ex-Pioneer – not a smart-arse from the Marines or Paratroops or from Hereford – he was given shit work to start him off, to let him know who mattered in his Baghdad world. He had picked up a blonde at the airport, had to escort her down to the UK embassy compound, and he was in the front passenger seat with the window down and the M-16's barrel jutting out and some kids had taken a blast at them, and he had let rip – might have dropped two. A month later he was called to the pool-side café in the Zone, and she had been there, in a pretence of a two-piece, her skin still damp from swimming, and she'd signed him . . . on a retainer, and easy terms for him to accept.

The guys from the pick-ups were vocal, in good heart and good voice, and were almost at the wire, and the shooting had gone heavy. What made them hard to beat was their apparent lack of fear, like they were merely on a road that was a diversion from the destination: fruit trees and meadow flowers and virgins with spread legs. Difficult to fight. No point in calling up again and demanding air support; no hope of the Special Forces troopers coming to the rescue with a bugle bawling and heavy fire power. The sun was high and the dead had swelled and the stench was bad. All of them holding Hill 425 knew the fate of prisoners. They would fight until they died, refuse to bug out from the position they had made their own and where blood had spilled . . . That fucking woman should keep her head down . . . The big man was up, scars dried on his skin and his voice hoarse with hatred, and the others followed him. No chance to think of 'sometime'. He aimed shots, but the big man was charmed and the machine-gun missed him. Coming closer and the noise was deafening. The kids believed in him, and followed him, and had trust in him: a big cross to carry.

Only aimed shots, and the line of them coming would seem to stagger and they would close the gaps – ever nearer.

'Need your back stiffening, Boot?'
'Just a little. Yes, I suppose I do.'

Boot had come to the one man to whom he gave considerable respect, whose judgement he trusted, whose sense of an almost reckless imagination he admired – and would try to match. He was in the process, through Daff's recruiting, of setting in motion a matter that could not lightly be reversed. He had come across London to see Ollie Compton. The coffee mugs on a low table in front of them might not have been thoroughly washed and the milk in the coffee might have been several days past its shelf life. They were in a first-floor bed-sit, on a street behind Ealing Broadway where a man – once a legend in the Service – eked out his last days.

'Your shout, is it? Praise if it goes well, brick-bats on your head and a rope round your neck if it fails? Is there big collateral?'

'Big, and not predictable. Would I be starting the Third World War, nuclear level, responsibility with me? Unlikely. Would I be shaking the tree, making a hell of a mess underneath it, stoking up some confused anger – sackloads of it? Sincerely, I'd hope so.'

'And it's a one-time opportunity?'

'I think so. Stripped to the barest bones it is this: Our problem is always "attribution", who the little bastards are and where to swat them. That I've cracked. Know who they are and where they are, and know there will be a conclave of their best and their brightest in St Petersburg. I cannot imagine there will be a similar opportunity again, that level of players and in a location only a hundred miles from a friendly border. The opportunity to swipe them is better than I've ever dreamed of in the years since I was given this bloody chalice of poison. Haven't been able to dent them, not raise a squeak, not till now . . . I fancy I can make them howl, or whimper, but anyway experience suitable pain. But a strike back, what involves serious violence over and above tinkering with cyber channels, comes with high-stake money – frighteningly high. But the chance won't come again, not in my opinion. Believe me, Ollie, the danger we face from these people would keep you awake at night, cannot just be ignored, nothing done because any response escalates the conflict . . . God help me, I'm setting it in motion.'

His host was in his ninetieth year. An automated e-mail message congratulating him on his anniversary would be sent from VBX to acknowledge the Big Nine. Otherwise there would be only one card on the mantelpiece, and that would be Boot's. The Service was supposed to have moved on and 'buccaneers' or 'pirates' were no longer held in esteem. The eccentric was seen with suspicion – except that the Big Boss, in a lofty office suite above where Boot worked with Daff and the Maid, had a streak in his make-up that Boot had discovered and could cultivate. That streak was for the bold and for the inventive, and for the recall of past days. Ollie Compton had left behind him a plague of diplomatic protests, fist shaking and finger jabbing, had executed assets and stings that had dripped angst and blood, and had been the prime mentor for the young Boot. It was like coming to a shrine.

'Can you push it through, get the sanction?'

'Would have to be economic with detail, and ramp up the "deniability factor". I'd win the day, stress the golden opportunity for the end of this week. The "eclipse business", won't be another one coming round and soon. I'm confident that I can.'

'So, why come here, looking for a comfort zone from a clapped-out buffoon?'

Not a pretty sight confronted Boot. The man wore shapeless trousers, pyjama bottoms protruding below the turn-ups, no socks, elderly slippers. A string vest, a shirt that had not been buttoned and might have been worn for a week, a dressing-gown, and a monocle over the right eye. Unshaven, with a sprouting of white hair garlanding most of his scalp that was camouflaged with old scars and laced with wide veins. No spare flesh on the body, and wrinkles patterning his skin. But a straight and proud back and bright and curious eyes, and a good speaking voice, and a mind that Boot would have called razor-sharp, and thoughts always worth assimilating.

'You said it, to get the spine stiffened.'

'Because you might lose people?'

'Might, yes.'

'You can live with that. Never bothered you in the past. Would not have shown a damn of interest in you if it had. Men and women taken behind the lines, beyond rescue, outside any orbit of safety. Tapes of their torture, the screams, sent for you to listen to? Have to come up with something better than that, Boot. All of your seniors disowning the enterprise, and you alone carrying a heavy old can of nasty-smelling stuff. Up for it?'

'I think so, probably.'

'I never gave a toss, Boot, for the debris I left behind. The old line used to be about omelettes and broken eggs. Never was mawkish. How it has to be. World without end, know what I mean, amen.'

'Suppose it's what I came to be told.'

'And it is worth doing, worth the sacrifices of men's lives, perhaps women's, while you stay safe and warm? In their lives, fucking them about, giving them a cheerio and nice wave. Is the job worth the possible cost?'

And Boot, in the quiet of the room, with the smell of old clothing around him, the window open in spite of the weather and carrying the scents of the cooking of various ethnic recipes, told it in greater detail. A tip from the Swedes, the interception of a young, scruff-arsed hacker with a St Petersburg address, a pause and a short résumé on the power of the Russian hack industry whether from Organised Crime or from state sponsorship and the growing fear that theft and espionage bred, and a sense of the helpless ... An impatient gesture from Ollie Compton's skeletal hand. Not much furniture in the room other than the bed, the chairs on which they sat, the table where the mugs cooled, and a wardrobe and a sink and a small electric cooker, and a plastic-walled corner concealing a shower. But there were piles of newspapers knee-high in a corner and a laptop on the floor. The gesture told Boot that what he said did not need explanation – as it would for the Big Boss. He repeated those grand and increasingly familiar words of 'attribution' and 'strike back', and the old head nodded, impatient because that was repetition, and the hair waved as if in a small breeze and he sensed the growing interest of the veteran, probably envy. The difficulty of target identification. The near impossibility of locating a den from which a hacker operated, the lack of an opportunity to hit where it hurt . . . a new warfare where one side had the freedom to roam and the other was stuck in a shelter and did not know how to frighten . . .

'Frighten, hurt, have them by the short ones, the curly ones, and grab what's there, and squeeze and twist and do some damage. You didn't just come here, Boot, to moan at your weakness and inability to dream. Get on with it.'

'I know when there will be this gathering of them – rats in a nest if I fancy that licence – I have the address and the time, and the quorum will be of many of the most sophisticated hack people from the St Petersburg district, and beyond. They'll get a briefing from the FSB liaison who deals with their Organised Crime principal, their GangMaster. All in the same room, together, and that is privileged information from a source, and Cheltenham can't put that together, and our ground people don't have it, and the best of the defence companies, good old private enterprise, are still faffing about in ignorance of this scale of session. We have an opportunity for a strike back, brutal and physical and not electronic, that will shake their complacency to the core, diminish the authority of their warlords. We put up with their shit, thieving from our accounts, stealing from our Research and Development, planning their capabilities to attack us, paralyse our life blood, and—'

'Steady, Boot. No need to make it personal. That, my friend is intended *irony*. When they poisoned that young defector in London, with that radioactive stuff, they thought he'd be dead and gone before the calumny was identified, they were using our pavements to defecate over, our kerbs to urinate in. Hurt them how much? A squib or a bang? Which?'

Boot sucked in air, and it whistled over his lips. He was observed closely and the monocle was in place and Ollie Compton's eyes were lit and his jaw hung in expectation.

'I think a bang,' he said. 'Quite a decent bang.'

A thin hand caught Boot's shoulder in a claw grip and he realised he had the approval of the old Cold War fighter. They talked on. Where the insertion should be made, how many personnel would be needed, the composition of the elements of the bomb so that if – God forbid – it failed, then the deniability stayed strong, and a situation where two crime groups would be in open conflict and believing that rivalries had overflowed, and what sort of man should lead the charge, and what his pedigree should be.

'Very calm, few words unless they're necessary. Able to fight his way out and, most important, able to lead. That's not a weapons freak, just a good man, and solid as granite, who can handle acute stress situations. Do we, Boot, still make them like that? Do we?'

'Daff and the Maid are working on it. Seem to think we can manage it.'

They stood. Boot wondered if he should take the older man's arm, steady him from the ravages of arthritis, but was waved away. They went to the door. Boot asked if there was anything he could do for Ollie Compton . . . and remembered that it was a good forty years since a wife had walked out with a reported final flurry of 'You love that bloody job a sight more than you love me', likely to have been a fair reflection of the marriage. And there had been some poor investments and there was the continuing inclination to back the slower horses going round Wincanton or Redcar or Chepstow. No wife, no money, and no one at the Service thinking if that depth of intuition could be tapped into. Boot, as a raw youngster, had hung on every word, and they'd chewed the fat at various checkpoints and border crossings while waiting for an agent to cross, and they'd gone heavy together to whip into line any compromised attaché from a Warsaw Pact embassy. It had been the saddest day of Boot's career when, on a Friday night twenty-four years before, the mentor's card had been shredded. It was he who had then handed Boot the Maid, and had given her the name – Marian, so natural – and he'd walked away from the little drinks event and gone into a spring evening for a pleasant walk along the Embankment . . . and had done more for Boot because there had been a Brussels stopover, on a journey back from Vienna, and the senior man had waved down a taxi and they had gone together to the battlefield at Waterloo, spent half a day there, and the taxi was almost off the clock when they were back at the airport, but Compton's expense claims were never queried.

'Thank you, grateful for your time. Keep well.'

'Bollocks, Boot, what else have I to do? Remember this – up there, where you'll be sending your man and the miscreants with him, it will be cold, wet, and the country is forested and rough, roads are few. Still a high security zone back from the frontier. When they're coming, after the bang which is not a squib, the chances are that – "best laid plans o' mice an' men Gang aft a-glay" et cetera – not everything works as hoped for and then the dogs of hell, each last one of them, will be unleashed. Your man all right with that?'

Briefly, a touch of embarrassment, Boot hugged him, then opened the door. 'Have to be, won't he? If we can get hold of him.'

Daff had done further circles with her pen around the initials G F H. The letters were fiercely underlined with messy doodles surrounding them. But she had moved on, and the Maid had taken over the hard yards of tracking the man they wanted. The two of them worked well. Both would have said, with a noncommittal shrug, that Boot's office would have ceased to function without their efforts. Each would have supposed he realised their value but neither would have taken the conclusion for granted. The Maid ran the office, kept Boot to his schedules, filtered the material that bounced on to his screen, restricted his visitor numbers, always permitted him the opportunity to think, ponder, consider. Middle fifties, a son just out of university, and travelling, destination uncertain, father unknown but rumours abounded, and a reported permanent guest in a small central London apartment, a parrot. She was one of those rare people who were content with what life threw at them, happy with her

lot. All those years ago, when he had first started out on obsessed
journeys in pursuit of the truths of Waterloo, the Maid had found
the framed print: the Duke's face rising from the big black boot
and capped with jauntily feathered headgear. The only decoration she allowed in his work space. And, for most weekends, the
Maid booked the train tickets and alerted the accommodation.
And, this – now – was important business because the rendezvous with the history and dreams, of the sodden fields where the
battle had been fought, had been broken. She sat on the edge of
the table, tweed skirt and high-buttoned blouse, bobbed greying
hair and cultured pearl earrings, and had a brisk voice as she
demanded of bureaucrats – the Ministry, Hereford, a company
employing private military contractors – for a contact point that
would get her close to the location of the man with the initials G
F H, and was not demure when obstructed. Quite a violent volley,
abuse, then she had her hand over the phone speaker, the secure
line, and an aside to Daff.

'Getting there, not quick, but getting there.'

'And me . . .'

An unlikely pairing. Daphne, Daff since coming as a nervous
young woman into VBX, took time over her make-up and seemed
to party late and not only at weekends, and dressed well, and
showed herself to the world, tight jeans and a low-cut jersey – but
wore no rings and barely holidayed. Blonde pony-tail that swished
in the wind, tanned skin and shoulders that seemed powerful, tall,
exuding health. Might have deceived, played a part, might have
been beset with loneliness. Early in and late out. There were days
when Boot barely seemed to notice her presence but her loyalty
to him was complete. She had certificates in unarmed combat
and for pistol shooting and had done weekend courses with
Special Forces, could strip a standard assault rifle while blindfolded, and reassemble it. Could do much, but had not snaffled a
man, and might have felt that a failure, but might not. She went
home each evening to a quiet, empty flat and ate junk food and
watched junk TV, and never voiced regrets. She had recruited the
young man who had done the escort run for her down Route

Irish, had propositioned him at the embassy's pool café in the Green Zone, and would have expected to sleep with him if a friendly corner of Baghdad had been found. She hadn't – would not have objected, but had not. Sometimes, she'd lie awake and reflect that she had recruited him, pretty much encouraged and facilitated him into harm's way, but the needs of the job came first, as they should, the fucking job came always first. The deal was easy, and seemed acceptable to him, and she'd reckoned him as isolated as herself. They should have been kindred, except that he seemed more taken by the gut-churning excitement – and fear – of close-quarters combat. Monthly payments went through a discreet account, and in return he had access to the fighting at any location that was useful to Daff's team, being shipped to wherever was currently 'interesting' – which was Erbil inside the Kurdish enclave, and leading a fight against the lunatics occupying Raqqah and territory south of Mosul. Raw intelligence came from him, not the sanitised material that the 'professionals' produced. It had a value, was cheap at the price. He had been there a little more than a year, had not been home, and she had not travelled to see him, and his material came – when convenient – written in pencil on lined paper, and they learned how well the enemy fought, who were the better locally based commanders, what munitions and ordnance were most needed. Truth to tell, with the little nudge he had from SIS, and Daff's team, he could do his fighting as long as he cared – no shortage of opportunities – and his killing. Now, the Maid was trying to track him and Daff was busy lining up the back-up.

'. . . two in place, now. Don't sound a whole tin of beans, but it's what we have.'

The phone rang. Not at a good moment for Toomas. He wore a fake mediaeval helmet with narrow eye slits, a short-sleeved tunic of close-woven chain-mail, and his legs were encased in scarred leather. He carried a five-foot-long battle sword, which only a man of strength who claimed to be a serious fighter could have used in combat. It was the dress of the Livonian Order of Teutonic knights who had been sold the strategic castle of Toompea by the bank-rupt King Valdemar III of Denmark around the mid-forteenth century. The castle dominated the city of Tallinn and was where Toomas scratched a living.

On any November afternoon, as winter approached, tourists who had climbed the hill through the Old City to reach the forti-fications were harder to attract, and Toomas had just corralled a couple – Germans. He would pose for them and then he'd take off his chain-mail and let the young man wear it, then the helmet, and finally he'd hand him the big sword to brandish and the young woman would oblige with the camera. And they would tip . . . The phone rang persistently, and his covert glance at it revealed he was receiving an international call. He had the young man kitted for battle, and the flash from the camera lit him, and he spoke briefly into his phone and asked the caller to leave him for three minutes, then try again. He hurried the couple through the ritual.

An inevitable diminished reward. Usually he expected ten euros. They gave him five. He had rushed them and the chain-mail had caught the young man's ear and nicked the lobe as he dragged it over his head, leaving flecks of blood. He put the mail and helmet away, locked them in his cupboard off the museum's hall, with the sword, and waited.

Not long. A cool, clean voice, accented Russian as spoken by a Pole or a Czech. A murmur of introduction and the brief naming of a client, a security firm in São Paolo. A recommendation from Gdansk. A brief shiver in his back, and the mention of the money he would make, and the throwaway that his friend, Martin, would be part of it. He accepted . . . could not have done otherwise. His bank card was blocked, his rent was behind, his meals were increasingly basic and his drinking curtailed. Bad weather loomed, when no visitors came, and he would be reduced to standing, over Christmas and New Year, outside the restaurants in Raekoja Plats in crap fancy dress, hawking for business inside, with the funnelled winds cutting him. Too many years back he had done the run for Kaliningrad out of Gdansk to spy out the naval base for the

Russians' Baltic fleet. It would be good to be with Martin again, and with Kristjan – the woman had said she would call him next. Their grandfathers had come back to their home town in Estonia after weeks of training and preparation from British instructors, with an intelligence shopping list and the equipment for sabotage attacks.

The patrol boat, on a stormy night with sleet blocking visibility and the myriad islands along with the popple of the waves screwing the radar, had put the three young men ashore: Martin's grandfather shot dead in the reeds close to the shore ... Kristjan's grandfather seeming to break clear of the cordon and reach the main street ... and Toomas's grandfather wounded by gunfire in a small park near the town's walls, and taken. Not to hospital, but to Tallinn, and brought to the building with the big basements on Pikk.

Now, above the basements, were what the For Sale boards described as luxury apartments, homes for the youthful élite who had made good money from the newly independent country. The building's past, as headquarters of the Soviet special agency, KGB, could still give encouragement to the ghosts of six decades before. Toomas's grandfather had come here, received no medical attention, had been drugged to give him the strength to survive immediate interrogation, had been questioned while the tapes had turned and the investigators had hovered over him. He'd died in Cell 9A, and been consigned to an unmarked grave. On his way to and from the castle yard where he dressed as a mediaeval knight and entertained tourists, Toomas passed the building. The windows to the basement were now bricked up. The images of a young man, in bloodied clothing, wide-eyed and hoarse and maybe trying to be brave; maybe realising in the moments before the release of death that the organisation he had believed in was corrupt and that he had stumbled into a trap, and, had had no chance. Light rain was falling on the city as Toomas returned to his lodging room and started on the preparations to fulfil the new contract. Good to be wanted, and rare for him. He was in poor condition and short-breathed, but did not think it important. He would be driving to St Petersburg, not a problem.

They barely spoke. Nikki sat in the big room that had the work surfaces for their laptops, and where webs of cables burst from wall sockets and were tangled chaos, and some smoked weed – forbidden but ignored – and some were on cigarettes, and those who did the longest shifts would have 'phets to keep them going through the night. Himself, he drank coffee. When he went to the kettle, he did not ask the Roofer or HookNose or Gorilla if they wanted some. They were adjacent but hardly communicated, and did not socialise. The Ministry defences against his cyber entry in Chile's capital city of Santiago were pathetic. He had already exfiltrated the necessary file on a contract's confidential fall-back position, and had passed it on. The kettle howled, and he stretched and arched his back, and his joints creaked. Close to him were some of the people he would betray later in that week . . . he did not know what part he'd play. He had no love for any of them, for nobody outside the building except his sister. He went back to his chair and put down the coffee, and did not look to either side. The Roofer was an urban climber, went each weekend to Moscow and scaled the tallest of the Stalin-era buildings, had been many times to the star topping the Kadrinskaya, and was a celebrity inside his circle. HookNose was clever, arrogant, and quieter now that his face had been 'rearranged' by a guard on the gate to whom he was rude when his entry processing was slow, but the fist and the punch had come from an uncle of the GangMaster. Gorilla had the body of a child, the physique of a weakling, was timid in conversation, and came alive when the lights flickered on his laptop's screen.

They did not share sandwiches, pizza slices, or girlfriends, but lived their own lives. They were certain of the fact that they – each of them – was the best, and the rest of the team were 'donkeys'. Controlling them was their GangMaster, Vasily, the *avtoritet*, middle-aged but regularly with a new suit of quality Italian fashion and a new woman sitting in the passenger seat of a new sports car, and always drumming up new contracts. In theory, Nikki – indeed any of them – could have shut down his laptop, tucked it into a rucksack, collected what monies were owed him – might be $2000 – and gone out into the dusk to search out a new employer, to fetch himself a new roof . . . not as simple.

The GangMasters, those who ran the city of St Petersburg, were seldom in dispute and seemed models of commercial cooperation. They did not often poach, unless the object on offer was clearly beyond the capabilities, for exploitation, of a lesser clan. Nikki might have admitted, to himself, that he was held by the throat – he was employed at a monthly salary a little in excess of $2000. They had tight hold of him. If he attempted to break free then a phone call would be made and he would have nowhere to run to because he could not abandon his sister whose passport they held. Nor did he have money abroad because the account was in lock-down. He had called Stockholm and tried to speak to the manager who handled him, but had been put off, delayed indefinitely, and when he had asked for a transfer of cash – to a bank in Copenhagen – there had been vague excuses about computing failures. Cold hands gripped him, tough calloused fingers were embedded on his windpipe, and they squeezed, and pain seemed to run in him, and despair.

They were all of the same stock, Nikki and the Roofer and HookNose and Gorilla. They were clever and rebellious. Had been rejected by the FSB recruiters looking for the disciplined ones who might be inducted and work full-time in a barracks. Had been offered the pick of courses at the university. Had either rejected the invitation or had lasted a year and then dropped out . . . all of them. The remaining twenty hackers on the books of the GangMaster were fulfilled when they crawled along the narrow tunnels and entered the affairs and scholarship of men, women and corporations, and slipped away through trapdoors, via the help of the Trojan Horses, with the bundles of passwords and credit card details. The opportunities were without limit. It had brought him little. There was a sound behind him, by the door, a shuffle of shoes, whispering.

He looked. Why did he look? Did he show concern? Should not have done, but he had eased back in his chair and had turned his head. The Roofer and HookNose and Gorilla had not, were still absorbed by their screens and the columns of numbers running riot on them. The GangMaster was there, and a man who wore the uniform of seniority in FSB: short haircut, a suit of poor fit but expensive cloth, a belt tight on a heavy stomach on which shirt buttons were stretched. They were watched, might have been animals that farmers were discussing considering which would get a better price at the city's slaughter-house. Nikki knew the FSB colonel by sight; he came to the building once a month and might have collected the thick envelope that was the price of a roof. The GangMaster coughed for their attention. They gave it, but not with grace.

'I would like to remind you of the situation confronting two brothers – shits – who lived behind an armour-plated door. Not any longer. They are in Kolpino and in the Kresty Two gaol, accused of stealing from a fund that supports veterans of the Great Patriotic War. They took some twelve million roubles that were designated to help the veterans in the final days of their lives. As officers used a thermal lance to get through the door, the brothers stuffed money and memory sticks and phones, all the paraphernalia, into the bog and tried to flush it away: they blocked it. It is a lesson. There are matters which are prohibited and matters which are not, but you know that, and all your friends know that. But two brothers did not and will now rot in their cells, and if they come out for exercise, and are pretty, and have tight arses, then they will be fucked hard by the older *zeks*. Yes? We should spit on them. Perhaps you read of it in the papers yesterday. I think it would be difficult for those two brothers when they are in Kresty Two and they have no friends to cry with, only sore passages . . . I thought you would like to know. Many friends come this week and we will discuss and plan for a big operation, and it has the highest sanction. Please, carry on with your work.'

The GangMaster eased back into the corridor and pulled the door after him. The other three had not stopped their quiet tapping at the keys. Nikki shivered, and felt the cold at his back, and the chill on his skin. He would have sworn he had heard the whispered last remark of the GangMaster to the colonel of FSB.

'Little bastards – I'd not trust one of them. Come and have . . .'

Nikki's next target – to provide cash for the money mules to launder – was a law firm in the city of Orléans, on the River Loire in the heart of France. He did not know whether it was a fine city or a rubbish one. What mattered was that the lawyers handled the financial affairs of many wealthy clients . . . like picking the pocket of a man with a white stick . . . and he did not know what he would be asked to do.

As a major in the service of *Federal'naya sluzhba bezopasnosti*, Danik could have demanded a chauffeur to take him from home to the headquarters building at Liteyny Bridge. He declined that privilege. Neither he nor Julia, his wife, attracted attention to where and for whom he worked. He did not have a driver to take him to the Big House, nor was their apartment – two bedrooms and shared with their thirteen-year-old son – in a fashionable quarter of the city, but in a narrow street off Nevski Prospekt. At work, he had a room that was without natural light or a view. All that he did without was of his own choice, and his wife was wholehearted in her agreement of the principles he laid down.

The Major was secretive about his work, not only with neighbours in their block – who would have thought him one more government bureaucrat and without influence – but also with his supposed colleagues. They had drivers to bring them around the city, had bigger apartments, and some owned small villas in the woods outside the ring road. They also provided for others – the 'roofs' that were an accepted benefit of such a position. His car was a Renault, with big miles on the clock, and if he wished to do casual surveillance – not put an entire team to work – it was a useful model. The woman he had tailed had not seen him the night before, nor that morning – and then he had gone home and, with his wife, completed the redecoration of the kitchen. Paintwork drying, she had left for the hospital where her expertise was dermatology, and he had gone to FSB.

The woman was a sporadic target, but interesting to him for associations – and stupid. Useful to see where she went and then park with an infra-red camera on his lap and watch for the people coming to that café, and build a better picture. Useful also for him to see that she went to the airport early and shivered on the concourse and waited for her brother to come through off a Stockholm flight and then had driven him to the heart of an industrial estate in Kupchino district. The Major had noted the strength of the fences around the place, the size of the guards and the ferocity of a tethered dog, and drew conclusions. Obvious to his practised eye. He did not have a better car because he was clean and was not rewarded with one from the BMW range, as were his superiors. Nor did he live in a smarter apartment, and have a second home amongst the pines because he had no clan leader who paid him for discretion. He did not have a 'roof', nor did he provide one.

She was a little mouse of a woman, and stupid. He had arrested her twenty months before, along with others from that vipers' hole, and she had faced Public Nuisance charges. The leaders of the group had been jailed, but she and two others had just been reprimanded by the judiciary. She had lost her place at the Conservatory and if she were taken into custody again she would go to a labour camp. She was a potential delinquent and was therefore of interest to the Major. His role was to stifle dissent among the crazy few who, he believed, lived off a diet of self-induced publicity and staged stunts that were juvenile but also offensive: the painting of the penis on the bridge in front of the Big House; the naked man nailing his scrotum into the tarmac-adam; another who stripped then bound himself in loops of razor wire; the gang that undressed in a public museum and performed sex for their cameras ... they were at the front of rallies that denounced the President. The Major monitored them, knew most of them by name, tolerated stupidity, but clamped hard when a dangerous message was preached. If in St Petersburg, a group of girl-kids such as Pussy Riot had danced and made music over the altar of the cathedral dedicated to Saint Isaac of Dalmatia, he would without a qualm have dragged them off, handcuffed, to the cells. He believed in the rule of law. The law said what was permissible and what was violation. He took no bribes, gave no favours, was passionate about the disciplines of the legal code. He was regarded by colleagues as a man to be wary of, and it was said that he had the ear of a general in the upper reaches of the organisation. They were careful not to cross him.

The girl was stupid. She had stayed in the company of the dissenters. Her passport had been taken from her and she had no future, living hand to mouth from the table provided by her brother. And he was Nikkolas, employed by a gang operating out of the Kupchino district, and that was another story, and another complication. There was a supposed 'red line' around the gang, around the building and around the criminality practised there – another story, because a 'roof' was above that building, and the source of the protection was a colonel in an office suite two floors above. A further reason for the suspicion surrounding the Major was that he did not belong to their community; he had been recruited from the KGB of neighbouring Belarus, had come from Minsk to work in St Petersburg, with his wife and school-age son. His loyalties, other than to the law he had sworn to uphold, were not to his more senior officers. Efforts had been made to draw him into the web of corruption that nestled in the Big House, the network of favours and indebtedness. His refusals had been blunt and without equivocation. He lived within parameters and did his own work, but was not a crusader.

In his office, the Major updated his file on the young woman, Yekaterina, and those she associated with.

How would it have been on that day, in the full beat of summer, two centuries before? The armies had started to catch the pace of manoeuvre as they headed towards the sloping fields by the village of Waterloo … Boot had brought back a timetable from Stockholm. In his mind, the meeting of the more talented hackers in the industrial park hemmed in by tower blocks in the Kupchino district of St Petersburg matched the day of the battle. Four days before the immense collision that so fascinated Boot, the great Duke, always belittled by his opponent, the Emperor, would have started to place his disparate and multinational force into possible blocking positions to prevent the march of the French into Brussels. He would have been anxious, uncertain of the outcome, and of what weight to put on the qualities of the supposed allies. The Duke would have known that the Emperor was on the march through northern France, but intelligence would have been poor to non-existent, and no HumInt source was sending written dispatches to him. A great army approached but he did not know which bridges it had crossed, what route it was taking, how many guns it brought, the strength of the cavalry, and did not know, in spite of protestations, if his own people would stand and fight when called to. Great forces of young men, the majority of them inexperienced in the shock of combat, groping towards each other at the pace of an infantry march, three miles an hour and over rough ground and farm lanes, tens of thousands of them.

If there were lessons to be learned from the Duke, then Boot tried to absorb them. Top of the list was calmness, no visible sign of anxiety. Not just the tactics of military manoeuvre interested Boot, but in particular the leadership displayed by that grand commander, and the steadiness of nerve, and the ability to think on the hoof, change direction. The loneliness of the Duke intrigued him, too. He sent men into danger, sometimes expected to buckle under the weight of it, then looked to the Duke for guidance and strength. Difficult, of course it was difficult, but Boot could hide his emotions. He had taken a train to the west London suburb of Willesden, then walked to his destination, a demolition yard. He had waited patiently until the main gate was unlocked and he was escorted past raucous dogs to a portacabin. A mug of strong tea was in his hands, and he told Dennis what he needed, and when, and to where it should be delivered, and what remuneration would be applicable, and what weight might be necessary for the job involved. The weight, the timer, the detonator were specified.

'Always a bit of shrinkage in this line of business – thank God – and always will be.'

The voice boomed at Boot. He assumed that deafness went with the trade. The man, usually called Menace but that was not a familiarity Boot used, was gangling and large-limbed and carried a shock of unruly grey hair, and wore a wide grin. He'd seemed genuinely pleased that Boot had made the journey to the site by the railway line where, far from view, was a concrete-reinforced bunker holding a variety of explosives of different origins.

'Not featuring in the books, of course.'

Several small jobs, destruction and disruption, had relied in the last years on devices manufactured by the Menace. He had the wealth of experience gained from initial work with bomb disposal in the Province, then from the IED curse in Basra, then on the freelance bits and pieces he put together for Boot and others in the shadowlands. Always seemed to get a good bang for the buck. There were many people whom Boot knew who would not have acknowledged to any investigator that they had met him or done business with him. The difficulty was that they were all – and Boot – an ageing clan and work was less frequent so they retired and went to live on the coast. The Menace would see Boot out . . . The timing on the trigger was important, and the description of the building, and where the meeting would be held and the thickness of the walls and of the ceiling. Always a stickler for detail.

'Usually a bit left over. We had a load brought out from Syria only a couple of months ago, and detonators, so it'll all be good and up-to-date Russian stock. Generally comes in handy. And basic stuff for the mechanism. Assume it won't be a trained operative with a finger on the button? Take it as read. And the delivery? A laptop, yes?'

The tea was foul, but the Menace seemed to thrive on it and showed mild offence that Boot had not drunk more. They did a brief handshake, a caveman grip that crushed Boot's fist, and the dogs leapt at him and he was gone. Another man had been roped into the conspiracy and would not know to what purpose his work was put; many others would soon be corralled and have joined the periphery of the matter. Some Boot might hear of and of many he would be in ignorance. As it had been from the start of his career and under the tutelage of Oliver Compton, and he'd not lose sleep over it. Never looked back at the detritus left behind and had never waxed emotional. A good day, so far, but it was merely the beginning, and the prime brick was not yet in place. The clock ticked, as it would have done for the Duke.

'If I don't have some "air" we're going to lose . . .' Merc yelled into the handset.

The shooting had died – as if the guns were exhausted and needed to rest – but it would be temporary. A few minutes, deep breaths from the attackers and a surge of faith or confidence or hatred, and then they would come again. They were closer, hard up against the wire, and had brought planks from the rear. He was less certain, if they came again – as they would – that the line behind the sandbagged parapets would hold . . . Merc knew an answer to a question he might have posed. He could have shouted to his right and down the line where three of his people were, 'If we bug out and give it to them, then survival is assured. Do we go back?' Could then have looked to the left, where the machine-gun was, with a couple of short belts ready to go, and where Cinar stood, poking her head up for a better view of the wire and the soft slope beyond it that led down to the track where the pick-ups brought more men for the next push. 'It's only a corner of dirt and goat shit, and its loss isn't going to lose a war, and we've made the price of it heavy to them, and we'd have our honour – whatever that means – if we went back out of here. Any takers?' Didn't bother. He would have cheapened himself and broken their trust. They were tottering, having to lean on the sandbagged walls or they'd have fallen, and they had caked blood on them from handling the casualties and from their own scratch wounds.

'Without "air" we cannot hold Four Two Five. Is that understood? Over . . .'

If he had, turned away from the wire and slipped off, crouched low along the length of the communication trench, he would have gone alone. They would not have followed him. A voice came into his ear, seemed loud because of the sudden quiet, and it dripped the reasonableness of a staff-man safe in a concrete bunker and well to the rear of the sharp end of the defence line. As things stood, no 'air' was available, but the situation was under 'constant review', and if 'circumstances altered', and there was 'availability' then 'air deployment' to the Hill would get 'fullest consideration' – a pause, then 'Good luck to you, friend, and we're all rooting for you and if you feel it necessary to withdraw then your action will be well understood. Out.'

Merc saw a shadow moving at a languid speed across the wire and loitered for a moment. It might have been an eagle or could have been the shadow of a vulture – both were regular scavengers on the front line. Suddenly, a sparrow was perching on a strand of broken wire. His grandmother had liked them, and scattered crumbs for them. Nothing as majestic as the eagle and the vulture, able to soar and then dive, but a humble little thing; he had not seen it there before, and wondered why it had come and what it would find and . . . A grenade looped past it, and the sparrow flew off. Merc yelled the warning. Their machine-gun started up.

The dark figures, could have been twenty of them, were up and off the ground and planks were hurled at the wire, and there were more grenades, and more screams as the machine-gun scored. Merc could see their faces, and the gaps where teeth had been dislodged and the brilliance of their eyes. Heard the shouts, some in praise of God and some familiar insults about screwing the defenders' mothers. The sparrow was gone, and the big predator that had looked to feed and would now have to wait, and the memories of grandparents. Merc cleared his mind and had the rifle's butt hard against his shoulder, and tried to compensate for the hunger and the thirst, and the tiredness, and to aim straight, pick targets for the cross-hairs. His own grenade was against his chest, the hook latched on to the webbing.

The sun was hot, and the ground in front of him stank from the bloated dead, and clouds of flies swarmed over the wire.

What was he doing here? How long would he be here? Not easy to predict. Where else had it been as bad? Not possible to think of anywhere. When would he call it a day, assuming it was his decision? Sometime, just 'sometime' ... Only one thing Merc was certain of, with the recoil hammering his shoulder and targets dropping, and more coming, there would be no 'air' soon, not in time to save Hill 425, nor a small force marooned on its summit.

3

He was about to fire.

Merc had the target in the V and the needle, and was squeezing and did the breath control that he had been taught years ago doing the Pioneers' basic marksmanship. He had a full frontal of the guy and the aim would be into the chest while the man struggled in the wire. Squeezed on the trigger – it would have been a fraction of a second before the bullet was fired – and jerked off the aim, sucking breath deep down.

The sparrow was on an iron pole that held the wire close to the parapet. All the shit flying, incoming and outgoing, and the yelling of abuse from both sides – Cinar's voice as loud and as hoarse as any – and the crying of those who had been hit and had lost the numbness of the initial impact and wound. Merc saw his grandmother peering through her kitchen window into the yard, watching a sparrow picking bread scraps from the bird table. That sparrow brought peace to an older woman's life, one not blessed with comfort, nor much satisfaction: the sparrow in the yard lived for ever because if one died or disappeared another took its place. His grandmother's sparrow had immortality. He fired. Merc didn't know whether he'd had a hit or whether the fighter had ducked.

The machine-gun had gone quiet. Not the curses of the pair who crewed it. The gear they had to fight with was rubbish. The machine-gun was old, a 12.7mm calibre DShK; they were trying to get the bar up and it was locked. There would have been a round stuck in the breach. The weapon jammed regularly. Probably had gone into the Iraqi military arms dumps in the late eighties, courtesy of the Soviet Union in its last tottering days.

Might have had an airing in the first Gulf War, and might have
been dragged out and dusted down in the second scrap, and
been handed to its rabble by the Baghdad pretend régime in the
hope of fighting off the IS mob: they'd run, so the IS would have
owned it, then realised it was crap, and ditched it . . . The people
who Merc fought with now were beggars and did not choose;
they'd have captured it on a rare success against their enemy,
and it was again in service – and was again jammed. He cared for
his own weapon with meticulous attention and he pleaded, or
shouted, that maintenance was crucial, and they smiled,
shrugged. It was Merc who had to clear jams, and would have to
now. The machine-gun was the lynchpin of the defence position
on the top of Hill 425. Without it the time would come for pulling
the pins on the grenades that hung on the webbing close to their
heads and throats and vital bits. He had to do it. No one else
would.

Merc was shouting that he had to be covered, and the weapon
protected. He heard Cinar, taunting them beyond the wire. The
worst thing that could happen to an IS guy, whether he was local
or from Chechnya or from Canning Town, was to stop a bullet
fired by a woman from the Kurdish force; he'd get no welcome
from the Paradise virgins, so they gave the women a hard time if
they captured them, as hard as was imaginable. He heard her
voice and saw her face, her chin jutting, eyes blazing, and the
tunic of camouflage colours bulged on her chest. She wore no
helmet, no vest. Merc had limited command of the Kurmanji
dialect she used, but it was foul and would have whipped up their
fury as they came into the wire, and might have made them better
targets as she sapped their self-discipline. Merc abandoned his
place at the parapet and went to the machine-gun.

He elbowed the two young soldiers aside, and grabbed the
weapon. Merc knew that the great powers talked big at confer-
ences on the issue of supply – but the hardware did not arrive. No
anti-tank, no field rockets, no short-range missiles, and few night-
vision binoculars or personnel mines. His head would have made
a target but he needed the height. The thing would not shift, and

the volume of firing told him that the attack was edging closer and that – Murphy's Law – one of the grenades being lobbed towards them was going to come into the trench. The machine-gun was their prime weapon, and the attackers must have realised that it was screwed. The boys and the girls who fought with him – up on the parapet, blasting and frightened – would have known that the big gun, the DShK, was silenced.

A machine-gun's bullet took off an arm and a leg or pushed the bowels out through an exit wound by a broken spine, or decapitated a man; it lifted the morale of the defenders and dipped the confidence of attackers.

The obvious option now was to get out his short-barrel rifle, the Kalashnikov assault job. He looked after it, it was important to him, it was the one he held on the ride down Route Irish, and on convoy duty in Afghan. He raised it like a club, and brought it down like he was a demolition man on the bar above the bullet belt. He swung again, and hit harder, gasping from the effort, and from frustration. The bar swung clear. He had his hands on the cocking lever, and dragged it back, and the cartridge flew clear. He replaced the belt, and clamped down the bar. A big guy – black trousers, black tunic, black scarf wrapped tight around his head, and a thick ginger beard – was pulling clear of the last of the wire coils, a grenade in his hands. The DShK was wrested from Merc's fists, and was fired. The fighter was cut in two: might have come from Mogadishu or Morocco or from an inner Manchester housing estate; the beard colouring might have been from a bottle or might have matched his mother's hair. The body fell apart, there was a fraction of silence and then the grenade exploded in his hand and his blood and body parts sprayed over them.

What did Merc know? Knew that an AK was a piece of genius engineering. It fired. He had clubbed with it, and it still fired. A ragged green flag still flew from a pole rooted into the ground beside the bunker entrance.

Merc saw Cinar. She stood on an upturned orange box and no longer fired aimed shots but had her Kalashnikov level

with her hips. She blasted and screamed obscenities at the
attackers, and some must have heard her and identified her.
Merc was behind her and could not have said how the bullets
missed her. She had good shoulders, and decent hips, and a
head that was well proportioned. Her hair had come loose
from its fastening, and flapped, ebony-black, and she snarled
at them. He hit her, whacking his open palm against her butt,
feeling the flesh and the shape of the bone and the tight curve,
and belted her again.

Merc yelled, 'Not much good if you're dead . . . If you want to
quit, go, go and roll bandages. If you want to fight then keep your
fucking head down . . . see if I care.'

Reinforcements were spilling out of two more pick-ups and
coming up the hill. His little army were all firing, every weapon
on the hill, and there was the thud of the big machine-gun, but
more were coming up towards the wire . . . Cinar's lip was
bleeding from where she had chewed on it, and the blood looked
good on her jaw, and she was aiming and was trying to kill . . .
They all were, had to be, or they would lose and if they lost they
were dead.

The sand from a punctured bag blew into Merc's face and
briefly blinded him. He wiped his eyes and went on shooting,
suppressive fire – 7.62 ball going from the barrel at a velocity of
2400 feet per second, and 1000 feet effective killing range, and the
targets were close enough, 150 feet, to see them, recognise them,
and hurt them . . . He never considered the 'sensible' option to
withdraw. He did not think they would survive the dusk. The low
sun was in their eyes. Another of them went down and no one
could abandon the parapet to comfort the flailing shadow of a
man, or stifle his screaming.

With the skills, instincts and purpose of a ferret seeking its prey in
a labyrinthine rabbit warren, the Maid hunted him down.

She would not have considered putting down her phone,
getting the screen save picture of the parrot – a Rainbow Lory
from Indonesia that was a foot tall and had cost her £400 – and

announcing she had failed to find him, that Gideon Francis Hawkins was out of her reach. The Middle East sections in VBX claimed no record of him; the Station Officer based in Erbil was home on leave and said to be wilderness-hiking; the Ministry of Defence denied knowledge of him; and the private military contractor who nominally employed him said they had lost touch . . . Follow the money. Close to Erbil was a front line more than a hundred miles long, and scattered along it were the riff-raff of volunteers, wannabe heroes and cordite addicts. Somewhere there would be a bunk bed with a table beside it, and on the table would be a Will and Testament in a grubby sealed envelope. The Americans would have done it on some damn great search engine. By following the money, the Maid came upon a bank in rural Buckinghamshire and roused a junior manager from the late afternoon job of closing shop. A call to head office; a suggestion that compliance was advisable: a PO Box address in Erbil, the Kurdish-controlled sector of northern Iraq, and a barracks where the envelope would be. The search was narrowed further by a conversation with the Adjutant's office in the Hereford camp, and a call-sign given for personnel who would know of him in that small and clannish society of foreign fighters.

She had spoken to Brad, faraway and faint. He had passed her to Rob, his soul mate. The Maid had stressed urgency, and already had an executive jet fuelled, with a flight plan filed, on the apron of the RAF's Akrotiri base. She had said what she wanted, not for discussion but as an instruction. Had put down the phone, had revelled in the clout her status gave her, and had crowed across the little room towards Daff and clenched a fist.

'Amazing, just like the old days and . . .'

A dry grin. 'The "good" old days.'

'Taken as read. We'll have him on board by the day's end. Piece of cake . . . sitting around in some distant corner, with his feet up – we'll be making his day.'

The Maid went to brew a pot of tea, and Daff's face lit up and she scribbled on her pad. Coming nicely together, and soon Boot would be back in the building, in time for the meeting on an upper floor, and the authorisation: a chuckle, 'never in doubt'.

She had a number. Had an address.

A town she had not heard of. Daff pushed it up on her screen, and her interest went rampant. Her lip curled and her tongue clucked, and she zeroed in on the map. They were a trio, almost brothers, and with a shared heritage and a smidgeon of experience. Probably enough, because innocence might be of more value than a calculation of danger. She had two of them in place – Martin and Toomas – and now went after the third. She dialled.

A man's voice answered, in what she assumed was the Estonian language that she did not speak, and the tone was stressed, impatient and irritated. In English, she purred a greeting.

Kristjan listened as an offer was made to him.

The young woman worked round him, and had already filled two bin bags and was loading a third. He stood in the centre of the room, his phone at his ear and his back to the bedroom door. She had cleared the bed of the linen she'd brought to his apartment four months before, and the wardrobe doors were open and the rail and most of the shelves were bare. Now her attention was on the photographs she was taking with her, and the personal items she had said would make the two rooms more 'lived in' and she had ripped the poster of a summer view of the research town of Sillamae – Stalinist, glorious, the uranium centre – off the plaster, exposing the damp patch and the mould. There was the blast of a horn from the street below. The phone call came with an offer of work. Important for him. He had tried to keep her, but she cost too much. Her clothes purchases went far beyond what she earned waitressing and what he made from shelf stacking in the supermarket on the main road towards Tallinn. His debit card was registering 'refusal' at the ATMs, and he thought she'd found a new guy to milk, and he was late with the rent. It had been good for a couple of months and then the bickering had set in, then the shouting; he'd regret her going if only because, at his age, it was not easy to find a woman with blonde hair, natural, and a good waist, and . . . Could he speak? He could. Told what was wanted, what the remuneration would be. How did the caller know of him? How did a company based in São Paolo, hear of him? Would he be alone and. . .? With his friends, with a team leader of quality, and only for a few days, not more than a week – and very careful organisation.

He agreed. Then realised that he had not seen her leave. He heard the block's outer doors creaking and closing, then a car's boot being slammed, then the engine starting up and the car pulling away. He went to the window, saw it turn on to the main road – and was alone. He was forty-three, and had – until the phone had rung – little to consider other than a partner walking out on him, taking most of the bed linen, half of the little that had been in the fridge, and all of the drink. He could see the ramparts of the twin castles, the one on the Estonian side and the one across the river on Russian territory, and he could see the far end of the bridge that spanned the Narva. His grandfather had been taken across an earlier bridge on the same site: would have been on the floor of a closed van, manacled and blindfolded and probably semi-conscious from the beatings. The other two who had come ashore with his grandfather would by then have been dead, but this prisoner had been driven to Leningrad, and then had disappeared. An unmarked grave, of course, after they had finished with him in a basement, and hosed down the floor; might have been a bullet that had sent him on his way, or might have been the scale of the injuries . . . He hated them . . . Because of his hatred, he had gone with Martin and Toomas to Kaliningrad. It would be good to be with them again, and to have money rattling in his pocket, and to remember what had been done to his grandfather.

He readied himself to go to work, the evening shift when he would load the shelves with produce for the morning – and wanted to pinch himself to prove that he was not dreaming and the call was genuine, that he was indeed wanted. And he had the

assurance that he would be with 'a team leader of quality', which
calmed him, someone to follow.

'You know what? You know what he said to me, Brad?'
    'What did he say to you, Rob?'
    'Can't credit it.'
    'Spit it out.'
A Special Forces team, Hereford and Poole, had ownership of
an annexe off the main command bunker, more of a broom
cupboard than a work area. The larger space adjacent to them was
for the air strike coordinators who could call in firepower from the
carriers in the Gulf or from Incerlik where the USAF had use of a
Turkish strip, and the British base on Cyprus. They had a fridge
in there and air-con and armchairs. Brad was a corporal and Rob
was a sergeant. They had taken the call from London, and now
had to decide how to reach Merc.
    Not friends, but had occasionally enjoyed a beer in the bar of
the International or the Marmounia back in Erbil and when he
was out of the line. It was a complex arrangement and one closely
monitored because of the Government's fear of 'mission creep'.
They were part of a training team, but occasionally did an unau-
thorised sniper mission, taking down a prominent target when
he went to defecate at dawn on the front line and was still bleary
and made an opportunity for the cross-hairs – and they taught
the fighters of the YPG the basics of field tactics, and had done
time with Fire Force Unit 47, and had met him . . . Shy, often
looking at his watch and indicating there was somewhere else he
ought to be. And could recall that he'd a place in their lives from
far back, in the glory days. He was not like those who'd come out
from UK on a 'crusade' and were looking to fight 'evil' and to
'save civilisation as we know it'. They'd seen him with spooks
and assumed that he was in bed with them. They'd talked of him
when the call had come from London and Brad had spoken to
the toff-voiced girl who'd seemed to assume that he didn't know
the Official Secrets Act, talked of him while they'd tried to work
out how to get her message through. Summarised: had arrived in

the Kurdish sector, had dug himself in, had made a name for himself which was quietly built and based on a bedrock of support from the people in the Fire Force who served with him; had no rank, and no bars on his arm or pips on his shoulder, but had been elevated to responsibility. Difficult for either of them – with their military background and culture of promotion and command ladders – to pigeon-hole him. Didn't talk about home, didn't have arms disfigured with tattoos, girls' names gouged out, didn't boast about kill rates . . . Seemed as happy to be in a corner with a stack of Mercedes car brochures, or with an out-of-date copy of *Auto Trader* or *Exchange and Mart*, but he listened – without interrupting – when they briefed on close-quarters combat, and the reinforcement of a fire position's defences . . . Just before Rob had raised him they had talked of where he was: a Forward Operating Base on Hill 425, a salient that stuck out from the main defence line and was of some use to the YPG, and some nuisance to the 'bad boys'. Rob had called him. Not a long call. The essence was the passing of the instruction of the toff-voice, and where he'd be met, and a few of the logistics details, and they might even go get him themselves when the relief shift arrived, which would make a welcome change from the stale air of the annexe. Brad had listened, waiting for Rob to say how it would work, what the schedule would be and . . . rare astonish-ment on Rob's face.

'He told me to go take a flying fuck.'

'He did what?'

'What he said I should do . . .'

'And explained?'

'Did explain . . . was on a shit heap. Was taking casualties. Was refused air support. Was not even going to consider quitting on his people who held that crap piece of ground against "human wave" stuff. Would not be leaving without them. Would not be leaving – any of them – and giving it up, Hill 425, to the opposi-tion. Was too busy to talk to me, would I get off the line and feel free to go take the "flying fuck". I could hear it all going on round him . . . I suppose he's gone native.'

'You'd better get back to the totty and tell her the good news.'

'And they were sending a plane from Akrotiri for him, the full works. Just said he wasn't shifting, not giving up on his team or his heap of shit . . . Actual words were "Leave the boys and girls? Not while we've got these people in the wire. What, have them put in a cage and the ground round them soaked in petrol and a camera running? You'll think of something to say, Bobbo", then he cut the link. Takes all sorts, Brad.'

'What'll they do about it?' Brad's voice tailed off because Rob was already on the secure line calling London.

It was why the Maid loved him. A brief window of insight into what she would have called Boot's dynamism, and she noted that Daff shared her feeling. Both of them stared at him, awe on their faces. Boot at his best.

The door of his office was open. He had not bothered to take off his coat, nor his familiar trilby. He had heard her out, the report of the call back from the Kurdish heartland, and the tongue-tied sergeant's explanation over a poor connection given no help by the scrambler filter. On the wall beside his desk, where he now sat, was the framed print of the Wellington Boot. Barely a day went by that the Maid would miss going in with a duster and wiping and polishing the glass, and then she would flip it over the set of dentures on his desk. Other women on that corridor, aides and bottle washers, bad-mouthed their chiefs; she had never done so. She heard him demand access to an operations cell in some ministry bunker tucked away in the Home Counties. He'd looked up, seen their wide eyes, and because of his trust in them – reciprocated – had explained.

'Why him? Why take the trouble? Why not cast the net wider? Because of who he is and what he is, and the sort of boy that Daff identified for us more than a decade ago has been worth monitoring. As if all the faith we put in him, and others, was for a culmination, this moment, what his talents deserve . . . Do they come on trees? Sadly, not. Something very steady about him, and a leader who inspires – not Henry Five stuff, but a man who makes "ordinary" people feel good, and they'll follow, and go extra yards. He's in a shooting war now, but that's not why we want him . . . Looking for that calm under pressure, the ability to survive when the odds are stacked, and the boy – what did we call him? Yes, *Hatpin*, yes – the boy will, as night follows day, wobble. One thing to agree to everything I say, but quite another when I'm not there and cannot work the verbal thumbscrew on him, do the psychological water-boarding. So he does not back away, I'd want *Hatpin* to have our friend, Gideon Francis Hawkins, right up alongside him . . . No one else, no one better.'

The little smile. The Maid watched, listened. Daff, beside her, was motionless. Neither woman had ever succeeded in lifting a veil and so understand the relationship, between Boot and his wife – Gloria, daughter of a long departed Assistant Director, manager of a bric-à-brac store in Hampton Wick, south-west London, widow to the obsession of a battlefield in Belgium – and he had never touched either of them who worked his outer office, or showed a sign of wishing to. After that little smile, his face had hardened and the link would have been made to whoever he had demanded to speak to.

No bluster and no wheedling, no raised voice nor deferential whisper. The Maid would have described his tone as that of a householder ordering a delivery of coal or heating oil. A clear voice, and matter-of-fact tone; couched as a request but that was for the sake of politeness. The authority was there, blazoned, and seemed out of kilter to those watchers in the outer office. Odd from a man who would not have stood out in a crowd and had a wan complexion and spectacles with heavy lenses, and grey hair that was thinning and wispy above the ears. What should be done and when . . . not 'why' because that was none of their damn business. He finished the call. No gratitude expressed before its termination. Boot stood and took off his coat and hat, and unravelled the scarf from his throat.

The Maid asked him, 'Would you like a cup of tea? Set you up nicely before you go upstairs. Probably what we all need, a cup of tea.'

*   *   *

'Something choice for me, Boot?'

Offices with grand views up the Thames and down the river, and the light was dipping over the London skyline, and artists would have thought the vista worthwhile but challenging, and the water was silver, and the roofs and jutting towers were bathed in grey gold. Boot never wasted a moment with admiration of what was laid out below him.

'Quite choice. I think you'll like it.'

Did he want coffee, water, a sherry? He declined and was waved to an easy chair.

'And time is against you?'

'Time, forgive me, is a bugger. Short of it.'

The Big Boss sat, loose-limbed, on the edge of his desk, jacket off and tie unknotted. He held a small knife, one for opening envelopes, and used its tip to clean his nails. His heels beat a tattoo on the desk's panels, and he showed the enthusiasm of a man who had once been a warrior and was now constrained by the limits and loftiness of his position. There might have been a gleam of envy in his eyes, also caution. Like two maelstroms that collided, and might then create true havoc . . . Envy, aloft in VBX, had an advantage over innate caution. He had reason to be wary because the man sitting in front of him was renowned for the silkiness of his proposals – but Boot was credited also with good triumphs, unpublicised. His host, whose sanction he needed, cut to the quick.

'Take it as read that I am exercised by the cyber business, exercised and frankly rather fearful, and I've read the last tract from your Trust, the young lions, which moves beyond fearful to frightening. You have a proposal. Give it me, Boot, warts and all.'

Boot did not gild nor economise with truth and facts. A quiet voice, and all done with the fluency of confidence. As he spoke, a device was being put together, of a size that would go neatly into a laptop, and he said what weight of explosives would be used, and its origin, and the same for the detonator. He listed the factor that confirmed 'attribution' and passed two photographs towards the Big Boss. One showed a pale, concave-chested youth, straggling hair and spots on his lower cheeks and tiredness mingling with stress in his eyes. The second picture was of a two-storey building surrounded by a perimeter fence, and he gave the date and time of a meeting and was able to point out the first-floor window of the room where it would be held. He took his time and was not interrupted. His own position was simple, Boot played the part of facilitator. The man across the Bokhara carpet from him was the can carrier.

'High-quality people to attend the meeting, as good as they have. A reasonable assumption, a specific attack on a scale rarely seen will follow: financial mayhem, possibly catastrophic damage to the infrastructure, loss of intelligence capabilities, our defences depleted. And we are in the front line. You know all that. I can justify this as a pre-emptive mission. And we wrong-foot them. It's what we do rather well, I hazard.'

A deeper breath, a pause that had theatrical effect, then an explanation. By the following day, mid-afternoon, what Boot described as his Brains Trust would report again – a couple of A4 sheets – on levels of infiltration from state-sponsored attacks, and there would be a paragraph on 'immunity' and another on protection and one that would be headed with the word for deception, *maskirovka*, and the skills with which the assaults by cyber weaponry were disguised. Stuff about danger, and stuff about the ever-increasing scale of the probing, and the vulnerabilities of UK infrastructure. And Boot escalated, ramped it, and his voice was compelling.

'We look at the new sciences, and they tell us how to defend ourselves, within tight parameters, and we know that we lose in more areas than we win. We can fry a few computers, we can wipe their memories, we can *inconvenience* but achieve little more. They damage us, we do not damage them. Forget the Americans' gripes, or the Germans, think only of UK. Imagine it, a meeting where our principal politician takes their President to one side, the two of them and an interpreter, and says, "Vladdy, I'm not happy with the cyber business and what you're chucking out from your territory. I'd like it reined in, wound up . . . You game for that, Vladdy?"

Would get a sneer of contempt. What I am saying is that we face their "Pearl Harbor Opportunity", riots on our streets, food shortages, power outages. It is in their hands. Am I carrying you with me?'

'Listening, Boot – but confess to nerves because of where you are bringing me.'

'I feel confident that the areas of anxiety are pretty much closed off.'

'Advantages, what should I look for?'

'We bring their world, the playground bully's world, crashing down around their feet – not something they will enjoy.'

The lighting was soft and there were gentle voices from the outer office that played through the closed door. Dusk was settling over the river, and the bridge below them was a stream of cars and lights. There could be rain within the hour.

'You're not asking me for a sub-committee's evaluation?' Almost a boyish grin from the Big Boss, and forewarned of the answer.

'Not on the schedule we are presented with . . . This is Monday. The opportunity is Thursday. Can I do the sort of risk assessment and mission statement that a sub-committee require in the next hour, and you have a team wheeled in . . . We need to be on the move tomorrow . . . It is in your hands, Director.'

A fist smacked on to the desk. Getting there, close to and ready to breast the tape.

'Open to argument, Boot . . . But I need to know – would we be making a difference?'

'It's an unpleasant and unwelcome shock for them. Disruption on a considerable scale, something to remember, a high degree of confusion that spreads unpredictably . . . And the buck passing and back stabbing would be wondrous to behold.'

'Nearly there but, please, more.'

'And we have "deniability". They love deniability, treasure *deniability* in the way elderly paedophiles do. Remember the deniability after they'd poisoned – an order given from the fulcrum of power – the defector. More deniability when their damned missile brought down that aircraft on to those Ukraine plains. I'd be giving you "deniability", by the wheelbarrow.'

'Are we talking, Boot, I repeat, about making a difference?'

'They'll be rats in a sack, hating each other, trust out of the window, and the big men alongside their chief will be scratching each other's eyes out. Easy to imagine that the "atrocity" is the work of rivals, not the poor old toothless lion, with mange on its arse. A major diversion, I'd call it, for that cabal of gangsters that call the shots there. We might leak a bit as well, through Helsinki or Stockholm, tit-bits about civil war among the inner circle. But, for that to happen, I have to have your ink on the paper.'

'Not galloping too fast, Boot? Assure me.'

'Think of the Duke. Everything was on the hoof. Moments of weakness had to be defended, moments of strength exploited. We have to react to the opportunity presented. Will you sign it off? It's a breathtaking chance, one cast in gold.'

'A good man?'

'Just putting that together.'

'A man of proven ability?'

'It's an old way of doing things, and they are often the best ways. Do I understand the arts of cyber attack, cyber theft, cyber espionage, and all the new jargon that goes with it? I do not. What I do understand is the value of robust response. Retaliation. And if the disguise cloaking it is approaching foolproof, then I like it even better. What we know of him, our man has the talents we require. Director, I have to know, and not tomorrow.'

He put an intolerable pressure on the Big Boss's shoulders. Acknowledged it, felt none the worse for it, and tried to imagine how it would be in the dropping light of a damn bloody awful day, with the last of the sun burning into their eyes, and in combat – which he had never known. Stress and anxiety, yes, never close-quarters fighting – and he thought he might have shouted from the rooftop, where all the antennae made a scruffy forest, that his man should hold on . . . just a bit longer, hold on tight. 'Don't quit on me now. Don't let those savages get their hands on your collar. Hang on in there . . .' Should have shouted it towards the rain clouds.

'You'll not quote me, Boot, never do that. God knows, I take a chance. Ruled by the heart and not the head. I share it, even sparsely, and I hit an immediate wall of "mitigation" – "mitigating circumstances" – and therefore a reason to do nothing, the Pitmans for "appeasement", and the hope that if we do nothing, make no fuss for their incursions, human and cyber, and look the other way, give them bloody tea and cakes and jam, then they will go away. That's the wall and I am, sensibly or not, prepared to skirt it and walk round it. See me before you deploy your dogs. Go for it.'

The Big Boss turned away, and Boot was up out of his chair, and away. Could permission be rescinded once granted? Possibly . . . He took a lift down, and seemed light-footed, and plunged out and into his own corridor and the blood pulsed in him.

He was inside his own area, his fiefdom. The women watched him, looked for a sign. He masked his features, was impassive as he went to his inner lair. Boot knew what he wanted, found them, held them in his right hand. He did a jig. Ludicrous and clumsy, using the dentures, the Waterloo teeth that had been a present from the Maid, as if they were castanets. He pirouetted, and spun, and the clacking sounds filled the room as the teeth of the young soldiers hammered together – perfectly preserved two centuries after the village women had been out on to the battlefield with their crude pliers. It would be a grand show, it would be the fulfilment of Boot's career. He sagged, and the teeth went quiet . . . They would have understood, pikestaff plain, that the operation across a frontier was approved, but neither Daff nor the Maid could match it.

'Is he clear? Do we have him?'

The Maid said, 'Not yet. We stay hopeful. Too early to know.'

He put the dentures carefully back on his desk, and his emotions were again concealed. He settled in his chair, and closed his eyes. Wanted that young man, and badly – but must wait. Could not do any other, and was practised at it. He waited to be told as the evening, and darkness, settled round him. It would be the summit of his career.

Nikki dropped it.

Was taking out a bag of crisps . . . Dropped a business card. Would have stuffed it into his shoulder-bag, missed it when he had cleared out the bag and made certain that the hotel bill, and the airport bus tickets, and the receipt from the restaurant, were dumped, not brought back to St Petersburg.

'What's that?'

The Roofer was behind him. Nikki swung in his chair. The card was the account manager's at the bank with the branch on Kornhamnstorg. Magenta with the man's name and contact details in embossed gold, one given only to a client of value. He swivelled his chair and reached down. Not fast enough. The Roofer had it. He tried to snatch it back and failed.

'A bank card from Stockholm, and gold—'·

'Give it me.'

'Do we have *please*? *Give it me, please.*'

One of those days. Raw nerves, tempers to be exploited. Amusement in short supply. Interest now from HookNose and Gorilla. Nikki was still in his chair and the Roofer was tall, a skin-and-bone body, his narrow arm held high, and the fingers extended, holding the card, beyond reach. The name on the card was read out.

Nikki pushed himself up. The card was in the name of the Account Manager Private Wealth.

It was an idiot's mistake. The blood ran in his face, and his breath came faster, and his colouring would have told them that the game might betray him. They were bored and it was the time when they'd have slapped shut their laptops and gone out into the evening. There would be little to match the discomfort of one among them who carried the business card of a bank in the Swedish capital. It was not in Nikki's nature to smile, make a joke – a rich girlfriend in Stockholm, needing financial guidance, big laugh, a great screw, but useless with money, roll his eyes – then put out his hand for the card, and say, *Please*. And they might have collapsed in laughter and made him talk about the girl and what he did in bed and ... Could not have, and might not reach the card if he sprang for it. His mind turned, but slowly. HookNose wanted to look at it. Gorilla tugged at the Roofer's arm.

Nikki jumped. Stood on his toes and pushed the chair back for more thrust and reached for it. Had hold of the thin fine-boned fingers of the Roofer, what he used in the crannies of a building to haul himself higher. Had the fingers, crushed them, squeezed them, and the card was released, and the Roofer howled and his face contorted. The card floated down. Gorilla would have had it but Nikki had his foot across it. The Roofer was squealing, and was hurt: he needed his hand for his keyboard and his climbing. Nikki crouched, moved his foot, pocketed the card that was torn and bent and had the street dirt of his trainer sole across it.

'I was given the card, going to use it, should be a good way in.'

Who would have believed him? Would not have believed himself. Gorilla would not, nor HookNose. The Roofer would have doubted that a fellow hacker would use such violence to defend information on a target. He wondered if the Roofer was about to hit him.

The GangMaster was at the door. The mood was hidden, but would not be forgotten. Fear made him loathe them. Nothing said ... The GangMaster talked about targets and the need for more material for the money mules, and seemed wary of them, like a keeper venturing into the big cat cages of the zoo on Alexandrovsky Park. Nothing said, but everything would be remembered. The evening closed in on the building and Nikki shivered, and had committed himself and did not know when he should have brazened it out with them, turned his back on the quiet-voiced Englishman in the hotel room, there had not been such an opportunity, and he thought that was the skill of the man who had impaled him. He said nothing, lowered his head over his screen, looked for another trapdoor. He had no friend other than his sister. The darkness of a foul winter night was outside.

The voice chimed in Nikki's ear. 'I'll hurt you for that, fuck you till you scream.'

In that exposed backwater of northern Europe, the night was around the house, and the wind came under the eaves and lifted those pieces of the roof that neither of the old couple, Igor and Marika, could make good, and draughts speared between the window-frames and the walls, and under the main door.

They had repaired the house themselves, but years earlier. Never married but had been together since she was eighteen, and he sixteen. If the logging man, Pyotr, had not come two or three times a week, and done their paperwork for them, paid the few bills for which they were liable, and helped them with the live-stock, they could not have survived there. Pyotr worked timber, was also a part-time sergeant in the militia and had arranged for them to live in the security zone beside the river, the border. The wind made music in the trees and funnelled down the Narva river, with powerful eddies branching off along the fire breaks in the forest and pummelling against the house. There was a saying among the elderly in those parts – five or six kilometres back from the river and hidden in forest: 'I want to see my neighbour's smoke, but I do not want to see him.' When Pyotr had a big fire in the yard beside the buildings where he kept his tractor and his flat bed and some of his tools, they might have seen it . . . except that Igor had long lost the sight of his right eye and boasted a glass one of milky blue.

They were peasants of Mother Russia, witnesses to the fero-cious history of that region that had been fought over many times and many times changed allegiance. They would not have known of the great power politics played out in that sector of their country but had suffered from armies coming along the mud lane between the trees, tanks and artillery pieces in advance and in retreat, and there had been the deportations of agricul-tural collectivisation, and . . . They had no photographs of the great men intruding on their lives, of Hitler or Stalin or Kruschev or Putin. The radio reception was poor in spite of Pyotr's best efforts, and the old generator was erratic and too many times the lights failed and there was no consistent signal from the wireless set. They listened intermittently to a concert because they liked to see the front of the set lit up, but both were deaf. Louder than the music, and the wind's howl, were the cries of the animals in the barn. A shot-gun stood behind the front door, and three dogs slept in front of the wide fireplace, where logs hissed, and they talked of when they might have to consider bringing the live-stock into their living area: a pair of cows, three pigs, two sheep and their chickens. No one would come that night and few knew of them and of the existence of the five-hectare smallholding. If the snow was bad they brought the animals in with them, and they loved them, all of them, and the dogs, even more than they loved Pyotr on whom they depended.

Close to the house built from felled timber were the four fields they had cleared. Laborious, back-breaking work, and they had dug the necessary drainage ditches in the soft bog and made beds where they grew vegetables and summer fruits. Farther away, in summer, the animals grazed. They had made it all and would not lightly let it go. When they were dead – an understanding that when one went the other would reach for the shotgun behind the door – they had agreed, unsigned, that Pyotr would take over the house and the land.

No phone, no gas, light from a generator, a log fire for warmth, no telephone or mobile, but neither would have considered that fortune had dealt them a poor hand. They had each other, and a sort of freedom, and no strangers came. The route to the river bypassed them by a clear kilometre and was used by smugglers of cigarettes and alcohol, and by the militia patrols, but Igor and Marika were left undisturbed. They had eaten their dinner, pancakes and omelette with potato, and drunk their well water that was discoloured but never did them any harm. The radio was loud and the dogs slept and the animals cried and no one came to intrude on them. Their lives were a long story but they seldom recited it.

The fire blazed and soon they would be ready for bed, barely undressed, and sleep.

Brad had the earphones clamped tight on his skull.

'They're on their way, five minutes or ten, but coming.'

Rob shook his head, bemused. 'Makes you wonder why he matters. No chance of a lie, Brad, they wouldn't do it for us.'

'Not arguing ... Young Merc – who'd have believed it ... Suppose we'll go and get him, soon as they've been and gone.'

He sat in his chair, no light on, and chewed at the stem of the clay pipe. He could not light it because alarms would have sounded across the floor and down the corridor, but he bit carefully on it, and imagined. Seemed to hear the roll of the wagons on farm tracks and the booming rumble of the iron-shod wheels when they lurched up from hitting wedged stones, and the protests of the horses that dragged them, and the cursing of the men who were bent under the weight of their own kit. They would not have known where they were headed and what the day would hold when the light next came. The quartermasters would have yelled at them to keep up the pace, and ahead would have been a myriad of small lanterns. Most would have had little or no food for the bivouac that night. They might cross the frontier during darkness, or at dawn, and then the great adventure would be launched. Veterans spoke of Brussels on their route and told the newest recruits, first time in a Bonaparte army, that they would be welcomed there, and have good whores. Earlier, they would have moved to the side of the track and manoeuvred the loaded wagons, but would not have sworn in protest because they had made way for their Emperor's carriage with its escort of clattering cavalry. They would have raised their headgear, held up their rifles, cheered him, and some might have seen him through the carriage window. And they would have been heartened ... He seemed to hear all that, and could see the teeth on his desk, and if he tilted his head could see also the cartoon rendering of the Duke and his Boot.

Nothing he could do. He put the pipe away in a drawer, stood up and shrugged into his coat, took his trilby from the stand, and wished them good night. He thought one at least would sleep there on the camp bed, mount a vigil until news came from some wretched front line on a horrid little corner of sand. He told them he was going home . . . Gloria had promised to serve a good goulash, which he fancied tonight . . . Nothing more to be done.

She bayoneted the boy. Merc saw it from the corner of an eye. Could not get a proper sight of it, the plunge of the blade, its disappearance into the black material, then coming free and the light shining on it, then the thrust repeated. The radio was by his feet and was a mess of casing and wiring, and the circuit board was stamped on and crushed . . . Pleased he'd remembered to do that, destroy the communications, because there would be prime call-signs and linking numbers held in it, and if they were over- run – *when* – it would be a good prize. He fired, and might have been down to his last dozen rounds, and had only two grenades left on top of the one clipped to the webbing across his chest. He saw Cinar stab the man with her bayonet blade, and it told him that she had fired her final bullet, and probably dare not go down on her hands and knees and scrabble into the dirt at the trench bottom, to go though the kit of any of the ones already too damaged to fight on, or the dead. Over the parapet, though, he had good visibility because there were flares fired high into the sky by support from farther to the north. But no reinforcements were spared, and a diversion attack was underway to the south of the Hill. They were isolated, and the enemy came for the kill. He might not have seen it well, but he heard it clearly and over the rattle of firing and the explosions and the screams – her voice loudest and her foul mouth worst – was the soft cry from the guy at her feet, This was his foreign field, and no one would even have known his bloody name. He yelled instructions.

Merc tried to lead, to be the example that they would follow. It was a hill, a pimple on a plain, and the blood drained away into the soil. They came again in a rush.

The instructions were to 'fire only aimed shots' and to 'stay strong' and to remember their 'families', and to 'take one with you'. It had not been as bad in the Afghan days, or going down Route Irish with the weapon on automatic and two magazines full and strapped together. The guys coming against them must have trampled the stomachs and spines, chests and backsides of their fallen friends, so many had gone down. A new sound intruded . . . The light faded and a flare died and the dark shapes came again and he heard the rending of clothing on the wire, but there was a new noise, first faint and then growing and gaining power as it approached. Two of them were in the trench. He saw the bayonet blade raised but another came behind her. Merc fired and the figure fell, but another replaced it. He heard nothing. The roar swamped his ears.

Merc could not have said whether they had Royal Air Force markings, or were American, or piloted by Jordanians, Saudis or Australians. They came low and dumped their cargo on to the wire, and Merc was cowering at the bottom of the trench and lay on a body and did not know if it was a friend's or an enemy's. The explosions came in a deafening ripple, and earth and wire and stone flew far, wide, high. Before the quiet came and before his ears had recovered they had turned and swooped again for a second bombing run and dropped more. Then they climbed towards the stars. They showed the fire heat of their exhausts, and headed for home.

In the light of one last flare, Merc could see the retreat down the hill. Some carried their wounded, some hobbled, some crawled, but most were left on the perimeter defences of Hill 425. He shouted at the top of his voice and could not hear himself, and the few he led came to him as if he were their talisman. The value of what they, he, had done? He supposed it mattered.

He led them out, the dead and the living, and a skeleton force waited to take the position from them, but the battle for the Forward Operating Base was considered over; it had been held and the flag still flew unseen in the darkness above the trench. They stayed close to each other, and the grenade on his chest bounced against his ribcage, and Cinar was ahead of him and did not turn and did not look and did not talk, stumbled twice, refusing help. They followed the route of the communications trench and none had the strength to speak or to cry. Merc was surprised that so high a price was put on him, but had the proof of it.

4

His people followed him out of the hospital.

They had left four there, and two more were in the mortuary and the funerals would be later that morning in the quarter of the cemetery used by the military. Merç was shaken at what he had seen inside the Emergency Reception Centre, but masked it. Was good at that, of hiding emotion. They had gone to the hospital first, and the two guys from Special Forces, Rob and Brad, had trailed them, but not intervened. Not claimed first call on him, going pompous about the importance of a waiting flight out, were experienced enough to know that a sequence mattered. What Merc kept hidden was evidence of the ripple of shock that had engulfed him.

He had no mark on his body. His ears rang and his eyes watered from exhaustion and his legs were cramped up. The others who had manoeuvred the gurneys down the corridors, not permitting the trained staff to take over, carried scrapes and superficial blood smears but were whole. Cinar had been on the back right handle of the lead stretcher, on which lay the girl who had taken the stomach wound. They were almost at the first of the examination tables when she had lurched. Might have hit the corner of one of the instrument trolleys, and had gasped and gone down and had been on the floor, the energy flooding out of her, and only then had the hole in her tunic, immediately below the flak vest, been visible. The blood must have been trapped above the tight belt at her waist, against her skin, and now it spilled on the tiles and loosened the mud their boots had brought in. They had been waved clear, had left. Merc had not looked back at her, had not spoken to her, nor knelt beside her, had not taken her hand. He had been told to leave and had gone . . . Had not asked the question that most often provoked a lying answer. 'She'll be all right, won't she?' and a doctor mouthing through a cotton face guard 'Of course she will, she'll be fine.' Near to him, the young woman who had been on the DShK machine gun, feeding the belt – only two bursts left when the 'air' had come – had choked a little, wheezed, then stayed strong. It was not Merc's war but there never had been one that was his. He was paid to fight and it was convenient in London, from a citadel of power, that he be there. He did not deceive himself, did not claim to be press-ganged. The sun was peeping to the right of the fortress that had defended the town for 3000 years, and he blinked hard, but against the brightness and not because there were tears in his eyes.

A couple of pick-ups took them across the city and to the barracks where Fire Force Unit 47 was based. The boys followed, still respectful.

He checked his weapon into the armoury; and one magazine was empty and the other had only a fistful of rounds left. He unclipped the grenade from his webbing and it was laid gingerly in a box. A single syringe of battlefield morphine was retrieved from his rucksack, and would not be dumped for lack of hygiene, too precious. He walked to the hut where he was billeted, and his room was an apology of space, barely enough for a bed, a chair and a wardrobe close to collapse. Merc had no civilian clothes, had long since donated them to one of the camps for the displaced on the outskirts of Erbil, but he dumped his vest on the floor and his rucksack, and the webbing harness. He gazed at himself in a mirror above the shelf on which was a picture of his grandmother in the yard where she fed the sparrows. They stood by the door, watching him. He took his last *Auto Trader* from the rucksack but left *Exchange and Mart* at the bottom with some foul socks; someone might look after the socks and get them washed, and someone might enjoy the read and the pictures. He went out into the corridor, into the growing sunlight. The boy who had used the machine-gun was there – he had saved their lives. The toll taken on the guys in black had been formidable, and the vultures were probably there now, skipping in the wire's tangles and the craters, picking at body parts. There were two others with him. Merc was quizzed. Was he coming back? A shrug. Was he leaving them? A grimace. Was he going to lead them when they were back in the line after a week with their families? A small gesture of his hand, uncertain. Was he going before the funerals? A nod.

He thought he knew his mind, but did not share it. The engine of the Land Rover was gunned, the reminder that he was called home, and an aircraft waited for him and a small flotilla of fast jets had sprayed the line in front of the parapet of Hill 425 to enable him to go, conscience salved . . . Merc was a Gun for Hire, and his grandmother would have said that *He who pays the piper calls the tune* and some other poor beggars in another beleaguered position would have begged for the expertise of the bomb runs and gone without. What was worse than being wanted? Not being wanted? He was hugged and dust-dried lips brushed hard against his cheek, they seemed to hold him for extra seconds as though recognising this was the escape clause for him, and the 'sometime' when he would quit . . . He walked to the vehicle.

Brad would drive and Rob would do shotgun and he swung himself into the open back and squatted on the metal and it felt strange not to have a weapon in his hand, like his trousers had dropped or he wore no boots. He waved briefly, then stared ahead and shut them from his mind, and tried to do the same with the vivid image of the bright colour on the scrubbed floor of the area where he had left her, and had asked no questions.

Brad accelerated. He was passed a cigarette, took it, dragged on it and he was driven through streets that he did not recognise, as if his life had already moved on. Not the first time, or the last. A picture played in front of him, not the jammed traffic and the scream of horns and the yelling of hawkers. He saw his father, saw 'Hold the Line Hawkins', lieutenant in the Corps, proud to be a Pioneer and give the army some sangars to shelter behind and latrines to squat over, and something of a legend because the last dreg force to be called on to the jungle of lanes and alleys and cul-de-sacs in the Creggan Estate in Londonderry was his. He had led a platoon of lads unprepared for combat duties, and the local kids had rained half bricks and milk bottles on them. They had made a perimeter while an ambulance evacuated an old boy with ticker trouble. Police were with the ambulance team because it was the Creggan. The army were deployed because the police were there. In the name of the 'unity of Ireland' the kids pelted them with missiles. His father had shouted to his lads *Hold the line, the Pioneers,* had shouted it at the top of his voice as a rallying cry, and then they'd launched some gas and the mob had backed off enough for the ambulance to get clear, and the police in their armoured Land Rover, and the Pioneer platoon in three packed Pigs. One of the police had told a senior NCO of the shout 'Hold the line, the Pioneers' and it had gone into the folklore of the Corps, because they had too few battle honours. All the rest of the years his father was in the military he had carried that title. He hoped his father could have seen it from on high, knew of the defence of the trench on Hill 425. But Merc did little religion and was not sure what he believed in, could not have said whether his father knew or did not know. He had been three when his father had died. In the park, taking the family spaniel for a walk. Sat on a bench for a smoke, then toppled. Hoped his father knew, but the thought was lost against the screaming of his mother when the policeman called at the door and brought back the dog. There was a sign for the airport.

He soaked in his own silence. Did not know where he was headed, who he'd travel with, what would be the end game.

Nikki was early at work, first in. Had taken the key from Reception on the ground floor, unlocked the door, was hit by the usual smell of old food, old sweat, and old dirt – cleaners weren't allowed into that area, nothing was tidied and the mess decayed on the floor. He dumped his bag. He had the right to hack and probe and pry from his kitchen table, but had thought it better – as the count-down ticked towards the meeting at the supermarket car-park – to come here, to be seen, normal and nothing different. Kat had dropped him off.

He wore the same clothes as the previous day, what he had used in Stockholm. The card from the bank manager had been shredded, thrown into a street rubbish bin, but the fight festered, and the certainty that the Roofer had never liked him, and would now seek to hurt him: a promise had been given. Hurt hard . . . So obvious to Nikki that he was apart from the others. He had slept poorly, tossing and heaving, and for much of the night could hear the coughing from behind the dividing wall as Kat had tried to clear mucus from her chest. Churning in his mind was the memory of their GangMaster standing in the doorway and threatening them with the story of the two boys caught by the police, who had ripped off a bank, who were going to go down and for many bad winters, in a camp, half-starved and probably raped. Nikki did not know, could not have done, whether he was merely the GangMaster's toy thing, a young rat played with by a powerful cat, taunted. He flicked the switch and heard the murmur of the laptop's power . . . Could have been that the story was dangled in front of him – boys who cheated the system, too greedy, lined up for punishment – and he would be watched to see if he broke cover. Waiting and watching, the GangMaster and the police and the FSB, and no one would stand beside him, and no one would protect Kat. He was cold and was shivering, and hit the keys clumsily, and aborted the trapdoor entry. He heard a footfall behind him. Nikki did not turn. His fingers slammed down on the keys. HookNose stood beside him. The shape of his nose, from the angle on its bridge, was as sharply bent as fisherman's hook for hauling eels from the Neva River.

Nikki could not have explained the differences between himself and the core of the little group – the Roofer, HookNose and Gorilla – who worked in that communal room and hacked there and ate there, and swapped cables. They talked in stilted jargon about problems of entry and exit and extraction, exchanged details on the better defended targets they were given, yet he was outside. He preferred to go home to Kat and have her cook him something than to go to a bar with them and sink beers and also, maybe, pills. There had been tension in the room all that week.

Did the GangMaster carry information on him? He started again, after the abort, to get his worm on the move, nudging it through the previously hidden entry points, and cautiously because this target area was scrutinised by a defence team at a military software contractor in southern France. The liquid flushed down on his head.

It would have been the coffee from a beaker left overnight on HookNose's part of the work bench. It was cold and the milk smelled sour. It ran on his hair, on his cheeks, over his jaw and dribbled to his T-shirt and . . . He swung his arm. A predictable response, and easily avoided. His fist beat the air, had no impact. He tried to twist in his chair but the vinyl was worn under the wheels and the wheels caught. A slice of yesterday's pizza was dropped on his lap, then the packaging and scattered crumbs and congealed mess. Coffee was in his eyes and he smeared them with his wrist. HookNose was at his place and staring at his screen. Nikki had never been a street fighter. He had not learned to fight dirty, fight tough, fight with deceit. Some kids did and some had practised the 'stay safe' way and had backed off and stayed in the shadows and had avoided the contact point. He didn't fight. He did not stand up, but wiped at his face and used his handkerchief to clean the laptop keys, and he put the pizza packaging and the food into the bin by his feet and said nothing, and boiled private anger and did not face the man who had humiliated him. He heard the clicking of HookNose's keys but made no eye contact, did not give the bastard the satisfaction of seeing his fear. HookNose was a full fifteen kilos heavier than Nikki, at least ten centimetres taller and would have enjoyed the chance to be provoked, have a blow landed on him, then retaliate.

Like it was a list of things to be done, targets to be attacked, in his mind Nikki ticked the box that was HookNose, and the box that was the Roofer . . . Kat was the one who would have retaliated, kicking and gouging and screaming and clawing. Kat would have fought but he had not, not then, not on ground he had not chosen.

*   *   *

The Brains Trust was in session early. Each spoke. Later, their digest would be on the Director's desk and would influence – predictable to all of them – a matter of significance. They seemed to rehearse arguments that took them outside the bubble of conventional thought. They were beyond 'attribution' and into the areas of 'strike back'. Their voices were soft, each fearful of the implications. Only an untidy watercolour of a Welsh upland watched them, only a basic coffee machine listened.

Bob, of the Security Service, addressed Article 5 and the definition of a declaration of war.

'Does a cyber attack on a NATO member constitute a trigger for Article five? Paraphrase, don't need the full jargon. "An attack on one is an attack on us all, and demands retaliation or at least an active defence to repel an invader." Got that? Simple. So the Kremlin puts tanks over the Narva River and into Estonia and has a one-day drive to Tallinn, and that is a declaration of war and we have no wriggle room, cannot kick a can down the street. We are in a combat situation – for a tank attack – under Article five of the NATO document. But anything that a tank does, or an attack aircraft, can be done better by a good hacker while he's sitting and scratching the pimples on his backside. There is an argument for saying that a cyber raid – equivalent of a storm squad of commandos – into our more sensitive private parts, or the Pentagon's, or our must-have utilities, is such an attack – and we are not talking about hoodlums and Organised Crime barons, but the Russian state. Provenance is what Boot has brought to the table for us to ruminate on. I'd say that we can be safe in an assumption that Article Five is violated by them every day and every week and every month. It is a breach of Article Five. Kremlin-sponsored theft, espionage, reconnaissance for the shutting down of our economy. Fraud is more damaging to us than armour and aircraft on the move, but they don't believe we have the appetite to go to the NATO council and call for retaliation, and they might be right. How hungry are we? What do we have the stomach for? Above my pay grade to be calling those shots. But cyber is an attack every bit as serious as bombs or bullets. We

could justify, as a NATO member, a strike back mission. Not with
trumpets blaring, but covert. Yes, we could justify it.'

Bob spoke in little more than a whisper, subdued by what he
brought to the table.

They had taken off, climbed fast, were soon at cruising altitude.
Disapproval, or something stronger, oozed round him.

He sat in a well-upholstered seat. Wore the same clothing as
when he had been in the trench for too many short days and too
many long nights, dirt caked on the fatigues from the pit of the
trench and dried bloodstains from the wounds of those who had
been Merc's comrades. The freshest stain was from the girl when
she had pitched forward as they had taken their own into the casualty area of the hospital.

Disapproval, dislike, was apparent on the faces of the two stewards with whom he shared the cabin. Neither of the cockpit crew
had come back to speak to him; he had not been told the duration,
the weather, the onboard food, where they'd land. The male
steward had brought a roll of kitchen paper, unwound a strip,
eased it under Merc's combat boots. The female steward had
worked around him with a battery-powered vacuum cleaner.
When she finished, Merc made eye contact and gave her his little
smile and it must have worked for her – as it usually did – and
she'd flushed embarrassment. He didn't ask for water or for crisps,
or peanuts or a fillet steak. He was not subject to the rank and
disciplines that governed their lives, was not a part of their world,
was free, a Gun for Hire. What he wore might also have stank of
ordnance, and of weapons' oil, and of urine that had run down his
leg because in a fire fight it was not sensible to turn away in
modesty and unzip.

They left him, and Merc soon slept, but lightly. The sort of
sleep where he did not rest. Crosswinds hit them and the cockpit
people did not look for a way round but ploughed through. His
sleep did not refresh him – his mind had locked on the sight of
the girl, Cinar, as her blood messed the floor and as the order-
lies stripped off her clothing and her skin was defiled by the

injury and the glaze in her eyes. Merc did not often take a casualty to heart, certainly not one who had so haughtily ignored him.

He was slumped in his seat, and the angle of the sun came through the porthole and lit him, but he was not at peace. Later, he lost the girl . . . New figures groped for his attention, but none had faces. They were men, women, not identifiable, and soon he'd meet them, affect their lives, but in his restless dream he didn't know them or their future.

Kat was not short of ambition. She had ideas for her status that were not yet achieved, but she harboured optimism. She met the group in a café across the river from the Big House. Not the best place for them to be, but the proximity of their enemy gave off an additional waft of excitement. She was not among the big planners. In fact, she was little more than a fetcher and carrier, a buyer of the masonry paint they needed for slogan daubing, and she distributed posters and pamphlets to other groups.

They believed in the power of 'shock', they thought they hawked 'ridicule', they believed that they had already achieved much, and that in the months, years, ahead they would inflict damage on the very fabric of the state . . . Not of course with bombs or violence. Kat drank the dogma that stated *shock* and *ridicule* were more influential than weapons or explosives. Few of them had employment, and they received no benefits from the state, so lived by a meld of donations and petty theft, and Kat understood her value because she was supported by the money paid to her brother. Not that he understood her friends and colleagues in the struggle. Not that they understood the importance to their well-being of attracting the sister of a hacktivist who worked under the direction of FSB, a criminal and an asset to the corruption of society. Dregs of coffee cold at the bottom of glass mugs. Biscuits long gone, and the crumbs swept up. Coats on because at that time of the morning, well short of the midday break, the heating was low. Rolled cigarettes passed around.

She had a class later. Nikki met the cost of her piano lessons.

She kept an eye on her watch. They talked of hopes for the future: the fall of the President, the sweeping away of the *siloviki* around him, the end of corruption, the start of liberty. The hopes were easy to accumulate, but methods stymied them. Not for them the sort of political rallies held in Moscow where arrests of principals were commonplace, direct protest with megaphones and banners. They talked of other means, and could be bold in their ideas but short of the enthusiasm that would carry them forward. Pride of place was the triumph just along the street, in view of the Big House, the *Bolshoy Dom*, where the great penis had been painted on the road surface of the bridge. There had been only thirty seconds to paint the organ's outline, sixty-five metres long, then the activists had jumped clear and the bridge had been raised to permit a freighter going upstream, and then the image had faced the main entrance to the FSB complex: an extraordinary achievement, but it was eight years ago and the people responsible were now scattered.

More talk . . . the filmed liberation of a frozen chicken from the Nakhodka supermarket, cameraman up close; a girl had crouched, lowered her underwear, had stuffed the bird inside her pants, then had walked out, bypassing the cash tills. That was also eight years ago, a mix of protest at the price of food, and their conception of an art form.

Endless talk . . . laughing at the former President, known as the 'little bear', and the orgy in the Museum of Biology in the capital, but that was ten years ago . . . and talk of the artistic concept of commemorating the theft by state and church when a man had dressed in the robes of a priest and wore a policeman's cap and had looted a food store, then walked out pushing a trolley, not paying . . . Babbled talk, and no one knew how to go forward. Some were bold but could not get others to follow, some preferred to talk but not act or strip. And Kat sat and listened . . . and remembered older fighters who had taken on the state in Moscow, a man who nailed his testicles to the tarmac in the great Square, another who wrapped himself, naked, in coils of razor wire, or set fire to the main doors of FSB headquarters – heroes. She did not know what she was capable of, or if mutilation in front of a camera was either a 'shock' to *them* or 'ridiculed' *them*. Would she have taken part, stripped and allowed herself to be screwed for the camera? Unsure. She looked at the men around the table, the hair on their hands, grime under their nails, the stains of fag ends on their fingers, and dulled eyes. Sure that she had no wish to do it with any of them, naked and with lights on her, and the clacking of camera shutters.

She cursed herself for her lack of commitment, saw the time, made excuses, left them, went to her piano lesson. They talked about damaging the régime, but it was only words – and all she did was talk with them. Her lessons were poor recompense.

Daff had learned the significance of Operation Jungle for the men she'd recruited. Bottled inside them, all three of the boys, was the sap of excitement of more than a half century ago. They would be picked up, off the southern headland, two kilometres from Haapsalu, at two in the morning. They had girlfriends. Dominating the excitement was the scent of high danger. Three boys, aged about twenty, from the same street in Haapsalu, behind the pretty painted fishermen's cottages. The boys were going off in the depths of that night to learn to fight a lonely, hazardous war against a régime occupying their country . . . or so they told the girls. Embellishment of the risks faced was hardly required.

The boys had set off for the rendezvous, had avoided Soviet troops and local police, had waited at the edge of a reed bed, then seen the shielded light to guide them out and up to their waists, had been hauled into a dinghy that had sped away to the mother ship. On board an E-boat, formerly of the German navy, now a prize of war and under the control of the British, they had been taken – too fast for Soviet radar and interception – out into international waters, then had headed west across the Baltic Sea for the old harbour city of Lubeck, near the West German/ Danish border.

While the boys trained in armed and unarmed combat and the dark arts of espionage, the girls' bellies swelled, and they threw up in the early mornings. The boys were familiarised with weapons and explosives and demolition, and would be a part – when they returned to Estonia – of Operation Jungle, and would join up with the Forest Brothers, and all three were as innocent as the girls had been. None had considered that Jungle was infiltrated by British traitors, was flawed at the summit. They had come back. The same E-boat, German crewed, had run the gauntlet – or so it had seemed – of the Soviet defences, and the boys had been put ashore from the dinghy and they waded together, bowed by equipment, into the shallow reed beds. Then the flares had been fired and the shooting had started.

No one who lived in Haapsalu would have heard the bubbled wheezing cries of the one hit just short of dry land, then drowning. No one who had walked past the KGB building on Pikk in Tallinn and heard the screams and pleas of another who lay on the floor of a cell with a window at ankle height on to the pavement, would have slowed their step, and gone closer. No one would have raised their head if they had been trudging across the bridge that spanned the Narva and had heard frantic banging on the inside of the steel frame of a prison van as it headed east for the more sophisticated interrogators in Leningrad.

Two years later, and forty-five agents' lives thrown away, Operation Jungle – regarded as a fiasco, but the traitors left unpunished – was suspended. By then, pregnancies had gone full term and babies had been born and three girls, older and wiser, had been taken to camps far into the steppes of the Soviet Union.

Jungle had relevance, and Daff knew the facts. Harry's turn, to contribute and influence a Director's decision. Needed to be clear, unequivocal, and foolhardy or, perhaps, brave.

'If an agency were minded to hit them, the sort of painful kick that would confuse, disrupt, now is as good a time as any to utilise strike back. Our experience is that they continually upgrade their defences, are harder to locate and identify, are more secretive, take more precautions to avoid identification and the cast-iron evidence required before countermeasures. They believe that disguising their ownership, particularly through the use of proxies, renders them safe from the use of force – what we are now advocating. I quote from an interview I read, apposite: "They don't want that trail of breadcrumbs to lead right up to the Kremlin." This is an extraordinary moment because Boot has produced the whistle blower. We have an insider, have the date and time of a meeting where a whole gang of them will be sitting round and receiving a briefing on state-sponsored targets and that is *manna* and did not fall from Heaven. The best kit we have can sometimes put the hacktivist into a district, sometimes – rarely – into an estate of perhaps half a dozen tower blocks. Cannot put it into a particular bedroom, nor can it identify an ordinary building in an ordinary industrial plot and behind an ordinary window. That is HumInt, and that is what we have. I am not privy to what is intended, but can state, categorically, that I would not take a crystal ball and say when another opportunity like this might beckon. I have the freedom to say this, talk retaliation, but we are supposed to think outside the loop. It is what Boot wants to hear. It is an opportunity for violence . . . Cannot believe I said that. But I did.'

Harry's fists were closed, the knuckles white, and he squeezed his eyes shut, and absorbed what he had called for.

The Maid did logistics.

She made Boot's travel arrangements, and planned how the 'incomer' would journey and what weight of baggage he would need, and where a package from an industrial estate in west London might be collected. She would remain at VBX as long as Boot was employed there, had an affection and respect for him that were greater even than she gave to her parrot. He was, she would have said, a rarity in the community of the Service: had resisted the vanities of promotion in order to remain at the level of a field officer – operating at the front line of operations, making decisions where responsibility could not be dumped in the lap of a sub-committee, adjacent to danger, not buried under welters of analysis, expenses dockets, leave charts, minutiae – and clever enough to have gone for better paid consultancy in one of many sprouting risk companies. Intelligent enough to have earned big money in the City of London, fresh enough in attitude and stamina not to have coasted towards a retirement pension . . . He was, God forbid it was ever admitted, her hero.

This mission – still short of a name – caused her anxiety. It had none of the usual comfort of thorough planning. Done at speed and without the rigour of a Lucifer's Advocate to challenge concepts, create difficulties, real or imagined, but that needed consideration. The Maid could manage a fierce tongue when appropriate. She might have said to the parrot: 'It's not amateur dramatics, for God's sake, it's not enough to hope it'll be all right on the night. You need luck, but luck is always earned.' Was Boot too old to be doing this, taking the responsibility for the success of an operation, for the survival of the men and women he sent forward? Would he not be better sticking to those weekends in the Belgian countryside, winter or summer, rain or shine, and being where cavalry had charged and cannon had boomed and the squares had held fast? It would be down to her, not his wife, to pack the bag for him. He seemed not to notice her, but she knew that the seeming lack of appreciation was bogus. She had a box of chocolates each Christmas, probably wrapped by his wife, her handwriting on the tag, and never a cheek pecked on the evening before the start of the festive holiday, but needed nothing more. She was fearful, would admit to it, and across the room was Daff – different to herself in many ways, but also wearing the crinkle lines of anxiety.

A greater fear, in the Maid's life, was reaching the day after his retirement and her gone with him, when her ID would no longer be registered at the entry point into the building. Their voices played the telephones, their fingers tapped keys and, watching them from through Boot's open door, was the Duke, sprouting from his boot, and with a small smile 'A Damned Serious Business', yes, indeed.

Daff's printer spouted out maps and aerial photographs and road reports, along with images of a building with a glistening flat roof where overnight ice would have melted and light specks flickered off what would have been the barbs of a perimeter fence wire. And she had close-up pictures of a supermarket's car-park . . . All clear, straightforward, easy for her to produce. It was what was taken on trust that caused her difficulty, knitted the frown on her tanned forehead.

She was less successful than the Maid at disguising worry. The bloody four-minute warning could have been sounded on the roof sirens and the Maid would have looked up from her screen, shrugged, then carried on typing so that the message she wrote could be received somewhere in the post-Armageddon society. Once, the wail blasting through the building, Daff would have thought she'd have been sprinting down the corridor and hunting down the first available male, and maybe doing it right there beside the coffee machine. Now, she just fretted. All about *trust*. The boys were on 'trust'. How they would be, Martin and Toomas and Kristjan, was uncertain. The Polish sister service had been fast with the recommendation, the Latvians had had nothing, nor the Finns, and fluent Russian speakers with reason to detest the régime and with practical if brief experience were hard to find. She sent them the message detailing where they should be for the rendezvous and when she would meet them. Their money was in transit – important because they'd want the assurance of where they were going, what was intended of them.

And Merc – Gideon Francis Hawkins – was also taken on trust. She concentrated on her screen, kept her eye-line clear of the photograph of him from the file, the slight smile playing at his mouth, widening his lips, lifting his nostrils; he seemed to mock her. She did not know how he would be . . . Those years before, hammering down Route Irish, she'd noticed that his hands had no tremor as they held the weapon that poked from the front passenger window. So calm, and none of the giveaway signs of 'phet abuse. Also remembered seeing him at the pool, and her in a skimpy bikini, and other girls from the personal assistant ranks at the embassy drooling, but she had not shagged him, and afterwards had told herself the fault lay with her, she hadn't tried hard enough. Had seen him once when he was convoy driving on the

northern reaches of the Kyber, had missed him when he was on
escort along the Salang tunnel road, and one more meeting – business and starchy and in company – at the embassy in Ankara
before he had left Turkey for the 'wild west' of Erbil. In the years
since, she had seen his reports concise, bare-bone stuff, and better
HumInt than most of the young men and women on the second
and third floors of VBX managed. But, Daff could not say how
he would be and what the toll of the battlefield had done to him.
She had talked him up, and Boot had accepted her judgement. It
weighed heavily on her that Merc was taken on trust.

And the kid who was Nikki . . . Boot had grimaced and had
remarked that any youngster in the 95th Rifles, after three days'
march along the road to Waterloo, would have smelt as sharply.
She knew the story of the battle, as did the Maid – it went with the
job. Nikki was taken on trust. Nikki, little hacker scumbag, might
by now have been telling an ingratiating story to any FSB major
who'd listen, jabbing a finger on a map where a supermarket was
marked, and a car-park, and talking of a meeting – trying to save
the skin on his back, attempting a deal of immunity. In the code of
MICE – *money ideology compromise ego* – the compromised people
were always the least reliable and the kid might have a greater fear
of his own security people than of an older man of mild appearance, who was Boot. She took Boot on trust and he took her on
the same basis, and neither would know how the other would
perform at the frontier.

A rare moment for her, an aberration of indulgence, Daff
scrawled the words on her pad: Taken on Trust. Looked at her
watch, squealed, grabbed her bag, and ran. The plane would be
starting to drop, not yet on final descent but beginning to come
down. Ran hard and with a tail of fair hair flying after her and feet
clattering along the corridor.

'Have to give it to her,' Arthur said. 'A great little mover – and
knows it.'

He and Roy were near the end of their shift. She'd not skirted
them where they stood at the principal gate into VBX, and they

hadn't backed off, and she had been precious near to impaling herself on the foresight of Roy's Heckler & Koch. They had watched her run through the traffic, not looking right or left, and then bury herself in a saloon parked by the station entrance. It powered away.

Rob said, 'She's one of Boot's, right?'

'And him out all day, gone at sparrow fart. Arthur, know what I'm thinking?'

'Thinking, my old cocker, that there's a show on. Bet the house-keeping on it.'

'Too right, a proper show. A show that matters – Boot's. Spot on.'

And they grinned and felt a little of the elation that did not come often. The weapons were heavy on their necks and flak vests, and Arthur sniffed – like it was danger he could smell. They saw plenty at the gate, it was like a top seat in the stalls.

Leanne had never met the Director, imagined rather a jaundiced stereotype, but her quirk of mischief suggested he might want to be liberated from the straitjacket of conventional retaliation. Not her role to offer up the cautions of his staff officers; there'd be enough of them queuing up to urge a turned cheek in the face of severe provocation. She'd give it hard, and rather enjoy the exercise.

'Let us put the situation into context. I get told most days of most weeks that terrorism is now on a back burner, just simmering in a pot, and that cyber has gone up and past it in threat terms. Top of the tree is Russia, more so than the Chinese, North Koreans and the kids in Iran. Russia has the infrastructure to put bums on seats, do it cleverly and outstrip the competition. We can talk – this is what comes across my desk – about a catas-trophe on the scale of cyber's Nine Eleven. Not necessarily deaths, but assuredly the destabilisation of our societies. Think of the Trojan Horse . . . Where's the threat? Cannot see it. Victimless? I don't think so. The malware is inside our energy distribution and our telecoms and our finances and our whole range of logistics. We are talking about Sourface and Eviltoss and Chopstick and Jabber Zeus malware. Millions, hundreds of millions, of personal details that have been siphoned, which is the unimportant bit for a state-sponsored operation. Anything that damages this march towards domination is welcome. In our language we are not permitted to refer to an enemy, only to an adversary. The adversary is better than us and we are throwing billions at the problem and are not yet matching with parity. They are not bound by rules, have not heard of old Queensberry – but we are, libraries of them – and we have to consider the dangers of a vigilante defence which is illegal. In the private sector, the Christmas present that everyone wants, the defenders against the aggression, is a nicely wrapped up, pink ribbons, "nuke from orbit" button, but it doesn't seem to get put in our stockings. Sorry, and all that, but things are actually quite bleak. If we can hit, have that chance, then we should.'

A damp and chill wind in the air, and the tang of the sea, and he needed hard advice, without varnish coating. The meeting place was a compromise. Boot had chosen Fort Monkton, on the coast west of Portsmouth. The sergeant had driven from Poole, farther west.

'How to get in, my problem. The river's three hundred yards wide, flushed up high from the rains, a fair speed on it. Going on his own. Others with better cover are already in place. It's a frontier, so how to cross and how to get into their territory, and cold, first snow of the winter about to fall. How?'

Wellington might have been here. The Fort had been completed two decades before Waterloo. It had been integral in the defences against Napoleonic invasion, and the old ramparts had been well maintained. The Service used it for the field training of recruits, and for pistol shooting and lectures in the arts of unarmed combat. Tucked away, discreet, and a good place to talk. He wanted to know if the river banks were patrolled, covered by electronic surveillance. The sergeant was a man of experience, could have risen to a higher rank in the Special Boat Squadron, but he'd never made the Officers' Mess. He stayed at an acceptable level and had, it was claimed, limitless common sense. Wanted to know the age and physique of the man going across. Was told what the most recent files, sparse, had thrown up on the border's security. Asked for detail of the terrain on the far side, Russian sovereign territory. Boot took his tablet from his briefcase. Daff had loaded it. He put up the images of the river and the deep forest on the far side, where few roads ran, and the loggers' tracks were hard to see. They were absorbed.

Cigarette smoke blew into Boot's face and he would like to have reciprocated with a stuffed bowl of his clay pipe but it lay in his office. What was the time schedule? Assumed covert, were there bad consequences for capture? Boot gazed into the leathered face of the old warrior, veteran of Basra and Kandahar and Sierra Leone and others, and wished that the man could be added, temporarily, to the payroll, and gave his replies briskly. A certainty – if their boy were taken – that it would be Not Confirmed Not Denied – NCND – a major creed in his work. Not worth thinking of if he appeared in a lower court in Pskov or Novgorod, then was heaved off to a holding cell in St Petersburg, in that ghastly building overlooking the Neva. He'd be out on his neck, holed below the waterline, drowning, taking many with him because the collateral would be fearsome. If it worked, then a sherry and a chuckle with the Big Boss, and on to the next project. Would not have had it any different.

'Assessment of the chappie who's going over?'

Boot gave it him. 'We think of him as special. He's leading a team that is rubbish but it's what we could put together in the time. He's acting in concert with an irrational and unmotivated kid who we have our claws into and who will need prodding into place. We think of him as a leader, someone who others want to follow and will believe in. We've dragged him out of a combat situation where he is – to all intents – a mercenary, but the money is paltry and what I will pay him is not much more than loose change. It's all cheapskate, how we live these days. He has no home, no close family or full-time relationship. He's footloose, and probably we, the Service, are the most precious item he relates to. Which is like me and like the ladies in my office, all the people that are, in my opinion, worthwhile. I think highly enough of him to have ensured that air strikes destroyed a planned attack on a sector he had taken responsibility for. I twisted arms, kicked shins to get the aircraft up. I look upon him as remarkable, and what I am asking of him is quite unreasonable. But we have a one-off chance when we can act or sit on our hands and do nothing and wait for another twenty years to pass. It's a meeting of high-value targets and the location is within range. Too much to hope those will be repeated factors. A leader makes things happen without fuss, no drama in a crisis . . . A good man. This is Tuesday, late morning – the opportunity for us to make a valued strike is on the afternoon of Thursday, and the location is one hundred and twenty klicks across that river, and it is a stampede and—'

'Thank you.'

They walked and a chain of cigarettes was lit, then tossed. Boot typed, one finger, and the detail was committed to the tablet's memory. Every few sentences the sergeant would peer at the screen, back to the satellite image and magnify a portion of it, suck hard on his cigarette, then speak again. He rapped with a gnarled finger.

'It's where I'd go, and how I'd do it, and nothing is guaranteed.'

'I think I know that,' Boot said.

'It's plenty that you ask of him.'

'I know that too.'

'And the way in is as good a way out, and tell him to come back alone, in charge of his own destiny. No passengers. Perhaps, when he's back – think on the bright side – bring him down. I'd like to meet him, after the talk-up you've given him.'

'Perhaps I will.'

The Major called an O Group meeting for the afternoon.

Then sat at his desk and drank water and ate a sandwich, spiced pork and pickled gherkin, that Julia had made. Wiped the crumbs from the desk top and spread out the files. There was still a generation in the Big House – the Major among them – who harboured basic mistrust of the computer, preferred paper and demanded photographs.

His wife, a sweetheart since childhood, would now be at the clinic where she met private patients on a Tuesday. Dermatology was now desirable to prominent St Petersburg players; the smoothness of complexions mattered, money was available, and she was gathering a nest egg for the day when he would write his resignation letter. They would then return to the countryside north of Minsk – ignoring the rampaging corruption in his country's governing élite of Belarus – and he would take a small boat out on the lakes in summer and fish for big pike, and in the winter he would sledge and ski with her, and with their son. A dream but attainable . . . First, the work of the day.

Nobody in the Big House could fault his efforts to ensure the laws of the country were observed. The Judicial Codes covered 'dissent'. He tracked the young men and women who breached the law. Had no hatred of them, nor did he admire them. The Major thought the girl on the periphery of the group was the most interesting. When she had sat opposite him before, in an interrogation room, he had weighed her anger against her intelligence, decided that together they put her in a different league to the men in the group who talked and planned, but acted feebly. He thought he could exploit her, learn more from her; and she had an anger that he had found moderately attractive, and an innocence. A second imperative governed the arrest of the girl – her brother. The Major did not directly infringe on the areas of Organised Crime, but if an investigation, properly mounted, created awkwardness or wrong-footed his superiors then it was welcomed. He started to draft his briefing.

Dunc had the Brains Trust's last offering, reckoned he followed hard acts. Thought that those who had tasked the Brains Trust were uninterested in arguments other than the striking of a blow against their opponents.

'Forget the politics and the military, just look at the theft. We estimate the annual cost of cyber crime has reached an excess of four hundred billion dollars a year. Credit card details sell in the black quarter for some four dollars each, but they have extracted millions of them. The information regarding a good savings account in middle Britain or Germany or the Eastern Seaboard, codes and passwords, that holds one hundred thousand dollars will be bought for as little as three hundred dollars. The man at the top of the FBI Most Wanted took one hundred million from accounts on a botnet scheme. A gang did a crypto-lock and shut down a whole range of accounts, and companies, then asked seven hundred and fifty dollars from each victim to "open the door". A company refuses, loses the originals and it costs them seventy thousand to replace the files. A US police department was more street-wise and paid up, did a transfer of seven hundred and fifty in notes. That's the big and the small. Who does it? There is a cyberpunk ideology. The characteristics are rebellion, anarchy, hatred of authority. Stereotypes are applicable – we have them where we operate and pay them big money – and they leave a trail of half-eaten fast-food, set off the smoke alarms with their fags, and they have utter belief in their own brilliance. The "script kiddie" is arrogant, conceited, intelligent, and moves freely between state-sponsored and Organised Crime. In Russia, he is part of an élite and more useful than a Special Forces regiment. By the age of twenty-eight, he is on a garbage heap, his skills are blunted, and another teenager will kick his butt and shift him out. The best will have been sighted, tracked by the Eighth Directorate of FSB, and will be guided into the arms of the gang bosses who cooperate. A big part of the attraction that goes with the work is the knowledge that we are hunting, chasing, screaming frustration, coming after him, but he is ahead. We say cyber defence is DLPI – Delta Lima Papa India. That's Denial Luck Prayer Ignorance. By the way, the script kids think we're rubbish, seriously second rate. I'd like to think of them suffering severe shock, thrown off balance, but that won't happen if we only fry a few laptops. Has to be heavy . . . obvious. We should get all this typed up for the customer.'

They broke, separated, began to hammer at their laptops and tried to make something coherent from their knowledge. Dunc thought he might insert the statistic of the east European gang, who had never been to the southern hemisphere but who had stolen 500,000 Australian credit cards, with a face value in terms of spending limits of 400 million sterling, then had sold them off and pocketed a profit the equivalent of 16 million sterling. They would keep their joint report simple, not confuse the Director, or Boot.

Boot came back into London.

Seemed to see, not the traffic in front of him, but men in columns coming from the ferry boats and disembarking in the port of Antwerp, bowed under the weight of their knapsacks and carrying long-barrelled and muzzle-loaded Baker flintlock rifles. The horses struggling to clamber on to the quayside, and the heavy cranes hoisting the cannon. And, with a shrug, the Duke would have said – because many were raw and untrained in European warfare, and the best of the army were in Spain or in Canada and could not return in time, 'We have what we have'. And seemed not to hear the shouts and horns and screeches of brakes around him, but heard the yells of the quartermasters and the drawl of the officers as their precious personal baggage was brought ashore, and the creak of the ropes and the curses of the troops who were off to war. Must have faith in their leader, in his plan . . . His leadership, Boot's, and the young man's. Faith, the great commodity in Boot's world, and in the Duke's.

He walked towards the building and nodded to Arthur and Roy and could have sworn that he was greeted with a fractional wink from Arthur, like sharing a confidence. Went inside, hurried to find the Maid and track what he had learned.

She drove him over the bridge and he had the chance to gaze at the building. She said nothing and Merc had nothing to ask her. It seemed vast, ugly enough for the sense of strength to be enhanced. She had been on the tarmac to meet him and the plane had taxied towards her car, and the steps had been lowered. Neither of the stewards had wished him well but one of the pilots had opened the cockpit door and had nodded to him, might have been a small gesture of respect. He had not seen her for more than a year and a half and thought she looked well. She had given him a passport and they had gone through brief formalities, the pages not looked at, and the Customs section was closed and they had gone back to the car and headed towards London. He had felt an idiot wearing combat fatigues. She'd looked at him a couple of times as if to query whether he wanted to talk, then decided on silence, and the traffic had been a bastard and it was good that she concentrated.

Over the bridge and past the entrance to the building, she had taken a side street then had parked outside a modern block. She'd fished in her bag for keys and had told him about a service flat, second floor, then had seemed to eye him over, like she undressed him – the same look she'd given him when he had met her beside the pool in the embassy's part of the Green Zone. She said there was a street market in Kennington and she'd go and pick up some clothes for him. Almost the first time she had spoken, except for swearing at other drivers, and greeting him on the apron. How was he? He was all right. She had not required a bulletin, nor a sit. rep. on a battle for a forward fire position she would not have heard of. And she had not briefed on the mission he was required for, nor why he warranted the evacuation from Hill 425. She said when she would be back with the clothes, and told him that the brief would follow and who would give it – a name that Merc had heard, no more . . . and told him not to get too comfortable because he would be moving on that evening. He'd shrugged, and did his smile, the trademark, and asked if she could get him the latest *Auto Trader* and also an *Exchange and Mart*. She was a good-looking girl but . . . there had been blood on the floor of the emergency area and breathing becoming irregular and pallor settling.

Merc took the keys and went through swing doors, and the place stank of fragrance sprays, and there was a pain in his shoulder from the bruising of the recoil. He wondered if he would ask 'Why did you come for me, why not one of the other guys, must be a thousand of them?' Wondered if he would. And wondered when the 'sometime' would be, the 'sometime' when he walked away, or whether it was too far beyond the horizon.

In the flat, Merc stripped, folded his clothes, sat naked in an easy chair, and waited for her.

5

She brought the clothes.

He had dozed, might have slept, naked and uncovered. Daff had not knocked, not called out. She had said that her name was still Daff. She had used her own key to the flat, and she had stood in front of him, carrying the clothes. Not a semblance of a blush.

Merc did not do personal modesty so did not hide himself. She laid the clothes on the bed, turning her back on him, and described what she had purchased: all High Street stuff, remaindered to the market. Merc stood, grunted his thanks, and she passed him a docket and he scrawled a signature: could have been his name, or Brad's or Rob's, or that of any of the girls and guys from the trench, or of the young woman who had bled so badly and who had no time for him. He went to the bathroom, and stood under the shower; first cold water, then warm and then scalding . . . Had been a time when she might have joined him, under the shower, or on the evening after the meeting by the pool, or when she had been in a hotel in Qatar or Dubai and done the debrief after the Afghan period. Hadn't then, didn't now. He towelled himself and shaved, using the plastic razor beside the basin. He chucked the towel on the floor and came out.

Merc wondered who had last been there, and where they had been headed or where they had come from, and who might follow him tomorrow, whether they would sit in the chair and let time pass, shiver and care about the day, 'sometime', when they'd called time on it . . . Saw the big fellow who was caught in the wire, and saw the grenade that had bounced and then wobbled and then lain still on the trench floor, remembered when he had lost sight of it under the boy's body, and remembered the jam on the belt, and the flag that flew above them marking Hill 425. Remembered the feeling of her rump when he had smacked it and told her to keep her head down . . . Daff sat on the bed and used nail scissors to cut away every label in the clothing. Merc dressed.

How was he? 'I'm fine.'

Had it been spectacular? 'The "air" coming in? Made a good show.'

Was there much time to spare? 'Not as you'd notice. They were near to taking us down. Ammunition was low. Came when it was needed.'

She grimaced, touched his arm momentarily. He supposed he told it – the fast jets coming over them with their ordnance – as if the matter were no more serious than going short of milk. He thought she was trying to read him, and hoped she failed.

Daff said he looked good. 'If that matters then I'm pleased.'

Time to go, and his gear would be taken care of. Then a little grin, like she'd brought sweets. In her big shoulder-bag were the magazines, and his face lit up and the smile cracked open and he almost gave her a snappy kiss on the cheek. She would have known his gratitude. She told him they would go and eat something, then he'd meet Boot, hear what made it worth flying him from a shit-awful combat zone, and learn where he was going. He'd shrugged. He said what he would like to eat and what he would not: no burgers and no fries, some fish and some salad, and maybe an apple, and juice to drink. Was he not impatient to know what was wanted of him, where? His grandmother used to say that watching a kettle did not make it boil faster. He said he was not impatient.

They went down the stairs and into the dull light of the early afternoon. She had brought him a conventional anorak, rain threatened, and she tucked her arm into his, and they hurried together. He thought she was an alone person – as he was. And that was the trait of the people *they* wanted. Always the best, *they* said, going into a place of danger, if you were unencumbered with emotion, unburdened by a relationship.

*   *   *

'It must have been an oversight.'

'Must it?' Not a chance of snow in Hades that Boot would have permitted Plimsoll – Antony Plimsoll – into his outer office, let alone the inner sanctum. The query was curt, on the edge of rudeness, and with a tone that indicated the intrusion interrupted important work.

'It must have been an oversight that you are drawing an expenses float in your name and for others in a team, and that notification of the personnel has gone to Human Resources, but required paperwork has not been submitted.'

'Has it not?' Boot let his gaze of indifference fall squarely on the individual whom he blocked at the outer door. Behind him the Maid was concentrating on her screen and the papers and maps that covered her desk, and Daff's, and more photographs, aerial and high-definition were Sellotaped to the walls.

'We have not received a risk assessment critique. It is compulsory, as you well know, to submit it after it has been signed off and . . .'

He knew Plimsoll. One more of the Eternal Flames now populating the building. One of the 'never went out' brigade, never posted abroad, would not know a frontier fence with a fresh-laid minefield if it stood up and bit him. Of course, there should have been a risk assessment, and the Big Boss should have agreed it covered the necessary ground – and signed on the line . . . Time pressed, and he was due at the Gate. In his mind was what he had to say, and the points he must hammer home. There was no risk *bloody* assessment, nor would there be.

'Short of time, apologies, rather busy.'

A pulled face. An expression of sadness rather than frustration. An intimation that no good would come from the contravention of best practice. 'Your application does not indicate where this unidentified operation will take place, the one that takes you away with a quite substantial sum of monies. We are, to put it mildly, light on detail.'

'Where? East of Cromer, or Kings Lynn, or Skegness – excuse me, have a lot to be getting on with.'

'I am doing my job to the best of my ability. As far as I'm aware, the days of ill-prepared cowboy jaunts are long gone. I understand you have verbal support from the seventh floor. My advice, don't push the support too far.' An edge was in Plimsoll's voice, and he cracked his finger joints for effect, emboldened. 'The advice – don't cock it up. Just don't, or you'll be hanging in the wind, twisting in it – that's good advice.'

'Would that be hemp or woven silk, the rope they'll use?' Boot heard a quiet titter from the Maid.

'Not just you, but plenty of others if it fails and there was no risk assessment submitted. The height of irresponsibility.'

Their eyes met. Each despised the other. Two men facing each other across the chasm that divided an old world from a new one. The cold was at the back of his neck, and the constriction at his throat, at the truth of what he was told.

He eased past. 'Then we should all pedal harder – to see it doesn't fail.'

He knew the footsteps. Nikki heard the approach of Gorilla up the stairs from the Reception area, along the corridor, then into the work area. Very few of the script kids were big men; most were wiry, small, skinny and with minimal muscle. Their status was based on their keyboard skill, not on squats and hoisting weights. Nikki thought Gorilla might have a degree of autism. Usually distant, harder to reach than any of them, but with an explosive turn of mood. Gorilla had a good relationship with HookNose, a better one with the Roofer, seemed easy with the GangMaster, and was generally tolerant of Nikki. Maybe poison had dripped in his ear. Early in the year, his temper tripped by a presumed snigger, Gorilla had belted two newer kids. One had suffered a split lip and the other had spat out a dislodged tooth. If it had not been for his skill on a keyboard and the angry persistence with which he followed entry routes into the better guarded compa- nies" computing systems, he would have been sitting out on a bench in a park in the rain with a view of a railway line and tower blocks. A high moment the previous year had been Gorilla's little squeal of pleasure – and they had come and taken turns to gaze over his shoulder and seen where his worm had reached: the Pentagon, a personnel section, a department dealing with the emoluments for senior ranking officers serving abroad, and a gush of email messages downloading. Not secrets at state level, but names and destinations and banks for salaries to be paid into, and confidential appraisals: the sort of material that GRU – military intelligence – drooled over, and that won the GangMaster praise and influence and further FSB protection, and Gorilla had taken them there. He could do as the fancy took him, would not be chastised.

The fancy did take, and the toxic in his ear had gone deep. Nikki heard him approach, hesitate, then Nikki was flying. The chair had been tipped back, the wheels had lost traction and it was upended.

He sprawled, his fingers failing to find a grip on the worn vinyl flooring, and his legs were above him and he'd had the mouse in his hand so had dragged it with him and the cable had yanked the laptop off the work surface, and it landed on Nikki's chest. Nothing said to Nikki, nor to the Roofer, and HookNose was ignored, and Gorilla sat, switched on his own power. And they knew nothing . . . it was the middle of Tuesday afternoon and sleet was in the air and the rooftops were hard to see, and they did not know who he had been with on Sunday evening and what was talked of. Knew nothing of Nikki's new friends, nothing of an account held in a bank on the square overlooking the quayside of the Swedish capital, nothing of the man who now controlled him, and what he offered. Had they known, then the Roofer and HookNose and Gorilla would have kicked him near to death. Their ignorance fortified Nikki. He was on his knees, reached up to put the laptop back on the work space, then pulled himself to his feet. That they knew nothing was the great strength he had . . . His stomach churned. He sat again, and powered up. None of them looked at him. He did not gasp or curse or threaten. Nikki ignored them. Nobody in that great city of Russian power knew anything, not even his sister who was the one person he loved. Nobody. And new friends were coming, would soon be with him and would value him.

'I had a grenade on my chest,' Merc said.

They were on the walkway on the south side of the Thames, and had been through the matter of detail once, would return to it again. The question asked of Merc had been how close they had been to their position being overwhelmed. He thought his answer adequate.

'And you'd have pulled the pin?'

'No hesitation, and everyone with me had one, sir, or a last pistol bullet. We'd not have been taken – and that's less than a day ago.'

He and the Six man were together and Daff was behind, like a protective back-marker, but twice she had been called forward, had skipped over the intervening space, responded to a query, gave the facts and had retreated. Merc did not care for 'hero-stories', kept away from those who peddled them. He could still feel, the weight of the grenade on his webbing and the little tattoo it had beaten on his vest when he had moved. He would have detonated it if the trench had been lost; he would have grabbed Cinar and dragged her down, his stomach on hers, then pulled the pin.

'Being captured alive in that little corner of the world – to me – raises quite horrific sensations. Captured where we are asking you to go would be uncomfortable for you, unpleasant, but unlikely to be life-threatening. The embarrassment to me and my ilk would be on a major scale. Don't call me "sir", my name is Coker – Edwin Coker. It's usually regarded as poor practice for an officer to give his real name to an "increment". I trust in you, and your ability to stay free, your resolution if otherwise in with-standing sophisticated harsh interrogation. I'm old, and operate in a kind of backwater, and if they had my name and my address and my wife's name, it would not be too disastrous to contemplate. So, I am Edwin Coker, but am known to colleagues as Boot. Just that – Boot – and not "sir", never "sir". If you were taken and it all spilled out, you would survive in a rat-infested cockroach colony of a gaol for a few years until we lifted someone they thought worth swapping you for. Not the colleagues. I do not think, in the modern holiday camp run by FSB, that the people you are with would come through. Bad for them, worse for my little compromised asset, the hacker. He would suffer greatly and death for him might seem pretty much of a liberation. If you wanted one, a pill, I could provide it. Do you?'

Merc did not want a lethal pill, not where he was going. They walked on. He spoke little and left the talking to Coker, thinned hair, spectacles that looked to have done good service, a jacket of tweed under a raincoat of fading brown, and a trilby plastered low on his forehead so that the wind would not tip it into the river. Never did talk much, certainly not when on Hill 425. Then, conversation was about infestations of flies, and kit, and the quality of the ammunition issued. They were comrades, but not friends, companions in conflict. He thought the man with him was senior and a decision maker, and likely to be obsessional about something, but not sharing it, and had hoped to be a leader – but now was vulnerable. A seasoned veteran but needing Merc, dependent on a man half his age who gained the most satisfaction out of *Auto Trader* and *Exchange and Mart* and studied the price lists of performance Mercedes saloons.

'Am I leaping ahead too fast?'

'You are asking me if I am on board – prepared to go?'

'I suppose so, yes . . . Rather took it for granted. Shouldn't have done.'

Merc supposed a spark of mischief was warranted. He was hooked, had been from the start. He always wanted to start, to be far from the briefers, make his own plan.

'At the end of the day, what's in it for me?'

A hesitation, then indecision, a near stutter. 'Good question, but it'll be a poor answer. Not much. A payment that will not reflect the importance of the work we ask for, will not alter your way of life. Quite miserly, but that is the way we are. What my wife often says about being coopted onto committees is that the only thing worse than being asked to serve is not being asked. I am not usually tongue-tied, but in this case I am short of words. What's in it for you, Merc – what my dear Daff calls you – is that you come with recommendation, your esteem will be enhanced, you will have the imagined medal for having done something that is "worthwhile". Am I getting anywhere?'

He thought him honest. 'Getting somewhere.'

'Thank you.'

Barges went by, then an empty pleasure boat, and the lamps seemed bright across the water and the bridges were a stream of headlights, and the grey of the cloud merged with the roofs.

'I don't speak the language, I don't know the ground, I don't know the back-up people, I don't know the man I am required to handle. It's not a promising start,' Merc said.

They walked on paving. Weeds were rooted where the grouting had collapsed. They had passed a beer bottle and several cans that rattled when the wind caught them, and fast-food polystyrene trays. All around him, separated by the river, were the great edifices of his country's power, its authority, its stature: they meant little to Merc. Merc thought he did not belong in such a place, that his last home was more important to him. The voice was crisp and calm in his ear.

'You raise difficulties, very fairly. As would anyone else with such a proposition put to them. The difference? "Anyone else" declines, sends me off with a flea in the ear – wants time to think on it, wants more hours to ponder than I have available. "Anyone else" walks away, a wave and a smile and back to the pub, or wher-ever. Not you, that's the difference. Three men travelling with you, Estonians but fluent Russian speakers, know the ground and the routines, and with an intelligence-gathering background. Did a good run a while back into Kaliningrad. Recommended by people who should know. You'll be protected and sheltered and your sole responsibility is couriering the package – and keeping the kid on side. But – first, foremost – you are not "anyone else", why we wanted you. And we're grateful you're on board.'

'Which makes me an idiot?'

'Not in any way. Makes you "old school", with a careless regard for the book and its strictures. For God's sake, there are people in this city today who regard the ultimate challenge they will face in the course of a working day as crossing the bloody road. You cross the road, Merc. You stand in a fire position, and all levels of shit are thrown at you. You make choices and they do not intimidate you. And you are not reckless with your safety or with that of the people who follow you . . . about "trust".'

His 'home' might have been in the barracks and the cupboard space allowed him, with the TV on the wall and the one chair where he could sit with his magazines, and the bed where he slept. Or might have been the trench dug out from the summit of Hill 425, and the dirt and the mess and the stains and the brightness of the ejected cartridge cases.

'What "trust" should I show?'

'All I have to offer is the guarantee that I have done everything possible, within my remit, to ensure this mission succeeds, has the best chance possible. That may not be enough. For God's sake, man, walk if you are going to walk. Are you in or are you out?'

'Never a question of—'

'In or out? Just for the record, I do not have time to go and drag another from anywhere, any damn place, put air strikes over him, get the Parachute Regiment on the ground to lift him, have a good woman bared and ready to go to enthuse him. I have no second option. It happens with you, or it does not happen – because of your record, your qualities, your . . . for fuck's sake, this is not a vanity contest. You won it. We chose you. Taking it or leaving it?'

And 'home' might also have been the hotel bar where he met Brad and Rob from the Hereford gang and passed over the notes he had made in a Forward Fire Position, done in a child's hand-writing and listing the complexities of combat at close quarters. The messages went back to the allied liaison team and might be shipped to London. Perhaps they were ignored. He had, for now, no other life and was not yet ready for 'sometime', was frightened of the quiet it would bring: kept it there in reserve, like a spare and loaded magazine, or the grenade on his chest.

'If I could finish, *sir* . . . Never a question of staying in or walking out. Never was . . .'

'It will be Copenhagen. Yes, Operation Copenhagen. Has a good ring to it.'

It was the second time they had been as far as Lambeth Bridge, and the flags across the river at Whitehall, topping the buildings of state, flew flat, and Merc seemed not to feel the cold, nor be rocked by the wind. He wondered why the man called himself 'Boot', did not ask, not important enough to waste breath on, but he wondered.

'Is this an act of war?'

'Entitled to ask. Might be, might be near to it, though not a concern of yours. Others will ferret through that consideration. Let it lie. Our opponents idolise the doctrine of deception. The covering of tracks. It will seem like internecine warfare between two gangs of rivals, of thugs, and will create uncertainty, confusion between the gangs that employ the hackers, and more uncertainty at the levels in the apparatus of state control as the men who do the protection fall out. One believes he is betrayed and one believes he is a victim. Lurking around them will be the heavy shadow of suspicion. Some brighter individual – always one investigator who is a tad above the intellect of the rest – will point a hesitant finger, but I'm confident he'll not be listened to. Could be said to be an act of war, aggression, same as they launch against us but they'll not recognise it.'

'It's important?'

'Not done on a whim. There is one last thing. Don't associate yourself on the way out with the passengers. If there is a hue and cry, and there's likely to be, come on your own, be responsible for yourself. That's it, thank you for agreeing to be with us. Important? Of course it is. It'll be a good show.'

Merc thought the man ill-equipped to muster a speech of inspiration, would have found it as awkward himself. But the light was in the eyes, and enthusiasm in the voice, and sensed also a ruthlessness that would come easier from being behind the lines, safe from hazard. They were halfway between the bridges and Lambeth was shielded by the low and scudding mist, and the colour seemed

washed off the yellow and green walls of the VBX building. The
tide was coming in fast and little waves rapped against the steps
leading to the grey and frothed water. The man that he called sir,
who called himself Coker, but known as Boot, hurried away and
was bowed and into the teeth of the wind and clung to his hat, and
his tie rippled over his shoulder. He had never considered hearing
the plan and then shaking his head. 'Regrets, but you've come to
the wrong man. Pity you went to all that trouble.' Never been in
his head.

Daff, from stalking the two men, had come up fast behind him,
and again inserted her hand in his arm, and they might have been
lovers or might have been brother and sister. Her voice was quiet
and close to his ear and she talked detail: the width of the river, the
security in the restricted zone beyond it, and the rendezvous with
the boys who were ill-defined quality but he'd whip them into the
shape he needed, and the character of the asset, and the size and
weight of the explosive charge, and the time of the gathering of
juvenile experts who were as good as they came.

He asked one thing of Daff – not for the use of a car to take him
to a terrace off the Oxford Road in Reading, or for a car to drive
him north and west and into the Buckinghamshire town of Stoke
Poges and be there before a bank closed, but he asked her to arrange
for flowers to be sent. What sort? Chrysanthemums, what his nan
had always liked, the gold ones and the merlot-red ones. Where to?
He gave the name of the hospital and the street it was on, near to the
Ministry of Justice. Brad and Rob would handle it. She typed it up
on her phone. Walkers passed them and cyclists and kids on skate-
boards, and mothers with buggies, and men sat on benches and
huddled against the weather and tried to smoke. They played the
game, and every now and again she would nuzzle against his ear,
did the acting well. She led him back to the service flat, suggested
he might try to sleep, told him when they would move.

'I can feel it in my water, Arthur.'

'What I always say, Roy, if old Boot's involved then it'll be a
right "good one".'

The two guards on the main gate had noted Boot's exit and his return; he seemed tense, alert, and in a hurry. The one they knew as the Maid, Marian, who worked for him, had come in carrying a heavy metal boxed case on a shoulder strap that had half pulled her over but she'd not allowed it to be handled by anyone else, nor permitted it on to the conveyor belt to the X-ray, and so it was locked now in a lead-lined storage box. Across the wide traffic flow they had seen Daff – could always spot her because she was tall and bronzed and had a pony-tail that was set off when it was windy – and she was leading a young guy who had a tanned and worn face, and was light on his feet. She'd come back alone from under the railway bridge, flashing the card on the lanyard round her neck. Bloody good-looking girl, with no time for a nod to them.

'On the final countdown, I'd say.'

'Sort of gives you a shiver, doesn't it, Roy?'

Then they were concentrating, or trying to, eyesight not as good and hearing impeded by the earpieces they wore, and neither was sure what would happen if the building came under sustained attack – suicide bombers, rocket-propelled grenades, a car bomb. But best guess was 'first-degree chaos, total cluster-fuck'. They enjoyed their prediction analysis of pending operations; it was like choosing lottery numbers.

Her attention was elsewhere. Kat was scolded.

Nikki paid handsomely for the lessons, and without the cash contribution of her brother, her fingers would have stiffened and thickened, the joints lost their suppleness, and the dream of playing in a concert hall would – once and for all – have been found a fraud. At the Conservatory she would have felt the quality of a teacher – not here, not any longer – would have been warm, and among fellow students all striving and feeding from each other's talent. She was insulted, was treated as a student devoid of talent: deserved to be.

Her arrest, the point of her decline as a musician, had been brutal. At home in the apartment, Nikki already gone because that

morning there was a concerted 'wolf pack attack' which he had
not explained, and she was alone, not dressed. The door had splintered, then caved. Just cotton pyjamas, no robe, uniformed men
and women filling the space, a fast body search, fingers cased in
plastic entering her, cold faces and no explanation, her brother's
gear tipped on the floor. They had known to leave his equipment,
not ransack it for hard drives, but could still violate it; she understood the extent of power and its limits. One day and one evening
in the interrogation room and a barrage of questions about associates, their plans, ambitions, the leaders. Still in her pyjamas and
with a stinking police station blanket across her shoulders, lights
in her face. A night in a cell with half a dozen other women who
were thieves and whores and a poetess who had written a work
denouncing the terrorism of despotic authority and had published
it on an underground press. 'Give them nothing,' the poetess had
told her. 'Fuck them and ignore them,' a whore had told her. 'Spit
in their faces,' a thief had told her. But, she had given them something: names that she thought were innocent, locations she had
never heard of, outlines of what was talked about. Morning had
come, and she been extracted from the cell, given bread and a
glass of milk, seen the smiling face of an interrogator, and had
signed a sheet of paper acknowledging that all the possessions she
had brought to the police station had been returned to her – only
her watch. She had been about to leave, confused and cold, and
had been handed a second sheet of paper, four lines printed on it,
had read it, and learned that the Conservatory had expelled her,
her student grant had been withdrawn, and items from her locker
could be collected from the main entrance on Teatrainaya Square,
and an illegible signature. They had allowed her to keep the
blanket, subject to its return the following week, and given her
sufficient money to take a train to the station closest to their home.
Her brother had wept for her.

She was useless. She wasted her tutor's time. She responded to
kindness with indifference. She did not deserve the opportunity to
be taught by a woman of distinction . . . All familiar accusations.
She paid $75 an hour for the lessons. Not an explosion of anger

but a calculated gesture . The woman was obese, wore a sack of a dress, and her scarlet lipstick was grotesque on her pale skin, and the ornaments at her neck were paste, and her hair was growing too fast for the dye, and . . . If the group wanted a 'clothes off' protest, she would agree. Strip naked, winter cold and ice on the ground, would do it, make a protest that was political and artistic. She had no passport, nowhere to run to, and could think of nothing with which to make her statement, other than bare and goose-pimpled skin. To hell with the system, the fat cats, and with the denial of freedom. What was freedom? Too confused at that moment to give herself an answer. Not confused enough to forgo the chance to slam the lid of the piano while the woman's hands were on the keys, and Chopin ended in a shrill scream. Might have broken the woman's fingers, but Kat did not stay to find out. She swept up her bag, left the money for the day's lesson on the table, and all her music scores, stormed out, kicked the door shut on the teacher's pain, felt relief, and had no idea where that could take her. She would see them that evening, make her declaration, demand a role, and convince them of her commitment.

The Major lectured his Operations Group. He had long ago succeeded in overwhelming any sense of mistrust among FSB officers in St Petersburg after his transfer from what they would have regarded as the primitive world of Belarus. Had done it with professionalism and with rigorous honesty, but he did not stray into areas that would provide conflict with the senior men who provided the well-rewarded roofs for the gangs.

He had the photograph of her taken in the police station, and others from surveillance teams, and could justify the commitment of manpower and logistics on the grounds that – sure as snow each winter and the freezing of the Neva – she would lead them to more important players, above the level of deluded kids. He had called his wife, told her not to expect him for the family dinner they valued each evening, had arranged for a part of the cell block to be freed up. He called her by her given name when he talked of her to his subordinates. He made no mention of her brother, or who employed him, or who provided the roof, the *krysha*, for that GangMaster and whose immunity guarantor was on the floor above the briefing room where the Major did his presentation. He used the given name because he knew that the juniors he would send out into the night responded better when they were more easily able to identify with a target. He stressed that Yekaterina – thin, wan, pale-faced, a stubbornness evident in her flashing eyes, hair askew – was not an important adversary in herself, but was like a pollen-gathering bee who would lead them to the queen. The young men and women who would make the arrests were patriotic, detested their targets, and worshipped the great man on the TV each evening who gave them pride in their Motherland, who was to blame for nothing, who was surrounded by enemies, who understood the value of their work.

'It will be a useful evening – and important dissidents and those who flout the laws of our society will be taken into custody.'

The principal photograph stayed on the screen.

She might have been a pretty girl, but made no effort. They always liked to have new girls in their groups, fodder for the appetite of the old men who led them. He was well known in the Big House for the diligence with which he hunted down protesters, anarchy-makers. She would be followed that evening and he felt sure that her tradecraft in searching out tails would be inferior to that of most of those she consorted with. A pretty girl, a silly girl and a useful girl and, the Major thought, an interesting girl.

His bag was packed, courtesy of the Maid, and contained clothing suitable for the extreme north. His wife had been telephoned at her work, and told he'd be away for a few days; he'd text her from the airport. Daff was fussing with her own kit, waterproof trousers and a heavy-duty anorak, and pepper sprays along with flash-and-bang grenades – banned from the upper floors, but drawn from a basement store. The Maid had turned to paperwork, what Boot needed and what Daff would carry, and the title under which they would travel. *Copenhagen*. A flicker of the Maid's eyebrows, like an alarm clock squawking, enough to tell Boot to be off and into the territory of the Big Boss.

Daff followed him, lugging both their bags. They took the elevator.

He had not needed a last look at his poster cartoon of the Duke. Had it clear in his mind. He had adjusted himself to a timetable of affairs, where he would be, and what stage his operation would have reached, and it ran alongside the schedule of Waterloo, the battle. Oddly comforting. He knew so little, and his intelligence capability was limited, and how it would be when confrontation occurred was beyond his comprehension. He could put his assets on the ground and hope – or pray. As it would have been for the Duke on that equivalent day. No location for that great heaving, shuffling groaning force that was his enemy, hidden from him and no agent in place to speed detail to him by a fast chain of thoroughbred horses. In the darkness . . . as Boot was.

In his hand were three pages, large print. The Big Boss disliked flicking electronically through reports, wanted paper. Daff was held at the outer door, would stay in the corridor. He was admitted to the inner office. Boot did not sit. He was launching that evening. It was *Copenhagen*, a good title and accepted, and the briefing notes – easy to absorb – were on the desk. The complaint, lodged formally by Plimsoll, was acknowledged, dismissed, chuckled over without humour, then the tie was loosened at the collar and the hands came together as if in prayer and the shirt-sleeved elbows rested on the desk.

'I'm backing you, Boot – I hope I should be.'

'Could not have done otherwise. It's to your credit.'

'A good plan and all in place?'

'Pretty solid.'

'And your man, a heap of trust given to him, Boot. Worth it?'

'First class. Tell you one factor I particularly enjoyed. He does not cherry-pick. No question of it. Does not labour a point of justification. We want it done, good enough for him. I'm very confident. You know that Burke quote? Of course you do. *People sleep safely in their beds at night because rough men stand ready to visit violence on those who would harm us*. I take it as having the same weight as a bible tract.'

'"Rough men" visiting, a solid justification for what you propose. God speed, friend.'

Boot left the presence. He felt weak, as if he might stumble, but cleared the door.

He breathed deeply when he got back to his office, watched curiously by Daff. Was he all right? Yes, he was fine.

'Actually, very fine. Now, let's hit the beast.'

The boys gathered. Regarded themselves as 'boys', and disregarded their ages.

They came in to the border town of Narva in the late afternoon. In their mid-forties now, it would be the sort of reunion where time was reckoned to have stood still, and the passing of the years ignored. 'How are things?' 'Things are good – excellent – things are going well.' They'd lie, and badly. What tied them together was their grandfathers, a street on the coast and the betrayal of trust, and of the mission that had sent the three of them across a defended frontier into the Russian territory of Kaliningrad. Since then life had not been good, and it showed.

Rumour and what purported to be intelligence had swirled but stayed unproven. The President had denounced the allegations as 'rubbish'. The mayor of Kaliningrad *oblast* had stated the claims were a 'dangerous joke'. The allegations and the dangerous joke said Russia had moved tactical nuclear weapons into the enclave sandwiched between Poland and Lithuania, the home of the Baltic fleet. There was supposed to be an understanding that short-range missiles with nuclear warheads would not be deployed there. The Pentagon said they had. The Poles, in the front line, wanted to know where they were, and sent three men, merchant seamen as the cover, put inside the enclave from a drifting fishing boat with 'mechanical problems' and landed on the sand spit running south towards Polish territory. The chosen trio were expendable, deniable and cheap, and the year was 2002. They had remained on the books of the Polish Service, not assigned again, until a message

– frantic because of a short-scale window of time – from that pretty girl in London: the one that all who met her wanted to bed. Three names. She'd seemed grateful.

Toomas travelled to Narva by motorcycle, through sleet storms carried by gales.

Long years before, they had gone into the Russian city, reached the base where the fleet was moored, and had trekked around it. Had looked like three guys with hangovers meandering in search of the fresh air that might swill the alcohol out of them. Had gone inland, had quartered the small territory and looked for road-blocks or areas that were surrounded by new barbed wire, had gone to the gates of a barracks towards the Lithuanian border, had pleaded they were lost and needed directions and had assumed that any camp where nuclear battlefield missiles were stored would have increased security, but had not found it.

Martin had used the train, borrowed the fare from a neighbour. He had promised, mother's life and all that crap, that he'd an opportunity to earn and would repay within two weeks.

They had started well in Kaliningrad. Had stayed inside the limits of the tradecraft taught them – had been waiting for a ship that was due to dock in ten days. The ship would be under the Finnish flag; they had its name and documentation. Toomas had drunk vodka and had a fight. Martin had fancied the 'fiancée' of a mobster, doing well from shipping heroin, transiting through Russia. Knives had been shown them and they had run into the night, run until they could barely breathe and no longer heard the patter of following feet. Kristjan had lost most of the subsistence cash given them, passed over the cash counter in the casino on Prospekt Mira, close to the Cosmonaut monument. They had finished badly. They had come out across the land border and into Polish territory, had run through the woods, and used bolt cutters on the fence and would have been clear by the time that tumbler wires identified their breakout's location and militia came with dogs and flares and helicopters. The flight, and the pursuit, added to the veracity of their report: prepared to take risks, go the extra kilometre. They had *not* located launch pads. Had *not* identified the heavy transport required to shift the missiles. Were able to recount the conversations with a Russian soldier, tipsy and indiscreet, who was *almost* certain he had seen them. Repeated gossip heard in a bar patronised by smuggling gangs, of the nights when their cargo was delayed because of military movements that broke the usual patterns and were believed to be the shipment of 'big hardware'. Had overheard, in a casino, an officer telling a naval colleague that he would be going home to Irkutsk as soon as 'my little babies, little but with the big bite, are safely tucked away in their new homes'. They had been told they had done well, had been thanked, had been paid, had not been given other work. Had stayed together, close, for the first years. Jobbing employment in Gdansk, then in Hamburg, and loitering in the old Cold War haunts where the officers of the various Services were supposed to come, like pimps hunting out girls, then had returned to Estonia.

Kristjan had left his quiet, empty apartment, had turned his back on a landlord demanding back rent, had said over his shoulder that he would settle in full by the end of the following week, and had pushed open the door of the café where they would meet.

They went slowly, held up in traffic, victims of the homeward journey of thousands of workers. Boot had gone. They had stopped outside a tube station. He had stepped out quickly from the front passenger seat, had touched the driver's arm with familiarity, and thanked him, then Daff had opened the boot and given him his bag. He had disappeared into the swirl entering the station's forecourt, not a backward glance, not a farewell, no encouragement, not even a shrug and a mutter of 'good luck, young man'. Merc appreciated the manner of his going.

'Will I see him there, before the jump off?'

'Shouldn't think so. You'll see him when you're back.'

Daff stayed quiet, but flipped through sheets of paper, and sometimes let her fingers fall on the back of Merc's hand, a kind of intimacy, and she used a small torch to focus on a piece of text or a detail in an aerial photograph. Merc liked the way of Boot's going. He'd have despised any 'band of brothers' speech, and had never imitated his father's call when they had fought to survive in the Forward Operating Base. Had few words at the best of times, and no words when they were not called for. He sat in near silence. He had learned its virtue, from when he was small. He had come in a taxi with his mother to his grandmother's home. His mother had been 'unwell', he had been told, and the house had been sold after his father's death. All his clothes and what possessions a three-year-old owned were in a small suitcase. The handover had been on the pavement, a fast hug and a fast kiss and tears, and the taxi had pulled away, and a moment later the front door had closed behind him. Cared for, yes. Loved, not as he'd noticed. He had heard, three or four years later, his mother referred to as 'a silly cow', and he had never seen her again, nor had sought her out. He had been good at silence as a child.

They went past the civil section of the airfield and on to the military wing. No security checks for them. Daff led the way through an empty terminal on to the tarmac, carrying her bag and the steel box. He had what she had bought him. The same cockpit crew waited on them. A thin-lipped smile from the senior pilot, nothing more. They settled in their seats, either side of the aisle, and Merc noted that the cabin crew stewards were not on board. They fastened their belts, and the cockpit door was closed and the lights dimmed and the engines went to power, and they taxied.

She rapped her fist gently on the box, and said, 'As well they don't know what's in here, or they'd have a collective seizure. Just for your interest, I asked Boot whether the plan we have in place would win. His answer, "It doesn't deserve to, but it might, might just win." That's where we are. Oh, and yes, I sent the flowers.'

A comment was not required of him, so he didn't give one. Boot was hardly going to use the F for 'fail' word. He would not disagree that the cockpit crew would be wary of flying with a live explosive device in the cabin, one that would detonate half an hour after an integral switch was thrown. There would be a Makarov PM 9mm in there, two full magazines and another twenty rounds, and an effective range of fifty metres.

He thought she looked at him often enough, attempting to evaluate him, and had probably failed to in the Green Zone and every other place they'd met. Two and three-quarter hours was the flight time. Merc closed his eyes and edged further down in the seat, tilted it back, prepared to sleep.

6

They taxied after a hard landing. The impact woke him.

He looked across the aisle and saw Daff filing her nails. Bright, high lights showed a line of parked A10s, the tank busters that always raised a cheer from ground people when they flew over the front line west of Erbil then darted down to hit targets. After them were Typhoons – Merc could see the Luftwaffe symbol on the tails – and then there was a building that looked deserted. Merc did little history, less politics. Abruptly his face set and his lips might have thinned. A Gun for Hire had no requirement of small sophistications: why were the aircraft here? He was poor on exit strategy, did not know when the 'sometime' would rear up and be impossible to side-step. The planes they passed as they taxied to a pair of parked cars had no significance for his mission, only told him he was near to a front line, close but not at it. The evening played out with a curious choreography.

He did not help her. She went first with her own bag and the steel-sided case. The senior pilot had the cockpit door open and worked the gear that put down the steps. Merc followed her, felt good, rested. The pilot looked hard at him, and Merc fancied that he did not take happily to performing chauffeur work. Merc did not thank him, or smile appreciation for the smooth flight over the western Baltic and a bit of Estonian airspace before the descent on to the Amari strip. Nor did the pilot offer to help Daff, would have known the gesture would be declined. The pilot probably wondered about the importance of a slightly built guy, around thirty years old, dressed first in filthy fatigues and now in High Street casuals, no swagger about him, lacking the presence of a decorated 'war hero', and just a couple of vehicles as the welcoming

party. Could wonder until it hurt his head, contemplate it all the
way home to Northolt. Merc was certain that if he came home,
with a flute of champagne in his hand, or with the smell of failure
on him, or on a CASEVAC with a nurse holding a drip over a
wound, or in a bag in cargo, he would not be travelling on an
executive jet. Wherever home was ... Before he'd slept, Daff had
talked him through the device inside the steel-cased box.

A chill wind cut him at the top of the steps. He assumed that the
line of tank busters and the wing of fast jets were not there as a
circus turn. Nor was it part of a music hall act for him to go across
an international frontier, carrying a device – detonator inserted –
with a simple arming trigger. Built into the laptop was a sufficient
weight of explosive, high-quality, military, Russian manufactured
and liberated in Syria, to do more than cosmetic damage. That
was restricted knowledge. A car door opened. A man climbed out,
then reached back inside to stub out his cigarette, then walked
forward. They were off the steps, walking towards him, but Daff
slowed and again she was close to him, lips against his ear: the
locals here, she told him, had as good a counter-intelligence set-up
as anywhere in Europe and if they had not declared then they
would have been spotted, isolated, fucked around, expelled. She
had a good walk, swung her hips. He heard the grind of the steps
being raised behind him, did not look back and did not wave.

'Welcome to Estonia,' the man said softly.

'Thank you.'

'A good flight.'

'A delightful flight,' Daff replied.

No handshakes. Only basic courtesies. One of the vehicles was
a BMW off-road and the other was a household car, a Toyota
estate, mud-coated, a dark shade of green under the dirt and
utterly forgettable. The base was quiet and night had fallen. They
drove past the terminal and workshops and hangars that would,
thirty years ago, have housed Soviet aircraft, their technicians, and
repair yards. Merc thought Daff was tense, as if realising she was
operating above her level of competence. Took it casually because
where he came from – inside any Fire Force Unit and heading

west from Erbil – half of the guys and half of the girls would have been raw, why they came to depend on him. He hoped that the chrysanthemums would be in a glass vase by the bed. He was passed a bottle of water, sipped it, because where he came from water was precious. Scudding sleet was whacking on to the windscreen and the wipers had difficulty clearing it. They came to a fenced compound with a hut protected by the wire, were admitted. He thought that it had worked well, and that what he had asked for was in place, and told Daff that and was rewarded with a raised eyebrow, as if his praise was precious.

Together, they loaded the body board, and the folded compact bicycle that weighed, he estimated, a little under fifteen kilos, and a couple of wrapped packs of inflatable arm supports. What he had requested was easier to collect here than have her chase after them in London as the clocks ran down. Reality blossomed. Could not step back, not mutter something about it all being a big mistake . . . He would be going across the frontier the next evening. Daff had her hand on his arm and he did not remove it, and the gear was loaded in the back of the Toyota and Daff drove. They went out into the night and followed the tail of the four-wheel drive, and went fast. She said it would be two hours.

'Anything you need, anything, to talk over?'

'I don't think so, not before we're down the road.'

The fingers were on her lower thigh, kneading her jeans.

They'd seemed surprised when she had pitched up. Kat had made a declaration: wanted to be involved, believed in the cult of protest, demanded the right to shock authority. Had stood in front of the gang, and they had smoked and eyed her as housewives would examine a slab of meat. She had heaved back her chest and jutted her chin, had denounced non-violence, had spat vitriol at the criminality of the *siloviki* who ran government with nothing more altruistic in mind than the lining of their pockets and new villas in the woods and the rip-off from state industries. Had pleaded to be a part of them and allowed to contribute, was a convert to their anarchy, wanted to attack . . . Slight sneers played at the sides of their mouths, like she was fun and made a show. She recognised, too soon, that they regarded her as mild amusement and that might have been fuel on the fire. She was driven further with her commitment to assault the power of the state, and she rattled through the case histories of the nailed down scrotum, and the naked man wrapped in wire, and the show at the museum and the painting on the bridge. By now the piano teacher would have binned the music sheets Kat had left behind, and would have cursed her for the pain in the joints of her fat fingers, already multicolour bright with bruising. No way back . . . a career on self-destruct . . . And as she spat out her dedication, she could recall the first heady days with the group, and the excitement and sense of glorification at having broken away from the conventional. Could recall the arrest and the night in the cells, the cold sweat when she had opened the envelope confirming that the Conservatory no longer had a place for her, the simpering loyalty of her brother, who was a criminal. There were whispers and sniggers, and she was invited to go with them. Two buses, a darkened street in the Grazhdanka sector in the north of the city. Up the outside fire escape staircase and through an outer door into the sixth-floor apartment of a leader: a tall man, stubble on his face, strong fingers, a silk shirt, a knotted kerchief and fierce eyes.

They sat in a circle of hard chairs and easy ones and a sofa, and there were big cushions on the floor. He had gravely shaken her hand as if formality was necessary, had gazed at her, seemed to look behind her eyes, and it had seemed inevitable that she would sit beside him on the sofa. It was a show, his hand on her thigh, and she had stiffened, and pushed it away, but was ignored. They had talked – without her contributing – of a poster to be plastered on walls in the bus station, the train station, the principal Post Office, metro tunnels. The motif for the posters, drawn and coloured by a serious-faced woman, big glasses, big bosom, big mouth, showed a line of cheerful fleshy piglets feeding from a trough. They had discussed the slogan that would go with it: 'greed' and 'gluttony'. The others watched her, and the advance of his hand. It was ordained. She was without a friend, without a family – other than a brother who was a thief – and without a purpose. And had no passport. The leader, unidentified might have flicked his eyebrows at the others, made a gesture with them; if he had she had not seen it. She was rigid. Wanted sex? Did not want sex? Would be a trophy? They stood, papers gathered, the poster designs returned to a bag, and a woman collected the glasses, bottles, and the plastic plates they had eaten off and headed for the kitchen. Kat heard them being dumped in the sink. Kat tried to stand and watched them leaving, but the leader's grip was tight on her, and the sofa low, and she would have had to fight to get herself clear.

The door closed. They were alone.

He had a remote in his hand. Flicked it. Music exploded. Jazz from America, played by Negroes. If she did not want him, did not feel honoured to be served up as a sacrifice to assuage the lust of gods, what was her alternative? One hand on her upper thigh and the other roaming, undoing the buttons at the waist of her jeans and pushing up her sweater, finding more buttons on her blouse . . . They would be tittering as they made their way to the bus stop and the first leg of the return to their own quarter. She assumed that when she was no longer fresh and new, she would be dumped and then given to one of the others, and maybe handed down, and maybe . . . Her zip was undone and his hand was groping her; the other took her fingers and guided them on to him. The taste in his mouth was of beer and the smell of his armpit was of old sweat, and she rested her hand on him and he groaned, and . . . The door opened, flew off its hinges, came halfway across the room, bounced on the cushions and was blocked by the chairs.

The bastard . . . he did not snatch his hand away but let it lie there, long enough for them to see what was happening. They were laughing. Men and women of the police, or militia, or FSB – who the fuck cared – were laughing. She pulled her sweater down and her zip up and fastened her belt and her body shook. He was handcuffed. Kat was manacled, wrists behind her back and the pressure of the setting hard on the skin. They began to search the apartment.

She did not see what, if anything, they found. The woman had
taken away the poster design and the notes for the slogan to go
with it, and one of the men had folded away the map of the city on
which the transport hubs were marked in highlighter. The leader
ignored her now, but disputed the validity of the search warrant,
the justification for his arrest. The uniformed men and women did
not address her; it was as if she were a toy, of little interest to them.
She was taken down the main interior staircase, past the graffiti
scrawls and the wet marks in the corners where kids and derelicts
pissed, and out into the evening air, and the cold clawed at her
face. She might then, as she was heaved after him into the 'trash
truck', have realised the depths to which her life had plunged. Kat
stumbled into the police wagon and was driven away.

The BMW pulled in for a fuel stop.

One of the Estonians climbed in beside Daff and she gestured
with her thumb that he should ride in the big vehicle. She'd pushed
a sandwich into Merc's hand. Good English from the new driver.
Said he was from Kaitsepolitseiamet, KaPo, that he was from the
town of Narva on the border, and knew the ground on the far side
of the river. The suggestion was that he was familiar with the
ground over there because he'd gone over it, and not once. Said
that he dealt with smuggling of cigarettes and Russian vodka.
Merc ate his sandwich. The sleet had cleared, the road was clear
and straight, and there were roadside lights that flashed a warning
of accumulated ice. Merc listened.

'I am not permitted to learn anything of your operation, what
colleagues you collaborate with, what is your target, and what is
your intention when you reach it. We have a high regard for the
Six Service in the UK. We regard the Six Service as a valuable
friend but we do not perform joint operations. I am tasked to tell
you what I know of the terrain, and the security, on the far side of
the river. We have a reputation for success in our operations
against the Russians and that is because we have an understanding
of their culture, their methods. The dislike between them, with a
population exceeding one hundred million and ourselves, less

than two million, is mutual. They like to hurt us, we do what is in our power to irritate or wrong-foot them – so, within limitations, we help you. You will go in darkness across the Narva river. It is high and it is fast flowing, dangerous. On the far side are reed beds and then thick forest, too dense for daylight to penetrate. Along the river are high watch-towers: sometimes occupied and sometimes not, depending on what state of alert is considered appropriate. Something will happen, a diversion. Accept, please, that if you are taken you will be disowned. We will deny any knowledge of you and they will talk of provocation, and you will have a difficult time, *difficult*, believe me. Running due east from Narva, through their border town of Ivangorod, is the E-Twenty highway to St Petersburg, two hours by car. But you are not going through the border checkpoints. You are crossing into their territory further north, and there the first ten kilometres is extremely difficult ground. It is forest, bog, small streams, rain-water lakes, very few paths and those are for timber extraction. In the bog you could go down to your knees very easily, to your waist, almost you could go to your shoulders, and you might never be found. It is a closed area, and inhabitants, very few, must have special permission for residence, and visitors are not permitted. The security zone is patrolled by the militia, the armed force directed by the Ministry of Internal Affairs. Such patrolling is haphazard and we recognise few patterns. You may be fortunate and they are all in bed; you may be unfortunate and a commander has put his entire force on the ground. On this frontier, the Cold War is warm, and they take very seriously their border: not for smugglers or criminals, but for our people going the other way. They are armed, would shoot to kill, and they will defend their Motherland with courage. Travel that ten kilometres and you reach a road heading north that leads to the Baltic coast and there you must, no option, go south until meeting the junction with the E-Twenty. On that main route, you must rendezvous with those people who will drive you further towards St Petersburg – safe to assume the city is your destination? Don't worry, my friend, an answer is not expected from you. Another ten kilometres towards St Petersburg the road uses a bridge to cross another wide river, the Luga, at the town of Kingisepp. It is a chokepoint for you. On your little cycle at night you would attract attention, if you had not already been flattened by a lorry, and at the bridge will be suspicious security. The barracks is beside the bridge, far end, on Prospekt Karla Marksa. That is the start of the restricted zone which reaches into Ivangorod and to the Narva river. There is no other bridge that you can use unless you cut far to the south, but that is a different journey. I do not know, of course, by what route you hope to return, but I hope to hear you are safe and your mission a success. Good fortune, and may your God travel with you.'

A firm hand clasped his wrist, and then he was freed. Ahead were the lights, a drive-in fast-food outlet. He was returned to Daff.

They set off again, and waves of tiredness caught him. His eyes closed, a sort of peace came. More of his childhood reared, what had shaped him. His teacher, Mr Dyer, fierce and fair, had said, 'What you need, Hawkins, is structure. The ordinariness that comes from living inside the rules. Skiving off wherever the whim takes you, just not good enough. Get a job, one that needs a discipline, with a trade. What I'm saying, Hawkins, is that you should think seriously – if they'll have you – of going for the regular army . . .' Mr Dyer, decent old boy, could still be there, or could have taken refuge in his allotment; had cared about the kids – had not known that Merc's father had been made up from the ranks, was the Hold The Line legend, was a Pioneer, and gone too damn young. He slept, seemed to feel the comfort of a pillow, and it was a smooth run, at a steady speed.

Nikki was at home, alone. Not often that she was not with him; she'd be sitting with the radio playing good music, and she'd have made his supper. Kat cared for him, looked after him, shopped for him and drove him, and probably despised him. He worked in the industrial estate in the Kupchino district, made money for a GangMaster. Had made big money for himself which was lodged in the now blocked Swedish-based account. He was a thief. He stole, for himself and for the gang that employed him and for FSB to whom he was often sub-contracted. She knew nothing.

He turned on the television to break the quiet in the apartment. The President was big on the screen, inspecting troops on manoeuvre close to the Ukraine border, down by Rostov-on-Don, oozing confidence and power. Nikki had raided the fridge, heated soup, then eaten bread, some cheese. He did not know how to cook, how to wash his clothes, how to pay the utilities bills. The President spoke to the crews of an armoured regiment. Nikki had exemption from military service – the FSB officer who was the roof for the GangMaster would have steered through the paperwork. He fidgeted. Sometimes Kat did fried pork for him, with potatoes in the oil and dark cabbage. The note on the table said that she would be out for the evening, not when she might return. She was like a crutch to him but he kept much of his life a secret from her. If he had told her of the account in Stockholm she would have snarled contempt; if he had told her of the Englishman, from one of the British special agencies, who he had met in the hotel room, she would have said he was a fool; if he had told her of a rendezvous in a supermarket car-park, she would have denounced him as a lunatic and might have thrown crockery at him. He had to tell her, needed to.

The preparation involved the first moves to insert malware into a defence contractor based in Britain, but one with sister companies in the west of the United States, and in the 'silicon wadi' north of Tel Aviv. The initial brief before Thursday's meeting on detail spoke of back-door entry, and then insertion of malware, then use of a 'rootkit' that would hide the virus, then the extraction of material . . . Nikki had thought the GangMaster had read out the target areas from a sheet of paper, had not understood a syllable of it, was ignorant – but took the money.

The President was now in a viewing stand and used binoculars to watch the tanks cross the open ground far in front of him, firing continuously. The tanks, and the jets diving above them, and the barrage of short-range missiles were useless, a simpleton's weapons. He – and the bastards who were the Roofer and

Hooknose and Gorilla, and all the others – could have done greater damage than all the hardware that the President inspected – halted then toppled it. There was nothing more in the fridge to eat, all the biscuits gone: this was the evening, a Tuesday, when she shopped, took a purse full of money from him. He might have told her that evening.

Had to tell his sister. Had to tell her about an account at a bank on the quayside in the Swedish capital, that close to half a million American dollars was lodged there, blocked. Had to tell her about a mild-seeming man, with spectacles, thinning hair, like the old schoolmaster on English monochrome films, who had him tight in his fist and squeezed, twisted. Had to tell her about a stranger who would come to the supermarket's car-park, off the A-118, after the E-20 from the west, and close to the perimeter of the Pulkovo airport, tell her that he would bring with him a device, a small one. The pretence would be a flare in tensions between their GangMaster and neighbouring rivals who controlled the airport trade but also had their own script kids looking with jealousy for sponsorship from the state. Had to tell her that he'd be in flight, but hoped to get her passport restored and bring her out soon. From the viewing platform, the President applauded the distant tanks, and the demonstration of strength. The cost of it all was displayed on the screen – huge, crippling.

Nikki doubted that the President would have understood the world the hacker inhabited. Had to tell Kat that he was a traitor, had been bought . . . The picture had changed to the fighting in eastern Ukraine and the devastation done by the fascist army of Kiev, and the misery brought to good Russian citizens . . . Perhaps, he would also tell her of the violence shown, the bullying, at his work place. Much to tell her. Nikki had no one else to confide in other than his sister. He changed the channel. A film on the fate of 'national traitors' was showing, those who had betrayed their Motherland, had spied or defected, taken foreign money. Switched away from that channel . . . Football, in a rain storm, from Moscow. Nikki hated football, hated exercise, but hated the silence more.

He looked around him. There was mould on the wall, up in the angle near to the ceiling and close to the window, dark and cold. The linoleum was frayed under his feet. The floor under the sink, where the unit was askew, was stained by water from a pipe's leak. They had no pictures other than a view – romantic – of the river and skaters, no book case because neither read . . . It was a 'fucking tip' – he shouted it, and could have been better but she had no proper employment and a bucket of what came his way was spent on the piano teacher. He shouted at the top of his voice and the curses reverberated back at him from the walls and the sealed window.

The Major watched through the glass as she was brought into the interview room.

He'd have acknowledged that she had been of use. Good use. All the others, dumped into the wagons when they had emerged from the back entrance of the block, were in the holding cells, and were without value. She – Yekaterina – was important to him.

The Major understood the culture of the dissidents, could read the anarchists. Those inclined to lead protest, increase the chance of instability, might as well have worn a label on their foreheads. He could identify those who merely played at the culture, the group members who decided nothing, distributed leaflets, daubed walls, made up the numbers at clandestine meetings. There were those in the Big House who had seen him drafted from Minsk, had been suspicious of him, had doubted his commitment to the work of FSB. Then there were those who had noted the Major's blunt and unqualified refusal to accommodate the well-established *mafiya* clans of the city, to visit the *dacha* properties of more senior officers, to accept the best seats at the opera and the ballet, holiday villas by the Black Sea. Proven wrong in their fears. They had told him, to his face. He was not one of them, but had their trust. Deserved it because his pursuit of troublemakers and agitators was marked by a keen discipline, and a keen intelligence. She would be useful, little Yekaterina, sitting at the table, head in hands, trying not to weep but her shoulders shaking. So ignorant.

Had brought her in all those months before and had frightened her a little, not greatly. Had arranged that she would be dismissed from her course at the Conservatory. No longer a student of music, boredom gripping her. The Major had assumed she would be sucked deeper into the lifestyle and company of the dissident group, his assumption was vindicated. The others in that group, foot soldiers, had the basics of tradecraft. They moved with care, understood the procedures of police surveillance teams, were hard to tail and ate manpower. Not so Yekaterina. She had not done well when they had switched buses, wearing a bright yellow anorak which showed up well under the streetlights. They would have taken her with them to ingratiate themselves with a renowned leader. They called the target the Lawyer; he had no exam passes, no diplomas, or university degrees in jurisprudence, but had always defended himself in court and had the wit to make idiots of the prosecutors employed against. him. For two years he had been underground, and the prominence of slogans on walls and flyers in public places had mushroomed. He would talk with the Lawyer later, argue in court for a remand in custody, look for a significant sentence of incarceration. He heaved the strap of his bag over his shoulder, turned his back on the window.

It was the Major's habit that as soon as he reached home in the evening he would go to the bathroom and scrub his hands until the effort made him gasp. His work place was filthy, dirt encrusted, and there might be rats in the interrogation quarter of the building. Certainly there were cockroaches – the guard duty, at weekends, did races with them, and bet on them – and the drains seldom worked although the building was not old, not like Lubyanka in Moscow, and not like Detention Centre No. 1in his native Minsk. She would have realised, alone except for a silent guard at the door, that her situation was grave and – as the arrest reports told him – she had suffered the further humiliation of being almost undressed for sex when taken. He went down the corridor. Beyond two more locked doors was the section of the cell block where the others were held and he heard shouts, demands for release, for access to lawyers. On another floor, watched, was the Lawyer, awaiting his attention.

Since leaving university in the Belarus capital, the Major had spent his adult life working in similar places. The smell of the corridor revolted him; it was designed to break brave spirits. The Major swallowed hard, arrived at the door, was admitted. He sat opposite her. From his bag he took her passport, and laid it in front of her, the red cover and embedded gold letters and the symbol of crown and eagle within reach of her hand. She stared at it. He saw the swollen bags under her eyes, the make-up around them hardened in the streams of her tears. He saw little fight in her. The Major gave a wintry smile, of disapproval and disappointment, not enmity – which would have augmented her status – and reached forward, opened the passport, and showed her the page with her name, details and photograph. She had applied for it only weeks before her arrest and its confiscation, and might have gone to a summer camp in rural Finland or a concert in a resort town in Sweden. He dropped it into his bag. He stood, told her he would see her the next day, or the day after, told her she would be permitted one telephone call, two minutes' duration, in the morning, and wished her goodnight.

The Major would go home, would sit with his wife after he had washed himself clean of the cell block, and would talk of her day, and his son's, and tomorrow's weather, and the prices in the street market, and perhaps look at a holiday brochure together. He had big plans for Yekaterina, but they would wait for the next day.

'You have support, I assume it, for – in effect – an act of terrorism?'

'Yes, I have support, support from where it matters.'

Boot drank a weak gin, and his Swedish host sipped with little enthusiasm at a non-alcoholic beer. Boot had been met off the plane and driven into Stockholm and the bar was across the road from his hotel. The street outside led to the open square where the asset, Nikki, had been picked up.

'They are bullies and expert at handing down pain and confusion, but I think they make a poor show of absorbing it themselves.'

'They are due for pain, and for confusion.'

'To gain it, the "support" you required, what argument? An inappropriate question?'

Only very occasionally did Boot permit himself, in company, a dry and humourless chuckle. Such a moment. He spoke of deniability, and the certainty of attribution. Spoke of clan warfare inside the *mafiya* groups of St Petersburg, and the potential of serious eye-scratching among senior FSB officers who controlled and profited from such groups.

'Easier than I thought it might be. A bit of predictable wobbling, a query as to whether I led too fast. Truth is, I gave my superior what he wanted to hear, always best.'

Spoke of the damaged relationship caused by the assassination of a British citizen in London by poisoning, the killing of another who was a refugee and granted safe haven, spoke of lies and distortions involving intervention in Ukraine.

'They complain, like a bloody dripping tap, about a new Cold War and spend their limited cash building main battle tanks, spitting a fresh generation of fighter aircraft off the factory floors. They have as many – could be more – agents tripping round our streets as in the dark days half a century ago, tasked to steal information, and to finance their cohorts, the hackers, with the frauds from credit card theft. Yes, a sharp kick to the shin bone should be administered with a hard-tipped Wellington boot.' Another chuckle.

The Swede said, 'We have little appetite for confrontation, so they abuse us. Their submarines are continually diving in our territorial waters. They have flown a simulated nuclear attack over Stockholm itself, in daylight. We are deluged with their spies . . . and we are frightened. A little frightened also, perhaps, of what you hope to achieve, dear friend.'

More to drink? No, neither wished for that. Was Boot able to amuse himself for the following day? He was. His host left him. A silly conversation, but inevitable, and both had offloaded small rants. Necessary to justify, in some slight way, what he did and what the Swede helped him to do. He crossed a darkened street to the hotel, old and expensive, and climbed the stairs, past old prints of Swedish mariners, and went to his room, closed the door behind him . . . and pondered. Transported himself. Was at the municipal cemetery in outer Brussels. A dark, dank place, heavily shaded by evergreen foliage, with little sunlight and much rain: the only British memorial to the battle. He took himself there most weekends that he travelled to Belgium, perhaps by taxi from the station, perhaps by bus. A great gloomy work in age-stained bronze that was topped by a larger-than-life female, flowing robes ensuring modesty, and holding a long-handled trident. Below her was a crush of fallen infantrymen and savagely wounded horses and discarded rifles and dying lions. On the schedule he imagined for himself, it would be over within 100 hours and then – of the bright young men surging into the Belgian city – 17,000 would be dead and injured, and the medical staff accompanying the army would be overwhelmed. Food for thought, but a commander could not allow himself to be deterred from action by the prediction of how many would be lost. He would usually find time to go into the musty, leaf-filled crypt underneath and would stand in front of the stones commemorating a few of the dead, and imagine them: Captain William Stothert, 3rd Royal Foot Guards, or Sergeant Major Edward Cotton of the 7th Hussars, and many others. He undressed, prepared for bed . . . He believed implicitly, and Oliver Compton had hammered it home, that the prospect of casualties should not deter a man of war – or an agent handler – if the end-game was worth the effort.

'All well?'

She was startled. He had come silently to the doorway, found it ajar, seen the light on and eased it open. She faced him, the Director – Big Boss – surprised to see him still in the building.

'I think so, sir. Heard nothing to the contrary.'

'A good paper he sent me, read well. Simple and direct – hard to argue with.'

'The work of bright young people. What Boot attracts. And his plan is sound, sir.'

The Big Boss looked past her, but the door to the inner office was closed. He might have expected to see the cartoon poster, Duke and Boot, gold spurs and a feather-capped hat, or perhaps the set of Waterloo teeth, but was denied. The Maid knew him as an isolated figure, promoted too high to have access to field operations, no doubt yearning for a 'whiff of grapeshot', or the crippling uncertainty of waiting safely beyond a frontier for an asset to make it back. Herself, she had a camp bed she could set up, and would do soon, and there were toilets and showers down the corridor, and she'd a set of night clothing, and a dressing-gown, in the wardrobe behind her desk, and he was away and so was Daff, and a neighbour would feed the parrot. He showed no sign of leaving. She wondered if he wanted coffee from the machine, or a sandwich made for him.

'They're launching from Narva. Don't know the place. Just a map's name to me.'

'Not to worry. Interesting town. Slap on the interface. Up to the river, one road bridge, and permanent aggravation with the big neighbour. The Danes built a fortress there eight centuries ago, and the Russian one went up a hundred years later. Two strong points and within cannon range of each other. A massive World War Two battle and a series of amphibious landings as the Red Army pushed the Axis back. In 1944 there were five hundred and fifty thousand casualties on a small front line, mostly in the depth of winter, and more than three-quarters were Russians. The town was flattened by air and artillery, but held for six months. Much of the defence was from Estonian units who sided with the Germans, and there were Dutch and Norwegian volunteers. Interesting that Estonians from the west of the country thought it their duty to fight alongside SS divisions, held up the Soviets long enough for thousands of their families to get across the Baltic to Sweden. Rebuilt after the war and scores of Soviet citizens drafted in to work in the uranium extraction mines. Narva appears like any other insignificant Russian town, ugly and with few historic buildings, endless apartment blocks. Nine in ten speak only Russian and so have no integration with Estonian culture. Against the country's tiger economy it is a backwater, and a place of old people. The young Russian speakers have gone abroad. High alcoholism and high drug dependency. There is a large Russian consulate, there will be a sizeable FSB presence, and the frontier runs down the river's centre. It is a depressed and helpless community but better off than the sister town of Ivangorod. The river is a formidable barrier, still is, and that's going to have to be crossed twice by our boy. The increments will go by car, "grey" passports mean they do not need visas to travel into Russia. A morning's drive from Narva to St Petersburg, it's very close. Quite exciting really – a bridge, a river, a no-man's-land, watch-towers and a restricted zone, a jump-off point where personal security matters. That's where Boot will be when he's ready, and where Daff is now – and our boy . . . I doubt they'll eat well, not much chance of it. Anything else, sir, I can help with?'

He shook his head. He seemed unwilling to leave. Quite a good looking man, a strong face but sad.

He said, 'We had to do something . . . Not looking on the black side, but if things should go, know what I mean? Not work as per the plan . . . if he does not make it out, if—'

The Maid cut across him firmly. 'Do we have something in place – what to leak, side of mouth stuff? Of course we do. All taken care of. He'll go into the river tomorrow evening for the first crossing. I'm sure it will all go well. It's first class, sir.'

The Big Boss left her. 'All well'? It had been put together in the barest minimum time. She thought the cold there would be bitter and the street lighting hardly adequate, and the streets near empty. She searched among the papers on her desk until she found the picture: fatigues, a cigarette at the side of his mouth, hair cut short and stubble on the cheeks and a chiselled chin. She lingered on it . . . Alone, the quiet returned, unwatched, the Maid fingered the crucifix hanging at her neck – hidden most of the time because it was viewed as a religious symbol that might cause offence to other, ethnically diverse, employees – and held it tightly and said words, silently, that she thought important.

*　　*　　*

They drove into the town, used the main E-20 route from Tallinn
and then swung right and on to Alexander Pushkinisi, and Merc
saw the darkened windows of the Old Trafford bar, and a few kids
were on a bench and might have been close to hypothermia, and
they headed towards a major church with a major tower. Around
a quarter of an hour before, Merc had woken from a good sleep,
and a comfortable one – his head seemed to have found a pillow
– and he realised his head had been on her shoulder, might have
been lower and there had been softness under his ear. An
on-coming set of vehicle lights had shown him the amusement
that crinkled the sides of her mouth, and she had grinned, raised
her eyebrows, taken a hand off the wheel and had reached with
her fingers to tweak a fold of flesh on his jaw, then had retrieved
her hand and laid it back on the wheel. Ahead was a street called
Igor Gravof and Daff swung the BMW's wheels and parked.

They emptied the vehicle: first the steel-cased box, then their
bags, last the fold-up cycle and the board. The building, plastered
ochre, was two storeys high with one narrow door, and puddles of
water lay beside the step. The sewage system stank, and water
dripped from a gutter overhead. She said they were to the right,
ground floor, that it was a KaPo property. They went inside. She
did not switch on the light but navigated the darkness, hit a low
table and swore, and reached the window. Merc saw, over Daff's
shoulder, the flash of a cigarette lighter. One of those Zippo
versions that went with old-fashioned Marlboro packs, what
soldiers and cops and fire teams smoked. Its flame lit the inside of
the BMW saloon. Showed the faces of the occupants. They were
parked under a tree, and in the lee of another block some seventy-
five metres away.

Daff came close and put an arm around him so that her mouth
was against his ear and whispered, 'We'll screw them for a bunch
of . . . Back in a bit. Ferret in my bag and you'll find some food,
milk, tea bags. Won't be too long.'

Predictable that local security would want to keep them in close
view. Predictable also that they should be free agents and not
report in with details of their movements and conversations, just

use the KaPo as facilitators. She crossed the room and went down
the corridor into a darkened kitchen. He heard her wrench at the
window fastening and something snapped and came away, and
she'd sworn again. She'd have hitched herself up on to the window
sill, and the wind coming in was ice cold, and he shivered and
heard the scrape of her feet landing and the window being pushed
shut. He switched on the ceiling light. Two bedrooms. He chose
one, left her bag in the other.

Merc sat in a chair, and waited. In his *Auto Trader* was a feature
on a Mercedes-AMG 63, the coupé, £125,000. It said it had
'musclebound performance' and 'addictive character', and was
said to be in a 'slugfest fight' with its Audi rival. He did not know
how much he would be paid for going to the edge of St Petersburg
with a turn coat and a laptop stuffed with high-grade explosive.
Had to hold faith, believe he would not be swindled, could not
have imagined haggling. Didn't know if all the shares that the
bank in Stoke Poges held were sold, how easy it might be to raise
the money for that Mercedes model. He saw her sitting beside
him, the wind lifting her dark hair, as he hammered the country
roads in Buckinghamshire and out into Oxfordshire, or maybe
north on the motorway as far as Warwick. He might get the frown
off her forehead and the fight out of her eyes, might get her to
soften, and if the slipstream lifted her T-shirt then he might see the
puckered scar, neatly closed. It was what he dreamed of.

'Bloody hell. This is what I've signed up.' Daff let the words choke
in her throat.

She faced them. Spoke cheerfully, in her good accented Russian.
'Good to see you, boys. Thanks for getting here on schedule.'

One was asleep, head on his folded arms on the café table, and
another had turned towards her and showed interest, summarily
abandoning a conversation with a girl at another table – like Daff
was a better offer. The third played a card game, against himself.
Other than the arms and the scattered cards, the table was covered
with bottles, empty, and two ashtrays, full. She recognised two of
them from the photographs supplied her by the Polish agency, old

but relevant enough. They might have waited two hours, and drunk enough to empty their wallets. They'd have cursed her lateness and wondered whether she would come at all, whether the promise of easy money was a fiction. Blotched eyes, large with suspicion, greeted her.

'Come on, boys, let's walk a bit.'

Cold outside, bitter and frosty. She took control, would employ an old adage: *never explain and never apologise*, handed down to Daff by Boot, and he would have inherited it from Ollie Compton. She gestured at the door. The bar owner hovered near them, had come from the cash till looking for payment. They had stood and the girl at the next table was now 'yesterday' and the cards were tidied and pocketed and the third guy smeared a hand across his eyes, and they were groping for wallets and small change. Daff looked hard at the owner and he'd have recognised her authority and he did a sign with his fingers as to how many euros they owed. *Good bloody try, my old chum.* She took a roll of notes from the hip pocket of her jeans, peeled off a couple, half of what he asked for, left them on the counter, and she was through the door and they followed – stumbled a bit, looked sheepish. Told herself that in the circumstances, time available, they were the best available. Tried to believe it. She put a swing in her hips and thought that might interest them. Her hair would be coursing out in the night air and she heard them stamp their feet, close up on her. In front of them was a viewpoint. It would have been a cannon's battery position three centuries before. Two kids sat on a bench; might have been there to shoot up or pop some pills, and she told them – good Russian – to get lost: they scurried away.

She worked for a company based in São Paolo, Brazil that dealt with internet security. They would escort an Irishman and get him to St Petersburg where he would meet a whistle blower, and then bring him back to Estonian territory. Their passenger would be collected at a lay-by on the E-20 highway, two kilometres short of the junction between the principal route and the 41K-109 minor road going north, at Pervoye Maya. A car would be hired in Narva, able to carry five people. On the far side, a set of number-plates would be taken, and would replace those on the hire car.

Their job was to drive, to use tradecraft that would identify surveillance. They would do the necessary Russian language speaking at road checkpoints. The Irishman would be travelling with an appropriate Dublin-issued passport along with a valid visa for entry through Ivangorod, with a stamp already in place. They should use limited force necessary to break clear of a block, but could not carry firearms. They were to follow the Irishman's instructions, no hesitation and no dispute. Did they understand? Cross the bridge tomorrow, Wednesday. Sleep in the vehicle that night, off the road. Collection on Thursday morning, drive to St Petersburg. Questions?

From the viewpoint, Daff gazed out across the void. The river, far beneath her, ran in a gradual curve and disappeared down-stream into darkness. On the far side, gaudily lit, was the casino. Side streets lined with small houses led away from the water; they had dim lighting and looked little more than tracks and no one moved on them. The Narva castle was floodlit but only a small part of the Ivangorod fortress was illuminated. The road bridge, spanning the divide, had seemed deserted until she spotted the lumbering progress of a timber lorry, heaving a trailer with stacked pit-props. In its headlights she saw straggling pedestrians using the bridge's walkway and leaving the checkpoint at the Russian end of the bridge, noted the lowered barrier, and men in uniform. Daff thought it a collision point in two worlds, tectonic plates, where great forces either tolerated each other and stayed apart, or collided. She gave each of them a wad of money, individual shares. Then handed to Martin, who looked the safest, the float for the hire car. Each of them, she insisted, signed a docket for the cash. Questions?

None. No questions? None. No problems? None.

She took them on trust . . . took the whole bloody thing on trust. And Merc would take her on trust. She turned away and her fore-head knitted. They – Martin and Toomas and Kristjan – were on her watch. She walked away, didn't care if her bum waggled and her hips swayed. She understood, first time and late in the day, what Copenhagen meant, where it was going, and the risk it carried. She ducked her head and walked fast.

Always, last thing, Igor and Marika went outside and checked the barn doors. They had already been to bed, but it was their routine to have the alarm sound, get up and wrap themselves in blankets, go through the front door and head for the barn. They did it in the height of the summer when the mosquitoes bit, and it was light that far north. Did it in the depth of winter, whether it rained or hailed or snowed, even if the temperature was many degrees below freezing. He could barely see and she could barely walk. He carried a storm lantern and she guided him, but her principal task was to bring vegetable scraps for the beasts and a fistful of grain for the fowls. If there was already snow, and more was forecast – and they had been warned by Pyotr, the woodsman – then they would bring the animals into the house and let them mill and cluck close to the fire and some would crawl over their bed. Igor went with great care because only a week before he had stumbled, landed on the lantern and burned himself, and it had been a great effort for Marika to pull him to his feet. Without the other, neither could have managed this nightly ritual, and if they had not gone then neither would have slept for worry over the beasts and the fowls. He had the padlock key on a a string necklace and opened the barn door with difficulty. A wonderful welcome that gratified both of them: the cows and the sheep and the pigs and the chickens surged around them, and the dogs had tailed them from the log fire in the house and stayed at the barn door, growling softly. At the edge of the light's beam, the food was distributed. Now the animals would be quiet for the night, feel secure, as would Igor and Marika. The padlock was fastened, a good and solid one that Pyotr had purchased in Ivangoród. They retraced their steps, ploughing through standing water, and the damp from the flood plain snapped at their bones under the blankets, and they splashed in rain-water puddles that could not escape into the saturated ground. They went back to bed. Had shared that bed since they were teenagers, and their parents had been killed by the warring armies – German or Soviet – and at first it had been for warmth and then for a type of tenderness that neither would acknowledge. Last thing, before killing the light, he made certain his shotgun was loaded and close. Nothing was new in their lives, nor had been for many years. Soon, in the darkness and when the weather worsened, they would sleep.

She came back through the window into the kitchen.

He had made himself tea, one bag, and washed the mug in cold water, and left it upturned on the draining board, and she'd dislodged it. It shattered on the floor. She grunted in anger. Merc lay on his bed and had reread half a dozen times the page about the Mercedes coupé. If she wanted to say something she would say it, he felt no need to prompt.

She shrugged, grimaced. 'I think it went all right.'

'Good.'

'Met up with the boys. Told them what was wanted . . . hoped you'd be asleep.'

'Was, nearly, not quite.'

'Can I say something? Not maybe what you want to hear. Can I? I was always taught to spit, not bottle. Doesn't make me successful politically.'

He sat up, the magazine across his knees. The blankets were piled over him and the room was cold, the damp bedding, seemed to cling to him. He knew he needed to sleep, would not again for perhaps three nights, and the worst decisions on the hoof were those taken when exhaustion kicked in . . . Standing and fighting on Hill 425 for the preservation of a Forward Operating Base on strategic ground had not been clever, not when they were perhaps fifteen minutes from going under. Merc did not answer her, did not need to, she'd tell him what he'd not have wanted to hear.

'What I should say to you . . . The boys. Merc, I'm sorry. I picked them and I found them – most important, I hired them. They are what we have. They are arseholes. Polite way would be to call them "works in progress", but we don't have that time. One was pissed, one was trying to get his leg over, one was . . . It's where we are.'

'Thank you. I usually encourage people to front up. Thank you.'

'We were never going to have Hereford or Poole, not an option.'

'When, if, it screws up, I'll address it – not before then.'

'I'll chase them in the morning, and—'

'When it's stress time, people tend to behave.'

He turned over, lay on his side and faced a wall where old paper peeled and where a picture of a rampant lion with a castle wall in the background was brown and crinkled from condensation. She went to the door and switched off the light and he heard her pad next door, heave at her bag – must have been dragging out her night clothes. He was thinking of the river, and its width, and the forest beyond and the usefulness of the foldaway bicycle. His mind churned with the sums, and with the problem of launching the board and keeping it afloat, and directing it so that it did not take him downstream where he had no reason to be. Concerned also with what sort of diversion she could get the KaPo to make. Worried because the ground on the far side of the river was hidden under the canopy of the evergreen pines and there would be winter lakes and bog where his boots would be sucked under, and he'd have a head torch that would project a beam a couple of metres in front of him, and he'd rely on the compass, and . . . He heard her feet, bare and slithering on the floor. The blankets behind Merc were eased back, the bed bucked under her weight. She wriggled down then pulled the blanket so that both their shoulders were covered. Her arm reached over him, held him close, his back against her stomach. She was warm and gave him comfort.

'You'll be fine, Merc. Sure of it. All you need is some bloody sleep.'

A long time since he had been with a woman. A UN girl – not sure whether she was from Romania or Bulgaria, or might have been Moldova, and after a party in Erbil that Brad and Rob had taken him to. A bad shout, but the Fire Force Unit was having its first night off from a spell in the front line trenches a few kilometres south of the Hill 425, and a mortar shell had exploded and there were casualties and . . . He was not supposed to care, was a Gun for Hire. The UN girl had spoken poor English but the guys there said she was a proven ride. That was the last time, and he had not stayed late with her, and had gone in the morning to the armoury and drawn his weapon and been drafted back to the line. The warmth was good . . . There would be no warmth in the river, or in the forest.

'I've an attack of the nerves, Merc, pathetic. Are you afraid often – where you go and what you do – afraid?'

Said nothing. Did not lie and did not boast, and tried not to give himself time to be afraid. It was not in a mercenary's job description to freak out, back off.

'My chief, Boot, he's a Waterloo groupie. He has a Wellington quote that he likes to dish up: "The only thing I am afraid of is fear". I suppose it's infectious, fear is, has to be stamped on.'

Letting her snuggle against him, Merc tried to sleep. Would never have admitted to fear. It caught him, gnawed at his gut – and he would quit 'sometime', but not tomorrow.

7

She had gone, where she had been was cold.

Merc padded off in search of hot water and a working shower. He washed himself but did not shave. Found the tea bags, and a bread roll that she had left in the fridge with the groaning motor.

He looked out of the window, a dull morning that exploited many shades of grey – the ground where kids had worn down the grass with games, the football pitch that was a morass, the apartment blocks across the open space, the tall church building, and then the skies. Where Merc had come from, earning his pay, there would have been fierce sunshine and it would have peeped from behind Hill 425 and thrown forward the shadow of their flag, a dark wobbling shape among the coils of wire where the mines were . . . New men and women from the Fire Force Unit would have been in the trench with the sunlight careering down the slope to soak warmth into the bodies that were on the wire and close to where the personnel mines had been planted. Other shadows would have roamed over the field, those of the vultures that meandered overhead, and would gather in the thermals before diving to gorge.

He saw an old man coaxing a dog to defecate so that they could both get back indoors. Saw shapeless old women wrapped in heavy coats, clutching their shopping bags and moving warily for fear of slipping, and a few kids who must have skived school. The BMW eased away from near the church, and another vehicle, same make and same colour, slotted into the position, and a little of the grey was brightened by the glow of cigarettes.

He dressed, yesterday's clothing, that Daff had bought for him.

He was, wouldn't say it, grateful to her for coming into his bed, being against his back, sharing her body's heat. Merc had slept better that night than he could recall. Might have been days, weeks, and he had not moved, had not kissed her, nor she him. Better than a pill, a decent and natural sleep.

The rooms were cold; the radiators squealed but threw out little heat. Not helped by her having left the kitchen window ajar, the broken arm carefully placed on the floor below the sink. He had not heard her wash . . . Merc shared a sort of life with her. There had been guys round her when she stripped down to her bikini at the pool café in the Green Zone: diplomats and UNHCR and junior officers who did liaison. More in Kabul: at the Park Palace Hotel she was stalked, propositioned, and he'd seen drunks fight for the right to sit beside her. No encouragement given. Like himself, two of a kind, living a life that did not depend on others. He had washed, dressed, and eaten and she was out and at work. He'd valued her honesty on the quality of the recruits. Did not concern Merc. He reckoned to breed purpose in failed men who had lost the will, or taken the money but then looked to back off.

A piss awful day. The Brecons in south-east Wales were wind scoured and open, without shelter when it was needed in winter or shade when the summer sun burned on the poor bastards doing route marches with heavy Bergens. Not often that the Pioneers were involved in paratrooper levels of fitness assessment. Had been that day, a new commanding officer's diktat for his detachment. Eight of them starting. Six of them pushing on. November and sleet cascading on to them. Merc at the back because he kept station beside little Trotter, who was overweight, short, little eyes behind big spectacles, a joke as a front line soldier. One NCO had led and another must have lost them in a brief white-out and it would have been reasonable for Merc to have turned around and helped Trotter back to the start line because the guy was incapable of going forward with the weight of the Bergen on his back. About nine miles to the end point, and only two and a half miles done, and the sleet was heavy enough to obliterate the tracks left by

those ahead of them. The NCOs should have had control of the
group, kept them corralled together. They came in at last light.
Merc carried his own Bergen and Trotter's, and held up the failing
soldier, and there was one vehicle left at the rendezvous point, and
Sergeant Arbuthnot was there with his thermos and his fags. Had
they started a search? They had not. Why not? Because Sergeant
Arbuthnot, in his wisdom, had decided if helpless Trotter was with
Private Hawkins then he would come through and be looked after.
They had driven back to the camp and the sergeant had put him
in the front, Trotter bumping in the back with the Bergens, and
had said, 'Never in doubt, you bringing him back . . . I watch you
and I see your language, could not give you better advice than
what you know already. Friends, comrades, fellow sufferers and
moaners in the unit are the most important handrail you can cling
to – not officers, keep clear of them. Stay close to your mates.'
Good counsel. Trotter had gone within a week, and someone had
said he'd trained as a brickie in Hartlepool. Merc had not stayed
long after that either, had gone off after the better money of
working for a private military contractor, and more excitement –
and no one he'd ever met had heard of his dad, 'Hold the Line'
Hawkins.

He wasn't anxious about the boys, whether they were considered by Daff to be useless and crap. He sat in a chair and did
his kit check, down to the strength of the laces on his boots;
dismembered the Glock Makarov, cleaned it and emptied out
and reloaded the magazines, then reassembled the pistol, and
started to check the aerial pictures they had brought. He reckoned the plan was sound, as far as that went. Achieving it was
possible. Make the contact – offload the device – get it put in
place – wait until the contact came back to him, running at
hell's own speed – all aboard, and the boys doing the necessary
of winging through the blocks if they were already up, and
going fast for the border – and dropping off near the bridge –
doing his own thing of getting over the river, second time . . . all
possible.

★   ★   ★

Daff blamed herself, could turn her anger nowhere else. They were her hirelings, she had found them, recruited them.

The Maid had found her the price of a hire car from a Narva firm – a basic Nissan estate, no frills. She knew the rental rate, and Martin had passed her the paperwork from the garage, and Toomas had challenged her with his look and Kristjan had smirked. They had taken a forty per cent rip-off. She swallowed it. They already had her money, could get out of the car, leave it in the street, keys in the ignition, and walk away. Walk fast, walk straight and never look back, and she was just the bitch who had provided the beer kitty that would keep them going for a month. She wondered how Boot would have handled a fraud – and reckoned he would have done nothing. They looked for her reaction.

She said quietly, 'Good shout, guys, a clever one that pockets a few euros . . . What I always tell anyone I work with is that they should remember something very simple: we have a long arm, the São Paolo end of our company has many friends . . . and with a long arm goes a long memory. Most people I work with get the idea of that, and quick.'

She smiled. Boot's smile, if he'd said it, would have been wintry and would have sent a shiver to anyone it was directed at. Hers was warmer. She handed back the receipt, then they had the map out and she went over the location of the lay-by on the main road that was fringed by forest. One of the instructors at the Fort down on the coast, when she had been a recruit and before being assigned to the Green Zone, had said '*Never lie to someone who trusts you. Never trust someone who lies to you.*' Then had laughed, had explained it was about one-way relationships. The agent could lie to an asset, but if the asset lied to the agent then he, she, would never be trusted. They had lied, had made a few euros. One was a painter-decorator, when he could find work. One wore mock mediaeval armour so tourists could take selfies with him. One was a shelf loader in the town's principal supermarket, and the money they were paid was crap. She had trusted them enough to have charge of Merc's safety. They could go up the E-20 highway and get to the block at the Kingispill bridge, and could pretend to go for a pee, and could ask for a light from a militia goon, whisper in his ear, could blow Merc out . . . She was in turmoil.

He had not woken when she had slipped from the bed, had dressed silently, had gone and found the boys. The signs had said more beers had been drunk, little sleep taken. There had been a steady rhythm in Merc's breathing, a sort of peace. Daff prided herself that she might have helped him rest. The fear now was about trust . . . She looked hard into each of their faces, and learned where the moles were and the weaker chins and the teeth yellowed from nicotine, and the furtive eyes. Saw little pride and less to trust. They could, all or one, denounce him and hope to save their own skins, or maybe hope to bring in a better pay-day.

She briefed them again. Sometimes they yawned, or scratched, or picked at a spot, and sometimes they listened. She said what the cover for their visit was, and was exact in the duties of driving and talking, and emphasised the point about not attracting attention. Boot might have gained their respect, but she did not. Martin tried to make eye contact with her, blatant, and she'd have liked to poke out his eyes. But she smiled, and told them when she would see them again, and where, and went back to wake Merc.

One call allowed, two minutes permitted. A poor line. She sounded hoarse and her voice was distant, and desperate.

He imagined a telephone on a corridor wall, and heard background shouting, and a man's screams – what an addict did when kept from shooting up – and she said where she was and who held her, and that she was not yet charged, had not faced interrogation, and . . . probably her time was exhausted and the call had been terminated. He had sat up and had waited for her. Nikki always did if she was out late. He had drunk coffee to stay awake, had failed to, and had fallen asleep at the kitchen table. Had woken and gone to Kat's room and would have joked with her how quiet she had been on her return, not waking him . . . but the bed was empty. She had no boyfriend that he knew of. He had gone back into the kitchen, had waited for her steps on the corridor outside the apartment door . . . had heard the old woman with the cigarette kiosk on the esplanade of the river go out, taking her hacking cough with her. The two girls from the other side of the hallway who lived with their parents and worked in the Pushka Inn hotel on the Moika canal came next, and were laughing loudly; if they had seen him they would have ignored him, rated him beneath their attention and did not know he was worth close to $450,000. And there was the man who drove a trolley bus but had a two-bedroom apartment to himself because his nephew had a good position in Customs at the airport. The building was springing to life, but he had not heard her. Did now. A small voice, attempting to hide fear from him, staccato sentences. He tried to remember what she had said, where she was held: under arrest but not interrogated and not charged.

Nikki splashed water on his face.

He snatched up his coat and scarf and his anorak, and the bag with the laptop. He slammed the door after him, chased down the stairs and out into a grey morning with ice sharp and glistening on the pavement. He found her car parked illegally in a restricted zone outside the block that should have been left clear for refuse collection lorries. Most days she took him; only occasionally did he have to go by bus, or trolley. He travelled in the opposite direction to the Big House, where the cell block was in the basement of the building, where natural light did not come . . . He hated them. Hated the world around him. Hated the men and women and children on his staircase, on his floor, and would betray them. All of those who had ignored him, bad-mouthed him, were to be betrayed. He had not told his sister, and if she were not freed then she would linger in those cells, with the whores and the thieves and dissidents. Because of the betrayal, the next day, he had to free her.

He pushed open the special door. Gone past the guards at the gate and inside the perimeter fence and had skipped past two heavy saloons with chauffeurs and bodyguards, low from the weight of armour plating, had waved his ID and they were too bored to chase after him. Did not knock on the oak panels. Nikki opened the door as a receptionist attempted to block him. He elbowed her aside. His worn trainers sank deep into a pile carpet. The smells were of rich coffee and of small cigars. A low light was on the desk, and at the edge of its orbit was the glint from the gold-plated barrel of a Kalashnikov mounted on the wall, a symbol of a former retreat over the frontier and out of Afghanistan by a veteran. Framed near to the assault rifle was a target of concentric circles drawn prominently over the face of the then enemy, a tribesman, and pocked with crude holes where bullets had punctured it. There was a nude, gilt-framed, on a far wall, provocative and hairy, and unfinished, and the word upstairs was that the woman, at that time his wife, had become 'friendly' with the artist as she sat, and rumour said the artist was dead, lost in a flyover or under a piazza's paving in one of the city's eastern sectors. There was a safe, open, and folders were visible and thick wads of dollars and euros and roubles, and ... Security was at the door and behind him.

The GangMaster was at his desk, shoes off and feet in good socks balanced on its surface. Opposite, on a leather sofa, was a paunchy figure in a civilian suit: a colonel, the roof of the GangMaster. It might have been the day that payments were made – or the opportunity for conversation relevant to the tasking of the hacktivists at the meeting thirty hours away or less. He was a traitor to them. Had they known it, both would have mutilated him, used a hunting knife or electrodes or lit cigarettes or forceps to take a sliver of skin and start to peel, or pliers for his fingernails ... Neither man showed surprise at his entry, nor annoyance, nor interest, and Security and the receptionist were waved away and the door closed. He was not invited to speak, was greeted with silence.

The words came in a spurt, blurted out. 'I am the best you have. I bring more money, more reward, than any other. I am superior to the Roofer and to HookNose and to Gorilla, and all the rest that you use. I deliver. I have a brain and use it, and you do well from my work. Something in return for the way I have enriched you. My sister is everything to me, my whole family. Is talented, a musician, also stupid . . . Mixes with a scumbag gang of dissidents. She is infatuated by them. She is Kat, Yekaterina, she was arrested last night. She has not been charged, is being held, not yet interrogated. I ask for intervention. She is in the FSB house. Please . . . I ask it, please . . . please – because you value me and value my work – use influence . . . I want her at our home. I do what I am asked, I fulfil every task given me . . . She is a very little piece of an idiot organisation, no threat to the state . . . please . . . Thank you.'

Tears in his eyes, Nikki spun on his heel, ducked his head in respect, left the room and closed the door quietly after him. The guards watched him balefully, as if hoping for an instruction to batter his face, but none came. His laptop bag was hooked over his shoulder and he went up the stairs to go to work . . . and felt a pulsing exhilaration at the scale of his deception, and what he held over them and would do to them. The betrayal would be so sweet, but only after his sister had been freed, and after he had told her of a meeting in the car-park of the supermarket farther west on the highway.

There was a toilet but it was blocked. Beside the toilet pan was a bucket which Kat used. She sat on the mattress, knees clasped to her chest. She had wrapped the two issued blankets over her shoulders.

Nobody came, other than the guard, a stout woman with a starched uniform and a face showing neither sympathy or contempt, who carried a small metal tray. On it was a plastic bowl of a thick porridge, *kasha*, made from millet or barley stirred into boiled water, and bread and bottled water. The guard had not spoken to her, had put the tray down and turned her back. Wrong, not bottled water, water from a tap poured into a used bottle, and a chlorine taste in it. With the chlorine was the scent of the disinfectant round the top of the toilet pan, and on the sides of the bucket. She sat and she thought.

The first time she had spent a night in the cells, Kat had imag-ined that news of her arrest would have moved quickly among her group and others who were comrades or had loose affiliation. She had even believed there would have been a cluster outside the main entrance of the Big House, and she had strained – unsuc-cessfully – to hear the sound of protest chanting, and had imagined reactions similar to those when Pussy Riot were held or when Navalny or Nemtsov was arrested. A delusion, as had been her ambition to play the piano in concert halls . . . She had wanted to protest, to fight, had not wanted a cell and no questioning and no attention, and one feeble phone call. She did not know why her brother had seemed distant from her, had assumed his work was dishonest, hiring himself out like a hotel tart, a *kurwa*, a *shlyukha*. She had pleaded for his help, as she had done for money to pay her piano lessons. She had taken one spoonful of the porridge, had drunk a little of the water.

There were voices beyond her cell door, commands and tearful screams, and the spitting of a hose as if a cell floor was being sluiced clean. For fuck's sake, it was her country. Should have been permitted to protest against corruption, against criminal gain, against what the foreign media called kleptocracy. Films on the TV showed the glamorous centre of St Petersburg and fashion shops on the principal streets, did not broadcast images of the block where she existed, of the druggies and the drunks, of the vagrants . . . Had the right to protest, but sat in a cell and no one came to hear her grievance. Might be for a day, might be for a week. She stood, rocking on the balls of her feet. Sucked in the fetid air, and shouted at the top of her voice.

'Come here, you bastards, pigs, come here – let me out of this fucking cell. I have rights. More rights than the thieves you support. See if I care. You are just *serfs*, you don't think, you're ignorant and without minds, you're shit – and you do what a *czar* tells you. Stupid, cowards . . .'

Kat's breath ran out. She stopped, lungs emptied, sagged and seemed to hear the echo of her voice as it died in the corridors of the cell block. What she knew: she would not have been heard on any of the eight floors of the building above her. Would not have been heard on the street outside where six lanes of traffic ploughed about their business. The final gesture was to lift up the metal tray with the plastic bowl and metal spoon and the filled bottle, hold it high and hurl it at the door and hear the slight impact and the rolling rattle of the tray on the concrete.

No one came. No one shouted at her and demanded silence. No one called for her interrogation, even bothered to slide back the peep-hole and examine her. A little moment of brittle amusement for Kat: they could charge her, under Article 319, with *insulting a member of the authorities*. Could lock her up for that, except that no one seemed to care.

Tears exploded. Kat was on her hands and knees on the floor, putting the bowl and the bottle and the spoon back on the tray and using her fingers to pick up the spattered porridge, and knew she faced defeat. It had not taken many hours, and the shame gripped her, and she could not help herself.

'It is a small thing, Danik. An unimportant request, but I make it.'

A colonel had come to the Major's office and wore a good suit wrapped around a solid belly, and the smell of a cigar was on his breath. No appointment made through their two PAs, but the senior officer had appeared at the door, had smiled and had asked if it were convenient for him to take a few moments of the Major's time.

'I have not yet questioned her. She is a minor part of a complex investigation.'

They were wary of him, all of the senior officers from the floor above. He did not come to their parties, was not a recipient of small envelopes, did not have a refuge in the forests around the city, was not a friend – but he was liked in a distant way, and had earned respect.

'I tell you very frankly, Danik, that in the interests of the state she should be freed.'

'She was in association with a known anarchist, also arrested.'

'Done soon, Danik, the release . . . She has a brother.'

'I know of her brother. Not part of a dissident movement, employed by a crime syndicate. Outside my area of responsibility.'

'Inside mine, Danik. The brother has doubtful liaisons . . . but he is also an expert at the accumulation of information that is important to national security.'

'National security? I have that guarantee, in writing?'

'A project involving ourselves and GRU. Sufficient, yes?'

'No charge pending, complete release?'

'Just a window, enough to calm the brother . . . I don't have to explain to you, Danik, that these are serious times for the nation, and we are hemmed in by enemies, and we must stay vigilant, strong . . . We are in a race for technology and this boy is able at what he does. I anticipate you will not disappoint me.'

And a sweet smile. They did not stamp on his feet. It would be about a roof. A building needed a roof to protect its interior from bad weather. A criminal gang needed a roof to safeguard its activities from the attention of law enforcement. So simple. A roof was a *krysha*. A woman who kept a kiosk must have a roof who would ensure her kiosk was not firebombed by a rival. That man, too, must have a roof to ensure that his territory was not invaded. Might be a more powerful criminal conspiracy, might be a middle-ranking officer of the police, or the militia, or the FSB in the Big House. It went on up, far into the clouds. This officer, the colonel, would be the roof for the GangMaster who employed the brother, Yekaterina's Nikki. Higher up the ladder, deeper in cloud, would be a senior clan leader and a brigadier in the security forces, and then a man who ran enterprises across a whole sector of the city along with a general – and a politician . . . The roofs went to the great buildings of state, and pickings were taken and for various men there was immunity from prosecution. The Major accepted reality when it stared him in the face. He winked as if to a co-conspirator.

'I have a proposition for her, but she will be free by the morning.'

'Thank you, Danik – a good compromise.'

The colonel was on his way out.

'My colleague has a villa close to Sochi. I am sure at Easter it would be vacant. Could be of interest to you and Julia. It would be very comfortable.'

The Major smiled grimly. He was not dependent on bribes, shook his head.

As the colonel went through the door, the Major believed he heard him mutter, 'Pompous little prick' or similar. But he had plans for the girl, and would put them to her, and would watch her writhe like a pinioned snake.

'Have you somewhere else to be, something else to do?'

A crisp answer from her. 'Yes, I have.'

'Go there, do it.'

Merc wanted her gone. No pleasantries, just an instruction. He slipped out of the car, did not look at her, did not wave, and went on down a small path that might have been made by picnickers in summer, or fishermen. He heard her car pull away. She had ferried him twice up the length of the road north from Narva, past the big cemetery and up to the spa resort on the Baltic coast where the river went into the sea. Had come down towards the town again and twice stopped to explore that section of river bank, then had climbed back into the car, no explanation given as to what he had seen, satisfactory or not, and they had driven on. Each time he wanted her to stop he had flicked his finger on the dash in front of him. It was a wide, straight road and followed the line of the river, and little traffic was on it . . . He thought the KaPo car had given up on them or had not bothered to stick with the surveillance. He had found a place among the trees where there was a graveyard among tall, straight pines, bright with plastic flowers, and close to it was a memorial to the Russian dead in the 'liberation' of Estonia: bigger than life size and showing a powerful young man in a heavy greatcoat and, beside him, a full-faced woman who would have been drafted to the front and they'd have fallen together. There had been another memorial to the Red Army downstream, with more plastic and bright red flowers and wreaths. She had started to talk about a battle, casualties, but he had shushed her, did not want conversation. Merc knew about battles and casualties, and more knowledge of them would not help him. They had come to a freshly painted T-34 Russian battle tank, high on a concrete plinth. The star, symbol of the Red Army, was vivid on the turret, and there were more flowers, fresh ones. Close to the carcass of the thirty-ton tank was the path he had taken.

She would be back in the late afternoon, with the kit. Nothing more needed to be agreed. It was not Merc's way to debate what he might do, look for confirmation or criticism. Never had been . . . Like the times on Route Irish, with a VIP civilian onboard and near messing his trousers with nerves, and Merc – ridiculously young to take such decisions on a diplomat's or construction expert's life – would seem to sniff the air and either decide to go, or that they would lay off, take an hour's rain-check. The guys with him had believed in the value of his intuition . . . once, because another crew had not listened to his concern, a run had been started, and an armour-reinforced saloon was hit with an RPG round: all dead. The principal lost. Merc's legend enhanced. She was gone. He was alone. Light rain fell. The temperature was three or four degrees above freezing, less when he went into the water with the cover of darkness round him. Merc sat on his haunches.

He had a small mono-glass, tidy enough to fit in the palm of his hand, and he scanned with it, and learned the life of the river. An hour passed, and another.

On the far side of the water, 300 metres away he estimated, was a border marker, striped green and red. Short of it was a reed bed, thick and noisy to penetrate. Upstream from the marker was a high observation platform – he had seen half a dozen of them on the reconnaissance journeys up and down the road. Between the marker and the steel pillars supporting the platform was a gully where the river came into the reed bed and split it, and a grey-feathered heron fished there. The heron was calm and had found a promising feeding place; every few minutes its head would dip and rise, a slithering shape in its beak, then the expert tilt of the throat: Merc might have sworn he saw the bulge go down the neck. The heron told him there was no track on the far side down which a foot patrol came, let alone a jeep.

The mono-glass showed him song birds on the far side. They quartered the small area of shore he could see in the reeds' gap. Looked for worms or grubs, would need to feed hard before the snow came and removed their sustenance, but they would have flown off in a panic if a patrol had been close.

A launch flying a Russian flag came and went. Two on board, and they'd have been bawled out if their officer had seen them because they trailed a lure from a short rod and would have been after pike or catfish and stayed close to their own bank, showed no alertness, but had weapons hooked on their backs.

Hours passed, and a stiffness was gathering in his hips. Well into the afternoon, and the light starting to fade. Within five metres of Merc, a ferocious tusked beast. A wild boar that would have been a hunter's pride and joy if shot. Would not have reached that size by an accident of nature, would have relied on cunning, suspicion and the taking of few chances. It came to the water. It would have crossed the road behind, having listened for the approach of a vehicle. It drank. Merc thought it would not have wanted stale rain-water from a puddle, but the freshness of the river. It would not have exposed itself had there been movement on either side.

Time was sliding. His gut was knotted, and he was cold, rain pattering around him. He could sense the darkness and density of the forest behind the watch-tower and tried to imagine how it would be under the canopy, how much bog. The map showed old drain ditches that would now be flooded. He had the clearing that he would make for, and then a track to follow.

A small deer tiptoed through the song birds and eased close to the heron but did not disturb it. Merc wondered if another would join it, or if this was a lone creature. The heron would have sight and awareness, and the deer would be blessed with the best hearing . . . and the day drifted, and hours slipped by, and the light dropped. Anglers went by in a small boat and were watched closely by the heron and the deer, but the boar was long gone.

He watched the water. The flow was hard and fast; he saw flotsam being carried down and so could gauge its speed. He calculated how far down the bank he would have to be, upstream of the little gap in the reeds that was the heron's place, and the deer's, and where the song birds were. He had help from a small navigation buoy that had broken loose from its mooring, drifted towards, then past him. It was the best place for him and he had learned much. But Merc was still not certain how his board would cope on the water with the weight he must carry. The forest wall beyond the reeds had given up no secrets, and would be difficult.

He was happy to be alone, always had been and always would be – perhaps. A slow smile on his face and he imagined, briefly, a vase of flowers. Then ducks flew low over the water and called to each other, and the dusk came. The rain had come on harder.

Boot was the tourist. The light was failing and the attendants imitated sheepdogs and rounded up the last visitors of the day, and sent them out. Boot declined polite suggestions that closure was imminent, would stay to the bitter end.

He gazed at the bulk of the beast, a monument – he reflected – to over reaching *hubris*. He had done the palace and the changing of the guard, but did not know if he had watched his colleague's son on the parade ground. Had taken the ferry and was at the museum for the warship, the grandest in the world as it existed on that August day 390 years earlier, and only 1400 metres into a maiden voyage, well within sight of the slipway. Such pride in her, yet such ignorance of the tenets of ship building, and the arrogance of leaders who believed they knew best and would not leave complications to those best equipped to engage them. It towered above him in a dull light, and the timbers still seemed pristine and the gun ports were clean cut and the heraldry on the prow was typical of the grandiose conceit of a Swedish monarch, a tinkerer with blueprints of warship design, so the thing had capsized and the king and his acolytes were humiliated . . . Boot detested interference. Kings and political leaders and the Big Boss should stick well to the rear. He liked the lesson of the *Vasa*, and the story it told of the frailty of ambition.

Daff did not need him in Narva. Better out of it. He would only have fussed, been in the way.

He gazed up at the timbers, and marvelled at the workmanship, flawed but magnificent. The Duke, on the schedule that Boot had set, would have been – as the light fell over Brussels – preparing for the Duchess of Richmond's ball. It was said that the future of Europe would be decided in the next forty-eight hours by force of arms, but the Duke would be seen, admired, calming faint hearts by being there, taking to the floor, talking with the richly gowned young women of Britain's greatest families, banishing panic. So impressive. The orchestra would have been tuning violins and fiddles, and the girls – shipped in from the aristocratic homes of London – would have been fussed over by their maids ensuring their beauty was clear to all, and the young sprigs of the army – cavalry and infantry – would be thinking of a blush, a kiss, and not of the surgeons busy sharpening their implements. Always good to have distractions and to keep stress at bay.

He had seen enough. The centre of the Swedish warship's gravity had been too high, the draught too shallow: silly mistakes.

Boot felt calm . . . believed Daff would cope, and well. Hoped the mercenary would and needed him to. Was at peace with himself, but accepted he was vulnerable to 'events', things that might happen that were not anticipated, always the enemy. Nor could he predict, subject to those events, which individuals – unheard of and not factored into any prior assessment – would stand in the way: a traffic policeman, a car-park attendant determined to issue a ticket, a suspicious *babushka* peering from an upper window and ranting suspicion . . . anything. Which made the game unpredictable, inexact – perhaps worthwhile.

* * *

'You'll be fine, boys . . .'

They had loaded the car. A decent shiny saloon with Martin behind the wheel and Toomas beside him, and Kristjan sprawled across the back seat. She had supervised the checklist, down to their tickets for the hockey match at the Ice Palace. The spare plates were wrapped in a blanket and stored with the spare wheel, Russian-issued and easy to find in Narva. The loss would have been reported to the police at this end but would not have filtered across the river and into the near-obsolete computers available to the police or militia on the road to St Petersburg. Daff did confidence well, her glass was always half full, and she fancied they needed the encouragement. It was Wednesday, late afternoon, and a clock ticked, hands jerking forward.

'It'll be good. Pick him up, do the run. It will work well,' she said.

They were in the big square opposite the tourist office and with a rear view of the castle, with low walls for the cannon emplacements facing them, and ahead was the Estonian customs and border control. They would not have wanted to talk. They were nervous and it showed . . . would have been all right for her, except that it was not expected for Daff, at her grade, to go into harm's way. Had she done so, as a UK passport holder, Daff could have claimed diplomatic status, and might only have been mildly roughed. Soon enough, she'd be frog-marched to one of those out-of-sight crossing places and swapped. The experience would make a fine story for her to tell if she trekked off to Ollie Compton's pad, put a take-away curry in the microwave and told him her tale. Not the same for the boys. They would go into harsh régime cell blocks, then to the camps up in the regions of permafrost, where they would have become skeleton-thin from hunger. They would have done better than their grandfathers, but after a few years beyond the Arctic Circle, behind the wire, they'd have thought it a relief – a blessed one – to be dead. But they were paid, and almost generously, and were lucky, in her opinion, to have been given the work . . . They weren't her friends, did not need to be her friends.

And should not have been her friends. Daff's home, as a teen-ager, had been an estate, remote and land-locked, in a harsh corner of Scotland. A grey stone house built to withstand the worst that winter weather could throw at it, and for half the year smoke blew horizontally from the stacks, and the pastimes there were stalking red deer – which she did well and was a fine shot – and fishing the Conon waters and Loch Meig. She knew the sons and daughters of keepers and the people who farmed tough cattle and hardy sheep and was fond of them in a limited way, but they were not friends. Ollie Compton went up there, had a week on the river in March, and she'd sit beside him while he smoked or ate a sandwich and broke from casting, and he'd said, 'You pay them and you use them, and they are never your friends and – God forbid, my girl – they are never in bed with you. They are the "hired help". Forgotten when their usefulness is exhausted.' Ollie Compton had been her entry marker into the Service, and her parents had thought it the right move for her, a curb to her bolshie teenager moods. Daff fancied that Merc would be kinder to them, and would win their loyalty in a way that she did not. They were paid, and would have believed a company in São Paolo would be more than grateful on their return.

The window in Martin's door was closed. Their cigarettes were lit. The car started. None of them looked through the rear window to give her a wave. They moved towards the Estonian check.

Daff hurried. She climbed up on to a bastion, built in the seven-teenth century by Charles XII, a Swedish king. She went along the wall, slithering on the mud, and came to a street that would lead to the viewing platform. She was short of breath when she reached the wall high above the river and overlooking the bridge. Daff thought herself a veteran, but was not. She had never done what was asked of Merc, what was expected of the boys; she had not been over the line into the territory of a supposed enemy, been beyond reach. She had been a decorative addition to the Green Zone café by the pool, had flitted in and out of Kabul and been ferried to the city by armoured helicopter and had worked in compounds, was a regular in Erbil and Beirut and Amman, but with a security detail minding her.

The car edged forward, slowly, lit by floodlights. It passed the last of the day's small entrepreneurs who went backwards and forwards to bring cigarettes and vodka into Narva for sale on street corners and in the housing estates. She thought they went too slowly, and sensed the nerves in the car. It reached the barrier. A red and white pole blocked them. A figure in a greatcoat, a shadow and a shape and anonymous, bent over the driver's window and would have been handed their papers, and would have started to scan them. They might, inside the car, try to make a joke with him, because of the fear . . . Daff did not cross into hostile territory; those she had met who did had always told her that the checkpoint was the place where the smile froze, and sweat chilled. The papers would be returned, the barrier raised, and then the anxiety would increase as the vehicle limped forward and all inside tensed for the shout to 'Stop'. A change of mind. Daff felt the fear. She watched the car moving off and out of the light from the arc lamps and it seemed to be close to the casino, and she lost it there, could no longer register the tail lights. It might be back the next evening, Thursday, or the morning after. It was now beyond reach, had gone across.

She went to her car, drove fast, went north and downriver.

She was brought to the interview room.

'Please, sit down, Yekaterina.'

She stood.

'I have invited you, Yekaterina, to sit down.'

She stayed standing.

'I have had a long day, Yekaterina, and am looking forward to being at home with my family. But they are used to eating alone and used to me being late. It is not important to me, and I am in no hurry. Sit or stand.'

She spat.

'Unnecessary and vulgar. I would have thought better of you, Yekaterina. Not even straight at me, but missing and only messing my carpet.'

She was flushed. Poor aim, and a feeble gesture. The guard by the door, Kat's escort from the cell corridor a floor below, took a pace forwards, her hand on the truncheon attached to her belt. He waved her back to the door, then with another gesture, slight and without fuss, closed the door behind her.

'I want to go home. Perhaps you want to go home. Why have you had to wait before I was ready to see you, Yekaterina? Because I have been talking with other members of your group, and with the one that you call the Leader. I talked to them about you . . . Some I find conceited and some are committed and some are confident, but they all have one difficulty. Let me tell you about it. You are certain you do not wish to sit?'

Still stood, and he thought she shivered but the radiator was turned high and the motion would have been from uncertainty, not cold.

'You have already, Yekaterina, been useful to me. We had difficulty, I confess it, in locating the one you identified as *lider*. We owe you thanks. That group have good tradecraft when they move and practise anti-surveillance techniques. Let me explain. It is difficult to follow without being observed if certain obvious tactics are used, and we would need perhaps ten or fifteen operatives. Expensive in overtime payments. But I had you, and you do not have the techniques. You might as well have blown a whistle. You led us there and I am grateful. We have been looking for him for eight months, since his participation in a demonstration in Moscow. Because of your help we have found him, and we have the full caucus of the steering committee – and you were there. Why were you there? I think they tried to please him. If I go out with my wife to friends for dinner, to their home, we take flowers, also some chocolate as a gift. They brought you. You were the gift. Someone he had not seen before, not fucked before, something fresh and clean, a diversion for him. Please, Yekaterina, you did not assume you were taken as a reward for the quality of your intellect? You did not? Taken, as in some primitive societies it might be a chicken or a goat, perhaps for sacrifice. You were a diversion. Are you quite happy to stand rather than sit? And if you feel the need to spit, please do.'

He kept his voice deliberately, soft. She would have had to strain to hear what he said, and his tone and his manner would already have perplexed her, and she would have forgotten the nuances of his questioning when she had first been brought before him, and treated as an errant child. The Major had long been puzzled that the interrogators of FSB, as in the old days of KGB, wanted to be feared, to hurt their prisoners and have them huddling in the corner of a room, wetting themselves, sometimes with split lips, fractured ribs, bruised eye sockets. She did not smell of the overflowing toilet and the bucket beside it – that specific cell with its plumbing problems had been allocated her as soon as he had been told the identities of the catch – because he had ordered she be taken to the wash-house, given a short but warm shower and a nearly clean towel to dry herself, and they had found a tracksuit for her. Most of the fight had gone from her. The defiance had ebbed . . . Had she been punched or kicked then she would still curse him and struggle, but his apparent gentleness – he thought – perplexed her, and the chance to wash and put on clean clothing over her own underwear.

'You have no passport, have nowhere to go. You have no piano teacher because you have lost your place at the Conservatory and have burned boats with your private tutor. A small matter but she spoke freely to me today . . . Your brother who is a criminal works under the direction of an organised crime chief. The chief has liaisons that do this country no honour. I am requested to free you. You should know, little Yekaterina, that I do not take bribes, am not corrupt. So if I return you to your home, then I do it because it is of advantage to me. I am not at the beck of a colonel in this building, nor a brigadier who has become rich from such liaisons. Do you want to return to your apartment, have the possibility of renewing your studies at the Conservatory, have your passport given back to you?'

She stood at her full height, thrust out her chin and drew back her shoulders, tried to recall the light in her eyes – did not succeed. Almost pitiful . . . He questioned her again, but bleakly.

'Or do you wish to be taken back to the cell block, have that clothing withdrawn from you, go to a communal holding area for women prisoners, and after a court appearance be remanded to a correctional facility? Is it a difficult choice?'

The Major had many agents within the ranks of the supposed dissidents, all subject to his careful, calm approach. He thought himself a fair man, without malice, and that the forces of protest in St Petersburg were limited, ineffective. A photographic portrait of the President adorned the wall behind his desk; he had no loyalty to that man, only to the laws of the country. She ignored the chair but sank to the floor, sat cross-legged and her head drooped. He told her that he would go and have a coffee in the canteen, then would return to hear her answer. He stood, put on his jacket, called for the guard to watch her. Smiled.

'You are at a crossroads, can go to the right or to the left. Think on it – but it comes at a price, little Yekaterina, going home tonight . . . not going to the cell block.'

Dusk fell over Narva.

Men and women hurried home, clutching plastic bags weighed down with the day's purchases. Kids were back from school and it was too cold for football, too bleak to pop pills. Buses thundered towards destinations . . . The brightest places, were those fronting on to Ivangorod and the Russian city across the river. The castle was a world-famous historic building, restored from the Second World War's devastation, a beacon. At the base of the castle wall was a pathway, paid for by the European Union. No one walked on it but it could be seen from the Russian side and seemed to boast success. The new money heaped on Narva was cosmetic. The town was rooted in the past. It had cemeteries and monuments to great and long-dead rulers and was a place where hope was rationed, coupons scarce.

The last lorries of the day crossed the bridge. The last pedestrians were checked and passed through briskly, towards and then past the white line, barely visible halfway across. The wind grew in strength and rain spattered. A harsh night was promised.

*   *   *

A dreadful night to be sending up fireworks, lighting the touch-papers and having them spear towards the low carpet of darkened cloud from which the rain tipped. An unlikely night for a celebration, for an engagement to be welcomed or a birthday marked. Local men did it, from the KaPo unit supposed to be watching over Daff's movements. They had trouble getting a cigarette lighter's flame on to the short fuses for rockets, for ear-piercing explosions, and for the cascades that climbed high enough to pierce the bottom layer of cloud, then disappear from sight, then come back, sinking down, and seeming to reignite. It was a good show, more than a token. The launch site for the diversion was upstream from the tank memorial and on the edge of the conurbation of Narva, in a far corner of the Wehrmacht graveyard, away from the squat dark crosses in stone. When some of the lights fell, the bright plastic flowers laid against the stones became visible. The two men charged with the work did as Daff had asked, and it would have been pretty enough and noisy enough to distract anyone on the far side of the river.

Merc went into the water. And sank.

The board slid away from under him and dipped and swivelled and tossed him off and he had to grope for it, holding his breath. He clung to its edge, and the folded bike had gone. He surfaced and shook and coughed and chucked up river water. The flow was hard against him and tugged at the board. Not possible for Daff to shine a torch for him, help him. He heard a sharp choke in her throat.

He hissed, 'No bike. Too heavy. We were wrong on the buoyancy. Going for it again.'

Instead of cycling he would have to run. Instead of finding a loggers' track and fixing a compass route and going through the forest on wheels towards the E-20, he would have to jog and maintain his speed. The rucksack was on his back, and the laptop shell that had been retrieved from the steel-sided case was wrapped in decent plastic and knotted at the neck, and another bag held his clothing. Murphy's Law, they called it. Good guys for gallows humour, Rob and Brad, said something always went wrong despite Murphy's best laid plans. He could hear, far away, the impact of the detonations and there were screams as rockets soared, and over the trees there were moments when the base of the clouds was lit up.

Nothing about 'good luck' or 'safe back' from her. Not a murmur of 'hope it all goes well – and the bloody thing works' from Daff. His 'Going for it again' were his last words to her. She was up to her knees in the water and had hold of the end of the board and seemed to steady it, and he'd manoeuvred himself until he was flat along it, and his wetsuit seemed to slither on its surface, and she gave the thing more than a nudge, propelled him out and into the start of the flow. He was gone, and to Merc she was history . . . He seemed for a moment to see the girl on the floor of the Emergency Reception area and the blood and the gleam, only a moment – and paddled with his hands.

He went further out from the bank. Had the nightmare moment. Darkness behind him and darkness ahead of him, and the force of the current pushing against the board and no light to guide him, only a dulled memory of what the far side had looked like, in daylight, where the deer had stood and the heron fished. Felt a great weight on his shoulders, swung hard with each outstretched hand to get leverage in the water, and spray bounced into his face and eyes. The nightmare was that he would paddle and push himself through pain barriers and seem to get across and would beach and would then see the lights of a car and hear a speeding engine through the bank's scrub bushes and know that he was on the same side as he had started from. Perhaps, then, Merc would yell, but no one would have heard him. A few more of the fireworks exploded upstream, and that – he realised – gave him the clue required, told him the direction to take. The flow tugged him and the wind lifted wavelets across him, and the rain pattered on him, and he rocked and swayed and twice he thought he had lost his grip and that the board would slide away from under him. Much of the time the board was an inch under water, but the wetsuit, filled with air and bulging, kept him afloat. Easier options?

Could have sat in the car with three guys that Daff rated as 'crap'
and be subject to incompetence or treachery when they went
through the most difficult of the checks – the block at the end of
the bridge. Could have been entering the Control Zone and having
a live device on the floor between his feet, and not speaking a
word of Russian, and having bogus documents, and not being
able to answer a question. No 'easier options' existed, his opinion
– and Daff's and Boot's. Merc felt the ache in his shoulders from
the paddling. He no longer heard the firework barrage but sensed
a soft singing sound and a riffling and could not place it and
thought he was hemmed in with obstructions at the sides . . . Then
was pitched off the board, and went into the water, and scrabbled
frantically to try to keep himself afloat and realised he thrashed at
mud. He crawled forward. The singing had been the wind catching
the tips of the reeds and blowing them back. He had gone into a
gap through the reeds and was ashore. He lay on the mud –
thought it the place familiar to the deer and the heron.

The force of the wind was around him and the rain beat on his
face and on the wetsuit. He gave himself the luxury of a short rest
and the chance to draw air deep down inside him. He was on the
far side and beyond help, reliant on himself, no back-up in place,
and not many cared enough to lose sleep when they had a Gun for
Hire over a far frontier . . . He thought that Daff, if she had any
sense, would go back to the apartment in Narva and rustle up hot
water from the shower and stand under it, and hold a drink in her
hand, and maybe call Boot.

'How did it go, Daff?'

'Don't really know, Boot, but he was all right leaving me.'

Merc stripped out of the wetsuit, untied the neck of the bag in
the rucksack and the clothes inside were dry. He dressed fast.
Then he opened the second sack and let his fingers linger on the
laptop shell: no water had penetrated. He listened, heard only the
wind and the rustle of the trees and the choral sounds of the reeds.
Looked back once and saw only darkness. Had his boots laced
tight. He slid the board into the undergrowth, and the wetsuit in
the clothes bag after it, then covered both with pine cones and

needles and the flotsam that the river had deposited after the last season's flooding. Last, he ripped a handkerchief in half and tied it to a branch. It would be his marker.

He did a compass reckoning, then loped away. An owl called at him. Might have shouted back, 'Hold the Line, the Pioneers' but did not. Went into the night, put the river behind him.

8

If he had not had an arm across his face, Merc's cheeks would have been lacerated.

Branches whipped him. He had careered into a tree's trunk, and had tripped on a fallen log, sprawling full length. The faint scent of wood-smoke guided him. His balaclava, of thick black cotton, had first been ripped, the threads hanging loose, then it had been torn off him. He kept going, had realised that the forest of close-set pines was not crossed with tracks, and had found the saplings growing under the canopy could flick with deadly force. Was it better to use a torch or to blunder against the trees and the scrub? His decision was that the noise he made could have been from a small bear or a deer.

He would get back, would round up Rob and Brad, have done his terse greeting at the hospital, placing another bouquet without ceremony on the bedside table, then been with the guys. He'd tell them about what a shit place it was, joshed with them that they'd not have lasted there ten minutes, called in on the satphone and demanded a heli-ride out – and would have won guffaws of laughter. Merc was sorry that they were not with him: only those two guys, not others. Neither spoke a word of Russian . . . he knew that because some days the big radios berthed in the command bunker were hooked on to the wavebands the Russian military used, when their special forces called in coordinates for the air force to start bombing. He'd tell Rob and Brad about the forest, the ditches, the fallen trees, about how his heart had damn near stopped when a creature had bullocked away from him: it would have been a wild pig. And there might have been wolves, a small pack, and possibly a lynx. If Merc had said to Rob and Brad that he was going through a forest, in total darkness, a storm blowing in the trees, just a compass to guide him, then it was certain one of them would have told a story about a lynx and how it hunted, sitting on a branch and jumping down on to the shoulders of its prey, a deer or a small pig. They would have liked to tell a story and try to frighten him. Not much did. Truth was that he was unnerved by the forest and its sounds, the crack of branches above him, and the wind's whistle. There could have been patrols in the forest, a track that a vehicle could negotiate and where the goons would cut the engine and listen, or they could have been on foot. Merc did not know.

He had all the hours of the night, would be at the lay-by before first light. He edged between trees, and he was wet and did not go fast enough to warm his body and had long miles yet to cover. The burning wood scent was his first target, as good as a light in the darkness, and guiding him.

A big bird clattered clear of his approach – would have been an owl. A furious wing-beat and the feathers risking damage against the branches. Merc looked up and saw nothing, only heard the effort to get away from an intruder, and was careless, and fell. Crawled and tried to find a branch to cling to, to get upright, and did not find one. He crawled farther, and started to slip lower. He was pressing down with his hands, attempting to lever himself up, and the mud was loose and sliding between his fingers. He had no purchase; the bog had closed over his knees, engulfing his boots. Rare for Merc to get even close to panic. He flailed with his arms to find something to hang on to. He heaved to raise his knees and draw up his boots from the saturated mud of the bog hole and he arched his back to make a greater resistance to the pit that seemed in that moment – as the degree of panic spread – to have limitless depth.

Anyone would have felt the fear. Even Rob and Brad who had been through the rigours of regiment selection, and even Cinar. And his nan as she fed the sparrows in the backyard, and the bank manager who would go home in the evenings and tell his wife about this strange 'little beggar' with a nest egg maturing and a tan to die for, but with fearsome scars. Anyone would have felt fear, and the verge of uncontrolled terror ... Might be where it all ended.

A forest that nobody came to. A victim that could not be declared missing. A body slid under, down into a sinkhole. A failed mission, and a bomb lost. No service held. Not in the big church in the Kennington Lane, St Peter's, where Daff said they did quality recitals at lunch-times, and not in the Cathedral of St Joseph that was out on the road to Erbil's airport. She would not know, nor Boot, and not his nan. After a year or two, the bank manager would consult with seniors as to what to do with a dormant account, and a room would be cleared and back issues of *AutoTrader* and *Exchange and Mart* would be binned.

'A good guy, but distant ... Useful at what he did, selling his trade of fighting, and earning what he was paid ... never saw under his skin, kept himself private ... nervous of friendship, I reckon, and frightened of women ... what he always needed and never had, a good woman ... must have made enough money to have quit but that sort never do, quit ... couldn't let go, one contract too many.'

Merc had a sunken root in his hand and tugged on it, dragged himself, inch by inch, from the hole, and came clear. He heard the mud give a belch, a gurgle as it released him.

The smell of the burning wood seemed stronger. Merc headed for it.

The girl giggled, told Martin his accent was 'funny' and his Russian old-fashioned, what a schoolteacher spoke, and his hand was on her thigh and she had not shifted it.

Across the table was Toomas, drinking. And over Toomas's shoulder was Kristjan's back and Martin could see the roulette table. He did not know what stakes Kristjan played for, how much he had won – a snort of derision – and how much he had lost. Nor did he know how many vodka shots Toomas had downed, and how many chasers of bottled Baltika. Nor did he know how much longer the girl would sit close to him and let his hand stay on her

leg before the heavy guys by the door came over and suggested
that he might care to pay up or get the fuck out. She laughed at
the way he spoke, and then her make-up seemed to crack in lines
away from her mouth. Kristjan turned and he caught his eye. He
supposed, because he drove, that they looked to him as their boss,
would do what he said. Precious few people in Haapsalu did. He
yawned, and the girl bored him and he wasn't going to have her
that night in the back of the car, while the rain pelted down and
the wind blew hard. He needed the money from the Brazilian
security firm, needed it when he returned to the coast. Lights
strobed and music blared, and there were few drinkers and few
gamblers in the casino on the road out of Ivangorod. They should
have eaten. Asked to describe himself he had told the girl that he
was a travelling salesman, trading in vacuum cleaners. If asked to
describe himself to *himself* he would have used one of the many
Russian slang words for 'arsehole'.

He should not have stayed in Haapsalu. Martin, back from the
Kaliningrad venture, was shunned by respectable company. It was
a society that dripped a self-satisfied comfort that came from the
tourist season. Shunned because of his grandfather. Old people
had known him, and younger people had been told the stories. His
grandfather had left an under-age girl pregnant, had gone on a
madcap adventure. The girl had been shipped to Russia. Old
people in Haapsalu did not regard his grandfather as a hero, a
freedom fighter against Soviet post-war occupation. The 'resistance' in the countryside had been known as the Forest Brothers,
but it was claimed – with new certainty – that many of then were
criminals, thieves and extortionists, sadistic lovers of violence and
lawlessness. Said that if a bus with Soviet troops on board was
blown up by explosives then the driver would have been Estonian
and innocent. As Martin understood it, most people in the town
had co-existed alongside the Soviets. There was a generation of
kids who had Russian fathers, then another generation with
German fathers, and then another – like strata in a rock face –
who had Russians bedding their mothers ... all accepted,
understood. Their men had gone to camps, fascist or communist,

and the women found comfort in the arms of the occupiers, and fed well on it. Martin's grandfather had been disowned. Martin had been marked out at school. His mother was the bastard child of a terrorist. He had gone on the mission for the Poles and thought he had done something to avenge the cruelty visited on her, and it had been a dream. He had come back to the seaside town and had lived there as a stranger. Should not have stayed and did not know how to leave.

Toomas was waving to the waiter, gesticulating with another fifty-euro note from the diminishing wad in his hip pocket. Kristjan had heaved back his chair and was starting towards the grilled hatch where tokens were bought for cash. Martin's hand came off the girl's thigh. He stood.

He jerked the note out of Toomas's hand and shoved it in a pocket. He dragged on Kristjan's collar. He said they were to stay close, make a wedge, and the guys on the door hesitated, and they were through. Martin could have screwed the girl and Toomas could have had another drink, and Kristjan could have won big time on the spinning wheel – and pigs might fly.

They crossed the car-park and rain spattered on them. Martin said, 'I just called myself an arsehole, and nobody disagreed ... We hate these people, so let's go hurt them.'

Had he had a good day? He had, the Major told his wife. Had she had a good day?

And she had. He kissed her cheek, was led through to the kitchen.

The dish was *knish*, a favourite from Minsk, and made by Jews there. Mashed potato covered in dough and baked, and was quick and could easily be heated again for him when he was late home. Both liked Jewish cooking. Close to midnight and the block was quiet. It was a building where many of the more junior officers of the police and militia and FSB lived. Teenagers were kept in check and it had a faded respectability, and was what the Major and Julia could afford. She poured him a beer. Told him of new funding for her weekly clinic in the hospital for dealing with teenage disease, and the money came from a 'businessman' and he snorted derision when she named him – called him *mafiya* – and she said the devil in hell could make cash available and she'd take it, and there was a child who'd had meningitis B symptoms and was improving, and she had chaired a meeting of her speciality subject, dermatology. Yes, a busy day. And his? A shrug.

'You achieved something? Of course you did, always something. What?'

Old habits died hard. The radio was always on when he confided in her, the volume high, or the television, or they would be in open parkland, or in the centre of the Mikhailovsky Garden, or – best – on a punt together, on a lake near Minsk. A game show played raucously around them.

He told her of an offer, named the colonel. 'A villa would be available for us in Sochi, by the sea and close to a beach, a week in the school holiday period, for next Easter.'

'You would never take anything that is "free".' She grimaced, mock resignation at the chance of a vacation week gone begging.

'The price was interesting. I turned it down, of course.'

'What did they want from you?' She took his empty plate, scraped out the bowl in which she had cooked, gave it back to him.

'They required the freeing of a troubled girl. Troubled because she is confused, also troubled because she is thought to have a talent in music but prefers to run alongside the dissidents, believes she has a place with them. I can charge her with "conspiracy" with "association" . . . It is my job to confuse them, and to defend the law. She has a brother.'

'Who has influence? Who has a roof?'

'The brother is a cyber criminal. They say, if there is another war, a big war and not a surrogate clash, that the front line will be defended by geeks, the children with the religion of the computer. He is a criminal and on the permanent payroll of the crime chief of the Kupchino clan. He must be important because a colonel comes and smears soft soap on me and asks, as a favour, for the release of this girl in order that her brother is not distracted from important work. They flit, the best of the hackers, between two masters: the clan, and the colonel who brings with him protection and also a shopping list. An important list for it to be necessary to massage the discomfort of this boy.'

She peeled an apple, then divided it. 'Did you bend?'

'A little.' He ate half the apple and she took the rest.

'But she is freed?'

'She is going home.'

'So, the criminals rule, they can shelter under the roof – yes?'

'They would think so.'

He thought his wife pretty, serene. But her face showed the weariness of work and worry: she would have benefited from that week on the Black Sea, on a lounger in the sunshine, and he worshipped her loyalty: she would never have demanded the holiday and the compromise.

'They would be wrong?'

'Two times wrong. First, the sister has been in a cell where the sewage rises in the pan, where the floor and the bedding are filthy, and the effect is to diminish her commitment to revolution, and I have recruited her. She will be the little bird that sings for me. Second, the brother is dependent on her for love, for affection, and for the conduct of his life and he will talk to her, will confide. As I drove home tonight I gave myself a solemn commitment. I will hit the Kupchino clan, will embarrass its roof, my colonel . . . Maybe a traffic violation, maybe Class A narcotics possession, an illegal firearm. Why? Because soon we return to Minsk – and maybe then move on. Who knows? I will hammer them, dear Julia, and I will not break my promise. Hammer them.'

He thanked her for his supper. Her fingers ruffled the hair on his neck. He kissed them and pushed back his chair. Both faced another busy day, but not a difficult one. He went to their son's room and the child slept well.

He was yawning and she was starting to slip off her clothes as they went towards their bedroom. A promise mattered to this man who his wife called 'obstinate, awkward, stubborn, principled and lovable'. Would not be broken and would not be ignored. He was pleased with the outcome of the day, and would soon have his

song bird in place, humming *cantatas*, and providing the evidence
for the hammering he would dish out. After he had undressed he
laid his service pistol, loaded and with the safety applied, on the
table beside the bed: another old habit finding it hard to die.

Most of the lights off, sitting among shadows, Nikki stayed up.

And listened. He heard the press of vehicles on the road below,
the shouts of the drunks returning from bars or sessions in the
parks, the sound of televisions and arguments and laughter and
singing, but did not hear her footsteps on the last flight of the stairs.
He knew what sounds she would make as she climbed, and he had
trained himself to register the noise as her key-ring rattled, and the
scrape if she missed the lock, and the squeal of the door opening.
Listened, and did not hear what he wished to. And agonised. Knew
what he would do. Seemed to see the flash that blinded his eyes, and
the thunder that would kill his ears, and the hurricane wind that
would flatten him – and did not hear her. He was manipulated, a toy
in the hands of the man who had taken him off the street outside
the bank, who had threatened him, who controlled him.

And agonised because it was still possible for him to approach
the villa where the GangMaster lived, a top-of-the-range Italian
car in the driveway for his wife and an armoured Range Rover
for himself. Ring the bell at the electrically controlled gate, and
tell a guard who he was and that his message was of great
urgency. Could do that. Go inside, stand in a hallway. Say that a
foreign intelligence team, enemies of the state, planned a provocation at the meeting the following afternoon, had sent people
who he would meet in the parking area of the supermarket off
the junction where the highway came in from Estonia. The
message would be passed, and FSB would escort him to a
holding centre, and what would he have achieved? Sweet fuck of
nothing . . . A promise had been given. He had believed it. A call
through to the Big House and bank statements from Stockholm
arriving. His fraud exposed, his sister dumped. Nothing to be
done, and the Englishman would have smiled at the depths of his
dilemma.

He could not work. Usually, when she was out late with her 'friends', and he stayed up for her and felt the loneliness, he would have tapped at his laptop keys, played the games of simulated 'honey bombs' and prepared mock attacks of malware. Tumbling into his lap would come the details of debit cards exfiltrated with spear-phishing. And he did 'zero days' assaults: went through the stages of *intrusive* and on towards *disruptive* and followed with *destructive* which could take down a country's utilities, darken it and blow out its capacity to function – and hide all of it because the policy was based on deception, *maskirovka*, and the need of it was taught them each time they fulfilled a state contract . . . Not that night.

They would have evaluated him, the GangMaster and the colonel. Should he be humoured? As if he had crawled on the floor to them, grovelled. He strained to hear. First the sound of her footsteps, and the stamp on the concrete, and then her voice and the hum of the chords of *1812*, Tchaikovsky's woodwinds and percussion and brass and strings replaced by a small defiant sound. He flopped into the lumpy filling of the sofa seat. She missed with the key and ditched the *Overture* and cursed, and the door creaked as it opened.

The light was snapped on. If she was grateful that he had sat up for her then she hid it well. She went to the fridge and pulled out a milk carton, looked at the expiry date and cursed again, swigged then turned and faced him. She stood, weight on her toes, her hands on her hips, and her hair a tangled mess, then he saw the light of her anger.

'Don't ask me if I'm all right,' she said. 'Want to know how I am? They might as well rape you, hands all over you, any dignity taken, fingers in you. Yes, I'm all right, yes.'

'I have to tell you.'

'And me tell you.'

On the sofa, close, big slugs of vodka to embolden them, darkness around them broken only by the street lights below. Arms around each other, like lovers, the brother and sister clung to each other.

Kat's mouth close to his ear. 'They don't own us.'

Nikki's voice, a murmur against her cheek: 'Everything I do, have done, is for us.'

'They think we belong to them, are slaves to them, and they play with us.'

'For you, what I have done and will do.'

The last news bulletin of the night had started on the TV and came through the thin wall from the adjacent apartment of the woman with the cigarette kiosk: martial music and the heroic commentary which meant that tanks would be advancing or aircraft offloading their bombs – somewhere. There were times when they beat at the wall in frustration at the noise, or exchanged angry words in the lobby, but that night, the start of a new day, they barely heard her. She could not remember when she had last allowed him to hold her, close and warm: she had thought him a criminal, artistically dead, with the principles of the rats that scavenged in the waste bins behind their block. Together, each feeding warmth to the other, and the alcohol coursing in them, giving courage.

'My first thought, how to get out . . . no passport, impossible.'

'Hear me.'

'Go, turn my back on this place, society, its control . . .'

'Listen to me.'

'. . . because it suffocates and stifles, and it watches and listens, and imprisons and persecutes, and cannot be beaten, and I should go – leave you, whatever. Say that "I am defeated", say "I cannot change anything", and try to walk out, maybe go north and through the snow and the fence and into Finland – but that too is impossible. My first thought.'

'Do you want to hear, listen, or finish?'

'Second . . . do we all leave? Give Russia, my country as much as their country, to intelligence men and the persecutors, fascists, and to the serfs who think still it is the *czar's* time. Say that we are too small, irrelevant, can do them no harm, and give them the freedom of the field? Accept defeat? Or stay and fight them . . . the other option.'

'Are you ready to listen?'

'They offered me a pass out of the gaol. The cell is disgusting. They do not have to beat you, the cell humiliates. In the cell you live in shit . . . They let me out and pushed me clear and I am on the pavement and the wind is in my face, and some of the rain, and it might snow next week and they think that is a sort of freedom. I walk on *their* pavement, cross *their* street, use *their* bridge, all by courtesy of them. The price? Always a price is charged by *them* . . . I was to be a *stukach*. That is what it costs, to go that low, be that level of scum, an informer. *They* were very satisfied with me because they believe they have a new "tout" who will give them gossip from meetings, stay near to the people who actually do something – even if only to strip off and make a panto-mime, or draw a penis on a bridge, but something. I let them think that I agreed because I was frightened to be sent back to the cell. I am ashamed I agreed but what else could I do? Remember that story, of the child, aged thirteen, betraying his own father to the police for anti-Stalin remarks in his own home? His father was shot in the Terror, but others in the family took the child, and cut off his head with a forest saw, and then they were subject to the "highest measure of social defence" and put in front of a firing squad. They wanted me to be like that kid, Pavlik Morozov, an informer . . . Fuck, what am I to do?'

'Be with me tomorrow – that is what else.'

'I think it is better to stay, stay and fight. Not accept defeat. Whatever the cost, fight them. I have to be braver. With courage I can survive the cell block. One day, think of one day, imagine it when the mass of people are no longer serfs, have the same courage as us, will fight . . . It is what I thought as I came home. Stay and fight, go to prison, fight there . . . How else can we struggle against them? No other way but protest with pamphlets and paintings on walls, and meetings. We have to.'

'Hear me.'

And he passed the bottle to her and she swigged it, and he drank and felt the glow of it, and felt brave. Thought also that she did not listen to him because she had never reckoned anything he said worth waiting to hear. She spluttered, and the power of the alcohol silenced her, and the TV in the next apartment was off and it was quiet. The defining moment. He paid for her life, her music, her food and her crap existence alongside the 'dissidents', and did not have her respect. Yearned for it.

He talked, matter of fact. The word he would have used was *priznaniye* – confession, a purging of secrets, and gratifying.

Her eyes widened. He talked of what he would do in the day, and who he would meet. A gasp of astonishment. Spoke of the bank on the Kornhamnstorg and what was lodged there, and coming away and a car door opening in front of him, and being pushed down into the back of a car, and an offer made and a threat given. Her arms on him, gazing into his face. He described a meeting, and who would be there – the Roofer and HookNose and Gorilla, and a colonel of FSB and the GangMaster who led them. And he felt her shiver. Told it calmly and in a sequence, and seemed to know the outcome.

'Is it for real?'

'It is what will happen ... why should I doubt it? They are professional people. I think that they are, have to hope it.'

He came to the barn. A storm lantern hung outside it, swaying in the wind. The house, wood and clapper boards and tin-roofed but with a brick chimney at the end, was beyond the barn. The smell from the burning wood on the fire was fainter and it would be dying and the smoke from the stack was occasional. He blessed the fire which had been a better guiding star for him than the compass.

Merc answered his own questions. Where the building was, and how far it was within the forest, and how long the track would be, and what time it would take him to cover that distance, and then how much farther on was the lay-by. He thought he had three hours ... His clothing dripped, and was filthy from the bog and his boots were sloppy with mud, and the rain pelted him and the wind sang in the trees.

The main building was single-storey and dark except for a glimmer from the window at the far end, below the chimney. The lamp outside the barn was guttering, would not last. On the barn's door was a new padlock. . . . What was Merc good at? Good at getting across a river not quite in spate, good at coming through a forest without a torch and without a path, good at sniffing out the value of a fire in a hearth, good at killing, good at deflecting thoughts of 'sometime' when he might be ready to leave the life of a Gun For Hire, and good at dealing with simple locks. He had a spike on his penknife. He extended the spike, thought he might find hay bales, but could be a heap of old sacking. A deep cold bit into his body and the wind lashed his sodden clothing. The lamp gave him sufficient light, and he lined up the probe on his knife.

Merc thought of the bank manager. 'You know, Gideon, if you don't mind me calling you that, because after this length of time that you've been coming in here – well, *Mister* Hawkins is so distant – I think we know each other tolerably well. You are a puzzle to me . . . not in the armed forces or your salary would say it, not anything illegal because you wouldn't want to come in here and discuss investments if it were ill-gotten gains. I think that what you do is dangerous, far beyond anything I'd be capable of, and I also think that what you do helps in some way to protect myself and my family. For the risks you take, I believe you are moderately well recompensed. I don't suppose it often, if ever, happens, Gideon, that people thank you for your work: anyway, whether it's a first or not, please accept my gratitude . . . Goes without saying that the account is ticking, not dramatic but these are not easy times. You have a decent nest egg accumulating – and I hope you intend to use it, get the benefit from it, have enough time to enjoy what you have earned from your work. What am I saying? Something like, "If it's possible, get out while the going is good", something like that . . . But I don't know what the pressures are on you, Gideon, and doubt you'll share them with me . . . Enough said. As always, a pleasure to see you . . . Stay safe, Gideon – wherever you are.' He'd be asleep, and would not have heard of Narva, nor its river, and what use he would find for the spike attached to his penknife. It went into the aperture. He worked the handle of the knife round, used slight force to twist the padlock's innards, then heard the metallic snap, as if a clamp were released. The bar flopped open, and he eased it off. He worked one of the twin doors, had to struggle to lift it an inch clear of the mud, and felt a little wave of heat escape through the gap and linger on him for a moment. He took a step forward.

Noise clattered above him and a feather wing lashed his face and a chicken screamed.

A pig yelled and fled from him. He reached back and dragged the door shut, was surrounded by darkness and by the sound of animals and the fowls, and their warmth seemed to settle on him. He used the torch from his pocket . . . a good beam. Merc thought he might have ended up with Noah, on the Ark's lower deck. Eyes peered back at him. There the noise of cattle, and sheep, and pigs, and chickens flew fitfully around his head.

Merc switched off the torch.

After setting the alarm, a low pulse beat, on his watch, after checking that the Makarov issued to him had not shipped water, after running his hands over the outer surface of the laptop – still dry inside the plastic packaging – he began to undress. The temperature outside might have been a degree or two above freezing. Everything off. Coats, fleece, shirt and vest, trousers and underpants, boots and socks. He squeezed the moisture out of the wettest, and he laid the clothing on the straw by his feet. Then, Merc put straw over them and bent and rolled them hard and tight and hoped the bedding would suck up more of the moisture. The livestock pressed around him, had no fear of him . . . He could not easily calculate how many hours he had been in the front line trench on Hill 425 and had tried to kill men before they could kill him, but the animals sensed no danger from this intruder. He made soft noises and the darkness cloaked him. He lay on straw and covered himself with two sacks that might once have carried grain for the pigs or cake for the cattle.

A few minutes of restlessness, and grumbling from the beasts at the interruption of their night, and some defecations and cascades of urine, and foul smells – all familiar to him from life in the Forward Operating Base, and some came to sniff at him, then the

quiet gathered. He did not think about the mission, the boys up
the road waiting in a lay-by, nor about the laptop that was inside
the soaked outer fabric of the rucksack and the device built into it
– nor about those who would die, be mutilated and live, nor the
bereaved, nor about the flowers beside a bed. Thought about
nothing – and slept.

The Maid had stayed calm, usually did. The camp bed was hard
but serviceable. There were rooms down in the basement for staff
needing to overnight – with long lists of regulations to prevent
assignations, same sex or differing genders, and a hawk-eyed
attendant who, it was said, 'never slept, not a wink, could have
been bloody Stasi' – but she preferred to be on her own territory,
with her own phones and secure computers. She had heard
nothing, always good.

   A deserted corridor was beyond her locked door. Later the
cleaning staff would come and noisily polish the corridor floor,
and others would refill the sandwiches and hot drinks machines.
Sometimes a cat came, seeking out vermin dinners and with the
run of a back staircase and a route out of the fortress, known to it
and very few others, and a way down to the gardens or the Thames
mud at low tide. The cat was known as AalZ to a select group:
Ayman al-Zawahiri. The heavily hunted figurehead leading
Al-Qaeda was known to many but hardly ever seen. If the cat
sensed she was behind the door then it would howl and scratch for
entry, and she might let it in. But to most in the building the cat
was only a rumour. Her friend, down the pecking order from the
parrot, would not expect a call from her and only visited by
appointment. He was a representative and sold tins of fancy
biscuits, for special occasions . . . The phone did not alert her, and
she had no ringtone from her computer. All satisfactory. Bad
news, on a race-track, always outpaced good tidings.

   And extraordinary how good news and bad percolated at speed
through a building dedicated to secrecy . . . Ollie Compton had
been in old Century House when news had broken, on discreet
links, that Oleg Penkovsky, '*our man*', had been executed in the

Lubyanka and had said that many were in tears, and others broke out the whisky . . . She, herself, should not have known anything of the successful exfiltration of a KGB colonel, but the tale that he was safe across the Finnish border had raised cheers through the building . . . But bad news had the edge, in speed, on the good. She had heard nothing.

Would sleep – her head was close to Boot's locked door – would sleep well.

He passed the ferry boat's disco lounge.

Boot had chosen an eccentric route to Estonia, was on the night crossing from Stockholm harbour to the port of Tallinn. A strange choice but with purpose: lack of trust.

The music blasted at him and lights spun in bright circles from ceiling attachments in the bar and a few couples were on the floor. He had to be there, in place, at the end. It was required of Boot that he should be on the bank of that wretched river that divided the cultures and histories and régimes of his world and Moscow's. Duty ensured that he was available either to welcome back and then hustle away his team, or that he should be present to take responsibility for the dismantling of overt evidence of the mission should the manure be in the ceiling fan . . . Not something that Boot would have delegated to Daff . . . And there was the matter of 'trust'. Good people, the Estonians, and with a proven intelligence-gathering apparatus, and blessed after the years of occupation with an understanding of what was across the river, the enemy. Boot had never shed that word from his vocabulary, *enemy*. But . . . *but* . . . the KaPo ranks were still inhabited by older men, buried away and barely noticed, career officers who had collaborated with KGB until the Soviet Union's collapse. They'd still furnish the dead letter-boxes around Tallinn. He'd have risked being noted had he flown into the Estonian capital's airport, and Daff was already there and a degree of cooperation would have been required for the launching of the fireworks a few hours earlier. So, without fanfare, he would come off the boat in the morning with a few tourists and some businessmen and the drivers of the big lorries. He would come in like a shadow.

He paused. Music blasted his ears. Boot seldom danced with his wife. There was an annual dinner for local traders and shop owners and it was understood between them that he escorted her, but stayed firmly in his chair when the band played. Plenty of other men walked her to the floor . . . On their schedule, the great battle and Boot's little skirmish, this was the night of the Duchess of Richmond's ball, the society event of the year in Brussels, and the Duke was there, and many of the girls of London society and the cream of the cavalry and officers from the Guards; the Duke maintained an austere calm and give no cause for anxiety. Messages would have come to him continually, and some say he was distracted and poor company for the girls, others claim he rode the evening well . . . His ears were dinned by the loud-speakers' bar music but Boot stayed by the door, was a *voyeur*, and kept a watch and some danced serenely and others hurled themselves round the handkerchief-sized floor . . . and they did waltzes and the gallopade, and there were sword dances by officers from the Gordon Highlanders, and one more message had come, brought by a mud-spattered courier and carried across the floor, past the Duchess of Richmond, and given to the Duke. A frown perhaps, a moment of gritted teeth; the despatch told him that the French armies were farther forward than he had believed, had gained twenty-four hours' advantage. The epic quote: 'Napoleon has humbugged me, by God'. And girls abandoned as wallflowers and officers leaving in droves to rejoin their units and march or ride away into the night, and some young men would fight, and would die in their evening dress . . . Boot turned away, sought the elevator that would take him up to his cabin. Perhaps because this was, in his opinion, the most significant mission he had launched in his professional career, he had taken the parallel timetable of the battle, his amateur obsession, and woven the two together, dovetailed them. He would walk alongside the Duke on Copenhagen, close to his stirrup, and would learn. Learn from a consummate leader. Was he *humbugged*?

Boot did not know. Was he tricked, deceived? Had arrogance betrayed him? Boot could not say.

A strong wind blew across the Baltic sea, and the ferry ploughed forward and he no longer heard the disco below . . . At that time, as the band had played on, the young men would have left the girls, perhaps with a locket on a chain hanging on their chests and under their finery, perhaps with a lock of hair secreted in the breast pocket of an undershirt, and the wagons carrying the cannon and their ordnance would have been on the move, and the cavalry, and the carts that brought forward the implements of the field surgeons.

Boot doubted he would sleep.

Could not say if he were humbugged, and could not intervene in any worthwhile way. Always the same when an operation was launched, the waiting for news and the vacuum of knowledge . . . It might be a great day in his life and might be the worst he had known. Boot undressed carefully and lay on the bed. He was in the hands of others, as the Duke had been; raw and exciting and pivotal. He switched off the cabin light and heard the rhythm of the engines and saw the bleak darkness through the porthole.

Best foot forward.

Daff had counted the number of lit cigarettes in the car. Three. Probably meant they had two cars but had come together for warmth, for conversation, and to salve the boredom. Always the best response when the subject of a stake-out . . . She used her heel to shut the front door of the block behind her.

Her bag had been partially packed by the Maid, and included a small jar of cocoa and another of Bovril, and one of coffee, instant. On the tray were two mugs of cocoa and two of Bovril. She walked away from the block on Igor Grafov street and towards the bulk of the cathedral. The wind buffeted her and the rain lashed her and she thought it a foul night to be huddled in a surveillance car . . . and a worse night to be loose in a forest and heading for a rendezvous. She did the carrying expertly, and liquid hardly spilled from the mugs and her hair blew behind her and her coat splayed, and the car went dark and she would have created a devil of confusion, all fags squashed out. The ground squelched under her feet, and when she slipped she held on to the tray.

They might have wondered at first, after she had emerged from the building, that it was chance that took her in their direction. Not when she was halfway across the open space and was the only person out on a bad night and coming with gifts . . . Would they have known, the surveillance boys from the KaPo, about the dangers of a wooden horse? Of Greeks bearing gifts? Would they have assumed that she, with her tray of steaming drinks on a night when the wind came from the snow-bound north-east, whipping the Baltic, was a 'hostile'? They should have, but did not. A rear door opened.

'Thought you might enjoy these, boys.'

Space was made for her on the back seat, and the drinks seized, and she was thanked, was everybody's friend, and the cigarettes were out again, and she'd taken one. They'd talk, she was confident. Might not get much sleep – but then neither would Merc – and they'd gossip and she'd listen, and the cocoa and the Bovril would warm them, and the clouds of cigarette smoke would thicken . . . She wanted to learn their fall-back position if it went wrong on the far side of the river, and if it went wrong what degree of help could be expected. It might go wrong and most would be scrambling to protect their backs, and she needed to know if aid would be denied her.

'Really grateful, boys, for the show tonight, the fireworks. Excellent stuff.'

She was a hit, a star, and talk flowed: she learned a bit and they learned nothing. Laughter rang from the car, and the rain sluiced on the windows and leaves were blown across the open space towards the cathedral and flew past the windscreen. Daff was good at her job, but was far from the front line.

'You ever been scared, like this?' Kristjan's question.

They all laughed, none meant it. Toomas was the eldest and Martin was the youngest, and they were all past their forty-fifth birthdays and short of the forty-seventh, not kids, not frightened of the dark. They were parked in the lay-by and the night was close around them. The wind seemed to funnel up the road. They heard trees break in the forest, like pistol shots.

'I never felt scared like this – not even in Kaliningrad.' From Kristjan. 'Not even when we bugged out from the roulette place . . . not like now.'

'Not always easy, Kaliningrad, but not like I'd shit . . . Sorry, guys, sorry. Feel bad here.' From Toomas. 'Worse . . . and stuck here and waiting, and older.'

'Young in Kaliningrad, and it's a long time back, and I remember the goons in the bar, and she was great meat, and I was in there, and . . .' Martin said it, quiet but hoarse. 'Not ashamed, I am scared bad.'

Headlights came from behind them, a vehicle travelling from Ivangorod, and they were on full and Martin, who was in the driving seat, had his hand up to shield his eyes, and swore, and Kristjan beside him swore but softer and said it was the police, and Toomas had a paroxysm of coughing that was stress. An interior light showed two police, uniformed; the vehicle stopped alongside them and the driver eyed them and the passenger climbed out, looked reluctant and clamped his cap on his head. He was bent against the gale and came to the near side.

A squeak in Toomas's voice. 'What the fuck do I do, what do I say?'

'Tell him to go screw your mother – how do I know what you say, just—'

Martin did not let Kristjan finish. He wound down his window. 'Hi, officer – you always have this weather? The worse weather I know about. Heh, thanks for stopping by, we're just killing some time. We're fine, not a problem. Don't want to get to that big lovely city in the dark. My friend is an idiot with navigation, so we'll head on when it's dawn . . . We have good tickets for the Ice Palace, for SKA . . . That makes us lucky dicks. Thanks for checking up on us, we really appreciate it.'

And Martin showed his appreciation, and the rain fell hard on the uniform, its back and its shoulders, and Martin reached out with a fifty-euro note in his fist and slipped it into the officer's hand, and then his cap came off and was blown down the road. It was retrieved, the police car drove off.

Martin said, 'We should not have done this.'

'I feel I want to throw up.' Toomas trembled.

'Should not? Try this, don't have to.' Kristjan stammered.

'What is "Don't have to"?'

'Easy . . . Turn around, get the hell out. Go back, get over the bridge . . . I'm doing shelves by lunchtime . . . Tomorrow Toomas is getting cash off tourists, all in his armour, Martin is opening up his paint pots again.'

'Just walk out on it?' Martin rolled the words.

'Just walk out . . . Who is going to come after you? Some crap people in São Paolo? They going to come and get their money back? How they going to do that?' Kristjan clapped his hands, like it was a done deal, no more argument. 'I learned it quick. That goon walking towards us and the pistol bouncing on his hip – and Martin was fantastic – and what I learned was that I have no stomach for this. I say, turn around.'

'We don't owe them anything. Don't owe that woman anything.'

'I been more scared than I can remember. Are we agreed? Turn around? Pity about the Ice Palace . . .'

The door opened beside Kristjan, and the night and the storm flooded the back of the vehicle, and the ceiling light came on, and the stranger pitched in a rucksack, eased himself inside, and slammed the door shut.

'Morning, guys. Thanks for waiting up for me.'

''Fraid I'm not much of a sight, slept in a barn. Stink probably, animals in with me. And my clothes, they smell too, mud and wet . . . I'm called Merc – not a proper name but what everyone calls me. An understatement, pleased to see you guys . . .'

He needed to calm them and knew it. Sensed the mood, and saw their faces: no welcome.

'Anyone have something to eat? I've some fresh clothes in my sack. I'll change in here. Don't suppose you had much of a brief? Nor me – but the money's useful – yes?'

He had watched for twenty minutes. Had seen the police draw up alongside and check them over, had been on his stomach and close enough to have noted the hand snake out and palms meeting. A lorry had gone by and had lit them . . . deep in talk. If it had been squaddies, or contractor boys, there would have been gallows' laughter and joshing, but this had been serious talk, and none of them had seen him break cover and come forward. The driver's fingers had been on the ignition. He spoke English to them and they understood him well enough . . . He thought he'd interrupted a conspiracy.

'Hardly want to strip off in the open. It's the last of my dry stuff. They didn't think it clever for me to go head to head with the border control so it was across the river and through the forest, and here I am. Guys, just let me put some fresh stuff on and then I want to get you up to speed.'

Three men outside their safety zone, stress building. If he had stayed in the darkness under the trees, the engine would have coughed to life, and the lights come on. The vehicle would have edged forward and come to the lay-by's exit point, done the wide swinging turn and gone back up the road, towards the river, would have been at the bridge in fifteen minutes . . . and they'd have disappeared.

For him? Not a whole bunch of options, precious few alternatives to hitching a ride up the road, rucksack on his back – if anyone would stop for a guy who looked like a scarecrow and had slept in a barn full of animals. Then get somewhere he could hot-wire a car, sit behind the wheel and open a map and head for sunny St Petersburg, and try to pick out a supermarket on the way where there was a decent-sized parking lot. And if he stepped clear of the car with his bag and started to undress and get out the last of the dry stuff then it was likely they'd head off. He'd not have run after them, not with his trousers in the dirt and clean underwear around his ankles. He changed in the car, wriggled like a ferret . . . It would be about his voice and his manner, why they had plucked him off Hill 425, lifted him from the Fire Force Unit. He could not get the damp and cold off his skin. The one sharing the back with him refused to make any eye contact, stayed quiet, and those in the front had their heads down. His advantage, he believed, was their refusal to act, throw him clear. He had to lift them, would have one chance, had to get it right.

'No one told you much, nor me. We call it Mushroom Management . . . the big people in the company are not greatly interested in things down at our level, and in their opinion we are expendable, deniable. *My* opinion is different. Listen. We are not expendable – repeat it, *not* – not deniable. We get paid, poorly, but I'll change that, believe me. What is Mushroom Management? It is "kept in the dark and fed on shit". Not any more. What I know, I share . . . We go in, and I lead and make decisions. If I ask for advice then give it to me. We'll do what we are tasked to do, and get the hell out, back to Narva and safe, my first promise. My second is that I will get to that woman, the one who hired you, and me, and I'll get a pay hike out of her. We are a top team, remember it.'

Done quietly, no hesitation, not the crap that officers used. It was what Merc believed in, the worth of little people – he was one himself – and what they could achieve. He tried to exude confidence. They gave him their names, haltingly, and he made sure that he held each of their hands, Martin's and Toomas's and Kristjan's, and took a cigarette from the front passenger and told it like it was. Like he would have done on the Forward Operating Base bunker, or to the Afghan lorry men in a convoy he was escorting, or to the boys who rode shotgun on the escort detail down Route Irish . . .

9

He saw the creep of the dawn light.

Merc was alert, had not slept, would not have taken that risk. This suspicion of him did not surprise him. They would have smelled his body, and he smelled their alcohol. He had made the speech and reckoned it unwise to repeat it. The road was flanked by thick forest, dense pines and ditches were lapping with rain-water. Set back from the road were small homesteads; some already had smoke crawling up into the rain from stacks, and some had dull lights showing. Few cars passed them, and hardly any lorries were headed towards Ivangorod and the crossing over the bridge to Narva.

Merc understood them. A good idea at the time – out of money when the offer had been made. They had the map on a phone in the front and he had told them where he needed to be and when. They did not talk among themselves, and the one in the back with him – Kristjan – kept close to the door, made no contact. Out of the trees suddenly, and a swing to the left and they drove alongside a revetment that held back floods when the river burst its banks. Then a sharp turn to the right and the bridge was ahead. Daff had said it was the last river to be crossed before the straight run on to St Petersburg, and there was a militia barracks. She might as well have signposted it as a risk point, but had done it with a shrug. He'd seen towering pylons with long cables slack beneath them and a chemical plant that belched a grey-white smoke then merged into the cloud, and a sharper light waved at a lorry and van ahead of them, and directed them toward the control point.

How frightened were the guys? Had his talk made any differ-ence to them? The lorry's headlights caught the militiaman who was waggling the torch to slow the driver. It could be routine, what they did every Thursday morning on the outskirts of Kingisepp. It could be the result of an intelligence leak, and a mantrap for an agent of foreign power. He sat low in the seat, unshaven, his outer clothing caked from the bog and some of it still flecked with straw from where he had rested, and traces of sheep and pig droppings . . . not the average guy bumming a ride into the country's second city. The breathing quickened around him, and an oncoming lorry's lights showed the sweat on the driver's neck. Merc saw the chicane of white-painted oil drums. A torch was played on the cab of the lorry; it carried a load of new timber props, fresh-cut pine. He had a pistol . . . about as useless to him as a box of chocolates, and it was a dead weight in his pocket and he was considering dropping it behind the seat. Nobody did a course on going through a road-block: might be the check they did on that morning every week, and it might be random, and it might be the end of a run before it had left the start line. The lorry pulled away, and a van took its place.

The torch was raised. Papers passed. Fumes spewed from the van's exhaust. One uniformed man with the torch and another checking the paperwork, and they were next. The rucksack was between his feet and inside it was a laptop computer except that its innards were removed and good-grade, Russian-made explosives were packed in their place, with the detonator stick and the wiring, and the switch that would start a clock countdown. What to say? 'Steady boys, let's all keep calm. Don't show fear. Fear is recognisable, and they'll see it. Keep smiling, boys.' Didn't. Cut it. Merc tried not to speak unless there was a contribution in the chain that was of value. The van was waved on. The torch flashed towards them, indicating they should come forward, then stop. They wore high-visibility vests and had weapons slung from their belts, along with gas and batons and handcuffs . . . Merc pondered the issue.

How frightened were they? A casualty of fear was loyalty. Different to the lay-by when they had been checked and he had not been with them. The loyalty was about money . . . Money had bought them, Martin and Toomas and Kristjan. Money up front and money on completion. Enough money, or not enough? They were paid men; ideology would have been low on the agenda . . . One chain-smoking, one with sweat streaming, one with an uncontrolled slither of a tongue over the lips. Guns for Hire, like himself. They could put their windows down, gesture towards him, have the torchbeam play on his face, and denounce him. What loyalty could be purchased with $3000 dollars in advance? Men with their freedom or lives at stake were likely to ditch loyalty.

The torch shone on Martin and Toomas. Papers were passed, another bank note. The torch-beam played on him, and more talking, and he was the subject. The militiaman spat on the road. The papers were passed back through the window, not the bank note. The beam moved behind them, and the car went forward, dodging the oil drums, and they picked up speed.

Toomas said, 'It was about motor insurance. They said we had a faulty indicator light. Worth fifty euros for it to be ignored. They are shit.'

A bad few moments for Merc, but not as bad as when the big man, black overalls and an assault rifle, was on the last strands of the wire and trying to get into the trench where his people were, and Cinar. It helped him put into perspective what was bad and what was acceptable. They were no different from himself, the hired helps, what the Service officers called 'incrementals', there for the money and no respect. And he thought the body language had been good.

Merc said, 'Something to eat would be good.'

He was shivering . . . Kristjan told him that breathing the vapour from steaming potatoes was a cure; Toomas thought he'd do better by chewing garlic and onion: and Martin said the best thing was vodka laced with black pepper.

Boot entered Passport Control and proffered documents that had little relation to his true identity . . . This fledgling nation state, Estonia, boasted counter-intelligence excellence, but many officers of the KGB-imitating state security apparatus had been booted from their offices, put to grass, had found the change difficult to stomach.

Old networks had mutated. A man who had once enjoyed power and whose presence had created apprehension, could find himself doing work that was little more than basic labouring – sweeping the floors of the walkway between ship and terminal, neither passengers nor ferry staff sparing him a glance. He had lost dignity, status, but had not lost the acumen of suspicion and the ability to recognise a face: a seminar in Helsinki. Quite a senior man, and walking half a pace behind a considerable target from the old and chilly state of war, Oliver Compton. He was recognised by the bowed figure who cleaned the floor, ignored by those hurrying past him, and a conversation was remembered.

A telephone call. How would Boot have known of it? He would not. He had registered the man and had thought him a recovering alcoholic, plenty of them, and charitably employed, given purpose. A call made to the flower market.

Boot took a taxi into the heart of the city . . . had some hours in which he could walk, take in some sights. He felt calm, thought all in place – composed but not complacent.

'All quiet?'

She had been up and dressed for an hour. Before going to the canteen for fruit and cornflakes, the Maid had shaken out bedding, folded it, stowed it in the cupboard and dismantled the camp bed. The outer office was shipshape when the Big Boss looked in.

'Yes, sir, of course.'

'Nothing different overnight?'

'You would have been told.'

Something of a reprimand. She had heard that most of the offices had 'dragon staff' allocated them, women who ruled a minor fiefdom and accepted little interference. She supposed herself to be prominent among them, rather enjoyed the thought . . . Early for him to be on the corridors. A couple of his bag carriers were behind him. A meeting beckoned, and he'd needed reassurance. Not that she could have provided it. Nothing from Boot, silence from Daff, no protest squeals from the Estonian brothers. She shrugged.

'Thank you.' She considered which minefield he was about to enter, then resumed her work: expenses and holiday dates, and it was useful to hack at the administration of the office when a good one was running, took her mind away from it.

They were on early shift, and noted the movements.

Arthur said, 'In at a quarter past six and out at forty-eight minutes past. Got it?'

Roy had, nodded as he lowered the barrier for the Director's saloon to manoeuvre out of VBX.

'And Boot's still gone, and the leggy one from his office that's all bum and tits, and the top man is missing out on beauty sleep. All three . . . What's it saying?'

'A big one, and it's running.'

It was their game and played with pleasure. Sometimes instincts were confirmed, glum faces at the gate, and some unfortunate had screwed the job. Other times they'd be coming back in from the Royal Oak or the Pilgrim with cigars lit and step unsteady. They loved it and the game made a job of serious boredom worth the while.

'Definite, isn't it?' Arthur said.

'My shirt's on it,' Roy answered.

'Know that poem, Roy? "They also serve who only stand and wait". That's us, old cocker. Hah, rather him than me, whoever it is, and wherever.'

'I'd not take kindly to embarrassment, Jerry.'

'I would not estimate the risk to be great, Minister.'

'Nothing I should know?'

'That might blow up in your face, my face, the Service's face? I don't think so.'

'Delicate times, Jerry.'

'When have they not been, Minister – Anglo-Russian relations? Which century do you want to fall back on? Always "delicate times", us and the Ivans. Normal levels of dislike and mistrust.'

'I need to assure our Allies, correction *the* ally, that we are in step with their initiative. What's the word your people use? *Blowback*, that it? Nothing is going to "blowback", scorch me?'

'Not that I am aware of.'

'We have constantly to make new evaluations for future policy.'

'Always need open minds, fresh ideas.'

'Have to accept the world as it is.'

'And we should not permit little matters to obstruct our overtures.'

The Director, Jerry to his political master, did not add any minor or major impertinence, but could have listed the obstructions . . . Annexation of a friendly power's territory, murder by poison on our streets, downing of an airliner packed with passengers from our neighbours in the Netherlands, bombing Syria back to the Stone Age in support of a ghastly little despot, cheating at international sport with drugged-up zombies winning medals, the cyber attacks and daily difficulties fending off their hackers, intrusion into the democratic process, and the constant probing by their bombers . . . 'Need to concentrate on the big picture.'

'Dwight is anxious to brief us in person on the new initiative his government proposes . . . Don't take offence, Jerry, I was only crossing Ts, dotting Is . . . The time for us to exist in a state of near warfare, all this name calling, has had its day. We have to appear to be willing to live and let live, work with them, not talk only in a language of sanctions. I was thinking that the spirit of cooperation that keeps the Space Station aloft – Russians and Americans, and the occasional Briton – is an ideal to be nurtured. We want to consign to the bin this age of dissent and recrimination, find a way of getting along with them. I am not a Labrador, rolling over on my back and grovelling, but we have to modify a sulphurous posture towards them. I wanted you to meet Dwight, hear all this at first hand and not from the Neanderthals of the Agency . . . Ah, here we are. Thank you, Jerry, for the reassurance.'

They came in a phalanx up the stairs, wide and imposing and symbolising the United Kingdom: huge and dominating and 'punching above its weight'. Portraits and busts of great men, looked down on them, and on the Americans climbing the wide marble steps. The Director envied the spending power of the cousin across the water, but little else. He supposed that an accommodation with the Kremlin meant that neither Washington nor London – not Berlin or Rome or Paris – was prepared to commit to any further 'arms race' and therefore hoped to buy off the beast and use honeyed words and a gentle massage to achieve it ... Some damn hope. A few statistics bounced in his mind as the visitors came towards them and the Minister wore the fulsome smile of a restaurant greeter: Russia had 22,000 main battle tanks, some old. His own country possessed 227, Germany 225, Norway 52. For fuck's sake, bloody Yemen had three times the tanks of the United Kingdom, and the hackers ran free and ... He fixed his smile.

'Hi, Jerry, good to see you. Have to say, we are quite excited by what we have in mind, and hopeful. Optimistic. We have no place for moaners.'

He shook the hand offered him and they were led into a meeting room, duly swept that morning, to hear what the Director would have called 'bloody unadulterated appeasement' and the Minister and his guest thought of as the 'new relationship'. About *pragmatism* – he imagined that dear Boot, his chosen man, might throw up, vomit on that fine flooring, if asked to give it lip service ... and wondered how Boot's people prospered. He sat down, his attention polite and insincere, and murmured silently 'Over my damned dead body', and toyed with a biscuit. He kept the smile, like it was glued in place. Should he have demanded more time and more opportunity for reflection before sanctioning Copenhagen? Had he allowed himself to be stampeded? Was there still a chance to press an abort button? Over his dead bloody body ... not a chance of it. The fixed smile had a tint of the glacial ... Boot's people would be moving in, going for their 'ground zero'.

*　　*　　*

'Quit, or stay and fight?' Kat was bent over him. Still dark, the dregs of the night still clinging to the city's skyline. She had washed, dressed in tough old jeans and thick clothing and had dumped a waterproof thermal coat on a chair, been to the fridge and emptied everything from it that she could dump into a pan, and made a mess of an omelette and had carried the plate to where he slept. He had slept well, not tossed, the cough gone from his throat, and she had needed to shake him to wake him. 'Should I quit, accept they have beaten me, or stay to fight them – which?'

It was hard to believe what Nikki had told her. There was sliced potato in the omelette, and a tomato, and she'd used the last two eggs, and a piece of ham that had curled. Grated most of the cheese left on a shelf, and finished the fruit juice carton. He wolfed what she brought him, then boiled the kettle for instant coffee. She called to him from the stove.

'I had a dream. I think it was a dream and not just imagination, wishful . . . I read that, during the siege of the city, the nine hundred days, men and women dreamed that a great relief force had battered through the fascist lines, and broken the enemy, and behind our tanks were columns of lorries bringing food for the people. All of our grandparents, the great-uncles and great-aunts who had stayed alive by sneaking out at night with a sharpened knife and finding cats, dogs, rats, they could kill and skin and bring back. Then slicing meat from the stomachs and cheeks of the bodies in the street . . . My dream was of a great army of us, battalions of the people, marching forward and coming over the bridge and storming into the Big House, and spilling out and going down the corridors and sacking offices, spreading through the floors and destroying the files and memory sticks and smashing the computers, and then smoke rising from the building. Then, a gathering in the square, all of us in front of the Winter Palace and we started the march towards Moscow . . . We believed we would get there. Not the people who were with me in the meetings, people who have never achieved what you plan, Nikki . . . Then I woke and I was not outside in the cold but with an army around me, and *belief*. Do I stay and think I can fight, and that one day we might be strong – strong enough to paint a penis on a bridge, for a man to nail his testicles to the road surface, a band play on a cathedral altar, and think the police will tuck their batons in their belts, let us walk past them. Do I? Or run, be an émigrée, and have nothing for pride, and live off the theft from a bank my brother did, have the loneliness of a stranger in another country? Which?'

He used his finger to smear up the last of the egg mixture, then put it in his mouth and sucked it, then licked. She had eaten nothing. He pulled a face, then shrugged. Nikki had no interest in a dream of a rising from the streets; what the proletariat had done a century before was a tedious story. He would accept no blame for what he did . . . She could gaze around their home, all they possessed, as far as their ambition reached: mould on the wall, a faded print of a palace, a couch bed that was functional, a grimy window that overlooked another block, linoleum worn enough to have lost its pattern. In a corner was a piled heap of music books: if she was to play again in the city it would be because the FSB Major gave her permission to, smoothed a way, signed it off . . . Which?

Nikki stretched, yawned, coughed. He wore his underpants and his vest. He handed her the plate, then swung back the bed clothes and crawled off the bed. He reached for her and let his cheek brush against her face.

'You should pack.'

'What do I pack?' Kat felt confidence leeching from her.

'What you need.'

'For how long?'

'Two days or three.'

'Then what?'

'Then things are bought for you.' He was irritated and his forehead had knitted as though questions were unwelcome.

'Tonight, where will we sleep?'

'I don't know. How do I know where you will sleep tonight? Kat, you will not have another chance. You want the gaol or the opportunity . . . Fuck's sake, grow up, Kat.'

'Do I take pictures, photographs . . . our parents, our grandparents, diplomas, birth certificates? You are serious . . .?'

The bathroom door slammed. She heard the dribbling of the shower water, only a few seconds, then the slap of the toilet lid being raised and lodged. She went about her packing . . . Yes, some books, and some photographs – yes, and more clothes than she'd have needed for two days – yes, her framed certificate from the Conservatory, and shoes . . . The rucksack bulged. She had put in two extra sweaters and a sponge bag that could barely close from make-up and washing gear. The toilet flushed and the pipes howled as the water streamed back into the cistern, and the light was growing outside . . . She saw his own rucksack at the end of the bed as she stripped sheets and folded them tidily. Nikki's bag was light in comparison with what she planned to take. Kat was about to open it when he came out of the bathroom. He pulled on yesterday's clothes. Kat was not sure whether he had put on old socks or fresh ones. After he had smoothed the tangle of his hair, and had wiped his spectacles on his shirt front, he opened her bag. Most of the contents were tipped out. She made no protest. The radio was left playing. The outer door was locked and the key pushed back under the door. She crossed the landing in a daze . . . A neighbour, the trolley bus driver, opened his door and spoke cheerfully to her about the prospect of rain and her answer was a grunt.

They walked to her car, and chucked their bags on to the back seat.

Nikki gave instructions. Kat said she knew where they were headed. He said at what time they were to be there, and she said she knew how long it might take. He told her that she should check her mirrors more, and she flashed anger and asked if he wanted to drive. It could have been weeks, months, since they had exchanged as many words as they had that night, that morning. Most of what she had said had been shit. The idea of an uprising, and guys swinging by the neck on ropes hooked up to street lamps, was serious fantasy. But he had no other love in his life. The only item he owned as precious as Kat was his laptop. He had not, before today, seen her frightened.

She gave instructions to him, kicked his ego and insulted him,
but cooked for him and washed and ironed for him, and tried to
control him . . . But he had tipped her on a course of action that
she could only have imagined; she was beyond her grade of
competence and no longer had command . . . Nikki did, knew
what was to happen and how. He had seen her look behind her,
and knew she would have seen his half-empty rucksack. She would
have wondered how far he went with so little. On any other day,
Kat would have quizzed him . . . Not that morning. Thick traffic
obstructed them and they went slowly: she had started to hiss and
fidget beside him, and twice pulled out to overtake, changed her
mind and had been hooted and abused. Aircraft came in over
them for landing at Pulkovo. They were beyond the monuments
and plaques, cleaned and burnished, that marked the desperately
fought lines behind which the city had survived. Then they were
beyond the turning that would have taken her into the estate at
Kupchino where she usually dropped him off. He was happy to be
quiet; his mind was churning.

An Englishman drawled at him, showed him the punishment
and fluttered the promise of a reward. He was the victim of the
Roofer and HookNose and Gorilla, and would damn them for it.

A sudden stop, shrill brakes behind them, and some skinhead
bastard with bare arms in spite of the cold and the thickening rain,
yelling at Kat to 'get the fuck out'. He was aware that there was a
collision behind them, two vehicles or three, and the argument
was fiercer there than around Nikki and Kat, who were responsible. She had almost missed the turn to the supermarket, the
entry slipway camouflaged by advertising boards – for local beers
and a new brand of coffee, and durable nappies. They turned in.

He had been told where to go.

The spaces all around them were empty and the busy trade in
the supermarket had not yet begun, and he wondered about the
length of the fuse and, how many minutes, and the force . . . Nikki
leaned back in his seat and lit a cigarette, first of the day, and they
were well early. The man had said, *I am a man of my word, Nikki,
and it will happen, what you ask for*. Nikki had told him who would

be there, and the agenda for the meeting and had seen the flicker of interest . . . When they talked of *strike back* most of the security companies advocated retaliatory hacking into the computers used by their opponents. A joke. If his was hacked, disabled – or the Roofer's or HookNose's or Gorilla's – then a replacement was available from Computer World or the Key Computer Centre. Pick it up in half an hour, be up and running within two hours, back at work and wriggling the worm by the end of the shift. Nikki said she was going for a yoghurt. He told her not to be long.

He had been promised they would come.

The woman, his target – the bitch – had missed her turning, then had braked her VW Polo.

A pick-up behind her had stopped sharply and had swerved to the side and hit the kerb. Behind the pick-up was a BMW 7 series, glistening black bodywork, and a chauffeur driving. The FSB sergeant – new to surveillance – worried about a lorry steaming past him, had hit the BMW's fender, and had taken out a brake light. Normally, for a minor road traffic accident, the sergeant would have flashed his card and that would have been enough for any other driver to back off, except that the chauffeur drove a senior official from the Regional Governor's office. To admit the shunt was his own fault? Never. Nor would the chauffeur back down. They argued for a full ten minutes, and wrote dockets for each other. The sergeant was uncertain whether the target vehicle had gone down the slipway that led to a supermarket, or had gone on down the highway . . . He had lost it.

Difficult, so early, to get on his radio, explain to the Major a situation in which he – of course – was blameless, and had lost sight of the woman in her old VW Polo. He drove past the slipway, and the BMW disappeared ahead of him, wove among the lanes, and the accident had cost him a full ten minutes, and he sweated.

Toomas watched the 'foreigner' change the tyre.

Only fifteen kilometres beyond Kingisepp, and late – time slipping – and both Kristjan and Martin had claimed to be able to fix it, and had not been able to get the jack to expand or the nuts to loosen. Tempers had flared between them – and he had stepped in. Not aggressive, and without criticism. 'Think I may have handled this model before: always was piss awful.' The jack had gone up and raised the vehicle and the nuts had been rolled into the inverted hub-cap, and the tyre was taken out of the boot . . . all done well and feelings left marginally intact. Toomas noted it, admired what he saw. And had learned.

Why was the 'foreigner' called *Merc*? There had been a poor answer, something about 'always been keen, you know, on Mercedes cars. Can't afford one, but it's the dream . . .' What he had learned had more importance than a name. There had been the girl, calling his mobile when he did his show for the last tourists of the autumn, and the same girl – recognised her voice – coming to the café. He had drunk plenty, but remembered. Told shit, the work was for a company in São Paolo. A lie. This man was no casual freelance . . . His gait was a giveaway – strong, loping. His speech was another – economic, familiar with leadership. The wheel was the game changer – not interfering too early, allowing their frustration to build, then taking over and doing it without pushing Martin's nose, or Kristjan's, in the dirt . . . Toomas thought him a 'special services' operative, not casual labour pulled in by a Brazilian company, which meant if they screwed up, if they were held – then the cover was manageable. He thought the man was British.

Toomas's grandfather was killed by British action. Not beaten to death in the cell below the pavement on Pikk Street by British clubs and rubber truncheons, not electrocuted by British terminals clamped to his testicles, not losing his fingernails because they were dragged out by British pliers. The British had put him there . . . it was documented. The British had recruited his grandfather, then the dates of the landing were leaked by a British traitor to a Soviet intelligence officer. After the death of his grandfather, or Martin's, or Kristjan's, Toomas would never have taken money from a British intelligence officer. The wheel was back on.

What else? Could be the matter of the coat.

His grandfather's memory was worshipped by Toomas and kept alive by the aunt who had hidden, taped to the underside of a drawer, a photograph of a face with light stubble on the cheeks and tousled hair, and an openness and naivete about the eyes and the mouth – then just short of his twentieth birthday . . . Toomas liked to go to Tallinn to the tower block hotel where KGB officers had positioned a listening and observation post and monitored visitors. Their uniforms were kept on clothes shop dummies and the place boasted their power. He also liked to go to the Occupation Museum where they had collected the lightweight weapons used by the Forest Brothers, some with stick magazines and some with a drum holding the bullets. Toomas had tried to get work at both the hotel and in the museum but had been turned down for having insufficient academic qualifications. Often he had imagined the pain meted out to his grandfather, and the terror he would have felt, and wondered how much he could have withstood. Now there was the matter of the coat.

Merc had stepped out of the car and watched their first feeble efforts, then intervened. Had taken off his coat, dropped it on to the back seat, where he had been sitting and where the upholstery was still wet from his clothes. The tyre had been replaced, and he had been cleaning his hands in a puddle. Kristjan had lifted the coat, had passed it to Merc, and Toomas had seen the pistol bulging from the pocket. Just a glimpse but enough time to note that the magazine was snugly fitted . . . Toomas had no firearm, and Kristjan did not, nor Martin. They drove again, picking up speed, and headed towards St Petersburg.

In an old metal sink, with water from a blackened kettle hanging above the kitchen fire, Marika had washed the clothing they had found. Now, she hung it on a wooden frame, made many years before by Igor, and stood it in front of the hearth.

He would not have noticed the scrapes on the bottom of the padlock that fastened the door to the barn. She might not have done if the key, hanging from a string around her neck, had fitted easily into the slot and turned immediately. That morning she had

had to wriggle the key and had examined the padlock's base. His eyesight had deteriorated, hers had stayed sharp. She had seen the scratches . . . had pulled open the door and gone inside. Marika, in her eighty-fourth year, had never shown fear. She had witnessed the killing by the Red Army of her father, accused of harbouring and hiding deserters. And the shooting of Igor's parents by the same detachment, condemned for collaboration with the German forces. She a teenager and he still a child had seen it from where they hid, and in the night had dug the necessary graves: still respected. She had watched her mother die eight years later from depression and total exhaustion, had seen Igor beaten for opposing the cult of collectivisation, an arm broken and an eyeball detached, had taken refuge in the forest's depths when more deportations were ordered in 1960. All that frightened her was the prospect of her dying before him and Igor being unable to care for himself . . . they had been together for sixty-five years. She had entered the barn; the dogs with her, and had noticed that the animals were restless. The dogs had rooted in the straw, had found the clothing. If she had been afraid, she would have gone as fast as old, arthritic limbs permitted, back to the house, demanded that Igor bring his shotgun. She was not afraid.

She had collected a pair of all-weather trousers, socks, underwear, a fleece, and she had found wrapping that smelled of peppermints. The clothing had gone into the bucket, rinsed thoroughly and layers of mud scraped from the material.

Would she tell Pyotr what the dogs had found? Doubtful. A lesson long learned was that trust should never be total. He was due to come that afternoon if his duties in the forest allowed it – hunting the smugglers who floated vodka crates across the river in the inner tubes of tyres. When the clothes had dried she would fold them and lay them carefully inside the barn, out of reach of the inquisitive beasts, and where the chickens would not mess on them.

The rain fell hard on the roof of the farmhouse, rattled and beat on it, and the window-panes ran with water. She thought the stranger would come back, would find his clothing had been cared for.

*   *   *

They reached the outer suburbs of the city.

Merc thought Martin drove well; he was cautious and used his mirror and had kept calm when a police vehicle came up fast on their outside with lights and sirens, but passed them. The road carved through modern industrial estates and behind them were tower blocks, and the monuments to the defence of Leningrad, and bright flowers. Occasionally, painted artillery pieces marked an old front line. Toomas sat beside him using the map on his phone.

He talked. Not flamboyantly but positively. It was a given that the local boy would be there, nervous, and they should calm him. When they arrived at the supermarket, Merc said what they should do.

Martin sat in the car, the engine idling. Toomas and Kristjan were out of the car and 100 metres away, one right and one left, and scanning around them to counter surveillance . . . As he would have done at a Forward Operating Base, or down Route Irish, or planning a supply convoy going beyond Kabul and into the Bagram base. Never loud, but using his finger to jab into the palm of his hand for emphasis. What his signal would be if he decided on a 'fail', an immediate reaction to bug out fast, and how Martin would respond. And the alternative way out of the city avoiding the E-20. He used crisp sentences, and let his words sink in and looked each of them in the face to check their understanding, and they did not question him.

There was always a calm. After the calm came the movement. Pulling out of the lorry park in the armoured Land Rover and starting out on a road monitored by *mujahideen*, leaving the international airport's fortified gate, jumping down from the trucks that carried the detachment as far as the end point of the communications trench that led up to the Hill. He was good at calm, and looked to spread it. Make each of them feel wanted, and give them their tasks. Merc shivered and the cold clamped on his damp body. He had zipped his coat and felt the weight of the pistol hard on his hip. Toomas murmured into Martin's ear, there was a stab on the brakes and they lurched into the slipway.

'It'll be good, guys,' Merc said. Didn't know whether he meant it, or felt it appropriate. Nothing seemed to threaten. Other cars took the same route. Stocking up for the rest of the week, ordinary people and ordinary cars. The supermarket was sheltered behind gaudy hoardings and the parking area was off to the right near to the fuel station.

Merc had seen it, but Kristjan called it.

A VW Polo, correct colour, a small guy inside leaning on the front passenger door and smoking, glancing down at his wrist, and chucking his fag out the window, impatient. A girl was wiping the windscreen. Flags flew horizontally from their poles near the building and it would have been bad to be out. Hanging around, waiting, impatient, not knowing if the rendezvous had gone wrong. Merc factored it all in.

He had his own timetable and would stay with it. Between Merc's feet was the rucksack. Inside it – plastic-wrapped, knotted tight with a supposed waterproof seal – was a laptop, inside the laptop was . . .

Never hurry, one of Merc's sacred rules.

About as stupid a thing as they could have done would have been to drive straight up from the slipway, cross the parking area and pull in neatly alongside the VW Polo. As Merc had planned it, they went to a different corner, close to a store for waste bins, where the trees were shredded of leaves and weeds grew tall. They looked for a tail, for watchers.

Merc would not move until he was ready.

They liked to play the martyr. The Major thought this one – and many like him – preferred to be threatened, then roughed up, left in a corner of a cell with a split lip and a few teeth loosened, and the slop bucket not emptied and abuse from warders, interrogators: martyrs were heroes. Guards were outside the door and a button was underneath the Major's desk. A light would flash; they could intervene within seconds.

The Major despised this man. Already he had created confusion in the mind of the self-styled Leader. No violence, no

psychotropic drugs administered by hypodermic, no screamed
abuse. The man did not yet appreciate the gravity of his situation,
and would have thought himself able to debate – an intellectual
superior confronted by a low-level bureaucrat – and assumed his
opinion had importance.

   They had talked of the President. Of the *siloviki* who surrounded
him, of privilege and corruption and misuse of power. The
Leader, lulled by conversation, had begun to talk in growing
confidence of the 'uprising' that would come, the 'clean broom'
that would follow, the hounding out of the 'current clutch of
criminals'. Any such statement violated the laws of the land, what
the Major had taken an oath to defend . . . 'What happens after
the President?' Fallen under a tram, a heart attack while enjoying
his privileges, a plane crash, assassination by a rival: plenty of
scope for a job vacancy. The Leader was not on a hard-backed
steel-framed chair, but had been sitting on a deep leather-covered
sofa and had sunk back, a heater warming his ankles; the Major
was opposite him, in his office chair, his shoes resting on his desk.
The man flushed out his ideas of counter-revolution, the lynching
of those chucked from power, the confiscation of assets, and the
use of the military – after authority had been wrested from their
officers – to maintain order on the streets. The Major thought the
man disappointing with the truisms of his programme, empty of
ideas and of little value other than as a sacrificial example of state
authority.

   He moved on. The girl . . . Yekaterina. A snort.

   How did her rate her? As a screw? Was she good or bad or
indifferent? Did she know what to do? How was she to be valued
in the world of protest? How much influence did she carry with
others in the group? Again the snort. She was a hanger-on, a
groupie, a lost soul, without importance. She had been brought to
the meeting for him to take to bed, no other reason, like she was a
gift of flowers, or a jar of caviar, or champagne from the south. A
pleasant gesture . . . one night and she'd have been out on her arse,
but he'd have paid her taxi fare . . . It was important for the Major
to have that assessment, but he hid his disappointment.

His phone rang . . . surveillance . . . a target had been lost, his feelings were masked . . . but a target had been found, in a supermarket car-park, and the girl and her brother were there, but nothing had happened. He cut the call. Enough. The Leader condemned himself, would go to a Special Facility for many years, would have ample time to consider how he had been fooled in a small office in the Big House by an hour of politeness and courtesy. He pressed his bell. The man was taken away. The Major regretted that Yekaterina had failed to impress. He wondered why the young woman sat with her brother in a car-park, and who they were meeting: more likely to be a contact of his, from the hacker world. A quiet day had started, he predicted, but that evening he and Julia planned a trip to the cinema, and he had promised to be home early.

After decisions had been taken and boxes ticked, it was easy to lose sight – in a welter of detail – of the original 'mission statement'. Boot tried to lodge in his mind the image of *Hatpin* heaved off the street in Stockholm, dumped in a hotel room chair, and spilling information – like a conveyor belt – of attacks on utilities and government projects and military planning, and the great archives stored by the principal banks. All of it accounted for Boot being up on the ramparts of Toompea Castle and entertaining an American, an air force officer and colonel, who dealt in the murk of cyber defence, perhaps also of cyber attack. Boot paced alongside and listened.

'You have to understand, my friend, that Organised Crime up the road from here, beyond the frontier, is joined at the hip with the state. When the state does not need them the kids are free to filch credit cards, do the frauds. But when the state calls, they come running. They are beholden to the state. It provides protection on a level which offers total immunity from prosecution . . . We're talking hundreds of millions of dollars. We're also talking about criminal conglomerates that employ hundreds of men and women . . . The hackers are the equivalent of the Special Forces units, they're glamorous. Behind them is all the back-up they need. They have people who do their documents, provide passports, researchers looking for vulnerabilities. They put people inside the State Department, your Foreign Office, a principal defence contractor, and they search out weaknesses and email addresses and make friendships. They employ psychiatrists so that the bosses can evaluate the trustworthiness of the people they employ. It makes the Italian mafia groups look small beer. It is a hell of a problem, understatement.'

Old associates had met at a Brussels conference, had stayed in touch. And Boot would not be asked *why* he had travelled, *what* he planned, *when* it would happen.

'How hard to go after them, my friend, is a dilemma. Simple when the tank fires up its engine and starts rolling, bomb the shit out of it: a politician understands that. What about now? The men and women who do the authorisation of counter measures do not possess a cyber mind. They're not blessed with a lexicon including "firewalls" and "airgaps", and they'll want to know the likelihood of "blowback". I meet a political master and I try and read his mind, judge him, then I talk with him in kindergarten language – still I doubt he understands. What I do say is that an unclaimed strike back will lead – as night follows day – to real antagonisms among those paid to supply the "roof". Which would be pleasing.'

Boot assumed the American appreciated that a retaliation was imminent. He could not predict such matters as blowback or collateral. Had rarely done so in operations he had constructed ... nor had the great Duke. Would have slept a few hours through the early morning of that day in mid June, shaken off the tiredness from a night moving between the ball guests, fielding the anguish of the Duchess because her evening was spoilt, reading reports and sending young men forward. Then would have followed them, astride Copenhagen. Would have hoped for clear-cut victory, would not have known how the dice would fall within the next forty-eight hours. Fickle hours ahead, uncertainty and diminishing opportunity to shape events. Boot thought himself a pygmy but believed he walked – in a manner of fashion – with his shoulder close to the spurs on the heels of the Duke's boots, which gave him comfort. Going out into the dawn, not knowing ... He doubted the American air force colonel had heard of Arthur Wellesley, Duke of Wellington, or known the name of his horse. Eccentric, unhinged, or merely using a fine example of leadership as a mentor? He would not have tried to answer the question. He was glad of the conversation, hoped it would enhance his resolve . . . It was launched, for better or worse, and he could not have called it back even had he wished to.

'On the face of it, we are supposedly in a state of peace, but their attacks come in every day. We are the servants of a civilised society. Our citizens expect us to protect them from external aggression. The reality? We are making a poor job of providing it. What is strike back? In our terms, inside legality, it would be to introduce a honeybomb in their gear, done as a malware beacon . . . Is that the end of the world? For them, it's an inconvenience. To have weight, strike back is by definition illegal by all national and international legal forums – a big bang for a big buck – but, my friend, you know that.'

Coming to the end of their walk they saw a patch of lawn where several figures, draped in white overalls, were kneeling, their heads buried, and there was a moment when both men's eyes met and they laughed, and went for coffee.

At the table, the colonel asked the question. 'I have a fair under-standing of the men under my command. I'm not assuming you are in Estonia for health reasons. The classic stuff is putting guys across frontiers. I don't expect either confirmation or denial. The query – *hypothetically* – the ones who do the fancy stuff, what sort are they? Where do they fit in the general scheme of life?'

A pursed mouth, a deepening frown, Boot stirred his coffee. 'Same as me, but younger. Wedded to it. Special Forces mentality, unable to ditch the treadmill. Sad, a little or a lot . . . and, awful. I hope they're awful, and hard . . . awful and forgettable. That's a tough place to be, over there, and the cavalry won't come hurrying to lift them out . . . Disposable, of course. That's my burden. I'm grateful for your time.'

Just beyond the walls and the main gate of the Old City of Tallinn was the line of kiosks where flower sellers traded. Among them

was one on whom fortune had not smiled in recent years. He had
held a position of high responsibility in State Security, had often
received gifts – the best cakes – because his favour was advanta-
geous to many. Not now. Seven days a week, winter and summer,
he managed his stall of blooms; he was up before dawn to collect
produce from the wholesale market and he didn't finish till late. A
call had come . . . He had waited until trade had slackened, then
had slipped from the kiosk, and went where he would not be overheard and called a number located in a room at the back of the
embassy of the former power, and delivered the message. It
seemed to him of limited importance. But he did it, and the old
wounds of the collapse of power remained alive, still hurt . . . *A
British intelligence officer, name unknown, disembarked from the
Stockholm ferry this morning. Recognised as a bag carrier at the '92
Conference on Baltic Mutual Security to Oliver Compton, SIS. Today
had no VIP welcome.*

Merc crossed what he thought of as a no-man's-land. Had a rucksack strap on a shoulder and barely felt the weight of it.

Neither Toomas nor Kristjan had identified surveillance. Merc
could not have judged how practised they would be in that discipline. Martin had the engine running . . . He owed them nothing
and they owed him nothing. It was a financial arrangement.
Money was there to be earned, loyalty was rarely bought and that
was the nature of Merc's business. The parking area was now half
full and more cars came down the slipway.

The girl had finished cleaning the Polo's windscreen. Twice the
boy had left the car to pace around and each time he kicked an
abandoned drink can. His frustration was obvious.

He wondered about the boy's state of mind. Might be in the
'second thoughts' syndrome and needing persuasion. Might want
to back away, clear off, and had brought the girl to stand alongside
him, be his witness. Might wriggle and make excuses, even say –
true or false – that the meeting was cancelled, postponed, a
non-runner . . . And, might have been turned. Might have gone to
a friendly face, a captain or a major in the political police, and

spilled it, and was now the decoy lure . . . Might have done the deal and been the bait that brought Merc to the surface. He walked briskly and checked out the two women who chatted as they loaded a boot with their shopping and did not seem to hurry even though it was raining. Saw a man sitting in a car . . . saw another who had a dog on an expander lead and encouraged it to mess on the grass beside the parking area, and saw Toomas who was to his right, and saw Kristjan to the left, but no signal from them. . . . The boy was aware of him, had stiffened, and chucked down another cigarette that the rain extinguished, and must have called to her because the girl got out of the car.

The boy was short and his clothing hung loosely on thin shoulders. His face was wet and pale and his clothing was thin, inadequate, and his eyes danced right and left and were on Merc, then off him, and they raked the boundaries of the parking area. The girl gazed hard at Merc, her face laced in suspicion. There were two vans parked sixty or seventy metres to the left, and each could have held half a dozen men in body armour and SWAT team gear. Both, silently, challenged him.

'You are Nikki? It's Nikki, yes?'

A nod.

He said, 'I'm Merc. That's what I'm called. They told you I would be here, and I am. And I brought what they said I would bring.'

He let the rucksack slide across his chest . . . The girl glared at him, but his business was not with her.

10

'Good to meet you, Nikki. I'm here as courier, and to help. We have, both of us, to be strong.'

Should not stampede him, but not allow the meeting to drift. The boy blinked at him; might have wondered how deep in he was and where he could find an exit. Always the problem with coercion. The boy looked as if he hadn't slept or washed. Merc knew about coercion. Boot had said that the boy's fingers had been twisted, a tactic which had never bred loyalty.

'The meeting goes ahead this evening?'

A small voice, hard to hear, accented English. 'It does.'

'It is an important meeting?'

'It is.'

'Organised by the crime syndicate, and with FSB attendance?'

'They will be there.'

'It is a big thing we ask of you.'

'Yes.'

'We regard it as important, to send a message.'

'It is important.'

'And I take you out, and afterwards we offer you opportunities . . .'

'My sister comes out.'

A hesitation. 'Hold, on. We have to—'

'What I said, my sister comes.'

No passengers. A basic rule had been set . . . no passengers.

'I don't think that is going to be possible, but . . . well, we could offer consular help, and . . .' Unwilling to refuse, not outright; his mind churned. He could lie, then throw her out of the car . . . She looked defiant, and she might have heard their soft voices, intensity rising, and might have understood.

'My sister was released by FSB last night. She is an activist, she is persecuted. She comes out with me. I look at you. You sleep rough. You stink. Maybe you came across the river. She has no papers. I have, she does not. You take her back the way you came. Yes, or no? We do it or we do not do it.'

She pushed her hair off her forehead then shook her head brusquely and the rain came off in a spray. She was looking hard at him and seemed to Merc to weigh him up, consider what he represented, and whether he mattered to her. Her hands were at her hips and her feet apart and she challenged him. He had to field it. Merc was there to stiffen Nikki, hold his hand as long as possible – damn near walk him through the door . . . Had to be there. The sister had not been part of the equation. He thought they'd have talked it through, gone over it as a negotiating position. He had instructions – no passengers. With no documents, she could not go back over the bridge, through the checkpoints, past the guards and the guns. There would have been an explosion, and a headcount, and a list of participants at the meeting. Would have been an understanding growing, and suspicion building, that the one boy had clocked out early. Had not been at the meeting, was not in the casualty count, had not gone into a bag for transport to the mortuary, and it depended on getting the boy clear. Would have to be through the Kingisepp chokepoint, then on towards Ivangorod and on to the bridge before the understanding and suspicion hardened. What to do? He could not go back into the water, paddle himself across, see Daff, see Boot, tell them 'Sorry and all that but you said I was not to accommodate passengers. He wanted his sister to come, but she's an FSB target and has no documents. I said it was not possible. They called it off. We came home. Sorry.'

'I appreciate, Nikki, these are stressful times for you. You may be looking for, in your eyes, a justification in—'

'A justification for what?'

'Second thoughts. I am sure we can work round this.'

'You think I back away?'

'You'd be entitled to. Do we ask too much? I hope not . . . I have to say, Nikki, the people I work for are unpleasant, they can reach far. Not a threat – but, we are where we are.'

'It is an excuse? I use my sister for that?'

'We are sidetracking. We have much to talk on. The matter of your sister is not for now. The mission is for now.'

'Did you come to lift my determination? Are you like a drink, a pill?'

'Natural, Nikki, when it comes to that moment, on the brink, to stop, think again. Not surprising. We have done the planning, it's all in place. It will happen.'

Was on the point of kicking the business of a passenger far down the road. Promise the world . . . sort the difficulties later. The problems raced in his head, and he hardly heard the response.

'I'm doing it. Of course, I am doing it.'

'That's good, as we hoped.'

'You should not threaten me.'

'There are no threats, only respect.'

'You could have sent it by UBS, by Amazon. You did not have to come.'

'It was to help you get clear.'

The girl watched him, did not react. If he, Nikki, was as good as they said, then he would be rolled up fast and delivered to an outstation of Five or Six or on a quick bus to Cheltenham. They'd feed her up and put some paint on her face and she'd look all right for meeting clients in a Mayfair restaurant and escorting them to the tables . . .

How to get the sister out, no papers? Worry later.

'And her name is?'

'She is Yekaterina, Kat.'

'I will bring her out, and you. End of story and we move on.'

A small flickered smile. 'It is good that we agree.'

'Is she monitored by police surveillance?'

'Sometimes. Probably.'

He could see Toomas had taken a feeble sort of shelter behind some of the supermarket's rubbish containers, and he could twist and make out Kristjan against the trunk of a tree. He looked for a parked car that had the wipers going and a mist on the windows but did not see a tail. The sister seemed not to notice the rain, stood her ground, and her eyes never left his face. Merc said he wanted to see the ground . . . He made a small gesture; that would send the two boys back to Martin. He walked behind Nikki, who took a seat beside her, and Merc had the back and pushed aside food wrappers and old newsprint and a couple of hack magazines from America, Black Hat stuff. He had the rucksack the laptop inside; and she started the engine and Nikki hit a button for rock music. He lowered the window, waved for the boys to follow.

An official was manning the desk for a colleague on leave. The message came from the faint voice of an elderly man, and his speech was distorted. The official worked in the intelligence section of the Russian embassy on Pikk Street, but was not familiar with the caller's identifying codeword . . . all so long ago, and a report to be prepared for the afternoon on a meeting between the Estonian military and an American commander in town for planning. More than enough for him to handle. And the message was vague . . . a British spy of a former era, identified from more than twenty years before and then a 'bag carrier' had arrived in Tallinn by the little used ferry route: name, not known, nor business, no address. But was not dismissed. Never safe to take responsibility for spiking or deleting. The information was filed, went into that great ravenous mouth, and might, one day, be checked out . . . A meeting between Estonians and Americans, hard to crack, took priority.

Messages awaited the Major when he returned to his office.

A tail had been recovered, her car identified. The location where it was parked and her actions, and her brother's, dictated to the sergeant that he should not be close and he had stopped some 200 metres from the target . . . Nothing to report, no seeming purpose for them there . . . The Major had not answered any more calls requesting further direction. He had been in the interview room

with silly little people who thought themselves brave and important and were of negligible value to the next 'revolution', at the
lower end of any activist food chain ... Then the arrival of a
second car. It had parked 100 metres beyond the target. One individual, Caucasian male, mid-thirties, carrying a rucksack, dressed
in creased, dirty clothing. Had seemed to check around him, then
walked to the target vehicle. Had spoken at length with the target
male, animatedly. Two other males had left the second car and
taken positions where they could watch. The woman, the target
female, had then driven her brother and the unidentified male
away, and the second car, at a careful distance, had followed ...
Yes, yes, and what was the difficulty? The Major scrolled down the
screen's messages.

He found the problem. Both vehicles had been lost. How? An
old trick, taught in the basic surveillance courses of FSB in Russia,
of KGB in Minsk, and no doubt at the British camps for recruits,
or at Quantico for the Federal Bureau ... Old, and often successful.
He summoned the sergeant back to the Big House, would speak
with him later. There were a score of other messages awaiting his
attention, and the interview had to be concluded, and the charge
sheet prepared for the self-styled Leader. And he had promised
Julia that he would leave early that night, and not keep her waiting
for him at the cinema.

She drove. Nikki sat in the front.

They spoke in their own language and in quiet voices. Merc
had no comprehension of whether they talked about the price of
vodka, how big the bomb would be, or if it would snow that
evening ... They gave him account of the sights of the outer city,
most of them relating to the siege seventy-five years before, and
different stages of the front line, but kept them short. He had told
her what to do, she had done it – and the boys behind had
responded. No discussion, no questions. From the fast lane
heading for the city to the slow lane and the approach to the
roundabout. All the way around it, and again. Twice round, then
back to the fast lane, weaving, then off the highway.

He could not have said for definite if they were being followed. Seemed a good idea to take precautions. Martin had done well, had not shunted, but had created chaos and the second time round there had been a chorus of screaming brakes and horns but he had not seen a tail vehicle. Never done the course, but Merc had learned the techniques from guys waiting to set off on a convoy or get down Route Irish. Rob and Brad were deep seams of information and Merc was good at listening. He'd told her, and the girl had thrown the little Volkswagen across the lanes and almost seemed to disappear under the front wheels of the big articulated vehicles . . . There might have been a tail and there might not. One of Brad's maxims was: 'We have to be lucky every time, they only have to be lucky once', and it seemed apposite. They'd stopped in a side street and the boys had pulled up behind and Merc had gone to speak to them. Had tried to be relaxed, congratulated Martin on his driving, and he reckoned their debate was how far to follow him, or whether to ditch him. Not much he could do. They moved on.

He'd seen her confidence grow, and she'd splayed out a big smile when they had been a cigarette paper's thickness from scraping a heavy-duty lorry, and on the roundabout she'd squealed, like she had never done it before, not known such anarchic freedom, and Nikki was quiet beside her.

They went through a housing estate, and past the railway tracks and a shunting yard, and into the middle and out of the far side of an industrial park of big warehouses. The rain had slackened, now came back. Suddenly, Merc saw the chain-link fence and the single coil of razor wire topping it, and the gate with the barrier down, and two big men huddled in thick clothing and little of their faces showing behind balaclavas. The building beyond was unremarkable, functional, two storeys high and some of the ground-level windows had steel shutters closed over them, and all the upstairs windows had lights showing but blinds lowered. Merc saw a glass-fronted reception area and glimpsed two blonde girls sitting there, and more security at a side table, and he knew there would be hardware. The far end of the square, beyond the building, was ringed with big towers, maybe ten floors, and topped with antennae and dishes. She went slowly, but did not crawl, and the guys at the gate eyed the car but Nikki had turned his head from them and would not have been identified and they went on another 100 metres, then turned into the forecourt of a Kentucky Fried Chicken place. She sniggered, as if the outlet demonstrated a level of sophistication. She went off to the side and might have been clear of the throw of any cameras.

What had he expected? Pretty much that . . . what he assumed a crime gang would wish for. Anyone cruising more than once past the main entrance would be noticed, and efforts made at identification. They had gone by just the once. Two bays in the parking area, one of which she had chosen, had a view of a corner of the building, not much of one, but something, and of the stained concrete facing of the walls. An ordinary enough place, and Merc reckoned it was about to become a 'significant other' in his life. She didn't have to be told. Haughtily and with a swing of her hips, like they were not worth acknowledging, she led the boys into the pick-up area for fast food. Nikki turned, reached out, and with his thin bony hands clutched at Merc's coat.

'You'll do it, take her out?'

Merc understood. 'I will.'

'Keep her safe?'

'She will be with me. The same chance that I have.'

'And them?'

'Go separately. She is with me.'

He seemed to slump. The questions would have been wracking him. Merc understood. He lifted the rucksack off the floor, opened the drawstring, took out the laptop. He was asked the size of the explosive charge, and gave the answer.

'What will that do?'

'Big damage. Hurt people who are in that area, on that floor.'

Merc did not gild it, nor attempt to counter the resolve . . . They talked about the firing mechanism and how the laptop should be armed, and the countdown. Quiet voices, no melodrama, and no curses about an enemy or about the big gesture, nor of changing a world, and he wondered how great was the anger burning inside. The young man twisted away and the moment passed. Merc watched the exodus from the service counter and could see that Martin was close to the girl, might have been chatting her up and they had paper bags full of food.

A good meal, hot, and he did not know when he would next feed – or would want to.

Boot liked to walk.

Slapping stout shoes on the ground always gave him a sense of belonging. He had made a little programme for himself; no more conversations but simply a swallowing of atmosphere and place. He stood by the statue. A classic figure, Victorian in style but dating from the inter-war years in Tallinn, sited on a fortification hump below the main castle; it had become a symbol in resistance to the Soviet occupation. In fact, the story was from mythology: the widow was Linda, her dead husband was the giant Kalev, founder of the first settlement. During the Occupation, when the KGB had been here in force in Pikk Street, it had been an offence, punished by imprisonment, to lay flowers at Linda's feet and so keep alive the memory of those citizens uprooted and sent east to the labour camps and factories of Siberia. Boot would have said that he came from a society that was flaccid, one with little comprehension of real suffering. He enjoyed the company of monuments. He went down the hill and past a museum and the theme outside the entrance was of suitcases. Concrete ones. Shapes of suitcases with neat handles were laid haphazardly around main door. So many from here had packed their possessions inside a case of leather, or cardboard, had queued submissively, had been put on to trains, squashed into cattle trucks, had either gone to Auschwitz in the west or to the frozen regions of the inner wilderness of the Soviet Union. An image that helped him gain perspective if he were to play the part, moderately successfully, of a Cold War warrior – which once had thawed and had now regained its chill.

The rain had eased.

He was near to the KaPo offices, austere and without flags or fences or armed guards, but he did not call in. Negotiations were better left in Daff's hands – so capable, lost without her, so reliable – and at a low level. Boot was disciplined, could avoid glancing at his wrist, telling himself how long it might be until the meeting in the block inside the Kupchino district convened, and how long until the device, built by the old deafened explosives expert in a forgettable corner of west London, detonated. Time to kill. Had to be there, at the end, went with the responsibility. But the waiting was painful, and Ollie Compton had taught him that tourism was a fair antidote.

If he had not been there, that Thursday afternoon, if the weekend had already beckoned him, he would have been clear of the cemetery in Brussels, off the bus, checked in at the farm where they kept a room for him. The family rejoiced in what they thought of as his excessive eccentricity. He'd have been on his bicycle, kept in a shed at the back of the kitchen, and pedalling on the flat and straight Namur road, cursing the the long-haul lorries, might have been singing or humming, and would have thought himself blessed. Did not matter if it rained or was hot, or if there were ice on the road. He would reach a junction on the route from Charleroi to Liège, where the first action had been – at Ligny – close-quarters fighting. Not for long, but it was his routine; he would stand in a track and gaze out over the fields – ploughed or sown, flourishing or harvested. It was where the Germans had been surprised by Napoleon's army, and 10,000 of them had deserted and run for their lives, and the Duke had been dependent on those who had not fled to stand firm and buy him time. He would have seen the tower where the Emperor had watched developments through his spyglass. Would have heard the explosions of grape and canister . . . Said to have been the 'last honourable war' because a prisoner could be released on giving his word that he would not subsequently rejoin the battle. Fought in midsummer, hot; an almost dried-out stream running through the village of small stone homes, with a church tower good for artillery spotting. Not much water. The bullets of the day required saltpetre and needed their ends bitten off before loading. A residue stayed in the mouth, foul-tasting and parching. Fighting infantry, in summer, needed ten pints of water per day. Very unlikely that he would have met any other visitors, would have been a lone figure, at peace with himself, imagining the speed with which liaison officers charged back towards the Duke's headquarters down the Brussels road to report how the Germans fared . . . He would not hear yet from Daff.

A taxi took him out of the city and on to the bypass linking with the Narva road. Boot asked his driver to wait.

He went through the cemetery gates. Two girls in baggy overalls and beanies operated petrol-driven blowers to force rotting leaves away from the stones. At the far end, facing him, was a massive bronze sculpture. Not about occupation, but liberation . . . Always two sides to an argument, a version of life accepted by Boot. It showed a Red Army trooper, head bowed, his rifle slung over his back. Lodged in a bag on his hip were a red rose and a red carnation, both vivid and alive, and at his feet, beside his combat boots, were vases of new chrysanthemums; he marked the reverence of his people at the sacrifices made in the repelling of the German military. The statue had been placed in a noted square in the city, but the newly independent Estonians, enjoying the tease, had uprooted it and shifted it to this small burial ground, out of the way and out of sight. The reaction had been punitive. The Kremlin had not enjoyed such a gesture. A highly coordinated attack had been launched from Russian territory. Estonia had pretty much closed down for three days. Tanks? No. Air strikes? No. Ground invasion? No . . . A cyber strike. The government in Tallinn had seen its computer systems collapse. Banks had failed to operate. Businesses were left in digital darkness. Boot thought there was a nobility about the statue. Always good to appreciate significances from the past. A year later, Boot knew it well, another Russian cyber blitz had brought the former satellite state of Georgia to a shuddering halt: the tactic worked, was proven. The statue he stared at had a simple grace, understated dignity, and told a cyber truth – a country's functioning gone dark.

He returned to his taxi and asked to be driven to the train station. It would be good to see Daff. Did not look at his watch, but time was slipping and he carried the responsibility for the strike. Like the Duke, Boot believed the faint-hearted deserved little respect. He would need to chalk up a victory. He had thought his time valuably spent.

Sitting by the river, the rain pattering on her shoulders, Daff was silent, chain-smoked. And waited.

Close to her, in thin undergrowth, was a burned-out rocket, the other fireworks used in the diversion had been collected up and taken away. The one that had been missed would be the only reminder of the business she was about. Not much to bloody show for it: the carcass of a firework, a few boot indentations in the mud and, she supposed, if she looked hard, some used matches. Further downstream and nearer to the tank memorial would be more scarred places, his footsteps . . . Ridiculous; she was supposed to be as hard as an old and rusted masonry nail, and she was wrapped in her thoughts, and he dominated them.

She wondered how the time went for him. The water flowed steadily. A patrol boat had gone past and then veered away round the bend, would now be close to the bridge at Narva. Two older men drifted by, their outboards moter switched off, careful to stay on the Estonian side of the river; they had rods out but she'd seen nothing caught.

Her knees were drawn up to her chest and her arms were folded on them, taking the weight of her head, and she remembered conversations in Baghdad and Kabul and Erbil, and it might have been her peculiar ability to draw him out, and others, take them into regions of confidentiality over little cups of Turkish coffee or good Earl Grey tea bags, and sometimes even a glass of beer or a whisky shot. Had fancied him, not ashamed of it. What people did who shared those sort of lives . . . And recalled her questions, his answers.

What happens afterwards? 'Not a job you grow old in. Pack it in someday, switch the phone off. A place in the back end of nowhere

where people can't find you. Light a fire, stoke it up, just sit and let it all drain away. Hope someone's there who understands it.'

Doing what? 'Might do van deliveries in the winter, then take folks out hiking in the mountains, up north of Brecon, in the spring and summer. Nothing carrying responsibility.'

Who'll share that, understand it? 'God knows – someone with a skin thicker than most. You do this, are a Gun for Hire, and you get on the treadmill, but it's always going faster, never slower and making it easier to jump clear. Don't know how to find somebody who can think that way.'

But you have to want to pack the life in – sure you do? 'All I know is this sort of soldiering – doing the mercenary, telling myself it's not about being a crusader but it's for the money. Can't be escaped from. Mix with guys now – and you, Daff – like Brad and Rob, and they're good to talk with, and other guys on the convoys. Go back to UK and nobody knows what it's about. Why I'd have to lock myself away.'

What's the dream, when the 'sometime' comes? 'Have a bit of money stashed. Get a home that isn't just a barracks room, get down to the dealer, select the Mercedes. A C-Class Coupé or an E-Class Cabriole. Ride the lanes, hear its throb. Not to make the world a better place, but to drive a big car, have that power.'

I can hide, when I do anything that's over the edge, Merc, behind the symbol of the Crown and the State and the 'duty stuff', and you kill and with the greatest efficiency, and you take the cash, pocket it – how does that feel? 'I have to take you on trust, have to believe what I'm told. It's not the old defence of obeying orders because nobody gives me commands. End of the day, Daff, that's what I am – empty, hollow, and want to be something different and don't know how to start out on that. Who'd want me, Daff? God, I have the feeling I'm talking and no one has stayed behind to listen, the drunk in the closed bar and the cleaner working round his feet. It's hard, Daff. Bad and hard. You still awake? Who'd want me?'

He'd get that far, a deep breath, then gulp the last of the beer, and the mood would change.

'Good talk, Daff, hope I didn't bore the arse off you. Time I went to bed. Goodnight and all that, and thanks for listening. Another day tomorrow . . .'

She did not really know in the half dozen times, could have been more, that it had been acted out, what else she could have done other than . . . A hotel bar, a café in a new shopping mall, in a secure compound, and could have stood with him and damn near taken the shirt off his back and gone down his chest and let her fingernails rake his skin and tease the old scar tissue from where they'd plucked out shrapnel, and march him to the elevator. Get the bloody key off him and open the door, and maybe use an unarmed restraint to stop him wriggling clear. If he did free himself, there would be that soft slow smile and a duck of the head and the door would have closed in her face. If he didn't break away, and she was able to get him into his room – which would be a tip and heaps of gear scattered about, and probably ordnance among it, and likely she'd damn near stub a toe on a grenade – and get him on the bed, and get his trousers off and all the rest, and what she wore, then – nothing much. Like it had been, her belief, in the room of the apartment on Igor Gramov, and her hugging his back. Tight as a pulled string knot he would have been . . . Not for want of bloody trying for Daff – not for lack of hoping. Nobody who did not live the life, theirs, would understand. She supposed herself to be fixated, did not care. Supposed herself, also, to be unprofessional.

She doubted she'd change, and doubted he would. The rest of the usual big river flotsam and the fishermen with their drifting boat were long gone and the rain might have slackened but the cloud was heavy and low and the darkness would soon be shrouding them. She hadn't meant to stay at the river so long, she should get back to the apartment and make it more habitable for when Boot arrived. But she did not get to her feet, go back to the hire car that would have the surveillance guys parked in behind it.

It seemed colder, and there was sleet in the air. She stayed where she was, heard the river and watched it, and could see the failing outline of trees on the far side and a watch-tower stark against the cloud line . . . and might say a prayer. And time drifted.

They came in an unpredictable stream to the compound in the Kupchino district.

Twins, fifteen-year-old boys, were brought by their mother in a polished Audi wagon from the far side of the city and were already entered in an FSB-sponsored centre of education excellence. Both had growing reputations for original thought and aptitude.

A boy, tall and gangling as a high jump athlete, but with bent shoulders and a concave chest, was dropped by taxi, looked around him and seemed to grimace at the building, spat into a puddle, and hurried through the gate.

Another, just a week past his twentieth birthday, had come on a bus from the railway station, and wore jeans slashed at the knees – not decoratively, but through age and wear – and was said to be the 'best on the block', and to have three GangMasters courting him.

A short, squat boy who had a straggling beard and was not old enough to have thickened it, arrived in a Porsche sports model, and lifted out two laptop bags. He'd driven himself and when he stopped and climbed out, a girl manoeuvred herself from the passenger seat to the driver's and the guards at the gate gawped at what they saw at the top of her legs, and she was a trophy – as much as the car. She slammed the car door after giving them the finger.

Another, in his early twenties, was brought by his father, dressed flashily in a shiny suit, and might have managed this prodigy in the skills of vulnerabilities, zero days, traps and Trojans, and negotiated rates for him, percentages. He had the nervous look of a man in a higher league than was comfortable.

And the Roofer came, and Gorilla with him, and HookNose followed them inside.

A further half dozen went past the barrier and into Reception and were ogled by the girls; these boys, even the twins, would have been fancied more by the blondes, as meal tickets – forgetting the

smells and the 'peculiarities' and the obsessions – than even the
footballers on the books of Zenit St Petersburg. They were the
best and the brightest, the cream of their trade, and some had
quality education provided by the state, and others were self-
taught, and some were minutely supervised from the 'academy' of
8th Main Directorate of FSB, and two of them worked only for
the highest bidder, and some were the script-kids of the principal
gangs and had no formal education but came alive only when
their fingers danced on a keyboard. None yet approached the
status of Evgeniy Bogachev, on a Most Wanted list issued by the
Federal Bureau of Investigation in faraway America for whom – if
information leading to his arrest was lodged – a $3 million reward
would be paid, or lesser figures for whom the recompense would
be a tidily wrapped $1 million. All were protected . . . Last came
two sleek black German saloons which carried the men who would
task the group.

Inside Reception, the girls ticked them off . . . Only one name
remained unaccounted for. But there was still time, and the coffee
break continued and he was not yet abusing the schedule.

'So, what do we do?' asked Kristjan.

A shrug from Martin. 'Just sit, just wait.'

From Toomas, 'What else?'

'You have any imagination? You want to know who these people
are?'

Toomas blinked at him, but could barely see the face behind
him in the darkening car. 'You talk shit, Kristjan – always did.'

Martin, more reflective, asked him, 'What are you saying to us?'

They were parked close to the little Polo. Its windows were
steamed up and it was hard to distinguish the girl from her brother,
and the man behind them. None seemed to be talking, but cigarettes were lit. It seemed impossible to Kristjan that any of them
in the Polo could have shut their eyes, leaned back, nodded and
slept, even dozed. Impossible. His grandmother had been taken
across the bridge at Narva, pregnant and bulging. Would have
followed the same route as his grandfather, on a truck floor,

bleeding and semi-conscious and ready to 'disappear'. His mother had been born in a camp and years later mother and daughter had been allowed back and were resettled in the town, and she had married a peasant from Kazakhstan who was placed there, and that was a fair option as it gave a roof over the woman's head, and food on the table, and a beating if the man were drunk, and the streets were the territory of the militia and KGB. It was where Kristjan had been raised. The town – Russian-speaking and Russian-built and Russian culture – had captured him. Occasional visits out, and one journey far to the west had brought him to Haapsalu. He had made contact with Martin and a bond was forged. Enough to take him to Kaliningrad with them, but afterwards he had returned to Narva, and had struggled and had existed, stunted. Anyone raised in Narva appreciated the KGB's control and their reach.

'They are criminals. They survive because of their links.'

Martin said, 'They have links with KGB, whatever it is called now, but the same people. We know it.'

Toomas said, 'I know the power of KGB, everybody knows.'

Kristjan slapped the back of Toomas's seat. 'Imagine it. The thing goes early, a bomb – what it is they take inside. The kid, the little rat, is running out. They go to a state of emergency, they seal the roads. You think they are not efficient? What happens when there are blocks on all the roads, and the heaviest blocks are towards the frontier, what is for us? I have imagination ... Do you, either of you?'

A silence in the car. All of them looking into the Polo, seeing the glow of cigarettes through the mist on the windows. Kristjan leading and the others beginning to follow, no stomach for argument.

Three men of middle age, and the last time their courage had been tested was fifteen years before, in the enclave of Kaliningrad, and they had fled, crashing through a border fence. One was a house painter, one wore fancy-dress armour for tourists' selfies, and one kept the shelves full in a supermarket. Persuasive talk from a woman, her smiling confidence dripping on them in a café, and none had – then – dared to throw it back in her face. In the lay-by on the E-20, Martin had been close to gunning the engine, swinging back on to the road, doing a sharp U-turn and heading back towards the check at Ivangorod. A temptation, an apple on a plate, a chocolate on a table. Kristjan thought he shared out the fear and all three in equal parts could imagine a security man's fist clutching their collars and dragging them out, one by one, and kicks, blows, steep steps to fall down, and cell doors slamming, and camps where the ground never thawed. Easy to imagine.

'What to do?' From Toomas.

'We owe them nothing,' Kristjan said. 'Nothing.'

'Should we talk to them?' Hesitancy from Martin.

'He would kill us. He has a firearm, we do not . . . You see his eyes? A killer's eyes. He smiles often, and acts like a friend. He cannot hide his eyes, those of a man who kills.'

'And he is British and they lied to us.'

'And, long ago, they betrayed our grandfathers, murdered them.'

Kristjan said, 'Just slip away. Be through the road-block at Kingisepp . . . We have no debt to them.'

Kristjan thought her pretty, and thought her brother vermin, and thought the eyes of the man who had been sent to instruct and guide them were without love or fear, or feeling. The sounds of their breathing, and stress in the whistle of air between their teeth, then the single click as Martin turned the ignition key.

Kristjan said, 'We were paid to drive and protect him. We have done that. He has another car . . . we have no blame.'

Toomas coughed.

Kristjan shouted, 'Get the hell out and go.'

Martin did it fast, and none of them looked back at the Polo. They went out of the Kentucky Fried Chicken car-park and headed for the slip road that would get them back on to the highway.

Nothing said, nothing to say.

The tail lights moved away and were engulfed. All of them knew. Did it make any difference? Merc thought it an added problem, but not terminal . . . Any survivor from where he had been would not rate it a difficulty beyond handling. They were supposed to do cool driving, talk easily at a block in the road, and give them protection if a crowd came be there, calm and ready. Just back-up, but essential: local knowledge, culture, street-wise.

What did they know? Enough. Could go to the nearest police station, dial the local emergency number, stop a cop and shout something at him and then head for the safety of the bridge. And the deniability factor? Nothing Merc could do . . . He thought he understood what was expected of him . . . He had no need to be there, had expected to twist arms, apply pressure, but there was no need.

'What do you call that?' She had turned to face him.

'What you want to hear, or what I feel?'

'Are they different?'

'Them bugging out on us makes for a difficulty but no more.'

'Or what you feel?'

'A bit less than a shit storm, and less than a train wreck.'

'We go on?'

Not Merc's call. Could not answer her. The boy stayed quiet. Twenty minutes earlier, when she had gone to the facilities, he had used the time to go over the trigger and the timing of the inbuilt clock and the size of the charge, and what it could do in confined space, and he and Nikki had had the laptop opened and the switch identified, done it all again. One thing the boy had asked had confused Merc – little usually did, but this had. 'Do you know about the Wolf's Lair?' He did not. Was it a cave, somewhere in a forest, a place among crevices of rock? He had seen a half smile on Nikki's face, then it had been wiped . . . He thought he understood. *Thought.* Was not certain. The boy looked at his watch, then reached out. Merc clasped the smooth body of the laptop, lifted it, passed it over.

There could have been semantics, a word Daff had used: was he now party to an 'act of war' in handing over the device, or merely indulging in 'justifiable self-defence against an aggressor'? Not Merc's business . . . he was one of those happily simple

people, she had said, who concentrated on carrying out his
mission, and surviving. Nikki's hands shook and Merc thought
the laptop might fall from his grip. The laptop disappeared from
sight, swallowed inside Nikki's bag. Nikki gazed into his face.

'And you will take her?'

'I will take her,' Merc answered.

'Thank you.'

'For nothing. We'll wait for you.'

'Do that, wait for me.'

A car was powering into the parking area and the headlights
ground into the windscreen, and Nikki's face was lit and seemed a
pocked mess from the rain-water, and a light smile briefly flickered. How should he have been? Taut, tense, biting savagely on his
lip, or calm? Just a touch of hands, not an aggressive slap of the
palms. Nikki took the girl's hand and held it tightly. More cars
came and more lights speared them and seemed to emphasise
their vulnerability. Merc would not hurry them.

A final glance at his watch. Her hand was freed. The light
flooded in on them as Nikki opened the door, and kicked out his
legs as if accepting that the time for messing around was over. He
stood outside the car. There were no goodbyes, no waves to him,
no blown kisses to her.

The door closed after him. Using his sleeve, Merc wiped his
window, cleared the misted glass. He saw the boy break into a
loping jog, like a kid who was late for a class. He had a good stride,
and the rucksack bounced loosely against his back. Merc had the
weight of the pistol in his pocket and gulped some air, then groped
for the door handle and climbed out of the car and stretched. He
could see the top corner of the building, a dark shape angled
against the cloud. Usually Merc thought himself better than
average at choosing something pithy to say when a crisis loomed
– and had nothing.

He looked around and saw motorists eating in their cars and
people hurrying to and from the service counter. Ordinary
enough. Beyond the parking area, the main artery road crawled.
He would gladly, at that moment, have exchanged this place for

Hill 425, and taken the incoming fire and men charging the wire, for sitting in the Polo beside a girl and knowing that her brother carried a bomb into a crowded room . . . what he had been ordered to facilitate. He felt the wind on his face and the spit of sleet, and did not know if he was cursed.

Merc climbed into the front passenger seat. Another car manoeuvred and its lights played on Kat's face and he thought the glisten on her skin might have been tears. The car stopped beside them and kids piled out, laughing, shouting, and ran towards the counter; he supposed them now to be his enemy, and he wondered where Boot was and why the big men were never there. She took his hand and held it in a fierce grip.

She said, 'How long do you think he'll be?'

I I

Merc stayed silent and she did not ask again, but held his hand.

More customers now thronged at the fast food counter, and some were singing and some were drunk and some carried big radios turned up loud, and some were hurrying to get home from a day's work. The pressure of her hand did not slacken. He had the window on his side lowered by an inch and cold air flushed through the interior and some of the damp that came from the sleet. He needed it open so that he would hear shots, or explosions or ambulance and police sirens. Any of them would tell him, and her, that the boy was blown out, arrested or killed, or was running, or that the rucksack had been searched and the building was being cleared. 'Ordinary' people flowed around the Polo and none had a sense of threat.

She did not look at him, did not sniff back tears, but they ran on her cheeks. It was the burden Merc carried – amorality, a justification. There had been a 'good old boy' in Baghdad. Once of the Welsh Guards, probably busted out for persistent infringement of regulations, and he might have thought the young – green – Merc needed to get the compartments of his life better screwed down. Had sleeves of tattoos on his arms, and angry spots on his chest from steroids, and an overweight jowl, bad teeth, and a bulging gut, and could get sentimental – with a can in his hand – about childhood in Merthyr Tydfil. Where the rugby team played every day and the male choir sang every evening and the pubs never closed. He'd told Merc: 'You do your job. Others may take a packet, get hurt. Don't let it be you. Leave your conscience behind, under the bed, and forget it. Don't expect to be loved by those with you. And, who is the friend of the sniper? Nobody – that's today. Up the valley where I come from there would have been longbow men, archers. If they were caught they'd have their finger sliced off to show they were useless and couldn't draw a bowstring, and a slit throat would follow. Just as snipers never go into the usual POW cage but end up in a ditch, mutilated. And nobody loves you, young 'un. There's not the protection of the regulars. Better money but hung out to dry if it goes sour. And they ask you to do the dirty jobs, and they try to keep their own hands clean, and you'll be deniable, a firewall between them and you. They're big men who do the tasking, and they'd call themselves honourable men, but they spend their time looking for people who'll go down into the sewer. No morality involved. Chuck it, along with the conscience . . . And don't think, afterwards, you'll be able to walk into your local bar and be the same as those who never left the town. You're different, set apart, and it's what you carry. None of them have been where you have, tossing lives around, taking money for it, and without the shelter of military orders. You know who the lucky bastards are? The pilots. Steam along and chuck out a bomb and not see where it lands, who falls on it, what the collateral is, and go back and have a jar in the mess. You're up close, and its personal for you, which is where the big men want you. No medals on offer, and no hearse leaving Brize with the Legion lowering standards for it. That's the life, and you get on with it, and you don't feel sorry for yourself. And you then go off, quit, and sell retread tyres. Apologies if I've bored you, young 'un.' He had lasted six more weeks then had been blown up, a roadside bomb, the Nahiyet al-Rasheed district, usually regarded as safe, and had gone home in a box.

He did not twitch, or shift his hand, did not disturb the hold she had on him.

'And you don't know?'

'Sorry, but I don't know how long.'

'He'll arm it, and he'll run.'

'Not for me to call. He does it his own way. You have to be ready.'

'Because they quit on you?'

'Because they quit on me, on us . . . I don't pass around judgements. I thought they'd stay, they did not. End of story . . . You will drive. It'll be good.'

It was what Merc was supposed to do well, that flutter of a smile, only it was dark and she would not have to read his voice and would not have known if his expression was sincere, encouraging, or phoney. He remembered how he had bawled out the girl in the trench, with the tucked-up ebony hair and the wasp waist pinioned under the webbing belt and the bulge below the flak vest, and the look of contempt she had given him, and about saving her head from disintegrating when a sniper fired . . . He squeezed the hand, and he could see the corner of the roof of the building.

'Because they were frightened?'

Merc said grimly, 'We should not have had them on the show. A mistake. We move on. You'll be fine.'

'How do we get across?'

'I don't know. Honest. One step at a time.'

He would have liked to have had the banter of the 'good old boy' with him, who took pills that wrecked his body, and drank in excess, and never showed fear . . . Could have told her the old Special Forces saying: *The only easy day is yesterday.* She was close to him and he felt her warmth, and did not want to talk. He wondered what Wolf's Lair was. Did not ask.

He tried to imagine how it would be. Could not see Nikki, could not picture where he would be and who stood or sat close to him and where the rucksack was, whether he'd already taken the laptop out of it, if he had already fired the trigger. Merc considered whether the twin strands of information he had been given by Boot – weight of the explosive contained and its quality and therefore its effectiveness, *and* the length of time between firing the trigger and detonation – was true or false. Whether he himself was trusted to lie, or was fair game for deceit. Considered it. Merc surprised himself, felt no outrage, and had preached the message of Mushroom Management. He held her hand, and the tears came on stronger. As the Gun for Hire, Merc knew his place. Nothing he could say. He had barged into their lives, made an empty statement about taking her out and across the river, and did not know how it would be done, and might not have cared.

The corner of the building became more indistinct as the sleet grew heavier, and a little of it settled and the vehicles coming in and out left confused tramlines, and what he saw told him nothing.

'You are the best, why we have brought you together.'

It would have been unlikely, in Nikki's opinion, that the GangMaster had any idea of what they did, how they achieved it. They were upstairs, scattered around a long table and a cobweb mess of wires ran from wall plugs and adaptors around their chairs and then up on to the surface and were already hooked into their laptops: except that Nikki had two of them and one remained in his rucksack, down by his feet.

'All of you are highly recommended, and are expert in what we want of you.'

The GangMaster stood. There was an annex at the end of the room behind him, and an open door, and Nikki had spotted three men in there, smartly turned out, keeping out of sight. He supposed they'd have colonel's rank, maybe one was a full briga-dier. The GangMaster would have made his way up from the gutter by the ruthless wastage of opposition, and now had reached a pinnacle. He would have had little experience in speaking to an audience, and made a poor job of it; seemed to sweat, gazed down at his shoes. None of them would have been fooled by him. He would not comprehend the world of malware, covert intrusion into supposed secure computing systems. But one amongst them would have been his trusted eyes and his ears . . . Could have been HookNose, might have been Gorilla, and along the table was the Roofer: one of them would inform on moods, indiscretions, confi-dences, grumbles, and would be rewarded. Not Nikki. He had never been singled out for recruitment to informer . . . Because his sister was an anti-régime activist.

'Each of you will be given a separate task for execution tomorrow and over the weekend. It is a matter of importance to the State. I remind you, all of you, that the State can be a generous protector to us all – can be a brutal enemy if our actions fall below standards required in the national interest.'

He had no love for any of them. Nikki could not recall that any among them round the table had shown him kindness, had offered friendship. He was remote, alone: some had sneered at him, some had shown contempt, some had refused him respect . . . He did not consider whether he had offered them what had been denied him.

'Confidentiality is paramount. Our country is under siege and we have the right to defend ourselves. To fall short of the faith placed in you, would be stupid, and dangerous.'

He talked shit. The twins sat opposite him would not have heard; they had earpieces inserted and their machines were powered up and they were playing a game and were not repri-manded, and their mother was waiting in a room below. He had been late, the last to arrive, and he had seen cold anger on the GangMaster's features, and had been ignored by HookNose and Gorilla, but the Roofer had peered at him – as if uncertain. Who would be late for such a call, who would dare, and why? He was reassured to have the weight of the rucksack against his ankles, felt calm. He had browsed for it, the events of that early afternoon at the Wolf's Lair, a summer's day in late July, seventy-four years ago, had recognised the lessons. On his own computer, the screen-save image was of his sister . . . a decent picture and her hair smart and her smile wide and she had been at the Conservatory, the world at her feet; but she had tripped, stumbled, joined the bastards who had contaminated her. He was not on her phone. He had checked. She did not carry a picture of him. He stared across the table at the twins, had no quarrel with them, nor with any of the other strangers who lounged in their chairs. Some yawned and some had their eyes closed, and HookNose had belched loudly . . . like it was important for them to demonstrate their freedom from the apparatus that employed, protected, them. Big egos, big vani-ties, but they all needed their roof to be in place. Only he was free. Nikki did not belch, yawn, play bored, was calm, because he had read the detail, learned what it taught.

'We have a break – a piss, a coffee, some small food. Then we allocate work.'

The GangMaster turned away, and went to the open door behind him. Chairs scraped back. All of them were preening peacocks, craving status – not Nikki, had gone past that era of life. Only the twins stayed at the table. A girl had come in, a bold smile, and had started to work the coffee machine and had brought in open sandwiches on a trolley. Nikki could smell the bodies around him, and they might have smelled his; he had showered but not changed his clothing. A sign of the script-kids' conceit that they were unconcerned about appearance, hygiene, were too important for convention. All were addicted to the excitement of the 'break in', and some had started to smoke and there were no ashtrays but there was the floor. The windows were closed and the smoke hung and the blinds were down, and the blast would be contained . . . if the device fired. It was a matter that he must take on trust: that it had been prepared by experts, and that the confidence of the young man who had brought it was justified. The girl acknowledged him, the only one. She handed him a mug of black coffee, and he noted that his hand was steady when he took it from her. She did not smell like the rest of them, but nice – a scent from abroad. He hoped, later, she would have gone home, or at worst been far from the room.

All the time he watched over the rucksack under his chair, as if guarding it.

Not talking, nothing to talk about.

Not proud, nothing to be proud of. Not justifying, because none of them inside the car offered criticism. Not blaming, because the decision had been taken by all of them. Not thinking of decorating the interior walls of a block of flats, or pretending to be a Teutonic knight in the castle above the Old City, or of loading the shelves of the aisles. Their minds were all locked on the image of the darkened VW Polo left behind, of a girl behind the wheel and a man beside her – and no explanation offered.

Martin drove. Toomas was beside him, Kristjan behind them. Not feeling safe; the chokepoint at Kingisepp could not be avoided.

For want of an explanation, as a gas station loomed, Martin pointed to the dial. There might have been enough in the tank to get them back to Ivangorod, the bridge, and into Narva, but it was reasonable to be safe in case the dial was faulty. Not questioned, his decision to turn off the E-20 and go into the gas station. The traffic had been heavy when they had left St Petersburg and they might only have been a quarter of the way, but the road was now clearing and soon would be fast and straight and clear. The bridge, where a white-line marked the centre point, the frontier, was no more than an hour away.

Time for them to go to bed. The dogs had been out and were now settled by the dying fire. The wood was damp and spat but they didn't mind it.

They had made one last journey outside, had gone to the barn, Marika carrying the clothing, washed, dried, pressed with an iron that heated before the fire. Carrying the shotgun, Igor had followed her. She had said he was as stupid as a sheep because his sight had almost failed and he was quite likely to hit her, or one of the dogs – or himself – if he had tried to fire at an intruder. Normally she would have been grateful if Pyotr had found the time to call and to visit. They needed more logs brought in, and more pine rings split. He had not come. It made Igor happy to sit with Pyotr and talk, talk of the evils of the armies that had come through the forest. Might have been yesterday, or the day before yesterday, but not three-quarters of a century before. Any other day she would have welcomed him, wrapped her arms around him, smacked a kiss on his cheek. He had not come and she was thankful. It was difficult to silence Igor when there were matters best left unsaid, like the sodden clothing left in the barn.

The animals had stayed quiet. Pyotr said it was because of his failing eyesight that Igor retained better hearing than most men of his age, certainly better than hers. She had found where the man had slept, loosely covered with straw; yet the beasts had stayed quiet, and the dogs in the house, and Igor had heard nothing.

She understood the habits of animals better than she knew the ways of men or women, appreciated their suspicions. Yet a man had come amongst them, had slept there, had not worried them. Igor would have told Pyotr and Pyotr served part-time in the militia. She was pleased he had not come, did not know. It was obvious to her that the stranger fought the authority which had devastated her life, and Igor's. Not a criminal but an enemy of the authority.

Time for bed. She had warmed Igor with a bowl of the broth she had prepared – it had meat in it, and small dumplings. She expected the man to return because clothes had been left and they were near the river . . . Few tried to cross there, it was dangerous. Marika would cuddle Igor, and a little of the heat of his bony body would take the chill off her.

Owls called, but the animals in the barn were quiet.

She responded to the gentle knock on the door.

The Maid pushed away her plastic plate, a chilli dish from the canteen's take-out stock . . . Not supposed to bring food into offices, nearly as much of a capital offence as smoking. The door opened. Did he fancy her? Perhaps . . . Was his concern for the mission, Copenhagen, genuine? Perhaps . . . Was he a lonely old thing, denied the pleasure of the chase? Probably. The Big Boss would have been one of a generation of young lions beating a trail of covert mayhem across the outer Soviet empire under the tutelage of the veteran Ollie Compton, a few years ahead of Boot. His inner office staff, with the exception of a duty aide – young, bright, ambitious, and outside the loop – would have gone home, but he hung about.

'Not very good at this, never have been.' Almost an apology.

'Few of us are, Director,' she answered.

'At the waiting. Nothing through?'

'I don't have anything.'

'Nothing?'

'Not anything.'

Always correct. Could have fancied her, or could have fancied company, and was too lofty to go to the building's small bar where his presence would have shut down the exchanges of gossip, flirtations, complaints, rants. Boot, had he been there, would have pulled out a bottle of Scotch. She could have done, but would not. He grimaced, frowned, looked to her for reassurance.

'Forgive me asking, Marian, but is it quite a big bang?'

'No, Director, not very – just a bit more than a gesture.' Her sweet smile.

He said, 'I thought it, when Boot came to me, what we had to do, take action. Can't just scatter ordnance, if you know what I mean. Block and degrade their laptops. Ought to be on the ground, inflicting pain, drawing blood. Has to be done. The message they understand. Believe it, yes. He never gave me all the detail . . . Would have thought it better I stayed in ignorance, able to plead that defence if it fails – take the full rap himself. Why he's such a bloody good man. I don't know the innards of it, or the schedule.'

The Maid answered him coolly. 'You'll be told, as soon as there is something to tell.'

He left. She went back to the chilli dish on the plastic plate. She doubted she would sleep, any of them who were involved. A dark night ahead, and a long one, and nothing certain by the dawn.

'Evening, Dessie. Off home?' Arthur watched as the security card, the identification for the Director's personal chauffeur, was slotted into the machine and the gate blinked green.

'He's not going anywhere.'

Roy spoke out of the side of his mouth as he scanned the traffic, and his finger nestled against the trigger guard of his weapon. 'Second night in a row that he's slept in. Right?'

Dessie had only to get to Raynes Park, down a line from Waterloo. A crisp wave and he was off. They had another fifteen minutes then would check their firearms and be off home themselves.

Arthur said, 'Better believe it, going to happen, and tonight, and be a bit of an earthquake. What odds would I get? What you reckon?'

'Could refine it,' Roy said. 'Because Boot's still gone, and the totty, and they're where it's cold and the bollocks jangle.'

Another small surge was coming into the security area, a few from Middle East, some from Personnel and HR, and one or two from Archive. All passed through, all normal. Arthur reflected that he had never been in a place of confirmed danger, never fired his weapon for real, didn't know how he'd be. Sort of shivered, and the barrel tip, where the foresight was, quivered. Be a rough old night for someone, someone far from VBX's gate, quiet as a bloody grave here – thank the good Lord – but not for some poor beggar behind the lines.

Not an attack, but an exercise. It was explained.

Nikki bent, pulled loose the draw-string on his rucksack. The implication as he understood it, was that all of them would have been rounded up, put into lorries, then shipped into a defended military compound if it were an act of cyber war rather than an exercise. He groped with his fingers. He had practised twice during the coffee and comfort stop, but they were back at their seats, and the twins had returned to their games but played with less enthusiasm and listened.

When he had surfed on it, he'd read that the colonel – one eye and one arm and decorated, beyond suspicion and with the freedom of the Wolf's Lair – had had difficulty arming it, had had to shut himself inside a toilet. This device, the man had said, and had shown him, was simple, just pressure on a button. He had asked, 'Irreversible?' A shrug, not an answer . . . and 'The timing, exact? To the minute?' Another shrug, another grimace and the implication that nothing in a wonderful world was without a factor of error, and a murmur for an answer, 'Give yourself space, that good enough?' Good enough. Nikki had liked the man, had believed enough in him to have given him his sister.

One of the 'suits' from the annex spoke. The GangMaster had fixed an eye on Nikki as if fiddling on the floor with his rucksack showed lack of respect, but he had carried on, had needed to open the laptop enough for his fingers to reach the button between the keyboard and the screen's hinge. They were told that at any time, without provocation, no warning, a strike could be launched against their country. Many government agencies worked at great capacity to discover when such an aggression might come . . . A pre-emptive nuclear strike could not be countenanced, not 'first use'. Defence planners believed in an alternative. He ignored the glowering stare of the GangMaster and his finger rested on the button, and in the effort his face was on the table, his cheek against its surface, and he heard the hiss of annoyance, as if he was insulting the speaker.

A button the size of a fingernail. He pressed it.

No reason for Nikki to peer into the rucksack, look for a glowing light, feel a vibration, hear a connection run like water in an emptied pipe. There would be no indication that he had triggered it. He straightened, ducked his head as if in apology. Stupid . . . when, if ever, did a script-kid apologise? Regret? Not in the fucking vocabulary of the Black Hat high performers. The spots on his chin itched, should have taken his medication but had forgotten. He scratched, might have drawn blood . . . Four different pods and each would be assigned a different task: utilities, food distribution, Defence Ministry communications, banks and benefit payments. Just an exercise . . . Justified.

Nikki saw a clock. Hands moving. Could have been the one in the flat where his mother had lived after his father's death. Another was in the classroom for computer sciences where he had starred, and one at the university where he had been for a year, a solitary one: unwanted and uncared for and when he had walked out it was probably not noticed. And the GangMaster, standing across the table from him in his shirtsleeves, displayed a Breitling on his wrist. All the clocks in his life were working, the hands moving.

How far would they go? A question mumbled from the tall boy, hard to hear and he was made to repeat it. 'Not show out, that far.' Withdraw or leave it in place? From the smart kid who wore the casuals that would have come from the French-stocked shop in the Galeria Mall, and there had been a Porsche parked outside and a girl asleep in the driving seat. 'Best if – no show out – it stays in place in case an aggression is mounted by them, and is present and can be activated as retaliation.' Put in place it had the potential to disrupt or the potential to destroy, what level was wanted? A high, squeaky voice from the boy brought by his father who sat in an ante-room off the ground-floor lobby, with the twins' mother. 'A maximum effect, darkening, closing down.'

Where were the targets?

The rucksack was snug against Nikki's leg. The lesson, as he had learned it from the Wolf's Lair, was control of its position. His own watch was cheap, an unimportant gift from his sister. Time moved on. He estimated how much of it was left, how long the device would run before the built-in timing hit the trigger.

Were the targets all in Europe? Going into the USA? Asia? Just Europe?

Now they were interested. Had targets, were challenged, and questions came too fast for the official who had emerged from the annex.

The officer from FSB, brought in by the colleague who had the roof for the GangMaster, gave protection and took the cut, had not anticipated the grilling and was uncertain how far to trust the young men and teenagers in front of him. Most of the kids who piped the questions would have been younger than the officer's own children, and if one of them had been brought home to the *dacha*, a weekend guest for the swimming pool and the barbecue, then security would have chucked him out on his arse.

He assumed the clock worked, had no reason not to.

'And now?' She threw her cigarette butt out of the window, and the wind caught it, and the rain would soon douse the glow on the tip.

'We wait.'

'Wait for what?'

It might have been tiredness, might have been the weight of fast food in his stomach, it might have been her hostility. Might have been that she had not been factored into the business. Irritation squirmed in him. 'Wait for what happens.'

'And do nothing?'

Merc was outside familiar areas. Beyond a perimeter fence, on the convoys and the security duties, and even when a fire fight at a Forward Operating Base became critical, his opinion was not questioned. 'We wait. It unfolds, happens, then we react.'

'We sit here?'

'There is nowhere else to sit.' In Merc's world, men hunkered down on their haunches and scribbled notes to women, or had a crossword book, or turned the pages of a magazine – he had *Auto Trader* or *Exchange and Mart* – and would not have recalled a word of text or even the photographs. A few called up their God. All would have been too sensitive to the common mood for picking and scratching at what was known.

'You have nothing better for us than to wait?'

'Nothing. Not anything we can do. *He* is the player. Not us.'

He had smacked the palm of his hand across the backside of the girl, Cinar, because her head was too high above the parapet. He could not turn in his seat and slap the face of Kat, Nikki's sister and tell her to shut her mouth because she helped nobody with her prattle, and he recognised her fear.

'You, who have come so far, are you better than the goons you brought with you?'

Merc could have straightened, probably hitting his head on the Polo's ceiling in the process, and could have spoken with emphasis. 'I am not them, they are not me. I have come to bring you out, and will achieve that . . .' Nobody who'd done close protection or rode the convoys or led a Fire Force Unit in a salient would have been so pompous.

'I do what I can.'

'And them? They walk out on you, abandon . . . You chose them?'

'Not important. Bitching at it will not help.'

He heard her snort. A mixture of frustration, impatience, and the helplessness that was always the most potent in the cocktail . . . and he realised a truth. He fielded her anger but her hand was warm in his fist. He did not know how he would get her across, how it would be for himself, and the rain would have raised the river level and increased the current's force. One step at a bloody time ... He held her hand and she clung to him – and understood.

'Were you the best they could send?'

Merc could have said something sarcastic, did not. 'I'm what was available.'

'Have you done anything before? Anything special?'

'Just minded my own business.'

'Do you know what it is like to face danger, be threatened? In your life has that been possible, not to know of danger, threat?'

'I know, Kat, about very little. Believe it, accept it.'

'Why did they choose you?'

'Just sitting around, cleaning my nails, washing my socks. Someone had to, must have been my turn.'

'Are you able to do what you promise? Fuck you, because I am afraid. Bad fear. Like in a cell. Where they put me. You know about fear? Tell me what you know . . .'

He saw the wide eyes and the glistening lines where there had been tears, and her chin was pushed out. Where he came from, men did not talk fear, would have shunned it because of contagion, believed it was viral; could spread and destroy. A driver had – very deliberately, as the convoy had formed up and was in echelon and ready to pull out of a guarded compound – switched off the engine, cut the choking fumes spitting from the exhaust, had picked up his rifle and his jacket and the grenade sack, and had jumped down from the cab and had gone to the office, and had chucked it in. Would have been on the night flight out, and never spoken of again – that was the defence against the infection of fear. How to silence her? All outside his experience. One of the guys who did escort on Route Irish had gone off – not a word beforehand – to the sandbagged pit where the weapons were cleared and made safe, and had put the barrel into his mouth. It had been dished up to the company pen-pushers as a sniping victim on the road. That way a widow or a girlfriend or a mother would get a better payout. His room had been cleared that afternoon, the paperwork done that night, the corpse sent home and a a rider put on the box that the coffin was better not opened. Never mentioned again.

Merc kissed her. On the forehead and on the cheek. On the lips, full, cold.

He felt her swallow hard as if she had stifled the next accusation, or question. He doubted if Brad or Rob, experts in the world of survival, would have dealt better with it. Quite a gentle kiss, for comfort. She squeezed his hand. It was bad that the boys had gone. Like he had told her, not a matter of offering a judgement, but a loss in his armoury of options. Merc would never have countenanced denouncing a man for the 'crime' of fear. He pulled back from her, felt the wet on his face, and sensed her soften, but still she clung on to his hand. He could see the corner of the roof. Watched it. She might have understood, and he might have. He assumed the clock ticked in the device. Nikki would come fast along the pavement, beyond the hoarding on the bend and would be running for the car. She'd be flicking the ignition and he would be leaning back to open the door behind him. The clock would be going. He wondered about the Wolf's Lair.

She was quiet. He wiped his tongue across his lips, erased the taste of her.

The call came from the bathroom. 'Everything good . . . Did you see Olga? She is doing the supper for them . . . We'll catch something out.'

The Major's wife was at the basin, undressed, washing. He said everything was good: it was, nearly. In the kitchen he found Olga and their son. Something simple; eggs and potato and sauce. Olga was a trainee chemist from a floor below, a simple and reliable girl, excellent for sitting with their child when he and Julia went out. Not often because most evenings he was too tired and most evenings she was buried deep in textbooks. Absently, he kissed his son on the forehead and was rewarded with a smear of mashed potato on his face, and a laugh from his son and a giggle from the girl.

He went to change. An evening in the cinema meant jeans and a T-shirt and a floppy fleece and a leather jacket. Rare for them to be out and therefore more appreciated. One good moment in the day: he had been thanked.

A colonel had expressed personal appreciation for his actions. The one who had 'requested' that the girl, Yekaterina, be freed because she was the sister of a criminal hacker for whom the state had work. She had been released, but might as well have had a manacle around her ankle. A long time since he had last been thanked by a superior officer. The colonel had hurried away and caught up with another of the same rank, and a brigadier, and they had strode, in masterful fashion, down a corridor and into the main lobby and a car had waited for them on the kerb, with a driver. The gratitude had been fulsome, and he believed it reflected their feeling that he could neither be bought nor bribed, was his own man . . . Praise indeed.

He did not know where she was. And did not know who she had met. Did not know whether a rendezvous was for her interest, or for her brother. The film was *How I Ended this Summer*, chosen by Julia. Set in the Arctic, it would be dark and dense, moody and atmospheric. The critics had loved it, and she would probably let her hand rest lightly on his lower thigh and he would, think of why the girl had gone to a supermarket car-park to meet another group, unidentified, and why – afterwards and driving towards the city's centre – they had performed a relatively sophisticated procedure in the traffic. Second nature to the Major, to throw off surveillance, and to criminals, but not to the level of people that she associated with.

They left for the cinema, and she held his hand closely as if fearful that he might break free, go back to work. And, their thoughts merging, they laughed.

Daff left everything in place.

A fair assumption that Boot was able to get up on a kitchen chair, pull the window wide open, get his leg in and on to the draining board and lever himself inside. The chair had been left, and the window was slightly ajar, and lights were on and curtains drawn and music played. Across from the building on Igor Gramov, the far side of the park, the surveillance vehicle was in place, its engine idling, cigarettes lit. It was not that he had no right to be there, or that secrecy was paramount, more that his presence was none of their damn business. She was on the platform when the train came in. Independence and sovereignty had given the Estonian town a new platform, but Narva's station building was decrepit, the product of a hasty rebuild after the battle, months of it, for the the town in 1944. A drab, grim and poorly lit place, empty of welcome.

He looked so harmless. An elderly man with a slight stoop, carrying a canvas overnight bag, his overcoat unbuttoned and a scarf – might have been last year's Christmas present – loose at his throat. A three-piece suit that had a bit of fleck in the herring-bone and well polished shoes as if that were important, and a trilby firmly on his head. Looking so unperturbed, might have filled in most of a crossword on the three-hour train journey from Tallinn . . . And might have sent men to their deaths, and might be facing a volcanic inquest into decisions taken, and might have politicians cringing or the hierarchy of the Service consigned to 'gardening leave' – and might be presiding over a coup of legendary proportions, One way or the other, nothing neutral about the single man coming slowly down the length of the platform. She assumed that the time of detonation would be close. She had worked hard on the apartment, what her mother always did if relatives were visiting – and she went forward and took his bag, which seemed acceptable. He'd go to the stake if it failed, and others with him. Daff? Might just slip out the back door, avoid the poison and the back-stabbing, get a job down in the Gulf, arm's length, head down.

'A good ride, Boot?'

'Very fair, thank you. Thought where I would have been if not on this caper – at Quatre Bras, my dear. A very significant cross-roads.' He smiled wanly. 'Just like here, I suppose, significant, yes.'

*   *   *

That Thursday evening, standing with the farmer who gave him a roof to sleep under most weekends, Boot would have been at the crossroads where the traffic streamed between Charleroi and Nivelles and Brussels and Namur. The farmer never tried to make conversation when Boot stood half a pace in front of him, and gazed, and imagined. He knew Quatre Bras well. A place where 'quarter was neither asked nor given', a contemporary chronicler had written. The Duke was here, had met his German ally, and the plan had been approved. The Emperor, only a mile away, might have noticed a small gathering of horsemen, might have identified them, might have spat at the ground . . . Today, the roads were busy and sloping countryside sat astride the main route from the south, straight and Roman and well paved. A car-park, weeded, littered with broken glass, dog excrement, abandoned plastic bags, had a low earth wall. Boot usually stood on it, unless the rain was particularly heavy. Squares of infantry had held their shape and blocked the French advance, little hedgehog formations that bristled with the bayonets of the Brown Bess muskets, and for some moments Wellington and his staff had taken refuge inside a square, maybe ten yards by fifteen, sharing the limited space with the wounded. Where the French cavalry had charged there were now fields grazed by horses and donkeys . . . It was painful for Boot to be here, coming off the station platform, and not where – almost – he believed he belonged. The purchase of time was the significance of the battle at the crossroads . . . Time had indeed been bought . . . He would have gone back to the farmhouse, would have sat with the family and eaten, drunk local beer, then retired early.

'No news at this end.'

'How can one expect there to be? It was the time then, at Quatre Bras, for lesser men to stand up, be counted, and win or lose the day. The same now as then. Always that posture in combat . . . We depend, Daff, on the small people. You are entitled to consider me deluded, but in the car-park at the crossroads, where the squares formed, I can sense – and you would also – the heat and noise and drama of battle, and men then do superior deeds and win or are inferior and lose. Straight choice.'

She drove him towards the town centre. He did not speak again. It rained hard, had done that same evening at the battle site. He seemed to blink, shut his eyes, banished it . . . ditched the past and turned to the present, the future. Not that there was much, if anything, he could do, but it was right to be here, showed loyalty to the boys on the ground. He assumed the monitoring services would have the first news of an explosion, and there would be newsflash interruptions on the agency wires. He would hear soon enough, but his phone stayed silent, and he must be patient. Boot reckoned, at that moment, in the darkened streets of Narva, that his life as an intelligence officer teetered on the edge, might progress and might collapse.

Her trick of the evening, clever girl, was to take him inside an apartment via a kitchen chair and an open window, and near to a headlong fall, and then a glass and a pizza, and then a long silence, and he would watch the phone that was placed on the table.

'There will be road-blocks, everything stopped.'

'Police everywhere, and militia. It will be a net.'

'Nothing will get through.'

Martin said, 'We will go to gaol for the rest of our lives.'

Toomas said, 'One of those fucking *gulag* camps, like for Kristjan's grandfather.'

Kristjan said, 'Until we die.'

They were sitting in the car, parked beside the hoses and the air for tyres, and vehicles came in a stream to use the pumps.

'It was rubbish, the money they were paying us,' Martin said.

'For what was asked of us, an insult,' Toomas said.

'Shouldn't have taken it. Should have told them to shove it up their arses,' Kristjan said.

'So, we are agreed – yes?' Martin's question.

'Agreed.' Toomas's answer.

'No alternative, because of who we are – what happened.' Kristjan slapped the shoulders of the two in front of him. They left the fuel station, went up a slip road, took the main highway, were lost in the traffic, and went fast.

            ★   ★   ★

Nikki watched the faces.

The last time he had looked at his watch it had been thirty-seven minutes since he had depressed the button. He *thought* he had been told that the timer was set for forty minutes. He seemed to *remember* that the time was forty, but his recall was fogged. He could not sit there at the table and gaze at his watch and examine the scurrying movement of the second hand, and the slower minute hand. So, he looked at the faces, and bent his shoulder and his fingers scrabbled for the rucksack's strap.

They had been divided into hubs. Inside the hubs, each had a target area. The one allocated to Nikki was the banking system for benefit payments in the northern English city of Manchester. He thought it bizarre. There was no similar system in St Petersburg. Men and women either lived off their families or begged on the streets, were given no wage for not working. His was a city of survivors . . . It might be three minutes, or might be fractionally less, could be a little more – if the device worked and did not malfunction. He looked around him. He could measure the boredom. All individualists and all shunning any degree of discipline, and hostile to organisation. He gripped the handle of the rucksack and lifted it between his knees.

He had no love for the *avtoritet*, the GangMaster who employed him, who paid him poorly, who had tens of thousands, hundreds of thousands, of euros and dollars from his work. He was sitting at the end of the table and fidgeted and wanted to be gone, back to the annex where the officials waited, and then they would speed away and do a restaurant that evening, and the start of the hacked entries through the vulnerable points would begin, be coordinated, for the morning. He saw the nostrils of the *avtoritet* twitch as if he smelled them, his cologne not proof against them. He might be hurt, might be killed. Nikki did not know the power of the explosives inside the laptop, nor how much shrapnel would be spat out. He set the rucksack on the table in front of him.

The twins were the youngest at the table. He had no argument with them. Their faces were alive with acne sores and they wore identical spectacles with thick lenses. They wanted out, played listlessly with their keys.

In the Wolf's Lair, as Nikki had read, the officer had brought into the conference room, for the Fuhrer's daily briefing, an attaché case with the device primed and had put it on the floor. A midsummer day, and the conference had been held in a wooden hut, not the confines of a bomb-proof bunker where the blast would have been contained, maximised.

The tall kid had twice met Nikki's glance, had seemed lonely, isolated, had wanted contact, but each time Nikki had failed to respond. He wanted no sympathies to build, nothing that would destroy his commitment. What was it for? At one level, because he was compromised, but that was peripheral. At another level, it was because he had been promised that his sister would be taken out, offered a new existence. At the highest level it was about his hatred of HookNose and the Roofer and Gorilla. He had never before felt such power. The rucksack was on the table and the laptop was inside it. More power and less regret than when he had wriggled inside the bank accounts and taken out the clients' money, transferred it, gone to Stockholm and been treated as a treasured customer.

The officer, integral in a conspiracy, had left the briefing room, abandoned his attaché case on the floor, had not known that another man would see it, ease it away with his boot, push it against a heavy table leg. All part of the legend of the Wolf's Lair.

The smart, slickly dressed guy, with the girl and the fast car outside, or the one whose father had brought him, did not seem hostile, just indifferent. They were together, farther down the table towards the annex, and would catch much of the shrapnel that the device would throw out, if it fired. The officer had left, exited the inner compound, had been boarding a military light aircraft and was ready to taxi as the explosion ripped through the briefing room. He had taken off, been flown in a bubble of radio silence to Berlin.

He hated HookNose, who drew doodles on a notepad.

Had reached Berlin, had claimed to fellow conspirators that his target had been killed at the Wolf's Lair, that the moment of revolution was right, and did not know that a solid table leg had taken the immediate force of the blast.

And hated the Roofer who used the long sinewy fingers that could take his weight up a sheer stone wall with minimal crevices for his fingertips, and who now picked mucus from his nose.

Had left too early, and the reward was to hear the target's voice, alive but shaken, on a radio wavelength.

And hated Gorilla who chewed on gum relentlessly and took it from his mouth, every few minutes, and fastened it under the table top and extracted a new piece, grinding it between his teeth.

Had failed, but was fortunate to have been frogmarched into the central courtyard of the Berlin building, and propped against a wall and executed by firing squad. Fortunate because many who had followed the officer's lead would die from strangulation, hanged with piano wire.

Nikki glanced again at his watch and cursed himself for his impatience, and took the laptop out of the rucksack and laid it in front of him, then dropped the empty rucksack to the floor, and did not know how long, and saw the movement . . . The *Avtoritet* headed, as if relieved to be shed of them, towards the main door, and the two officials followed him, and chairs started to scrape, and panic began to grip Nikki. It took hold, and he seemed to see the room emptied and just himself and the laptop left inside the Wolf's Lair.

He raised his hand.

A strong, firm voice, the quaver controlled. 'There are matters that I do not find clear, and it is important that we all know exactly how far it is intended that we travel. An example, how important is secrecy, the enemy left in ignorance . . . One question, but I have others.'

He saw annoyance, felt contempt directed at him from HookNose, irritation from the Roofer, and heard an audible curse from Gorilla. He did not know how much time he had bought, but the *Avtoritet*, GangMaster of the Kupchino district, and the official who was his 'roof' and took his money, and the second official who had delivered the shopping list of targets, were in conversation, and they came back to the table and questions he might have to ask to win more time careered in his head, and the twins watched him closely as if puzzled by him, and suspicion might have grown. The laptop, benign, was in front of him, and he saw his sister and heard her rare laughter, and with her was the man who had given a promise . . .

Merc blinked.

Light shone in his face, then the angle altered and caught, full on, Kat's, and she turned away. The headlights swung towards a parking bay near to the exit point on to the slipway, flicked on-off, twice, and then were killed.

It was a moment before Merc regained his sight, could focus again on the corner of the building, and wonder why the lights had flashed and . . . More light, brilliant. The same illumination as there was when a flash-and-bang grenade was thrown but so much bigger, brighter. He twisted, saw her face and the wide-eyed stare. A fraction of time and the first signs of debris hurtling up from the roof area, then the light failed, died, and the noise came as thunder brought on the back of wind.

If he was coming he would have come. Merc couldn't tell her but she'd have known.

What to say? Nothing that was appropriate, that matched the moment. Merc knew how it was when men or women fell in the line, sometimes within sight and sometimes round a corner where the trench was in sharp-angled bends . . . the sounds of falling masonry and glass shattering as it landed on the ground. Then silence. Until the first scream. A woman ran towards the service counter of the Kentucky Fried Chicken franchise and her head thrown back and her skirt stretched with her stride and she howled in terror. Then the first cars revving their engines; many would have been queuing for food but abandoned it . . . She had removed her hand. Her lips, where he had kissed her to silence her, were thin, drawn. She would have known. A sharp look at him, and he nodded. Then the first siren . . . far away but coming fast.

He looked at the top corner of the building and a jagged bite had been removed from it and he reckoned the flat roofing had been taken off, cast away, and there were flames leaping where earlier there had been windows with lowered blinds. The car by the exit point flashed again, then reversed and was in place at the side of the slipway. She drove. An arm was waving from the car in front, the gesture for the Polo to slot in behind. The boys had come back.

They went on to the main drag clear of the city. Their headlights lit the car in front and he saw the back of Kristjan's head, then his face when he turned. Then, Merc lurched in his seat and his belt snapped tight and he hit her shoulder and she rode the blow. The boys had swerved into the fast lane and she followed and there was a cacophony of protesting horns. The needle climbed on the speed dial. More sirens. Vehicles belted towards them on the far side of the crash barrier and hammered past. Ambulances and fire brigade and militia. The boys coming back, then leading them clear, was ignored . . . He understood as she did. Kat had not protested that they left too early, should wait to see if he showed. He didn't see her face, could not have said whether she still shed tears or how far her jaw jutted.

They went fast, kept to the convoy, and Merc reckoned it would take them an hour and a half to the choke point. He did not say a prayer, did not think she had. In the trench on Hill 425 they always said a prayer, then laughed, then cursed the enemy, then did the fighting. Had to hope that chaos and confusion would blind the investigators long enough for them to break through, get clear, reach the forest.

12

Merc thought her driving bordered on reckless. Some ability, no fear. Astonished, accelerating, how they had not collided with other vehicles, hit the central reservation, gone off the road and into a ditch, or though the chain-link fences that surrounded factories and storage units.

Security vehicles and rescue teams powered noisily past. It would not be long before the blocks would be in place: there was always a window after a major incident but a small one. Where the boys went, Kat followed. Martin drove well. Might be a jobbing decorator but might once have owned a performance car, seemed to sense gaps and their width and be able to push though them. Possible for the lead, harder for the following car. They had twice overtaken the two lanes of traffic by going on to the hard shoulder – only wide enough for a cyclist – and their wheels spat gravel up from the verge. Had taken a mirror off a saloon car and fractured their own, now crazily angled and useless. A trail of debris and cursing was behind them, and siren blasts.

Could Merc have done it better? Not sure he could. Was a decent enough driver but there was usually a clutch of speeding tickets held in a *poste restante* down the street from the bank in Stoke Poges. But if handed a ticket and asked to give an address then he would give Hill 425, along with a GPS reference. Brad had done speed driving with the regiment, and always said it was about the chicken game: all the other drivers on the road would blink first, get the hell out of the way, not wanting to end up with a scratch on their bodywork. It was what Brad said, and Rob had the little masked grin, enigmatic, that said – even he – trained in close-quarters combat, damn near wet himself when riding passenger, or shotgun, with his mucker at the wheel. She would not have been on any driving course. She made little grunts, like hard swallowing. Tears ran unchecked down her face. The windows, both sides, were down and the wind came in and the rain, and the cold, and the noise of the big vehicles they left behind. Never more than half a dozen yards behind the boys' car, and sometimes Merc could see Kristjan turn, look at them and smile, maniacal.

She said, almost a shout, and staccato because she was crying. 'You didn't know about the Wolf's Lair . . . It's what happened, and why . . .'

He was told the story. Short, savage sentences. Good, expressive English. The uncertainty of a killing game. Gone too early. Failure. All understood, and the realisation that Nikki, hacker and drop-out with the sloppy shoulders and spindly arms and the hole that seemed burrowed into the centre of his chest, had performed an act of self-destruction for the sake of his sister getting a ride out of Russia. Nothing to do with a great plan concocted by Boot . . . The traffic seemed to thin. She didn't talk again.

He wondered for how much longer she would cry: not those theatrical tears that his mother used, which became the excuse for dumping Merc on his grandmother's doorstep with his case. Tears of the sort done in private. Merc had seen Rob cry. For a little guy, fat and short-sighted and useless as a front-line fighter and keen and able to make everyone laugh. Could not clean his rifle, and if he managed to strip it then had no idea about reassembly. Brave as a damned old lion when it came to crossing open ground to bring up more ammunition, might use a wheelbarrow and go at a snail's pace. And had stopped one in a trench a couple of miles beyond Hill 425 – and had died slowly and still fucking smiling . . . Brad and Rob had known that section of the Fire Force Unit, had trained them, had cursed the fat guy for his incompetence and seen him cringe like a dog, then come back and sidle up with fresh coffee, and anger evaporated. Merc had been there, had seen Rob cry . . . had felt his own tears welling, had stifled them.

She cried big, and drove the car fast. Should have had a cushion under her buttocks, would have let her see better through the windscreen, and the wipers were going hard and sleet gathered at the sides of the arc they made. Her body was rigid, her chin stuck forward and her hair was a wet mess from the wind blowing in through the windows. She held the wheel high with both hands, didn't go through the gears, hardly touched the brake pedal. They were out of the traffic. Fewer cars and fewer vans and fewer lorries. The boys had done well, had opened up the road.

She coughed, then tilted her head to wipe her face on the sleeve of her coat, then looked up. Merc saw that her cheeks were dry, and there were no more tears. As if a crisis had passed . . . He remembered they had not said goodbye. When the Kurd girls went forward into the line, their fathers, their husbands, their boyfriends, would come to the depot and stand outside the main gate, and the trucks would pull out and go past a knot of loved ones, waving and fluttering handkerchiefs. They had not touched, not clung to each other. More important to Nikki than to the sister, Kat, Fuck all business of Merc's . . .

A gasp, an involuntary shout, and she swung the wheel and just missed the back of the boys' car. They would not have reached first base of the escape without the boys, something to be grateful for. What they were there for – to get them through the road-blocks, and the choke point – essential to them. Merc wondered what had happened to make them quit, then stop, then retrace, then flick their lights and give the signal, wait for her to come out from the parking area, lead the charge. They had braked, and the lights had flashed, and they had dropped their speed, and the silly beggar – Martin – had hit the horn and done a little dance on it with his fingers, or it might have been Toomas beside him.

He would need them at the choke point, would need them badly.

He pointed his wife in the direction of a taxi queue. With the rank of Major and the ID of the FSB, he had commandeered a militia driver for himself.

About to go into the cinema. A phone had sounded, muffled in a pocket near to them. He recognised the head of Internal Security in the office of the Mayor, a face pulled, a phone snapped off, and a woman with her cheek pecked abandoned in the foyer. More ring tones. A woman, a general accident and emergency consultant at the Mariinsky Hospital, answered her phone. Julia knew her, and the woman's face had gone ashen . . . then the phone of a man he knew from the militia, a colonel, then his own.

From the Operations Room at the Big House, a curt message. They would have known that he had had a minor dissident in custody. Would have known she was under surveillance and had been 'lost'. Would have known that her brother was a hacker and used by the *mafiya* group operating from the Kupchino district. An unexplained explosion in a building used by that organisation . . . His caller lowered his voice, then an aside – had probably turned his head away so the words would not be picked up on the permanent monitoring microphone – clear that senior men from the building were present. A bomb. Casualties . . . The Major had hesitated. But the link captured him. He had been on a Civil Defence course with an official from the city's Fire Unit, and that same man had been across the foyer, and his phone had rung, and he had not hesitated. Something of an apology, not much . . . It would have been a good film but already the Major had forgotten its title. The foyer had emptied. Julia was already in the taxi queue; had neither criticised nor told him she valued his sense of duty, had not wasted breath.

He told the militiaman where he wanted to go, what part of Kupchino, then held the door open for two more to join him. They were driven away, and all had their phones to their ears.

A crowd had gathered, raw in anger, several deep. Some casualties had been taken away. Others were still being dug for. Some distance from the living, and the *triage* work of the first medical teams, were the black bags for the fatalities, already zipped but showing the shapes they held.

Alarms rang from cars and from the stricken building. All the windows were blown out and a part of the end wall, on the top floor, had collapsed and the roof was split wide. The sleet and the cold had access to an open area into which searchlights played. The fire teams had their first extended ladder in place and would have had a clear view into the devastation. The lights showed, to the crowd held back by increasingly nervous militia, a splintered and overturned table and parts of bodies, some intact but unmoving, and some crawling towards the ladder, jostling for safety.

A girl in a flimsy dress, and cloaked in gold foil, still sat at the reception desk and was white cheeked from the dust that had fallen on her. She gazed straight ahead and was deep in shock. Another girl sat in an open Porsche sports car and did not move and had no mark on her, and might have been sleeping except that a small dribble of blood seeped from her mouth and ran down to the cleft of her chest. A girl in waitress uniform, except that the apron she wore was no longer white but crimson, walked in circles and whined like a lost dog. Most were silent . . . but not all. One fuelled the anger of those held back by the uniformed men. He was the *avtoritet* of the Kupchino district of the city. He ranted at the crowd. He shouted of treachery, of rivals, of murder, of the revenge that would be taken on the 'evil shite', the 'fucking pig' – and named him – who ran the Ul'yanka district and had control of most of the cargo area of Pulkovo airport, and had his own roof. He was pale, blood stained, and had an open wound on his forehead. A sleeve of his suit jacket hung loose and was held at the shoulder by threads, and his trousers were ripped and showed his tanned legs. He made a denunciation, had the certainty of conviction. The official who might have backed him, and might have denied him, did not contribute, was being carried to an ambulance's open doors. Another official huddled in a corner, a blanket across his shoulders, shivering and silent. A woman, strangely calm and with her face scarred by glass shards, said that her twin boys had been inside, and she had not seen them since the fireball burst.

Many of those who gathered at the torn fence around the building lived close by in the tower blocks that ringed the small area of low-set industrial buildings, and owed a good living to the *Autorite*. They drove for him, did courier work, provided cheap muscle, pimped girls from whose work on their backs he took a healthy cut, and were dependent on his generosity for finding work for their children, and for the settling of disputes – anything requiring leverage with the city's administration. He was a popular man if not crossed, and he stood, bloodied and unbowed, and called down devils on his rival in the Ul'anka district, neighbouring his own territory.

In such circumstances – the attack on the commercial enterprise of a man with significant influence – few of the more minor players would wish to intervene. The *avtoritet* was known for quite scientific cruelty: none, at this moment, would wish to antagonise him further. The militia officers organised a cordon of uniforms around the fence and hoped that the crowd, teetering towards a mob, would not burst through and vent their resentment against the medical teams and the fire crews, and investigators. At that moment, few men or women in authority wished for prominence.

One came forward.

Because the Major was from Belarus, a foreigner and without a roof, and gave not a kopek for the city's endemic corruption, he stepped out. He took charge.

It was a crime scene. He secured it. On his orders, long rolls of tape were unravelled, and the fire and rescue and medical teams warmed to him, someone who understood the requirements of their work. He gathered the principals together, talked through the recovery of corpses and the injured from the building, little of which was safe. He gave them respect, they gave him effort.

A general came. It was the Major who briefed him. Leadership was not awarded him, merely seemed to slip into his lap, and lodge there. He was crisp and to the point. He wore his civilian clothing, had an armband over the sleeve of his leather jacket. It was to his advantage that he did not wear the uniform of his ranking; as a major, he would not have been listened to. The general approved of what he had done. He was told he headed the investigation.

With the general had been two colonels but they did not query the order. Did he have permission to go wherever the investigation led him? 'Within reason', he did, and the general's name was to be quoted if he encountered obstruction. Perhaps a word had been passed to the general's ear: this was a man without 'connection', without a *krysha*, without friends who carried influence ... Perhaps the general appreciated such independence. Almost at his car, he called to him.

'Is this clear cut, Major? Does it shout at you?'

'I don't know, General.'

'Thugs, turf war, crossing of boundaries, good enough reasons for an atrocity?'

'A meeting in progress. Its significance. The seat of the explosion ... also good enough reasons? I cannot answer you. Please, General, excuse me.'

The Major would have liked a good sergeant with him, reliable and enthusiastic and with a nose – and fearless. Would have to make do, when he could lay hands on him, with his surveillance sergeant, and there was a young lieutenant in the Big House who worked for him, seemed sensible. Had to get the scenes of crime team in, and the fire forensic people, had to have them crawling through the wreckage of the meeting room. Were there roadblocks in place? A shrug for an answer. Were there road-blocks in place on all main routes? No, not just to Ul'anka district, but on the roads into central St Petersburg, and the roads away from the city, north and west and south. And he raised his voice, unusual for him, and demanded action. Blocks on all the roads, and to hell with log-jammed traffic. What should the militia on the blocks be looking for?

'I don't know. I do not know what they should look for, but they must look.'

'When do we get a woman?'

'When do we get a drink?'

'When do we stop – and will the casino still be open?'

Peals of laughter inside the car.

They veered on the road, hit the barrier and bounced back because Martin laughed so loud. 'I want a woman, big gut and big paps, any shape, just a woman.'

Toomas chimed in: 'A litre of vodka, high strength, some beer to chase it, the rest of the night on a bench, and not wake until I am back on the hill with the castle and the tourists have come, and everything of this forgotten.'

Kristjan leaned between them, and the laughter bubbled spittle on his lips. 'Get there, get to the casino, clear the bastards out, win big. Put it on nineteen – every cent I have. Big odds – it was the age of my grandfather when he came on the fast boat . . . Let the wheel spin, the ball wobbles, comes to rest, can only be that number. Be there before it closes.'

'I accept the chance of a woman is slight, less than minimal.'

'Can't stop, fuck about – not at a store where they'd sell good quality vodka, or bad.'

'Would the wheel come up? But it is a dream. It is good to dream, what else?'

They went on down the road, and the traffic opened out for them and the girl kept close and the Polo's lights were full on and were in their mirrors. The thoughts of a woman, and of bottles full to the neck, and of a bouncing ball on a spinning roulette wheel, were like sand slipping through their fingers. Their elation had been strengthened by the chase through the lorries on the road, and Martin's driving skill, and the brilliance of the girl who had followed them. But the road now opened up and excitement had no place. The mood swing was sharp, felt by all three of them.

Martin said, 'We should never have come. If there is a road-block, what do we do?'

Toomas said, 'What we did wrong was turn back, then wait for them. Without us they don't get through.'

Kristjan said, 'Should not have come, should have taken their money, gone.'

They went down a long straight road, and all the time the head-lights stayed bright in the mirrors, and the girl tracked them.

★   ★   ★

Colder. The sleet had not turned to snow, but came stronger, spattered up from the road surface, and visibility was worse, but the vehicle in front kept a steady speed. They had skidded, and he had thought she had lost traction but she regained it. He did not know whether that was ability or luck. Merc usually reckoned that luck outweighed talent.

And she talked. Talked and did not stop. He thought it was the climb-down from the stress of the drive, and from the acceptance that her brother had died in the building, at his own hand or misjudgement of the length of the fuse mechanism. He was not referred to, nor was the drive out of the city. A monotone voice, devoid of emotion.

'We saw the fire, and heard the explosion. It was not a firecracker. It was designed to kill. A meeting of hackers, men or boys of the best quality, and controlled by the government. You wanted them destroyed, that was why you came, why you brought the bomb. You would hope to hide what you did behind the cover of a vendetta.'

A steady speed and they were tucked close to the car ahead, and that was behind two lorries, each with empty timber trailers, going fast, and a chemical tanker.

'I was in a group. I tell you, very frankly, we were pathetic. We dream of belonging, being part of a family.'

Clear ahead, effortlessly passing the lorries, trailers, and the tanker.

'The family has to make a difference. That is good, yes? To change a system, burn out corruption. To throw out the new *czar*, to destroy his court. Big, fantastic aims. We talked of how it should be achieved. How? The Leader will screw a new girl, and enjoy himself, and enhance his authority, and none of the family will question what he has written. We exchange a *czar* for a Leader.'

A deer crossed the road but she did not brake, would have collided with it, but it leaped for the shadows and disappeared in darkness.

'Do you know what it is to be crushed? Are you experienced in fighting, you would have told me. In our family we often spoke of our importance. I saw the explosion. It was huge. It would have killed many if they were in that room, upstairs, the end of the building. It was a blow against them. The room was filled with hackers. They are the people who strip assets from foreign banks, take hundreds of millions of dollars, euros, sterling, steal it, and there were people there who have tormented my brother. I thought . . . You want to know what I thought?'

Merc did not reply. A hand came off the wheel, was laid on his thigh, rested there. He did not move it. He would be told what she thought.

'I thought that it was heroic to go under the big bridge opposite FSB offices in the city, and when it is raised to allow a boat with a funnel to go under, then to paint on the under-side the outline of a penis – a dick, what the Leader would have shoved in me – and we regarded the man who came up with the idea as a lion struggling for freedom. It was to make a difference. You understand?'

And he wondered how many times, on deployments he had 'made a difference', and he thought of his father. The legend of the Corps, the elderly officer drafted off the routine duties of supervising the digging of latrine pits, or constructing sangars that were proof against a direct hit from an RPG -7's grenade, had been put on riot control, his platoon bottled, stoned, abused, and had shouted 'Hold the Line, the Pioneers', had gone into mythology. Had he altered anything? Her hand moved, stroked him.

'Make a difference. It was what we hoped. How? Find the courage and go out in the depth of night, have lookouts to spot police or militia. Look for walls not covered by the street lights. A bucket of paste with us. Certain we were not observed, we would slap on the paste, then stick small posters to it, the text written by the Leader. That was the extent of the counter-revolution. The limit of what we did. You are entitled to laugh in our face.'

Merc stayed impassive, and the wind whipped his forehead. He had saved the lives of men, and had ended the lives of others . . . He thought he had saved the life of a dark-haired girl who regarded him with indifference, or occasional hostility, and he had whacked her arse to keep her alive. Cats sometimes came into the bunkers, had been one on a previous posting to Hill 425, and the guys, the girls, always made a fuss of a cat, stroked it. Like she was stroking his leg.

'Did we make a difference, did anything change? Can you imagine it, a message goes to the FSB liaison officer, sitting inside the Presidential quarters at the Kremlin, or at his palace overlooking the sea in the north, or to the place built for him far to the south, and the officer shivers in anxiety. He goes immediately to the great man, to the *czar*, and tells him that posters have been put on walls in St Petersburg, and they denounce him as a tyrant. He would tremble? His hand would shake? His bodyguards would transfer him to a bomb-proof bunker? That was the best I could do, and I nearly screwed the Leader because I wanted to belong with that family . . . I am ashamed. I see what you have done. They will hear about it. He will be told about a bomb, but not about posters and paste. I am right?'

A bomb would be talked about. Lives had been taken. There was always the moment that the TV relished when a national leader was smiling in mid-conference, or was with flag-waving kids, or greeting guests at a reception, or perhaps squaring up on the twelfth or thirteenth green, then the interruption came. A stone-faced aide, a scrap of paper, the face clouding: confusion, anger, and a day wrecked because the authority of the man was hijacked. It was how it would be. What he might say to her: 'I'm not the man who can give you an answer. Just do as I'm told, what people of my rank always do. You know a chap called Boot? No? You should. Put your questions to Boot.' Merc said nothing. The forest was thick on either side, and no more deer came . . . He remembered how it had been at the choke point: the chicane and the oil drums weighted with concrete, the guns slung on straps from the goons' necks. They carried on down the road; there was no other way. The boys were ahead of them: entrapped by Daff, not the first and would not be the last.

Not idiots, the men in the surveillance car parked on the open ground across from the front entrance to the apartment on Igor Gramov Street. Daff didn't have to ask: they supplied.

'Some sort of incident in the Kupchino district.'

'Never heard of it,' she said.

'They're wary on their radios, a sensitive location and sensitive people.'

'None of my business.'

They knew of the river crossing, of the diversion created by fireworks being launched into a rainstorm. Knew that a woman such as herself was not visiting depressed, run-down, going-nowhere Narva because of the beauty salons. She had brought Boot in through the kitchen window, and they probably knew it, and knew also that she had bought enough food for two, but it would not be spoken of. She was in the back and the guy beside her fed her cigarettes, and the one in the front had a camera with a big lens and an image intensifier attachment. Charade games had been a part of her upbringing and she was easy with gentle deception.

'Explosives involved.'

'Is that right?'

'And reports of casualties.'

'Too bad.'

'Could be gang stuff, *mafiya* feud.'

'You always monitor their net?' A query, little interest, but polite, making conversation – and smoking – helping them pass a boring night. Playing at sympathy for the tedium, but they understood. Relaxed, like it was talk among friends, and both sides trawling . . . Better kept at this level, than alerting the spook desks in the embassies and their seniors. She wore a provocative scent, which usually coughed up dividends.

'Why does that local stuff get through to you boys?' An innocent question.

An innocent reply. 'If it is a gang fight, then the boss who launched it will want to get the perpetrators out fast, beyond reach of arrest, and we are just down the road. We have the escape route. It is the easy way to get clear.'

And the guy behind the wheel ducked his head and listened hard, holding the earpiece tight against his head. Would have been his Control. He straightened and turned to Daff.

'Their ambulance net is talking of fatalities. Interesting . . . when *mafiya* have feuds they do car bombs or sniper shots, take out specific targets. This is a big bomb, not the usual way for them . . . But as you say, none of your business.'

'That's what I say.'

And she moved on to safer territory: kit. What the boys always wanted to talk about – not sex or food, not books or films, but the quality of firearms, a Makarov set against the Walther PPQ, or socks or boots or . . . She'd stub out her cigarette, tell them it was her bedtime, and leave them with the thought of it, and grin, and touch an arm, let the scent linger, and be gone. And would take Boot out through the kitchen window.

Boot had a good view of the barrier. The area, the far side of the bridge, was well lit. It would be a new entry on Boot's list of battle honours. He was thankful for the quality of his coat, and had the trilby hard down on his head so that the wind did not take it. Its force was down the gorge, north to south, made between the ramparts of the twin castles, and for centuries men who were in effect mercenaries and with no immediate quarrel in that territory had eyed each other across the fault line, the river, had watched for signs of what they'd regarded as important. As he did. They had weapons at the barrier and a hut where papers were verified, but little traffic to occupy them at that time of night.

There had been Rozvadov, a point on the German–Czech border where he'd stood and waited with Ollie Compton, and another one where the two Germanys faced each other across a minefield and savage dogs, with watch-towers, outside Helmstedt, and various ones in Berlin of which the favourite to wait on was the Glienicke on the Potsdam side of Berlin. Good restaurants there, with a view, comfortable to wait in. And he and Ollie Compton had once done shivering time on the Soviet–Finnish border, at Rajapooseppi, inside the Arctic Circle, and the sad little man they had waited for had never shown: might still be there, frozen solid, if a bear had not had him. The first time at the bridge at Narva. Some in VBX might have had little flags pinned to a

map to mark the points, or a collection of fridge magnets ...
Always tough to wait, and a stretch on his patience.

There was much for Boot to reflect on. Principally, there was
the size of the bomb, as reported by Daff. Difficult to read, in
Boot's experience, whether a man in the field, up close and
personal with a target, would go squeamish. Stockholm syndrome,
almost appropriate. A look through cross-hairs or across a street,
seeing the faces and eyes of the potential casualties, often weak-
ened resolve. A man or woman might back off, lose conviction. He
had been economical, had understated the weight of the device, its
power. They would be running hard, a few kilometres away from
the bridge, and would need a minimum of obstructions. He
doubted he would rot in hell – hoped not to. It would have been
good to have been able to exchange Daff's company for that of
Ollie Compton, as he watched the bridge, and waited. It was
where her boys would come, the Estonians who had been hired, at
minimal cost, for undemanding work. The crossing places were a
narcotic to any field officer who hired agents – at the best deal
available, squeezing the expenditure – to wait.

The barrier was down. No cars or lorries were about to pass
through. Pedestrians crossed, the last of the day's smugglers –
tolerated by both sides – of vodka and cigarettes. They went past
the barrier, and headed briskly towards the centre point, where
the white line was clearly painted. When the boys came, Boot
thought – with blood on their hands – they'd have their heads
down after passing through the security, would not look behind
them, would dread the cry to 'Halt', and had to reach the line.
Then could dance, sing, punch the air, give a finger behind them,
be safe: just a line in the middle of the high bridge and the water
dark underneath and flowing deep and cold, and the rain spat-
tering on its ruffled surface. He had known better places.

It seemed, from the first report she had relayed, an operation
impeccably on course so far. Except ... except ... no chickens yet
to be counted. About deniability, about getting the guys back. All
about deniability. Boot should have been asleep, far from anxie-
ties, in his farmhouse billet – and Gloria away on an antique

dealers' junket – and dreaming contentedly of how it would have been thirty-six hours, or less, from the start of the battle. Two great armies abandoning retreat and pursuit, starting to form up within two, three miles of each other. An area of fields some five miles square and seething with 200,000 combatants, and their horses, their cannon and their baggage . . . thrilling stuff and he thought himself blessed . . . and he watched the bridge. A car came. Daff stood apart from him, allowed him to absorb the mood and atmosphere of the place. The car came painfully slowly towards the barrier, braked, the barrier was raised. The driver did not hurry, would not have dared. The car edged towards the white line, was within the range of an automatic weapon, and there would be loudspeakers to broadcast the command for the driver to stop, and order the vehicle to reverse . . . Sometimes they had come through and then hung on the necks of himself and Ollie Compton, and sometimes they had never showed, and sometimes there had been crisp rifle fire from beyond their field of vision, and sometimes a klaxon's howl. If deniability was lost then he had failed.

'Are we too early?'

She answered him. 'A little early, for them. Merc will be later, of course. Frankly, forgive the jargon, it's Kingisepp that gives me the squits. Know what I mean?'

The Maid locked the outer door behind her. She was well prepared for overnight office stays. She padded quietly down the corridor towards the elevator.

She wore an ankle-length robe, a shimmering silvery effect, that had been a present from the man who shared a small part of her life – less than the space occupied by her parrot – and comfortable fluffy slippers. She had tidied her hair before leaving. In the dulled light of the corridor, she could have been a ghost. A glance into the mirror to make certain she was presentable. Tapped in a code to get to the top floor of VBX; she was one of the few outside the inner circle who had access to it. A young man met her, an aide of the Big Boss, junior but well thought of. His Night Duty Officer.

She was brought through . . . He snored, quite loud, with catarrh lodged in his sinuses. She went forward, stood over the camp bed and shook his shoulder; he jolted.

She said, 'Just to get you up to speed. An explosion has been reported in the Kupchino district. A warehouse, office, used by a company described as dealing in import/export. Quite a big bang, fatalities, and several carted off to hospital. News agencies and local radio are not talking bombs but suggesting a gas leakage, but that's to be expected initially. No word of any arrests. So far so good. Thought you should know . . .'

For a moment there was a flash of excitement in his eyes; he would have given his right one – not his arm – to be in that little town flanking the Narva river, alongside Boot. She left him. The aide switched off the light. She did not think the Big Boss would get back to sleep, and would soon be pestering her for more news.

She went down in the elevator and along her corridor. A ghost abroad in the silence of the floor . . . All for nothing if one were caught, held and identified, and deniability failed. She wondered how sharp they would be, the adversaries, how clever, whether they could think outside the loop or were trapped inside it.

The Major now had his sergeant to drive him, and the young lieutenant. Enough . . . From the jeep he had already made the briefest of calls to his wife. Would not be home, did not know when he would be. She was scrubbing up in a hospital. No conversation.

He went to the Operations Room. A formidable area in a basement section of the Big House, the far end to the cell block, it dealt with all aspects of the security of the state: serious crime, the activities of dissidents, counter-terrorism, anything that pricked the formidable skin of the nation. An old lesson, one he believed, was that an investigator should always follow his 'nose', go where it took him, but always be prepared to stand still for a moment and raise his head, allow the wind to fan across his nostrils and sniff; be open minded, without the burden of preconception. At the desks that monitored the banks of screens watching over the inner and outer districts of the city, he was told the first blocks were now in place and traffic queues had formed, and he was informed, with ghoulish enjoyment, that tempers were already frayed. More blocks were now sealing the northern road towards the Finnish border, the E-18, and out to the east and the wilderness of forests by Lake Ladoga, the E-105, and towards the south and Moscow, the E-95. The road west out of the city, close to Kupchino district, the E-20, also had an outer block in position, within the last several minutes, at the town of Kingisepp. They showed him, on the screens, the satellite view of where the further controls would be placed. He was told, at Kingisepp, there was the river, and the expanse of chemical works, and both were impossible to by-pass. What sort of car were they looking for? He could not answer but the men inside the one that mattered would be in flight, stress pasted on their faces, would lie and stumble, show fear and . . . they would know when they hit the right vehicle. He moved on, to the far side of the bunker space.

The Major stopped behind a young man's chair, no recognition, no deference, and in response to the question put to him, lifted a phone and dialled. Would have spoken to the general, would have received choice words. A gulp, an acceptance without further query. The delay was regretted. What could be done for the Major, could he repeat his request? He did.

As if he cast a fly over smooth waters, sitting in his small punt boat on a waterscape outside Minsk. Did not know what he might draw up to the surface, or indeed if the fly he had tied was suitable. It was the Intelligence Desk. What was unusual? What was interesting? What had been received but as yet had no relevant pigeon-hole? Of particular interest to him was the E-20 because Kupchino was on that side of the city, and the border there, and . . . Fingertips clattered on a keyboard. Text played on the screen: a German national, with a press card, had tried to enter Russia through the bridge control point on the Narva river and had claimed a wish to visit the Ivangorod castle, and had been refused entry. Smuggling infringements on the border, amounts of contraband too considerable for the protocol. Two men out duck shooting on the lake, the Peipus, where it ran into the Narva river, and they had 'strayed' into Russian territory, gone past the marker buoys, and been chased back by a patrol craft. And a display of fireworks that . . .

'Fireworks?'

'Yes, Major, fireworks. With low cloud, and in heavy rain. Mostly rockets, but wasted because of poor visibility. A display of several minutes, considerable expense . . . reported from a watch-tower. Should I go further back, Major?'

He paused, a frown cutting his forehead. He asked where the fireworks had been launched. He was shown the map, then the satellite image, then a zoom took the picture to the river bank, the Estonian side, and the ground below a steep bank behind which was an open space marked as the location of a German military cemetery. The Major was told that the graves had been bulldozed in the Soviet era, but then landscaped following the new régime taking power in Tallinn. The Major was told also that the screen operator's grandmother had fought on that front in the Great Patriotic War and . . . A quiet click of his tongue ended the anecdote.

'And it was raining hard when they were fired?'

'So they reported in the tower. It was registered because it was strange to launch fireworks in such conditions. They saw no party in progress and no audience. That was all.'

And he was again shown the location, and he had a print-out done of that sector, and of the river banks closer to the town of Narva and also further downstream and towards the estuary to the Baltic. The significance of this? The Major was uncertain. Uncertain also whether an American journalist asking for entry to Ivangorod to investigate the condition of a mediaeval castle was relevant, or excessive smuggling, or two pensioners who were armed with veteran shotguns and had with them in their boat a spaniel and three dead ducks. He raised his head, sniffed and caught the waft of the recycled air and searched for a scent. He left with a promise that anything further would be passed to him.

Past midnight, the night deep over the city, and reports on the radio spoke of an explosion, probably the result of a faulty gas

installation, on the premises of a small company dealing with
chemical exports and imports. He demanded that the sergeant
who had done surveillance on Yekaterina the previous afternoon
and evening – now assigned to him – should go to the location of
the explosion. He felt little sense of outrage but rather a considerable pleasure that he had acquired – right place and right time
– what was, without doubt, the most prestigious investigation of
his professional life.

She said they were within five kilometres of the town of Kingisepp.
Added that there was an ammonium plant there.

He said there was a road-block at Kingisepp, with a chicane.
She said that the men on the block, at Kingisepp, would be dozy
bastards, and stupid. He said 'dozy bastards and stupid' ones were
dangerous if armed with automatic weapons. Perhaps that weighed
heavy with the boys in front. A road sign directed traffic towards
a lay-by, and Martin was indicating the turn-off, then pulling in,
and she followed.

She asked, 'How do we go?'

Merc answered, 'Not with them.'

'And . . .?'

'We are too far back now. When you need to know I will tell you.
But we have to be beyond the block, on the far side of it.'

'And I have an opinion?'

'No.'

'Because?'

'Because it is what I was sent for, to get your brother across the
Narva river. Instead of him it is you. Sufficient.'

She persisted. 'And I don't get to sanction how? Don't have an
opinion?'

'No.' He laughed. She was a failed concert pianist, and a failed
activist, and Merc was a Gun for Hire and brought out of somewhere near nowhere to do a job. Miracle, she laughed with him,
touched his arm, then drove off the road and into the lay-by, and
bushes screened the empty piece of road. She stopped behind the
boys, killed her lights. Merc opened his door. He was climbing

out, his coat in his hand, and the rain was now sheeting. She asked if she should come. 'No.'

The door was opened for him. He eased in beside Kristjan. Cigarettes were passed. No preamble.

'The block down the road . . .' Martin said.

'Which you have to get through,' Toomas said.

'Get through or you lose. You cannot come with us because the girl does not have the papers – and we don't know what is the degree of alert . . . Or you can ditch her, be with us, take the chance.' Kristjan punched him, lightly, as if he'd made a joke, a good one.

'Whose opinion first?' Merc asked, and the smoke eddied among them.

They might have read him already. It seemed so. It would have been his opinion first, then second and third. Only his opinion. He did not know why they had turned back and waited at the entrance to the Kentucky Fried Chicken, why they had led himself and Kat away through the traffic, nor why they were here now and allowing him to flesh out an idea. It was like a combat situation, fast moving, on shifting ground, as in any of the places where he had done time. He did not like to spread trust but accepted times, places, when the options ran short. He would not argue, not debate. He said what he wanted of them. Merc waited for a small avalanche of rejection, all of them bunched together in turning away from what he said.

'What we thought,' Martin said.

'Near to where we were,' Toomas said.

Merc reached into his jacket and found the weight, solid and comforting, of the Makarov – already loaded – and his fingers grasped the spare magazine and lifted it out of his pocket and held it between them. Kristjan took it.

A little grimace and Kristjan said, 'You haven't, but you ask why? Entitled to ask . . . I stack the shelves in the Fama supermarket off the Tallina manatee, address 19C, and my woman has gone with her mother, and I have no one I call a friend, and I am not held in respect, and I am a bum and I do not think that my grandfather dribbled excuses or cried to be spared. I think he spat in their fucking faces. Is that good for why? Good enough? I hope to do the casino tonight, do the roulette, then go home.'

Toomas said, 'I am a Teutonic knight, a fantasy. All of my life is fantasy, not this.'

Martin said, 'On Monday, I will be painting in an apartment, the bog end of Haapsalu, and I want something to remember if I am not to die from boredom. Exhilaration, like it was for us many years ago, and our grandfathers. Stay safe, and her.'

He was kissed on each cheek, all of them in turn. The car flooded with light when he opened the rear door and saw the ugliness of the pistol that lay on Kristjan's lap. Merc went back to the Polo. He told her he would drive. The lights came on in front of him and he flicked the ignition. Should have changed her seat setting, hadn't time, wasn't bothered. They went forward out of the lay-by, and turned on to the main road. He said nothing.

13

Engines idling, lights dead, he and the boys sat in their respective vehicles, and waited for the hands of their watches to reach the point agreed. The last delay, and ahead of them were the illuminated streets of a small town he had never heard of before the briefing. Chemicals and open-cast mines, and he remembered the smell from the day before. The boys had pulled in just short of the first street lights and nothing moved on the road or the pavement.

He'd asked her, 'This is where the block will be?'

'Here, where you came through the last morning. Inevitable after the explosion, but you knew that.'

'And it is Kingisepp?'

A small and brittle laugh. 'You should have the name and say it?'

'Why should I have the name?'

'Because it is where you *die* – or where you, we, are taken. Does it concern you? Die, or taken – at this place, so you must have the name of it.'

Merc thought she spoke the truth. He knew most of the hard yards on the Route Irish run, and also where the diplomats from the embassy compound in the Green Zone would go to in downtown Baghdad on an excursion – behind a wall of guns – to reach a ministry. Knew the routes that the escorted convoys would take, and where the bad places were for the IEDs or ambush points, had codename calls for the street intersections and all the roundabouts where they might slow. And had lodged in his mind all the places either side, north or south, of Hill 425, and Brad and Rob in Command and Control had the call signs and – if luck shone bright – might get the Warthogs in, circling and then diving to dump the ordnance, or the fast jets. He had no one here, at Kingisepp, other than her, and the boys in the car ahead who had stayed behind, earning the cash they'd pocketed, and flaky at best. Not a good place to be, but better for having a name.

Thinking about death? A bit. Usually did when the stakes were high.

All the guys did. The men who took the money, the Guns for Hire, had written wills and lodged them with the embassy's consular people, and had taken to fingering the phones with the pictures of divorced wives and kids who were growing up without them. All the guys who congregated round the pool in the Green Zone, or lived in a supposed secure compound in Kabul, had a hotel room and a barracks billet in Erbil, when things were likely to get 'difficult' took a cloak of the sentimental, and then would push the pictures round. 'Great girl . . . super kids . . . really well, she looks . . . lovely, lovely kids . . . must be proud of them . . .' That's how it was supposed to be. Everyone had an eyeful of the one-time wife, and the kids who are now trying to sleep while she's getting a decent shafting from the new bloke on the block and the sounds are creaking through the thin walls. No one says that the ex-woman and the brats look just like everyone else's. Off the next morning and might be the day to die, or the day to get a bloody awful mutilation wound, or the day to get taken and face big music.

It could be the day Merc died.

He had no phone with pictures on it. Did it concern him?

Her challenge, and the mischief in her face. The lights came on in front. Kristjan – ten or fifteen years older than Merc and the girl beside him – had given the thumbs-up. Might have been to wish them luck . . . Might need it.

Merc said, 'You do what I tell you, exactly that. Remember my promise.'

Bombast seconds earlier, but all of it flushed out. 'What did you promise?'

'To take you out – why he stayed in there, your brother. Because of my promise.'

'How do we do it?'

He did not answer. She had seemed to shrivel. Had been bold and sat up straight, and had now subsided. They were rolling. The Polo had good power. He stayed close to the fender in front and used only the side lights. Merc no longer considered a situation at the 'end game' and how it would be when they hit the block. No more dreaming. His forehead was lined with the ruts of concentration. He would have liked to have had the pistol on his own lap, but he had no weapon. Beside him, she was starting to pant, like the stress had reached her. They went at speed and Martin, in front, had lifted the pace and they probably broke most of the speed limits in the municipality of Kingispill, where he might die and might not.

A sense of age gripped him. Close to the 'sometime' when he should have jacked it. Packed a kit bag. Handed a weapon into the armoury. Sold off everything that he owned in Erbil, and Rob and Brad would drive him to the airport and grip his hand, hug him. Age caught all of them, might now have hacked into him. Might have reckoned himself past his sharpest, reactions a fraction slower, and no way to retrieve one-time youth: knew it and was frightened of it. She was close to him and he smelt her, thought it was her fear, did not think less of her, and closer as he felt the pressure of her arms.

She had lived off her brother who had been a criminal. She had wanted to be a concert pianist. She had thought of herself as a revolutionary, and had so little credibility that to be groped by the self-styled Leader had seemed worthwhile for an entry ticket to the movement. Her 'enemy' had thought her so worthless that he'd offered her freedom in exchange for touting, informing. She had believed herself brave. She clung to a stranger, and to give herself courage had taunted him, and was ashamed. They went towards the road-block, where he said there were guns and petrol drums in a chicane to prevent a car speeding through.

Kat could not hold his hand on the wheel, or his arm that swung with the motion of the wheel. She sank down to the rubbish and dirt on the floor, and hooked her arms around his leg, hands clasped tight underneath his thigh.

The town was a place of ghosts.

She saw, through the bottom of the open window, shadows on bicycles, most without lights or reflectors, looming from the darkness. A van was parked and two men threw bin bags in through the rear door. A woman, a winter coat covering her dressing-gown, swept the step of a shop front that was not yet lit. A police vehicle overtook them, blue lights rotating on the roof, and would beat them to the bridge where the drums were, and the guns . . . A drunk, or an acid addict, was sprawled half on the pavement and across the gutter and half in the road, and might – perhaps – have survived the night in the rain . . . Kat had been loved only by her brother, and she had seen the scale of the explosion, and he had not come running towards the car in the minutes before the detonation. She knew the story – and the lesson – of the Wolf's Lair. There was a road off to the right that went to the heart of the town, and a timber truck and heavy trailer, loaded with pit-prop lengths of pine, emerged from it and was nearly across the road. The boys pulled out and Merc followed. She sensed oncoming headlights and heard the scream of tyres and the yell of horns, and they missed it. She held his leg, clung to it.

She had made her own life. Dumped by her father, abandoned by her mother, had won her place at the Conservatory. Had ignored those who had warned her of association with 'negative elements'. Had known best, flouncing away after being told of her dismissal. Had gone to the group and listened to the 'new warfare' against the state and had volunteered to paste posters, in the dead of night, to the walls of public buildings . . . Had made her own mistakes. He drove faster. Kept close to the weaving fender in front of him, and it was nearing the time he had said when men on night watch were at their least responsive – half asleep, bored. She had not doubted him. Knew nothing of him, where he came from, but gave him the bundle of her safety, future, life . . . Must believe in him, had no one else.

'I ask you . . . My brother was targeted by the special agencies of Britain, who employ you. Why? He was negligible – a criminal who stole money from banks, from savings accounts. What importance did he have? He gave his life, for what?'

He did not speak. The car rocked at speed, she clung to him and felt each movement as he shifted in his seat. They were still among buildings, either side of the road, and she did not know how far it would be before they hit the block – and she thought him so calm, and if it were the start of the last minute of his life then she, too, would be dead – a ragdoll corpse and nothing to show from a cut-off life.

Martin drove, foot down. Toomas, beside him, did the radio. Kristjan held the Makarov. The lights were weak, the red seemed to be the brightest. Once the silhouette of a man passed across the beam, the angle of a rifle barrel jutting away from him. Martin asked them, a hissed question, if it was the right time; a moment of truth and the commitment was made. Whispered agreement from Toomas and a punch on the shoulder from Kristjan behind him. He had his answer, used the wheel stick to shut down the lights, giggled and said it was a rubbish car and that modern versions would not have allowed him to throw the switch. Martin went straight, held the wheel easily, breathed hard.

Toomas had flicked channels, had found what he wanted. A station from home, beamed out of Tallinn, He'd found the Raadio2 station on the ERR band, what he would have listened to after a day in the heat of the chain-mail armour up by the castle. He had Queen's 'We Will Rock You'. Freddie Mercury's foot-stomps and the May guitar blasting. The sound was turned high, like they were in the front row at a concert, right by the speakers. Could not hear, could not think, which was good. Toomas was a middle-aged man and his life was wrecked and he had once wanted to be an academic, and God alone had known in what discipline. None of them had achieved: not Martin as an accountant, nor Kristjan as a fast-footed boxer. They went down the road towards the block and the song hammered at them and gave them a cupful of courage.

Kristjan had the windows down, right and left of him, and had twisted on the back seat and had remembered which side of the heavy oil drums the militia goons had stood and he faced that way and made the pistol ready to fire. The cold wind blew on his face, and he held the weapon in numbed hands.

A light waved at them, its movement increasingly frantic – and Queen carried them.

He should not have been there. Pyotr was part-time in the militia, a reservist. He was beyond the drums and halfway down the bridge and heard the thudding of the music and thought it horrible, like a sow in difficult labour. Heard the shouting of the men who had been drafted in along with himself, there to augment the pair of guys assigned the duty.

Pyotr saw the wild swinging of the light Vladdy held. Vladdy was on the far side of the drums and it was his role to slow vehicles approaching the zigzag among the drums and wave them to a halt so their documents could be examined. Pyotr had received a text message less than an hour before. He had been at his supper, prepared by his mother, then would have been going into Kingisepp to spend the rest of the evening at the home of the widow, Anna, and they might have listened to concert music afterwards, and might have gone to bed and . . . He had not ignored the text message, would never fail to respond. There were two more men, neighbours, and both had hoped to be at home, beside the fire and with the TV bringing them the game from St Petersburg, the top ice hockey fixture, and some Baltika bottles and might have been still awake, slumped in front of the television. He was not warm in the widow's bed, and they were not sprawled among empty bottles, and Vladdy – he knew – had his uniform on over his pyjamas. The noise rushed towards him but the vehicle was not yet in the cones of light thrown down by the street lamps above the drums.

They did not know what they were looking for. An incident had been reported in the city a hundred klicks up the road, but no explanation.

Heavy on the strap around his neck was an old AK. A grand
one. The Kalashnikov assault rifle was more than eighteen years
old, had been in many hands, but had been Pyotr's all the time
that he had been listed on the reserve for the militia. The date
coincided with the start of increasing tension along the closed
security zone between the town of Kingisepp and the Narva, the
border with the NATO territory of Estonia, against which it was
necessary, as the President said, to show great vigilance. This
weapon was always assigned him, the younger men wanted a
newer, cleaner version. Pyotr loved the rifle, treated it with as great
a respect as he did his Stihl chain-saw, had fired it for real only
once when he had dropped a boar, as wild as the forest it lived in,
seventy kilos, seen it grazing beside the road on the way back from
duty down on the Peipis Lake. So much better than shooting at
targets; the foresight locked on the beast's flank, behind the
shoulder, one shot and barely a twitch. A wonderful weapon . . .
He was grappling for the strap, trying to free the weapon from his
collar. Pyotr was not a man who was used to acting at speed, liked
time to work through the process of what confronted him. He did
not have time. A vehicle came into the light, and he heard – with
the blast of crude music – the shriek of tyres as it began to swerve
among the drums, and heard the scream from Vladdy who stumbled backwards. He realised that there was a second car on its rear
wheels, no lights, coming at the same lethal speed. The rifle was
off his shoulder and he groped for the arming lever.

Merc followed the tail. Stayed close, two hands strong on the
wheel. The music serenaded him. The boys went through the first
bends; he was slower. He hit a drum and was flung to the side and
the Polo lost traction, was on two wheels and then lurched back.

His leg was held, tight as a tourniquet, and he thought her
fingernails would penetrate his trousers and puncture his skin. It
was as if he were the only safety she knew. Her head was down
and she would not have seen the next drum rush towards the near
side, and then another buffeting collision and the brightness of
sparks leaping, dying, and metal lifting away, and he went through.

He could count shots, and differentiate them. Three from the
pistol. He did not think them aimed. Just fired from the moving
car and the bullets would have gone high and clear, and anyway
the targets were crouching or falling, or ducking and weaving, and
he went into the last section of the chicane. Then the burst, semi-
automatic. A finger on a trigger, releasing it, then immediately
after it had slipped back into position, pressuring it, and repeating.
The fiercer, stronger sound of an automatic rifle . . . Knew enough
about them. Might have felt that the Kalashnikov, in its various
models and with refinements, had followed him for half his adult
life. Had known them all over, the primitive ones and the most
advanced, and all of the damn things worked well, did not jam,
were consistent with high rates of killing. The noise, with the background chorus of Mercury and May, was shrill in his ear. Also, the
whiplash crack of the round going overhead, and a ricochet's
whine off the tarmac or the side of a drum. She was down on the
floor and had contorted herself so that most of her body was
folded away in the foot space, and her head was buried, and her
arms gripped his legs.

The car ahead went through. For the last yards it was swinging
and manoeuvring, as if a drunk drove it, a fairground-ride. He hit
the back of the car, saw Kristjan thrown aside on the impact, and
saw the pistol in his hand. And bullets hit their car, and his. Not
organised shooting, not how it would have been if he had been
behind one of the AKs, and not deadly as it would have been if
Rob or Brad had been firing, or the big fellow who had been
stopped in the wire on Hill 425 . . . But they hit and each time he
felt the impact into the body of the car, and into the engine block.
They kept going, and there were more shots fired from the back
seat . . . Queen had died.

They were pulling clear. The steering was wrecked, tried to
lock. Merc needed his strength to wrench at the steering and keep
the wheels from aiming into the barrier on the side of the bridge.
They were out of the pools of light. He thought their best chance
was to have created enough panic, confusion, something beyond
anything experienced by the goons who'd manned the block, and

hope it had destroyed clear thinking, logic, the discipline of training, and to get on down the road. More shots. More whiplash and more whines, more sparks.

The car ahead had its lights back on. Intelligent and sensible. Full headlights, no dipping. A man in uniform in the centre of the road, daring to stand there with his AK at his shoulder, and he could not see because the brilliance blinded his vision. He fired, his shoulder sagging from the recoil each time, then he jumped sideways. Merc thought that the boys' front passenger side had clipped him, might have been at the hip or on the upper thigh, and the man screamed, and was lifted momentarily and then fell against the barrier at the end of the bridge.

Merc thought that with those last shots, the guy had ignored the blindness from the lights, had kept a degree of control, had fired low and straight, had probably cleared his magazine, and had done damage.

She was good, did not howl or swear, was still, but held him. He would have known if she had been hit. Enough times in his life there had been 'incoming' and it had dawned, never fast, that he had not been hit. Unlikely odds that he could have sat behind the wheel, upright and exposed . . . could not see well now because the windscreen was fogged, and he needed to punch it, do it full force, to break it . . . and not taken a bullet. A brave guy, but a stupid one, had fired aimed shots, weapon at the shoulder, had used the last moments before leaping for his life, and being clipped, but had done damage. The steering was going. The engine was coughing and becoming less responsive to his stamping on the pedal . . . They were off the bridge.

A last flurry. A volley of fire that might have been a dozen rounds or fifteen. They came over and past him. The best was saved for the end, always the way at the fairground.

Merc had seen the militia faces as he had come through, and their performance had been poor. He reckoned they had been challenged for the first time in their lives. But nothing for Merc to take pleasure from. There was one last burst of firing, targeting the back of their car. Aim poor, height wrong, no casualties. But . . .

The tyre went down fast. The steering was close to impossible. The engine power was sluggish, diminishing. Merc reached down, grabbed her collar and heaved her up. She was caught between the glove compartment and the edge of the seat. He yanked her clear. He told her what she should do. She was kneeling on the seat, looking through the back window, and told him that – what she could see – there was no one pursuing. She did not need to tell him that the tyre was shredding and that they were driving on the metal of the wheel. Did not need to tell him that the car was filling with foul engine fumes . . . He had thought they had come through well.

Ahead, there were no lights to guide him and he had lost the boys after the last brief flash of their brakes. Merc needed another ten minutes from the Polo. Needed another ten minutes to carry them five miles. Needed it before the pursuit was organised. A helicopter with image intensifier, cordons and dogs. Ahead of them was the river, in flood and bone-chillingly cold.

'Are you all right?'

Almost a laugh. 'Been better.'

The wind came at them, and rain splattered in off the Polo's bonnet and was funnelled into the hole he had punched in the windscreen. The noise from the wheel was raucous, and more sparks flew and he struggled to keep the car moving, to keep up the speed. He pushed the pedal on to the floor, and the cold was fierce and they listened, as best they could, and did not hear sirens. Nor did he see the boys. Merc knew them well, those times that went slow.

She said, 'Did we do well?'

Merc said, 'We've not started.'

They were going west, the way ahead clear. They were in the black dog hours of the night, and the trees of the forest seemed to press close to the road and funnel them forward.

Toomas was silent.

Martin drove. The rain had eased off and might have stopped. Cold wind chased the clouds, and with the clearing skies would come a fast, bitter frost. He had to strain to see through the wind-screen because of the fog that spurted up from the engine and was thrown back against the glass. The dials in front of him were banging at their limits and red lights winked messages. He did not know if the engine would explode, or would simply cough, choke, and expire. He was exhausted, his arms were rigid, his hands locked on the wheel, and his mind raced. If they went into the trees and the engine failed, then they must push it far and deep, must cover up the tyre tracks and take off the plates. All of that went though his mind, and he struggled to see the road and keep to it, and he might not have the strength, but Toomas would. The wind came in and he shivered and he thought their speed was slackening.

Kristjan was nestled down on the back seat, the pistol in his hand – it would have taken pliers to take it from him – and had said nothing. He looked into the void where the rear window had been smashed by three shots; the fragments were on him and plastered against the backs of the front seats. He thought he had done well and had fired almost the whole of the magazine. Though neither Martin nor Toomas would say it to his face, the firing from the militia had been haphazard, chaotic, and they'd have done even better had – no fault of Kristjan – the big fucker not stood in the road and aimed straight at the engine. Much farther? He did not think so, not from the engine sounds, with smoke spilling out, and the smell of scorching. They would not say it, so he would.

'I tell you it for nothing, I did good.'

Martin answered him, quiet, distracted. 'You were the hero of the hour.'

'Is that sarcasm?'

'Take it as a compliment or take it as shit – being a hero.'

Another question, like a dam had broken. 'Is that what we expected? That number of guns? And now, we do not just turn up at the bridge at Ivangorod, flash some passports, get waved through and ride over the bridge in a car that's holed, a kitchen sieve. Can't be done . . . Did we know how it would be? Who told me?'

Martin said, not turning, 'I did not know. The scene, a gang feud. Why a reinforced road-block a hundred kilometres down the road? I do not know. I know nothing. What does Toomas know?'

Kristjan chimed, 'Toomas, fuck you, man, what did you know?'

A moment of stillness in the car, and the smoke seemed to thicken in front of Martin, and the juddering of the engine shook Kristjan and the glass crystals jumped with the motion, and Toomas was upright but did not speak.

One hand off the wheel, Martin reached for him, shook his arm, felt the wet, let out a small oath . . . The only light to guide them was off the dashboard dials. The breathing was regular but the touch of their hands must have stirred something in Toomas's chest, because the first froth and bubbles appeared at his mouth and blood had soaked through his clothing, and still came, oozed . . . He was their friend, and should have taught at Tartu College or at the university in Tallinn, taught at any fucking place. They had dislodged him, and his head rolled. He was going under, like the car's engine.

'Sorry, boys,' Toomas murmured. 'Not good, sorry. A gang feud, what you said . . . and some bright shit reckons otherwise, not just a *mafiya* fight . . . sorry.'

Shouting clamoured down the corridor of the Big House.

The building, at night, was a cemetery, quiet and the first cleaners not yet there, the offices dark and locked. The Major was at his desk and had the sergeant to help him, and the lieutenant who had come off duty at two o'clock in the Operations Room had joined him. They were enough; he could manage. He assumed that, on the floor above, the general kept a vigil in his own section, but he did not interfere and gave him free rein.

The yelling was fierce, bitter, angry.

He had ordered that the forensic team from scenes of crime get into the building with the firemen to escort them so he could match the seating plan to the critical item of intelligence: the centre point of the explosion. Where had the device been? In what was it carried into the room? Detail was the necessity. He had the names around the table. He had biographies of the young men. Nothing was clear to him, everything fogged, no direction obvious. The success of his career, not in ranking but in status as an investigator – he maintained – was based on his refusal to carry prejudice, preconception, in his back pack. The obvious was seldom satisfactory . . . The noise annoyed him.

Uncontrolled and furious, as if blows were about to be landed, punches thrown.

The Major had glanced at the message from his wife: some injuries at the hospital were of desperate severity. Of course, Nikki was there. The brother of little Yekaterina had a place on the chart that put him halfway down the table, with a doorway behind him into the corridor to the staircase. He had the identities of some of those admitted to the hospitals, and several of those who were already declared dead and had been named and were unmarked. A peculiarity of bomb detonations was that some victims were dismembered, some were hideously disfigured by fire and shrapnel and might live and might die, but there were always some who carried no wounds and seemed at peace, asleep, and were dead. He thought the rescue teams had showed extraordinary bravery in getting to the first floor and retrieving those still alive, and those who were clearly dead. It would take longer to bring down the body parts, but they would show better where the device had detonated.

Other than Nikki, he knew of none of them. The Major did not stray into the world of cyber crime and knew little of the hackers beyond that each organisation employing them was given an expensive 'roof' as protection. His investigations probed only infrequently into areas dominated by Organised Crime . . . but all of it now was confusing to him . . . And the noise of two men, voices incoherent, came into his office and distracted him. He went out of his door to confront them. He was not noticed by either of them.

'Because of your fucking jealousy.'

'I did nothing.'

'Your fucking jealousy and your fucking greed.'

'Wrong, and you take that lie back.'

'Jealousy, greed. The contract was for my people, and you could not stand the fucking rejection of your useless people.'

'You accuse me of the explosion? Bastard . . .'

'Accuse you? I do!' Jealousy and greed. My contract, my contacts, my intelligence. You put in a bomb . . . You will fucking pay.'

One in the remains of a suit. The other dressed for a restaurant on the Nevsky Prospekt, with prices far beyond the declared earning power of an FSB colonel. The suit had lost a jacket sleeve, and the lower right trouser leg. The other wore designer jeans and a foreign shirt and a fancy sweater and had a shoulder-bag of Italian leather. One was blood stained and had cuts and slashes on his skin that had been cursorily cleaned, and the other was immaculate, except that now a congealing dribble ran from the side of his mouth. They had been standing but then had wrestled, then had fallen, and now rolled on the carpet and once down were unable to land the big kicks, punches, head butting, that both struggled to inflict. He understood. It was about the 'roof'. The one provided the roof under which the Kupchino *avtoritet* sheltered and in return for handsome remuneration was supposed to offer high-grade protection. The other offered the roof for the organisation that ran the airport and the cargo scams and was accused of permitting the attack on the premises of a competitor. That competitor had done well, had pulled in a lucrative government contract, had been attacked. The motives for such failure to provide protection were 'greed' and 'jealousy'. Both men lived well, had fine apartments inside the city limits, had substantial country homes in the forests, and both were linked closely to Organised Crime gangs, and they were fighting in the Big House. The Major thought it disgusting and turned back towards his office. Past four in the morning, and colonels fighting. He reflected . . . Few certainties existed. Was a vendetta a satisfactory reason for an act of internal war, a bomb to blow up a rival's headquarters? Would such blood-letting be permitted by the 'roof' for the reasons of greed and jealousy? They crawled to their feet and one staggered and the other used the wall as a support until he could stand, swaying.

The Major offered no explanations to his sergeant and the young woman lieutenant. He needed facts; without them was as his blind as two brawling superiors.

She was awake, he was not.

Igor snored softly, lay on his back, did not touch her. Marika sensed the rain had finished and through the drawn curtains saw the moon's trace. She listened.

She had heard the dogs stretch and roll on the rug in front of the fire, and the wind against the eaves, and had shivered and pulled the rugs closer over her body, and knew it would be colder that night and that the frost would gather and . . . She had taken an ironware dish out to the barn in the late evening, and he had been with her with his shotgun, and she had laid it prominently inside, and a bottle of beer and that he had jibbed at. She listened and the dogs were not alerted, did not growl, and the animals in the barn were not disturbed by an intruder. The clothing she had washed and pressed had not been moved.

The guttering on their home was plastic. Their friend, Pyotr, had installed it because the original ironwork had rusted and collapsed. Plastic guttering contracted and expanded when the temperatures dipped or rose, and creaked as it did so. She thought the cold would gather on them and would freeze their breath on the windows. But no one came, and the dogs did not warn her of a stranger's approach, nor did she hear any restless movement from the beasts in the barn.

What she did hear, other than the gutter's motion, was the big owl's call, which she thought reassuring. And needed to be. Little in the life of Marika, or of Igor, had been safe. Great armies had trampled over their lives, pausing only briefly in their fighting, then moving on, and officials had come and had threatened, and had tried to take them by train deep into Siberia and far to the east . . . She thought the stranger had trusted her, and had left his clothing, filthy and damp which meant he had come across the river, and she believed him to be a friend. She had not heard him come but twice a deer had passed by the front of their home, provoking a low growl from the dogs. She had looked out and the moon's light had bathed the open ground, but she had not seen the stranger, and the dogs had soon settled. She would not tell Pyotr that she had put food out for a stranger. Pyotr always preached them a message of caution, said these were changing and dangerous times, but she had ignored his warnings.

No one came. Igor slept on. She heard nothing.

Above the river, on the old Swedish-built cannon emplacement, with uninterrupted views of the bridge, Boot kept his vigil . . . Going through the front door at home, extracting the Yale key from the lock, dumping his bag and shrugging out of his overcoat, and turning off the outside light.

He did not have to be watching the bridge, could have been in bed, asleep, and allowing events to play out; here, he had no influence on them.

'Hi, darling, good trip?' Gloria's voice singing out from the kitchen, an extension of the three-bedroom home he shared with her, pebble-dash and mock-Tudor beams on the front façade and London brick on the rest, and a shared driveway with the Fentons on the right, and a common wall with the Turners on the left, and 150 feet of garden at the rear. They rarely used the dining-room, seldom sat in the 'front room', the lounge. Most nights that he was at home, and she, they shared the principal bedroom, but not if either were late and the other already asleep, and the third bedroom stayed empty because Boot did not like to have visitors overnight with them. He'd have answered, 'Not bad, all right.' She'd have told him that there was a cauliflower cheese, or a lasagne, something easy, ready for the microwave, and he'd have come in and bent over her and given her a perfunctory kiss – a measure of his deep-rooted affection. She'd not have asked if he had successfully wrecked anything, damaged anybody, done anything life changing and bad for them. Would have asked, 'Decent food where you were?' She might have looked up from her catalogues, antique furniture and sales rooms and new chemicals for treating wet rot, dry rot, infestations. 'Sorry, darling, where was it you were? Silly me.' He'd have smiled, retrieved his supper, brought it to the table, and she'd have cleared a space for him, and he'd have said, 'Oh, you know, somewhere and nowhere.' Then smiled again . . . he would not have queried whether customers had been sold dubious Jacobean or unproven Georgian tables, desks, porcelain . . . He did not have to be there.

Cold enough – as Ollie Compton might have said at the Glienicke – 'to freeze the tail off a brass monkey', and he shivered and the wind came between the great castles and skipped over the bridge and swept across the bastion. He could have been at home for all the use he was on the matter of Copenhagen. Would not have gone to bed, but would have sat through half the night on the stairs and Gloria would not have called to him, would have allowed him the time to brood, or suffer.

Boot could not have said from where the hunger came . . . He'd remembered Ollie Compton's last day before compulsory retirement, and a party had been arranged down in the atrium with a free bar and complimentary cava or prosecco, and the Director expected for a brief speech of appreciation, and the presentation of a carriage clock or a crystal glass decanter, and they had waited, and waited, and . . . the old bugger hadn't shown. Ollie Compton lived in a bed-sit in Ealing, near the High Street, and was almost sad. Out of character, but a brief affair with slow horses that came in expensively late, immature investments in the markets, had run up surprising debts, and much of his generous pension went to the creditors and he lived – existed – in near penury. A lesson there for Boot, and it told him always to do his work, but always, also, to have reserves in his knapsack.

No vehicle came from the east on to the bridge, he'd noted that. The vehicles from his side, the west, were held in a long queue that stretched almost the length of the bridge. He need not have been there but would have felt ashamed to turn his back on his people . . . and he had reserves.

Might have been enjoying a good meal at the farmhouse, just off the road from Quatre Bras to Belle Alliance, and the talk would be of dispositions made and forces placed where the Emperor or the Duke believed them most valuable. A discussion concerning the precursor to crisis: the conversation mostly from Boot, the farmer's wife long gone to bed, and the dogs asleep, and the good man humouring his paying guest and listening, and the virtual monologue in adequate French. Always an important moment in Boot's visit because it marked the time when a commander started to lose control of the field, and would cede authority to lesser men . . . A few junior officers and alert NCOs would have sought out a farmhouse, had done so with the one where he was billeted, and liberated cellars where wine was stored, or brandy, and perhaps found a choice ham hanging in a larder, but were the minority. He liked to think of them, ordinary men and similar to himself, bivouacked in the open, and with a hot and heavy day's marching done, an empty stomach and a dry throat, and no cover, and the first spots of summer rain. Wondered how he would have been, and would talk in the night until the farmer gave up on the struggle and let his head sag down to the table. It was a grand routine, and the visits to the fields of Waterloo were much loved, and valued. Occasional pedestrians crossed but the vehicles, all shapes and all sizes, were fixed, and he seemed to hear the drums beating, mournful and dispiriting, and he watched the barrier at the far end.

Daff was at his shoulder. She had been in the warm, smoking, with the surveillance people.

'A big bang. Blocks up the road. Shooting. Not much else that's clear . . . Nothing to do but wait . . . you all right?'

Boot said he was fine.

'Just that you looked a bit peaky.'

He was fine and his tone had an edge and she'd stepped back.

It had to be 'deniable'. If evidence was left in the gutters and its source was transparent, then the mission would be dubbed, rightly, as flawed. If none were taken and if the crime was 'clean' then it would be an occasion for a choral hallelujah, a brass band playing, and bubbles spilling. The loneliness of command – gone unshared by the Duke, and not spoken of by Boot.

'I did flasks,' she said. 'Coffee or tea?'

'That would be good, either . . . We've handed it over to them, they're as strong as the weakest link. Cold to be out and running. Dodgy old game, Daff, but we knew that.'

'I can't do it,' Merc said. 'Can't stay with you.'

Two cars. Two fires that seemed to overlap. A smell that was pungent, choking, but all of them off the road and up to their ankles in thick, clinging mud.

'What do we do?' Kristjan's response, bordering on hysteria.

They were a hundred yards into the trees. It was the hope that the density of the pines would mask the fire. The wind helped them.

'I think I understand,' Martin said. 'Did we ask you to stay with us?'

'You did not.'

'And we are better on our own, without you?'

'I think so, it's how it has to be . . .' Merc was paid to fight and paid to lead and paid to be the man that others wanted to follow. It did not go easy for him, was against every instinct. He had not needed them and they had not needed him, and a small bond had developed. Kristjan was jabbering beside Martin who had kept cool, and on the ground – and alive – was the third of them. '. . . Do our own. I don't know how you go. I don't know how I go.'

He had been nursing the Polo, had almost reached the lay-by where – twenty-four hours before, a flicker of time – he had been picked up, and she had spotted them. He had missed them with the fog fumes from the engine across his holed windscreen. They were into the tree line and pushing the car deeper on an old loggers' track, and in darkness and chaos. He had wrenched the wheel and found their tyre marks and had come up against their vehicle and had nudged and shoved, shunted it another forty, fifty, yards. Then his own engine had died, and smoke was billowing. Bare-handed, he and she, and two of the boys, had manhandled

both cars farther in, and had fallen, had slipped, and sworn. Again
she was the first to see what was relevant. Merc had not missed
the boy who dressed up as a Teutonic knight to pay his bills, buy
his beer and bread.

Toomas was on the ground and Martin and Merc had given
their coats to warm him.

Kat had no medical experience, she said. Martin and Kristjan
said they had basics from the training before they went into
Kaliningrad, but that was fifteen years ago. Merc knew what to
look for, expected to find a messy entry wound, that would have
carried clothing and fragments of the car into a hole that had no
exit. Merc reckoned him lucky, perhaps not, still to be alive.
Contractors, former military that Merc had known in Kabul and
Baghdad, usually well dosed on steroids and laden with more
equipment than they had hands to use, and they'd had the USMC
logo on their socks and their underpants and tattooed on their
arms and arses along with *Semper Fidelis* and The Few, The Proud
and Devildogs, and had them on their stomachs and their shaved
scalps: one constant message from them that reflected the fear
because they were no longer in the Corps but were civilian wage
earners. The fear was of a wound. From the wound came the
knowledge they had become a burden. The other guys, unharmed,
might have a chance to leg it out, but not if they carried a casualty.
Had they been in the Corps, the ethic said that a wounded man
was never left, would be brought out whatever it took – helicopters, fast jets, Rangers on foot. A wounded guy was never
abandoned.

Martin said, 'What happens to him? They hurt him, keep him
alive, needle drugs into him, hurt him some more, lie to him. He
tells it – they are good at that work. Tells about me and about
Kristjan, and about her, and tells them about you. My grandfather
was lucky, was killed at the start. He died in the cells at the HQ in
Tallinn after interrogation. Worse was Kristjan's who they took
back to their camps and would have had days to work on him, or
months. It is a bad outlook. He needs treatment, and care, and
drugs, and—'

'I cannot take him and I cannot take you.'

'And what your people fear most is that one or more are taken.'

Merc said, 'May your God keep you safe.'

Martin said, 'If He is minded to.'

'We should have a beer on the far side – tomorrow night, whenever.'

She knelt – might have been recognised and might have been remembered – and kissed the cheek of Toomas, then held his hand, stroked his arm. Then stood, tucked her fist under Merc's arm, and pulled at him. There were sirens on the road, loud and threatening, but darkness would be their friend. Darkness would help, while it lasted.

14

Martin called after Merc. 'What we've done, did it have any purpose?'

'No idea.'

'Was it a disaster?'

'Most of what they organise from behind a desk are usually disasters. Doesn't stop them . . . I'll buy the first beer.'

'We'll go south, get round the town, find a boat.'

'Good luck to you.'

'You'll go the way you came?'

'Perhaps.'

It was one of those dumb bits of talking that neither wanted, and neither would forego. No help to Merc to know how they were going, and bad for them to know how he had come across the river and how he hoped to return . . . Unfinished business. He took her hand off his arm, strode back. Merc had learned that anything important, a job that mattered, was best done by himself. The flames in the cars had slackened but were still alive and the smoke would have choked him if he had inhaled. He kicked at the two registration plates, and they were burned enough to fracture, then he went to the front and lashed again with his boot and dislodged the plates there. They were as reliable as a calling card. He could have asked Martin, or Kristjan, to bury them . . . should have remembered before . . . and they would have promised. The Polo was traceable from the plates, and the hire car – easy enough for their people across in Narva to trace a hire car, and get copies of the paperwork. Best done by himself. He lifted up the plates, held them in his gloved hands and blundered away into the dense wall of low branches, bent and pushed. He sank in mud, and kicked with his heel, and made a shallow grave for them, and used the toes of his boots to bury them. He went back to them, and all the farewells and good luck wishes were already done. Nothing more to be said. Kristjan shone a small pencil torch on Toomas's face. The pallor of the near dead; might last a day, or an hour . . . Would be blessed to reach an appropriate hospital – and stay deniable – within an hour or a day.

Merc passed them, did not speak, did not offer another hug, or a hand clasp. He took the girl's hand. Not from affection, but to lead her. He tugged, and she fell into step.

And he stumbled and went up to his knees in a ditch and she was chucked against him and levered him upright, and a dozen steps later she slid and he held her. They had reached the track along which the cars had been pushed. Merc did the best he could. His best was to snap off two branches and pass them to her, then another two for himself. The sky above was clear and the clouds had gone, blown to some horizon, and the dregs of the moon's light gave them a milky trail, faint but possible, and the cold was bitter. He held the branches hard against the ground, and she copied and they broke the outlines of the ruts where the tyres had been, and softened the indentations from their boots and her trainers and he said it was something, not much. The wind was a friend and it came into their faces and pinioned their clothes and coursed along the path, and blew away the fumes from scorched paint and melted tyres and the plastic linings of the cars. He heard sirens. It was important for Merc to have purpose, cleaning the trail and leaving it less prominent . . . Never before had he walked out on comrades in a state of war. Did not like them, did not have to, shared nothing with them. Might as well, if he had had the means, have shot dead the three of them and left them. Achieved 'deniability' and moved on. Might as well, except that they were comrades, and had come back. He could not have helped them, and the excuse seemed feeble to him, shaming. They reached the road.

Merc, no explanation, pushed her down. They were on the rim of a ditch and vehicles came closer, then big headlights . . . How

much did he know of her? So little. The section of road was long
and straight, and the engines merged with the song of the wind in
the trees and the crackle as frost formed. There was the cry of a
lone bird, and lights approached. He knew so little of her, could
not have sworn that she would not stand, wave down the vehicles,
denounce him. He felt the warmth of her beside him and heard
her breathing. Merc had promised to take her out.

Why was he there? He could not have said. What had he
achieved? Precious little that he knew of.

Two jeeps cruised past. Their lights burned on the road and the
trees and speared past them. In each, he saw two men in the front
and two in the back, weapons readied. He thought that when
daylight came and organisation had been reclaimed there would
be cordons and dogs. The darkness was a good friend, not to be
squandered. He led her out into the middle of the deserted road,
assumed that a vehicle tailback was building to the west and
another to the east where the bridge was and the block had been.
Had to take a chance. Did not give an explanation. His grip was
no longer on her hand, but at her wrist.

He ran, took her with him.

A white line lay down the centre of the road and the last of the
moonlight held it and guided him. He was combat fit, and she was
not. He dragged her, showed no kindness. They came past a junction that had been his target, and then were close to the lay-by.
He'd a good stride, and she'd have fallen but for his hold. She
sobbed for breath and he thought she tried to break the grip, and
she'd have gone down if he had allowed it. He was near to the
lay-by when the lights came, and he dived for the side and she
came with him, and they plunged into a mess of low bare branches
from birch trees, and crawled, then were into the pines. He looked
back. Another patrol jeep went by. He thought he had used time
well, and that the dawn would soon chase them.

Ice was forming on the puddles in the ditches.

She swore. He took no notice. She swore in her own language,
and then in his. She was tugging harder, trying to halt him. It was
her shoe. The shoe from her right foot. Where was it? Swallowed

by the mud . . . If it had been Cinar, without a boot, and retreating under fire, what would he have done? Would have slapped her arse, and hard, with the flat of his hand, would have made her run until her foot bled, then some more? She was sobbing, might have been exhaustion, might have been anger. He hooked her on to his back, went forward, and branches scraped him and wind cut him, and sometimes the sirens were loud.

Merc let instinct guide him.

A single sheet of paper was on the Major's desk. A little dribble came from the side of his mouth and fell, absorbed by the paper. Spoiled but still readable. The fighters had gone their separate ways, still snarling, towards opposite ends of the corridor. He had gone back to his office, had demanded the file on all that was known, had started to gut it, and had swilled down coffee. The first report was expected 'soon' from the explosion site, and 'soon' was of no use to him. Was needed 'now'. He had gone back into the loose threads of the file and had added to it the report sent by the sergeant of a meeting in the supermarket car-park, down the E-20 from the city, had yawned hard, and slumped.

A bright morning and ferociously cold, and men and women on the pavements below hurried, well wrapped, and workmen scattered salt and grit, but he saw none of that, and the traffic of the day built, and the young woman fielded his calls. The sergeant and the lieutenant had agreed he should sleep until he had rested . . . until a crisis call came. The surveillance report, under the Major's head, took second place to an event, linked, and with a genuine demand for crisis status.

She pondered, only briefly. She woke him, surprised by the force necessary to stir him, told him of an incident, and a location. He was – then – awake and alert and was coughing, spitting into his handkerchief, and rubbing at his eyes, and he took his side-arm from the drawer, with its holster, buckled them, snapped his fingers for the sergeant to drive him, took a vest from the cupboard, and was gone.

*   *   *

He had been brought a pastry by Daff, sweet and clogging round his teeth, and coffee in a beaker. Her flask was finished and she'd gone to find a café. Boot maintained his watch.

He blinked frequently and looked into thin sunshine. Almost gold, the sun rose above Ivangorod on the far side of the river, beyond the bridge, and the rich colour of the skies was misted by the first smoke from the chimneys and then peeled off into horizontal lines. Hard to look into the bright line of the dawn, and hard to stave off the tiredness. The first of the day's small-time smugglers were coming over the bridge, going from east to west, carrying heavy plastic bags that would be floppy, empty, when they returned an hour later having dropped off the early delivery of vodka and cigarettes. Most were old people, stooping, and the wind blew hard on them on the open walkway. A few were younger and braved the bluster of the wind, and did not need to clutch at a handrail. But the vigil was pointless because he could not see their faces. They were vague and blurred, and none stood out . . . Not that he had seen them for himself, but Daff had shoved photographs under his nose, and he'd have sensed them. Not certain they would be walking, not certain they would be driving . . . not certain if they were alive . . . and not certain if they were still at liberty . . . and not certain where the one who called himself Merc was. It weighed on him, and bowed his shoulders, and he had wolfed down the pastry, hadn't the heart to tell Daff that it had tasted foul, instead had grimaced by way of gratitude, and the coffee was worse.

She was his source of news. Daff had been down to the queue waiting for clearance to leave Estonia. Could attract men's attention when she leaned forward, even in the quilted anorak. There had been a shooting up the road, twenty kilometres away, would have been gangsters, bandits, hooligans; a militia operation had started. A shrug, more cigarettes. Anything on the radio? Nothing . . . Boot was starved of what he needed to know.

She let him drink the coffee, and then forgot herself sufficiently to take a small handkerchief from a pocket and use it to wipe crumbs from his lips and what had stuck in the unshaven stubble.

He'd have admitted that his collar, tight with a tie beneath it, felt dirtied and stale. Something of a liberty for her to nanny him, and he should have shown displeasure. She took the beaker and the pastry's wrapping, and binned them. A little light cough, as if it were time to move and he was merely humoured. There would have been many others who shared a similar situation that morning.

Might have been in Peshawar, and waiting for some poor compromised devil to emerge from the tribal homelands of the North West Frontier having slapped a beacon on the under-side of a wagon used by a *mujah'* commander. Might have been up in one of those little Turkish towns on the Syrian border and an asset late for a rendezvous, and time crumbling, and wondering if a video of a decapitation was already in post-production. Might have been in the Control Tower at RAF Akrotiri, awaiting the return of a Special Forces Chinook, which might have brought out a burned agent, and might not. Might have been in Kabul, or Baghdad, or up close to the poppy fields of the Triangle, or the coca leaf farms of Peru, and might have been in Grand Cayman or Turks and Caicos or the Virgins and looking for the key that would unlock the accounts of bad bastards. Little operations running all over the place, damn them, and had to be if VBX was to 'punch above its weight', be a decisive player in the grand game. Men like himself, and women, would be staring into the middle distance, into places of acute danger, unable to intervene – and were responsible and carried the weight of it with differing degrees of comfort . . . He had once seen a senior officer in the Service weep because a good family man, a source in the Iraqi police, had ended up crucified, with flies laying eggs in his wounds, and a woman, his junior, had slapped his face and ordered him to 'Get a grip for fuck's sake'. Or, might have been sitting, on the 07.38 out of Motspur Park and heading for Waterloo and a day in the comfortable company of a screen and a canteen lunch, and there were plenty who did, and plenty who knew little of the long stare into a fogged distance, and . . .

She held his arm, took him to the car. He reflected how much of his working life had been dissipated, wasted, in waiting. So much of it. Tried to pull Merc's face to the front of his mind, but failed. At the end of the short journey, the back of Igor Gramov Street, he'd have fallen on his face if she had not supported him as he climbed through the window.

Martin was on the right, Kristjan on the left. Toomas hung between them.

'You think, Kristjan, he meant that? A beer on the other side?'

'I think, Martin, he meant it.'

And Toomas's feet sloshed in the mud but he hadn't the strength to lift them. Toomas could neither help himself nor speak, was a limp weight.

'Would you want him, Martin, to get you an Estonian beer or a foreign one?'

'I would want, Kristjan, a local beer – any sort of piss, but local.'

Toomas was alive, coughed, had blood at his mouth. He was a burden.

'On the other side, Martin, I think any beer is acceptable.'

'Not Russian beer, Kristjan, any beer but Russian.'

They had found a narrow track, not adequate for a vehicle, good enough for them. Could no longer smell the fumes of the burned cars. The wind wove through the trees. If they had not concentrated on carrying Toomas, and if the big issue had not been the beer, they would drink in Narva when the Irishman put his money on the bar, then the clatter of the branches would have unsettled them. They would go faster without him.

'On the other side, Martin, which would you prefer him to buy you? A woman or a beer?'

'All the women there are Russian, Kristjan, so I would want a beer – not their beer.'

There had been an eyewitness in Haapsalu. She had lived in one of the pretty brightly painted wooden-framed homes, fishermen's, on the town's strand, and had seen the flares come down; she had been restless and had been smoking at an open window. Had seen the light descending on a small parachute, had seen three men who were cumbersome with the packs they attempted to drag through the reed bed. Had seen the tracer rounds that were fired, red streaks ... some said that she was a changed woman, damaged by it ... had seen two try to carry a third out of the reed bed, then had dropped him, had disappeared. An ambulance man on the scene said afterwards that the top of the head was sliced off, and that death would have been immediate. The two survivors would not have known it in the darkness ... Martin's grandfather who was dead, and Toomas's grandfather who was injured within the next two minutes, and Kristjan's grandfather who had tried to get home but dogs had brought him down ... And three girls, young and heavy with child, would have heard the shouting and the barking, and the sirens, and the gunfire. They did not contemplate leaving Toomas while he was still alive.

'I tell you the truth, Martin, I might drink any beer when we are on the other side.'

'Any beer, Kristjan – and I am not the accountant I wanted to be, and you are not the boxer you wanted to be – we are fucked up, but we are now agreed.'

'Any beer.'

'And I would open Toomas's mouth and would pour any beer down his throat.'

'Any beer, Martin, but not Russian beer.'

Laughter from them both. Nervous, frightened, laughter. They trudged on and the wind hurried them.

Dawn hesitantly broke, filtered to daylight. While men and women should have been scurrying to work, their kids heading for school, pensioners on the move to the shops or for meetings where they might gossip and smoke, on a main street between big accommodation blocks and leading to an industrial estate – on the outskirts of the second city – was the Major's 'incident'.

First a police cordon. Waved down, an officious bastard telling them access was prohibited, who had been shown an ID, and had then been ignored. A patrol car was skewed across the road, doors open. Its crew, male and female militia, crouched in a doorway. His sergeant had slowed, swung past it.

Then a side turning, and more men in uniform, some standing
and some huddled, and all clutching firearms and looking as
though the Third World War was either launched or about to be.
They had been shouted at, and the Major's anger had run
unchecked. He'd lowered the window, let in a blast of air, had
bawled for them to go shag their mothers, their aunts, their
daughters, whichever they preferred. Behind a van, windscreen
shot out and water leaking from a radiator, were four armed
men. Sheltered by a builders' skip were two more, one shoul-
dering an RPG-7 launcher. And more in the shadow of a refuse
cart, all with Kalashnikovs. And one other was easy to
recognise.

He had the torn suit still hanging on his back and ripped trousers loose on his hips and blood on his shirt. Must have been
immune to cold and had stained bandaging on his head. The
avtoritet of Kupchino held a Vityaz-SN, the most modern subma-
chine gun issued to the military and the police special teams – 400
metres a second muzzle velocity, effective lethal range of 200
metres – and was yelling at the open gates to a warehouse complex
that was barricaded by a flatbed trailer. The Major did not have to
be told that the building behind it would be the operational base
of the *avtoritet* who controlled Pulkovo airport's cargo movements
at the Moskovsky end of the airport perimeter. He had seen the
fist fight of the guardian angels who provided the roofs, and now
saw the pack-dogs who paid for the roofs to be in place, paid well,
and had been fucked, fucked hard and fucked deep. Then, some
gunfire.

A desultory burst, and two single shots in response.

A hero? He would not have declared himself as one . . . . He was
annoyed. Armed groups of gangsters lined up in the city suburbs,
emptied streets, residents hiding in their homes, children kept
from school, all irritated the Major – and he was tired, and might
not have considered further options. Above all, the Major felt
contempt for the men – senior to him – who had scrabbled on the
floor. Obvious to the colonel who placed the roof over the operations in Kupchino, and the boss who slipped wealth into his

pocket, was that the gang of hoodlums, trapped in their complex and behind the flatbed, were responsible.

He stepped from the jeep, told the sergeant to reverse, turn, then keep the engine idling. Tired, irrational, he had a poor consideration of the consequences. His pistol was in its holster, flap buttoned down, and he had no gloves; the wind scalped his face, and the cold was in his ribs. He would not shiver, would not let them think he was afraid. He walked forward. The vest carried the logo of FSB. He was covered by many rifles, sights were trained on him. He carried the authority of the *Federal'naya sluzhba bezopasnosti Rossiyskoy Federatsii* and he did not expect to be shot in the chest by the people from the Pulkovo *mafiya* nor in the back by those from Kupchino. None would have seen him before unless they had glimpsed him in the dark chaos of the collapsed building. He was not known, had no links to them.

The Kupchino crowd was fifty metres behind him, and the Pulkovo guns were fifty metres ahead of him and he had already skirted a scattering of spent cartridge cases. A wise officer put little trust in the quality of the vests offered to officers not serving on Special Operations; the best trained teams had the best equipment. The vest offered to a major dealing with dissident activity in the city would be unlikely to stop a high-velocity round from a Kalashnikov, even from the machine pistol held by the *avtoritet*. If he showed fear then he might be dead. At best, fear would earn him ridicule. At worst, it would bring him a funeral followed by an insincere crocodile of mourners who muttered asides of 'climbing beyond his status' and a 'fool's just desserts'. A deep breath. He did not shout. Both sides would have had to strain to hear what he said. Almost conversational, and the street had gone quiet and no bird sang – and no shot was fired.

'It may not be true . . . again, it may be true. I have the rank of major, and I am charged by General Onishenko, from the Big House, with the investigation into the explosion last night at the building used by the Kupchino *mafiya*. The obvious accusation is that a rival group – the Pulkovo *mafiya* – believed themselves to be tricked out of a favourable contract given to Kupchino by State

Security. In retaliation they – from Pulkovo – took a bomb into the building where a meeting of experts planned to carry out the tasking of State Security. The bomb killed several and wounded more. In retaliation, Kupchino has come to Pulkovo with guns and is intent on exacting revenge. Listen, if you wish to shoot each other then I will not object. I don't care . . . My own view is that the more you shoot, take each other down, then the happier I am . . . In the night I saw your two "roofs" fight on the floor in the Big House, one accusing the other of jealousy, greed, organising the bomb. I could give you all, perhaps, one full hour to shoot at each other, hopefully get some hits, then the security will be obliged to intervene. One option. The other option is that you put away those illegal weapons and go back to your rat dens. May I please give you another of my opinions? Not set in concrete, but having a certain weight. I have no evidence that Pulkovo brought the bomb to Kupchino. No proof. To be truthful, a small voice tells me I will not find that proof. When the trail is too obvious, my experience is to look elsewhere. I don't know. Only a small voice . . . You should put away your weapons because at the moment you distract me and use up my time. Put them away.'

Men emerged from behind the lorry, and from the corner of his eye he saw that others moved into the open and abandoned the builders' skip, and he saw that the wounded *autorite* turned his back on his rival and let his weapon trail beside his leg, and walked away. He believed he heard the sounds of weapons being disarmed. The Major went to his jeep, climbed in. His sergeant asked if it were true, what he had said, a 'small voice' and not finding evidence. Did he believe that?

'Perhaps, yes, a little. But I do not know yet where else to look. Perhaps, no. But it was the right thing to say.'

'And to say anything there, it was dangerous for you.'

'Perhaps, yes. Perhaps, no.' He hid the stress well, and his smile was slow and careful and would have been hard to read.

Merc judged her by her weight. Not by the tilt of her nose, thickness of her lips, the strength of her thighs that she had wrapped round his waist to grip him better, not by the size of her waist or her chest. He judged Kat by her weight. She clung tight with one hand. The second fended off the branches that bounced into their faces. The ground under his feet was slush and mud but the standing water was now freezing and a trace of sunshine came through the tops of the pines, showing him where to go but giving no warmth. He did it because he had given his promise.

Now, his instinct served him. A track drifted away in front of him. He paused in the tree line, eased her down, laid a hand on her mouth, felt the warmth of her breath, and she nodded her understanding and he eased it clear. He listened. She was good, did not speak. Which pleased him . . . None of the guys did, nor the girls, in the trench lines. Only spoke when it was needed. He heard the wind, and a distant engine, and also the call of cattle. An animal must have come behind them and been surprised by them and had veered away but they did not see it. He stood a long time, and listened, and the sound of the wind was constant, but that of an engine grew clearer. They were back among pines and in front of them was a screen of birches, then the track. It had scattered stones in it and the mark of tyres but was not well used. A whiff of wood-smoke was carried to him.

He felt a vindication. Some would have done high fives in acknowledgement of their skill in locating the one staging post he knew. Merc took off his glove, from the right hand, and lifted her leg. He put the glove over as much of the foot as it would cover, not much but something. There was sufficient light for him to see her face and realise it wore a gentle shade of blue, like a paint into which too much water had been mixed, and her sock was sodden. She stood by him, defiant, but would have been crippled by the cold. The engine sound was nearer. He pulled her back.

The vehicle was military, open, painted a dull green, and it came fast and scattered cascades of water from the pot-holes in the track. A lone driver, a middle-aged man, heavy and unshaven and wearing a uniform and flak vest. An assault rifle bounced on his knees. The vehicle swept past them and went on down the track and into the wind and the driver had no helmet, and lank untidy hair flew behind him.

The scent would be from a log fire. A slow fire, made with wet wood, and coming from the building beside the barn where he had slept. He remembered the time in the barn and the animals that had nestled around him, and their smells, and their grunted acceptance, and the fowls that had cheeped over him, and the warmth, and the dry straw, and the freedom from the cold . . . They would not go to the river that night. Too tired and his mind too numbed. On Hill 425, pretty much anywhere he'd been, Merc could hunker down in any corner and get decent sleep. But he would need a floor, and a roof over it, and the comfort of soft dry straw. She felt the cold worse than he did, and he felt it bad, and she had started to shiver and he could hear the little clatter of her teeth. He hoisted her up on to his back.

Merc went towards the scent of a fire, a place of comfort. He walked for ten minutes. The track straightened. He saw the barn and the farmhouse, and the smoke billowing from an angled iron chimney. The barn door was open and animals were out on the open ground in front of it, and some fodder was scattered for them, and a dog chased chickens without enthusiasm. The jeep was parked between the house and the barn. On the driver's seat was a Kalashnikov with a magazine attached. The militiaman had stripped off his military vest, dumped his cap, and was chopping logs. An old man, a shotgun leaning against a wall and close enough to grab, tossed him big rings of pinewood for splitting and the axe was swung lazily, but he paused when a woman came out of the house, elderly but walking well and carrying a steaming mug, and a second dog followed her and then the chickens hurried to her, and the sheep – and the pigs and the cattle.

'What do we do?'

'Wait and watch. Nothing else we can do because we have to sleep. Watch and wait, and hope.'

'And I am cold enough to cry.'

'Must live with it.'

She had to talk. Kat said, 'I have a dream and—'

'Most people do. Be quiet. Please.'

His back was against the base of a tree trunk. The pine's branches were around them, obscured the view of the farmhouse and the barn, the livestock and the log chopping.

'I have a dream of what I want to be and where, and—'

'It's not the time to dream, just to stay still.'

His glove did little to warm her foot. The chatter of her teeth drowned her voice. She sat across his lap and he had opened the zip of his jacket and had tucked her half inside it, and she had inserted her hands under his sweater and against his T-shirt, but the cold still bit at her. She thought that if she talked she would divert the cold.

'You, for what you do, are you not allowed a dream?'

'If the dogs hear you, they will come. We will be found, cannot outrun dogs. We will be shot or captured.'

He did not meet her eyes.

'My dream is to be an individual sufficiently important, radical, respected, for *them* to know my name. To be someone of value. A woman who should be heard. That is the dream. One day, my dream, I will walk with many thousands, be in the front rank – along with great figures, arms linked – and go into the square, confront the Kremlin, know that the big cars have fled from a back exit. Bring it down, pull it apart, their whole apparatus. They will flee – the new *czar*, and the new *siloviki* around him, and the new *apparatchiks* who are his servants. Am I not allowed to dream? Do you not dream?'

'I do a job, and am not paid to dream.'

She took slight warmth from him, not much and not enough. One hand roamed on the T-shirt material where it went around his rib-cage and towards the space above the angled hip bone, moved there without purpose. It was good to feel him, take that comfort, and she could see the dogs, and the shotgun and the rifle. The chopping had halted and the old couple and the man in militia uniform talked while he cupped his hands around the steaming mug . . . Her forefinger lingered on a roughened ridge on his skin.

'At first, the great man of Ukraine, our *czar's* friend, had an army of KGB to protect him, a brigade of special troops, a unit of the Presidential guard, and a team of bullet catchers. This is my dream . . . He fled. Helicopters, then a vehicle convoy, and finally he crossed into the Motherland of Russia, him and his woman, and there were only two bodyguards left to him. Everything else had gone, like old paint on wood that has wet rot. That is the end of a *czar*, and what I dream of . . . There is an old slogan, maybe you have heard it: "I disagree with what you say but will defend to the death your right to say it". That is freedom, that is my dream. You, how can you live without a dream? When you came, did you not have a dream of doing something that made a difference to lives, had importance? Can you be so shallow that you do not dream?'

'I do a job, try to do it well. If you alert the dogs then I will have failed in my job.'

Under the T-shirt, her finger was against the line of damaged skin, and at the lowest end of it was a small crater; a small coin could have gone into it, or a blunted pencil end. Quickly, as if to catch him by surprise, she pulled her hand back and opened the gap in his anorak and lifted the sweater higher, and eased back the T-shirt, and bent her head. White skin, not tanned like his face and lower arms and his upper chest. It would have been where a bullet had gone into the skin, breached it, then mined a corridor into his body, and the skin had been tucked down at the entry point, but would have been opened for a line beyond it and that would have been where they had dug, in the emergency room, for the debris and the shattered pieces, and perhaps to extract what remained of the bullet if it had not exited through the small of his back. She thought of where his spine was and where his lungs were, and she knew sweet shit of the biology of the human body. She could imagine it was long odds that a bullet striking there could have missed everything that was vital.

'Do I get to be told?'

'No.'

She took her finger away and pulled down the T-shirt, then the sweater, then closed his jacket tighter round them both.

'You are a fighting man. I assume it's a battlefield wound, not treated in a skilled hospital with time for cosmetic surgery, make it pretty. On a conveyor belt, and you sewn up and then the next stretcher carried in. Was this war? You have the skill to fight a war, are a fighting man – not a poet. Why they chose you, sent you?'

'To do a job, no more and no less.'

'And not to dream?'

'To dream would be an obstruction – except to dream of a Mercedes Benz, high performance, owning one, probably a coupé version . . .'

A smile flickered on his face. She kissed his cheek, then snuggled lower and the cold seemed brutal. She was grateful to have found the battle scar, and to learn something of him, more than he would have told. In front of them, the militiaman with the axe was talking to an enthralled audience. And the animals moved close to them, except the dogs who kept watch.

'Any of us could have been killed. They were animals. It could have been me, could have been any of us. They were ruthless. No thought for us, nor for themselves. No lights. Accelerating. We have poor illumination so they came from nowhere. Any of the boys at the start of the bridge could have been flattened by them, and they did not care. They were bouncing off the drums. What could we do? Nothing. Had to save our lives – well, almost all of us. We had been given no information from headquarters, just told to stay alert. Who was coming? Not told. What to look for? Not told that . . . We were very close to the end of our shift. They came from nowhere, devils . . . bandits, gangsters, perhaps from a smuggling gang. You would not know it because you live here, and are protected by isolation but – believe me – there are violent, despicable people in St Petersburg. They sell weapons, sell drugs, they sell protection which is extortion . . . criminals. And escaping towards the frontier. That is a place of thieves, across there. I tell you, it was me, Pyotr – your friend – who has done them damage. I was at the far end of the bridge, and the intention is that if the bandits, gangsters, criminals, push through the barricade there is one last chance to shoot at them. Me. The target was so hard to see, I could just fire and hope. Two cars, and I hit both, and I must have made at least one casualty. The border at the bridge is closed – and the river is in flood and no one can get across it, and all the boats – the fishermen's – will be chained and padlocked. Because I fired into the cars, I think they will be on foot, if they are able to walk. You should be careful, but you have the dogs and you have a weapon. Barricade the doors. Lock all the windows. They are desperate and dangerous, will show you no mercy. But I do not think they will find anywhere as isolated as this. I will stay as long as I can, but we do an extra shift this evening. New forces have been moved into the area and will work both ways along the road. We will find them, I guarantee it. My commander says that I did exceptionally well – may receive a medal. Now, more logs should be cut.'

He swung the axe with a new-found ferocity, his energy sustained by anger. He wished he had done better. If he had stopped both cars, or either of them, and if prisoners had been taken, or corpses offloaded, he would have been a hero among the men who did Reservist duty in Kingisepp, and the story would have been better for the telling. He cut a growing pile of logs, and would warn them again before he left to go back on duty.

Back in his office in the Big House, the Major finally studied the surveillance report. He had kicked off his shoes, his feet were on his desk, and he might give himself the brief luxury of closing his eyes, a few minutes' light sleep, and the opportunity – so elusive – to think. His phone rang.

'That is Danik? It is, yes?'

'I am Danik.'

'Leonid, from Forensic . . .'

'I did not know you were assigned. What news, please? I struggle on a dilemma.'

'I heard you had the backing of the general. I think Onishenko could be a good friend, no shit with him. The hackers, that's what they were, use first names, not family. You asked for ID on the one who was Nikki – yes, Nikki, I am correct?'

They were from Minsk, from Belarus, and both recruited by FSB in the same year, but their paths rarely crossed, and he shunned social life. The Major gulped, tried to kill the exhaustion. In front of him was the surveillance report. He remembered the girl – ineffective, posing little threat, anxious to please, and who'd built a fantasy world, but defiant and not easily broken. She had met with four men, had taken her brother, and there was vagueness on whether a package were passed or if that was the sergeant's imagination. It had been at a distance, the far side of two vehicles, and Nikki had carried a laptop bag. Confusing, difficult. Easy to evaluate consequences if it were gang warfare, and anything else was to walk into quicksand.

'Yes, the matter of Nikki.'

'My question, Danik, which bit do you want?'

'I don't understand.'

'My little joke. It is messy in there. He is in many pieces. Some on the floor, some on the wall behind him, some embedded in a wooden table … Some are outside the building which is possible because parts of the ceiling, and the roof, were detached and he flew with them. Well, bits of him did. You know those Chechen women who liked to go to Paradise where a nice boy or a dead lover was waiting for them, travelled via a vest and some explosives? They were spread so far that there were acute worries for contamination – could be HIV, dengue fever, hepatitis B. This is the same scenario. I am saying that the bomb was up close to your boy, your Nikki, when it detonated, and from the top of the table and might have been under his outstretched arms. It was inside a laptop computer. How much further should I go?'

'Go the whole way, Leonid.'

'Then I offer two scenarios. Perhaps your Nikki took the device into the meeting room in his laptop – or – a second individual was able to interfere with the bag and insert another laptop into it and know that it would explode while the meeting was still taking place. Are you there, Danik, are you listening?'

'Listening, considering.'

'Those diseases, did he have any of them – add in syphilis – all dangerous to my people, and to survivors, and there are more bits of him than a jigsaw. That means a considerable amount of ordnance, not a firework.'

'Fuck off, Leonid . . . He carried the bomb into the meeting, is that what you are saying? Blew himself up, took them down with him? It is your conclusion?'

'Was on top of it. I am not there, what else can I say, I offer reasonable hypothesis and paint a portrait. May I say something else?'

'Go on, please.' A sunny afternoon, and the cold outside was kept back by strong windows, double- or triple-glazed and the building's boilers kept his room at a reasonable temperature, and he had been about to doze. No longer.

'A meeting of hackers, and an *autorite* keeping watch on them, and men from your organisation there to ensure an agenda was in place, and the young people – I hear – all had grand reputations in their chosen fields, and are protected. Who would wish them harm? Have a pleasant afternoon, Danik.'

The Major eased the button on his phone. Rang off and felt himself a novice swimmer in a deep pool or a wide river, out of his depth.

'Afternoon, Arthur.'

'And a good one to you, Roy.'

They had met in their small fortified armoury, had drawn their weapons, ammunition, and grenades, and the sprays and the cuffs and extending batons, and had shrugged into their heavyweight vests, and walked together to the gate to resume duty. Not a bad day in London, crisp but the frost long gone. Nothing was out of the ordinary . . . an idiot had dropped a sandwich in the middle of the road, between them and Vauxhall railway station, and the gulls were coming in among the cars.

Interesting for a moment, then Roy said, 'Dessie's not been out, not taken the Big Boss to his club, wash and brush up.'

'Means it's not sorted. And always a big deal when Boot's away.'

A cyclist came through, sweating in his lycra, and cleared his card, and all quite unexceptional, except to Roy and Arthur who liked a little charade puzzle, personal and not shared. A chap from Accounts and Budget Analysis who'd have known less than fuck-all about the business end of VBX, but always friendly, and with a wave.

'I'd say it's still all to play for, and the nerves upstairs will be taking some scratch.'

The Maid, not like her, had underestimated the amount of milk in the fridge. Other than for toilet visits, and her dawn shower, she had not been away from the outer office. It was that time of day, when the light had begun to drop and the greyness had settled on the river, and the traffic was building, that she made a decent pot of tea. There was milk available in the bowels of the building but usually she'd find some at the tea point, at the end of her corridor. She had heard nothing. No call from Boot, no word from Daff. She would make the pot anyway, even if it were only herself who drank it. At the tea point were, courtesy of the management, small cartons of milk, far from fresh but drinkable. She looked, longingly, at her phone, at her screens, then hurried outside, locked the door and scampered to the far end of the corridor where the electric kettle was, and coffee sachets, and the milk, and saw them: the Big Boss and Plimsoll, deep in conversation . . . or conspiracy. She was jolted. The Maid had spent the morning working on the office expenses, and getting Boot's into order, and sorting the leave chart for the first half of the next year. Also receiving attention was the remuneration for a recycling company in Harlesden, and the payment that would go through to a Buckinghamshire bank for the services of Gideon Francis Hawkins. Precious little for where he was and what was asked of him, and what Daff had invoiced for, multiplied by three, and . . . She thought Plimsoll a snake, and his mouth close to the Director's ear. She went for the milk. She was not acknowledged. She gazed into the face of the Big Boss and he did not seem to see her, and into Plimsoll's face, but he looked away. She went back to her door, unlocked it. She sat and waited for the whistle on her kettle, and had measured out the right weight of Earl Grey and felt tears well, and smelled treachery, and the knock on the door was light. She dabbed her eye, acknowledged it. He was in the doorway.

The Big Boss said quietly, 'I recognise the scale of opposition, but I continue to defend. I do not second guess my first commitment to Copenhagen but the wind of change is in my face, blowing quite hard. It's the deniability factor that matters and can it hold fast . . . If Boot wins we'll weather it. Be a concern if he loses. Dear lady, stay constant.'

She had not quite put him to bed, but damn near.

Daff sensed his fatigue and encroaching age.

He had struggled to get through the window and had almost fallen off the draining board, and she had ushered him to his bed, and had seen his eyes close, and he muttered something about keeping a 'good watch', and had covered him with a rug, and had found herself a drink. And could reflect with the mug in her hand and the Scotch slopping in it, that had she been in London she might have been considering dinner, which invitation to accept, be like an Irish priest checking the day's funerals against the pedigree of the hospitality afterwards. And could reflect that Boot, had he not been here, would have been on that midday Eurostar, reached the farmhouse on his old bicycle, would have done a part of his ritual tour, would be facing the long evening, and would retire early with his guide books and his maps and his histories, known by heart. Would imagine now that he could hear the patter of the falling rain, as it had been on that night before combat. In Boot's mind there would have been darkened skies, the relentless storm soaking the men of both sides: thousands and thousands of poor wretches, almost in each other's pockets and unable to cook, with little or no shelter, their woollen uniforms sucking up the moisture, and what was precious to them was the powder they must use the following day and it would have been kept against their skin. A quarter of a million men, suffering. Often enough, he had told Daff how it had been . . . An obsession? A man who might just as well have stood on the end of a platform at Didcot station and taken down the numbers of passing trains, an addict. She assumed it brought him a degree of serenity, and she had not heard him curse, nor criticise, and she thought he had a peace about his life . . . and would need it. And thought, also, that Boot had learned from his study of the Duke of the requirement of commitment, and to hell with the cost: worth doing, worth doing right . . . quite a burden.

She would allow him a couple of hours, no more. Daff did not see herself as a care-home assistant . . . She would savour him, did not expect to meet his like again. It would have been brutal out in those fields, the rain tipping on them, and would be brutal, or more so, for the boys on the run from the hit – and if there had been shooting at a road-block then likely they would be on foot, and had probably separated. 'A tough old world, Merc,' she murmured, 'but that's why you took our shilling. Trouble is, Merc, you'll have to look hard to find anyone prepared to thank you, if you make it out.'

The day had gone, and the militiaman.

The heap of logs had been thrown against the barn wall. The axe had been taken inside. The militiaman had put his vest back on, had again seemed to lecture the old couple and then had checked his rifle. Climbed back into his jeep, waved, and bumped off down the track. Exhaust fumes flew in the gathering dusk and hung, and it seemed the first of the frost caught them. The couple had watched him go, the old man cradling his shotgun as the jeep had disappeared, then had stood watch for her. She carried something into the barn and Merc assumed it to be grain for the chickens, or whatever the pigs would eat, and the cattle and the sheep were herded in by the dogs. When she emerged, she had put the padlock on the catch, and he had keenly watched her. She had made her way back to the farmhouse, and the old man's eyes had seemed to probe into the trees where the light did not penetrate. The dogs stayed close to him.

Merc waited. More smoke billowed out of the chimney.

She was pliant in his grip, and in the gloom it was hard for him
to see the colour of her face, but he thought it greyer. He had tried
to warm her, and failed. He did not know whether she dozed, or
had lapsed into unconsciousness. The cold had cut him, and he
had the better clothes. Merc could not move because one dog, a
scarred face and with flattened ears, had stayed outside, its head
between its front paws, watching the open ground. He wondered
if a rat would come, or a rabbit, for it to chase. Simple things . . .

Brad and Rob liked to wax on about the 'small factors' if their
subject was Escape and Evasion. 'E&E', in their opinion, was not
about training but was about commonsense, and luck: luck had
the big call, they said. Worst thing, when luck was in short supply,
was dogs. Cattle were a nuisance and sheep always milling too
close, but dogs were the nightmare. No guy on E&E could beat a
dog's innate hostility to a stranger on its territory. He could lose
her because of one dog and Rob and Brad would have nodded in
agreement; he could lose himself . . . if she coughed or sneezed, it
was cluster-fuck time, what they'd call it. One dog that had a
miserable view of the world and had once been kicked by a stranger
and stood across the way that he needed to go, carrying her. Big
plans made by big people, important enough people to call up an
executive jet and have him lifted out of a combat zone, but he was
dependent on the mood of a dog, and . . . The door opened. It was
called, went inside.

He thought some more. Might not just be a dog that stood in
his way. Might be an old couple who had lived in a forest, isolated,
most or all of their lives, and who had a shotgun, who owed him
nothing and might block him. She was as old as his grandmother.
They might stand between him and where he needed to be. That
great building on the south side of the Thames, ugly as sin, would
have a brigade of men and women to lecture on infiltration and
exfiltration, and attribution and strike back, do all the smart things
with the problem that clever people did, and they'd flake away if
he put his hand up. 'Please, sir or ma'am, what do I do if a man
stands in my way, blocks me, estimate eighty years old, and his
wife, same age? Do I hurt them? Take them down? Within the

rules of engagement?' Would not sit easy with a fighting man off the trenches of a Forward Operating Base. Did a convoy driver on a road out of Kabul keep the pressure on the pedal when a kid ran out to collect his football? Ease off when a woman with a stick was crossing Route Irish? No one would tell him, or appreciate him asking. He had to get her inside the barn. No more talk about her dreams, silent. He had to be out of the cold, had to rest, sleep.

He spurted to the barn door. Had her in a fireman's lift, one hand clinging to her, the other across her mouth. If she cried out, Merc might have to kill a dog, or kill an old couple, or accept failure and the consequences. He disabled the padlock, as easily as the first time, hooked it back, and closed the door. He stood inside in darkness, the animals milling near, anxious and cautious, but he spoke softly to them.

15

A small dog was prominent in Merc's early childhood, but after his father's death it was given away, and there were no animals in the home of his grandmother, and they did not do animals in the military, with the Pioneers. He had no contact with livestock in Baghdad or Kabul or Erbil, and did not gaze through gates at cattle or sheep near Stoke Poges. He carried the girl inside and his feet slithered under him. Warm noses nuzzled and shoulders pressed against him, and the animals seemed about to dislodge her. Merc laid her down.

He had the torch with the pencil-wide beam, was careful and cupped it. He looked for a place where the straw was better than half clean, made a sort of bed that was dry, had some softness, eased her on to it . . . Merc had made a promise. She needed food, sleep, and warmth. His glove came away from her foot and the sock was mud-caked and her toes were cold. When he ran the light briefly over his face he could see her lips had thinned and darkened . . . Merc had seen the suicide deaths of those wearing the vest with the pouches and the explosives linked with wires to the switch held in the palm of a hand. All of them had a detached look on their features, like a mind-set had already killed them; recognisable from the blank eyes that had lost emotion. The boy, Nikki, would have valued the promise Merc had given him. All the men whom Merc had fought alongside had extracted promises that their bodies would be retrieved if they went down on what a schoolmaster had called a 'foreign field' when poetry was read to a bored, fidgeting class. Wives, sweethearts, would be visited, given bullshit about the death of a 'hero', courage and sacrifice, told with a straight face in some fuck-awful housing estate – and likely a new bloke already with his feet under the table. Nikki had his promise and would have carried his bag with the laptop shell into his meeting, and knew the story of the Wolf's Lair. The bag would have been off the floor, not against a table leg, probably on the table in front of him, and the promise sustaining him after he had activated it would have been the survival of his sister, her being brought out, and maybe an image of a piano-playing career – that sort of rosy crap. He would have looked around the table. Snipers always claimed they could engage the eyes of a victim as they lined up with the cross-hairs, watch the guy playing with the kids, going with his newspaper to the unit latrine, joking with his chums, then drop him . . . Unlikely that Nikki would have beaded on the faces of those at the table, or showed the hatred he must have felt for them. Would have been hard, counting down the last minutes. Tension as sharp as a razor's edge, and if he had showed it then there could have been an evacuation, or something . . . Nikki had only had Merc's promise that his sister would be lifted out . . . It had been a quality explosion. A good result for Boot and Daff . . . Nikki was not looking over Merc's shoulder, not watching to see whether the promise was kept . . . She had to be brought out. On top of the promise, she was a factor in the 'deniability' sub-clause of the deal . . . and the boys were, but they were beyond what Merc could cope with. Hands washed of the boys, not proud of it, and laid down from the start that they had the skills to get themselves through . . . And, not sure that he could get her across the river, or get himself over if burdened by her.

She looked helpless. Like a waif on a street corner, far from home and far from what was familiar. Her eyes were open. Merc took her hands, rubbed them, and the animals seemed about to walk on her, trample over the bed he'd made, and the chickens were on a rafter above. Merc did not know which of them had done it, clattered against something metal. Could have been a cow, could have been one of the pigs.

He smelled cooked meat. The lid had fallen against a mug. He was very still, as if he were watched. He lifted a small container, slow movements, nothing sudden, and laid it on her waist, where her coat was thick, and had her steady it, and the mug, and retrieved the lid, then found a plastic bag, lifted that too and inside were thick slices of bread, and that too went on to her lap, and he found the clothes. They hung on a wire frame. He had left them, hidden under straw, and they had been sodden, filthy. Trousers washed and pressed, a shirt meticulously ironed, and his pants and vest, and the hanger was on a nail from the beam that was the refuge of the chickens. He had thought he'd used good tradecraft, and had seen the old couple, the dogs and the shotgun, and seen the militiaman chopping wood for them . . . and had uncovered their deceit.

He knelt beside her. Merc poured the liquid into the mug, then used his fingers to pick out meat and pieces of potato, and they too went into her mug. He fed her.

Fed her, then fed himself. Felt his body grateful for the heat of the food, chewed longingly on the meat and crushed the potato in his mouth. Brad would have said, 'My boy, be thankful you fell on your feet.' Rob would have chipped, 'Because you had the angels watching over you, and you'll need the food, the sustenance, Merc, because of what's in front of you.' She ate and drank. If she shifted on the straw, the animals came closer, and he heard the soft tinkle of her laughter. The right response. It was extraordinary and unpredicted, that he should be running – with a passenger – and be fed by people who he had never met, knew nothing of. Wonderful food, right to laugh . . . He thought of the boys, wondered how they did: could not help them . . . She finished the mug, he wiped his fingers round the sides of the container for the last dregs, had her lick them off, and he put the mug into the container and replaced the lid.

She slept.

He took off the clothes he'd worn, changed into what had been left him. He could not explain the kindness shown him, nor why – as he assumed it – a militiaman was deceived. The wind filtered into the building and sang through holes and the frost came hard. The food might have saved them but the cold would come again. He lay close to her and – more to laugh at but he did not – a pig grunted, pushed at him with its snout, then subsided against his legs, and his face was licked . . . He had to sleep because of what lay ahead, and the promise made.

'I just thought you'd like to know . . .'

'Know what?'

Boot had heard footsteps, heavy on frosted ground, then the sharp rap. Daff had shut his bedroom door, gone to the front of the building.

'What had gone on up the road.'

'If you think I'd be interested.'

He'd heard the voices. And Daff had laughed, always seemed flippant, as intended.

'There was a shooting at Kingisepp. Kingisepp is twenty kilometres from the bridge. Late last night . . . I thought it would be helpful for you to know.'

'Any business of mine, a shooting up the road inside Russia?'

Boot eased off the bed. His sleep had been a life saver, had managed a couple of hours dead to the world. He felt a cough rising in his throat and tried to stifle it, made a poor job of the effort. It was a strangled sound . . . As he could hear the man at the door, assumed to be from the surveillance team, so that man would have heard his splutter. Often enough a chase for secrecy seemed pointless.

'Two cars came from the St Petersburg route and a block at Kingisepp had been reinforced after the explosion in the Kupchino district. The cars switched off their lights and went fast into a zigzag to get round the oil drums put there to slow vehicles. Achieved surprise and were almost clear . . . almost.'

'Only almost?'

He thought her attempt at indifference was plucky. He had slept but at the moment of waking he had believed himself to be sitting on his collapsible stool, in the shade of a tree or the shelter of an umbrella and had been looking down the slope and not able to see much because of the density of the smoke, and not able to hear much because of the barrage of the guns, and it had taken half a dozen seconds of blinking before the recall. Stuck in that dirty little room with the hideous wallpaper and the faded prints of the castle, and he had eased from the bed and had smoothed down his shirt and had done up the top button and knotted his tie, fastened his waistcoat. He listened.

'Were almost clear, but . . '

'They, who were almost clear, should I mind?'

'We have a good monitoring capability on their radio systems. The old and tried tactic at a road-block is to have one gun as a backstop.'

'Not taught at my school.'

'The backstop had hits, tyres and bodywork, and perhaps also hits to personnel.'

'Hardly my concern.'

Attempts did not equate, in Boot's opinion, to dramatic indifference. That the man had cracked the cover seemed to him to render the game merely stupid now. He went to the door, opened it, but kept back and was in shadow.

'Thank you, friend.'

'And you, sir, should be careful of catching pneumonia from the river air, and should get your sleep and get food. Also, sir, it is not necessary for you to act like a circus artist and climb into and out of the kitchen window. It is not dignified . . . Two cars have been found down the road from Kingisepp and both are burned out and the plates have been removed. It is on the militia radio nets. They will not search the forest until the morning because they are nervous of gunmen still alive and desperate. We venture to suggest that the haven of our border will very soon be harder to reach. We are concerned, also, that the opportunity to reach our territory may have passed, that the fugitives will be apprehended on their side of the river. You know better than us, sir, that the risks that follow what they'd regard as severe provocation, are considerable. However, there is still some time . . .'

Boot supposed now that he had been tracked by the KaPo since reaching Tallinn, and while he had spent time in the capital, and no doubt had been followed to and from the train. Each of his precarious climbs from the kitchen window had probably been observed, and the long hours spent above the bridge, compulsive for any of the old front line warriors of the Cold War. His preamble done at the cemetery, and the site of the Duchess's Ball, and at Ligny and Quatre Bras, he looked with excitement to erecting his stool to the left of where Wellington had been for much of the day and he would gaze out in any season over the fields and take in the distant high ground where the cannon of the Emperor were in formation, and would see the small end wall of the cottage where the Corsican had slept, poorly and with stomach ache. The day slipping, a wonderful dream and a happy one . . . And had seemed to hear between the cannonade blasts, the shouts of 'Stand Firm' and 'Stand Fast', and had seen Sir Thomas Picton, go forward and fall, and the advance of the Heavy Brigade . . . Breathtaking and always he was gripped with an excitement and a sense of perilous nerves, then had been woken.

Boot asked, 'The time? What is it of time?'

'They have poor coordination. Areas of command are protected by those in charge. They do not talk to each other . . . I explain. There was confusion in St Petersburg in the explosion's aftermath, described as a gas problem, then a suggestion of *mafiya*. Road-blocks in place but no indication of what the troopers should look for. We do not hear, yet, that lines have been drawn between dots, that Kingisepp is linked. It is the way they are, jealous of power, suspicious of sharing to prevent a rival gaining advantage . . . That gives time. Not considerable time. Time should not be wasted . . . But of course, it is all 'hardly my concern'. And to you, sir, goodnight.'

She closed the door. Boot went to his bed, smoothed it, tidied the sheets and blankets and did an institution's hospital corners and punched the pillows, and called to her.

'Daff, what's the schedule? When will he try, that bloody river, to cross it?'

'Has to sleep. Has to rest, cannot take it at the charge, and God alone knows what baggage he's bringing with him . . . My fear,

Boot, there'll be a man across there who can think, assess, then act ... Might be wrong.'

'You seldom are wrong. A "man across there who can think", very seldom.'

His screen was clogged with detail on the explosion.

No chance for the Major to go home, to sleep in his own bed. Late into the evening and more than twenty-four hours after the detonation, he was aware that a new incident room would be functioning by the morning, with a new team. The young woman in the office kept him upright at his desk, fed him stiff coffee and rough bread sandwiches from the canteen. He was a man of obstinate determination: a dog refusing to surrender a bone ... His screen now had the plan of the room where the meeting was held, the location of each hacker at the table, the positioning of the GangMaster, of the FSB officers. The most recent information to reach him was an analysis of the explosive used, Russian and from the Samara-Sefiev factory on the Lower Volga. He had CCTV of the building and who had come and who had gone, and pictures of confrontations in the ensuing chaos. The coffee sustained him ... Would he hand it over lightly, the file he created? He worked on, struggling to remain focused.

A courier brought it from the basement operations room. A single sheet of paper. A handwritten scrawl apologised for the delay in its circulation. He glanced at it, then dumped it on a heap of everything else that had been collected and categorised as 'related/unconfirmed relevance'. Another blink, another slurp of coffee, another hacked cough. He retrieved the sheet, read it a second time ... A one-time officer of State Security, sacked and now on hard times and cleaning the ferry terminal in the port of Tallinn across a nearby border, had recognised an intelligence official, British and elderly, coming off an overnight ferry from Stockholm. His fault, but the Major had asked for *everything* of possible interest – 'everything'. It had been diligently reported, and an officer in Moscow had gone back to the embassy in Tallinn on Pikk, and a further answer was given ... How had the Briton been recognised after so many years? Because two men, once equals, had discussed at a reception an area of military history and the importance of single battlefields: Borodino on the road to Moscow, 1812 and the blunting of the French advance east, or Waterloo, which had been fought thirty-three months later, quite an animated discussion. It was how the man was remembered, and he had come on a ludicrous route to Estonia, had slipped ashore with no official welcome.

The night dragged on. In the morning, fresh-faced men and women would rifle in his files, transfer them, forget to thank him, and he would be cast adrift. He returned to the surveillance in the car-park, as if that were a key, and a meeting and men still unidentified.

They thought he still lived, but he gave them no help.

Toomas was still slung between them. Martin had one of his arms over his shoulder and Kristjan had the other. They had little to guide them now the noise of the road had faded, and the last of the light had been lost hours before. They had not eaten, had not drunk, had not rested. The man who decorated homes in the tower blocks outside the town of Haapsalu had done nothing in years to build his physical fitness. The man who stacked the shelves of a supermarket smoked incessantly, never walked if he could ride. Toomas, whom they carried, his feet scraping on the forest floor, was a big man and suited to his pretence as a knight in Teutonic armour. They went slowly, blundered, and branches whipped their faces. Unsure if he still lived, they did not talk about whether they carried dead weight.

Both of them would have heard old stories of the sick and the infirm being pronounced gone, being buried alive . . . They carried him and barely talked of anything, saved breath and did not squander strength. Their grandfathers would not have abandoned one of their own. They had been three men, trapped in middle age, hope abandoned, and – who would admit it – when the girl had come with the offer of cash, the improbable chance had been snatched. They went due south, slowly, and skirted the eastern

side of the straggling town of Ivangorod, and the aim was to hit
the river upstream from the town and take an angler's boat, and
do the fast run across its width and reach the Narva's far shore.
Martin did not ask Kristjan whether he had ever been on a boat
on that stretch of water and if he knew how it was guarded, and
Kristjan did not ask Martin if he could start an outboard, or use
oars. The Irishman was forgotten, and the girl, and the mission
and the money, but they would try to take their friend home.

Pyotr had said, 'You must be careful, especially vigilant. I am on
duty, I cannot refuse it. I would be here if I could. They are
dangerous men. Tomorrow there will be a big hunt for them, with
a helicopter. Tonight you must be careful, and have the weapon
close to you, Igor. You do not open the door, Marika, and keep the
dogs with you. I will be back in the morning when I have finished
the duty.'

   Marika presumed it an act of treason. She had assured Pyotr
that the dogs had been free in daylight to roam the ground close
to the house and the barn. His parents, both of them, and her
father, had been killed as traitors, seven decades earlier, accused
of sheltering Red Army deserters. She knew of the weasel officials who'd come to their farm to collectivise them, and they
would have been accused – if found – of betrayal of the
Motherland. She had told her man what they could do, had not
asked an opinion of him. Pyotr had gone into shrieks of laughter
because the couple had driven to Ivangorod, and Igor had bought
new trousers and she had seen them, dismissed them as 'inappropriate, too tight for working', and had sent him indoors again
to change out of them, and had said she would cut them up for
cleaning cloths . . . and Pyotr had said, 'In this house, Igor wears
the trousers – but you tell him which trousers he should wear.'
The Soviet troops had come through their farms, then the
Wehrmacht, then the Soviets again, and bureaucrats had come
with police to enforce orders, and there were smugglers who had
trails in the forests and who brought to the river bank vodka and
cigarettes and cocaine and pills and liquid heroin. She had

decided, and did not care that it could be regarded as an act of treason. She had not seen him but had handled his clothing and had recognised that it had been manufactured outside her country, and he had come in secrecy across the river . . . He was, to this old lady in the twilight of her life, something of a 'hero'. She would have kicked Igor hard if he had started to talk of the clothing she had brought into the farmhouse and the time she had spent washing and pressing it, kicked him so that he could not have been able to walk if he had blurted anything about the food she had left in the barn. Would have slapped his face hard enough for the glass eye to be dislodged.

The house was quiet, the dogs slept, she had washed the dishes, and he snored close to the fire where the embers dulled. Around them, in old frames and old cases, were photographs and carcasses from the past. Pictures of their home and stuffed relics of fish he had taken out of the river and the antlers of deer he had shot and a mounted head of boar. Everything was of the past, and the future was minimal, and the damp and the years of rough work outside had aggravated his arthritis, and the cough on her chest hurt her more. She feared nothing but wanted to nurture a hero.

Pyotr had said, 'I give them little chance. I hope soon that they are dead. They would have killed me. I give them little chance because of the river. They will be trapped against it, or drown in it. They will be desperate. On no account must you open the door, and you must keep the dogs close.'

She heard nothing but the hiss of the fire and the wind against the roof and the call of an owl and the creaking of the beams of the wooden building.

'In God's name, where is Kingisepp?'

A clatter of the lieutenant's thin fingers on a keyboard. 'Major, it is twenty kilometres east of Ivangorod, on the main route from here to the border, the Narva River.'

'And Kingisepp is what distance from here?'

More clatter, a pause, then, 'Major that is one hundred and thirty kilometres. Direct on the E-Twenty route.'

He swore, shut his eyes, opened them, tried to focus. He said it
quietly, not a bark, and seemed to accept where blame lay.

'What is at Kingisepp?'

'You do not want the industry, the size of population. Of significance to you, Major, is a river, and a main highway, and a
road-block placed on the bridge, as you instructed there should be
on all routes from St Petersburg.'

'How long has this been with us?'

The young woman looked away, acute embarrassment. The
sergeant would answer for her. 'It has been with us five hours,
Major. It was shown to you, you acknowledged it, it was laid on
your desk. It was assumed you had read it, discarded it as not
important.'

He nodded, no more to be said . . . They had reached the middle
of a long night and the message from Kingisepp, relayed by the
barracks in that town and passed on to him by militia in his own
city, had been with him since just past the hour of dusk, delayed
by more than twenty-four hours. The same message had probably
passed across screens and desks in St Petersburg before being
diverted to FSB and some outpost inside the Big House, then at a
painful snail's pace it had meandered from office to office, been
delayed by the breakfast breaks and lunch breaks and dinner
breaks. It would have been known in the building, common knowledge, that two colonels had fought and one had accused the other
of murder . . . Too much for many to think of. The matter of a
shooting on the main road that would have been a *mafiya* route
was poor substitute for their domestic drama.

'It is a big river at Narva?'

The young woman answered him. 'Much wider than at
Kingisepp and faster at this time of year, more powerful . . . One
road bridge and one rail bridge, but the rail is for freight and for
gas wagons. It is a security zone on our side of the frontier, going
back as far as Kingisepp so entry is controlled. There are watch-
towers, there can be patrol craft. Anglers must be vetted if they
use small boats and are obliged to remove engines and oars, keep
them under lock. It is, Major, a formidable barrier.'

He had been told, his memory squealed at him, of fireworks being fired on the far bank of that river, under low cloud, in driving rain, and no one had been visible who watched the display, and no music played for a party. Militia on the border had been captivated by the display and watched, had reported on it.

The sergeant said, 'It is better than formidable. Unless a fugitive has a boat, the Narva cannot be crossed when the river's high, impossible.'

Nearly asleep, both of them, and nearly awake. In the barn, the movement and grunting, clucking and snorting, of animals and fowls made for calm. Not for warmth. Warmth, body heat, they had to provide for themselves.

She could have told him that it was probably the coldest night of the year as winter chased towards the Christmas holiday. He could have told her that they had frosts where he had travelled from, and snow in the high mountains towards the Iran border, but not the bite of the wind, not even on the convoy routes across the Afghan plains. They lay together, his lower arm under her head and his hand lodged against the small of her back, and her arms were tucked loosely below his armpits and clasped together against his spine. The moon was high and small beams of weak light came through a window-frame that had no glass, only rusted bars, and pinpricks of it were funnelled down through the gaps in the roof. Some animals seemed to Merc to sleep standing, others were on their sides and a few – shadowy shapes, not identifiable – were lying neatly on their stomachs with heads tucked down between their front legs.

They were not asleep, and, not awake.

Merc had not removed any clothing. He still wore the heavy anorak he had travelled with, and the sweater and the shirt and the thick T-shirt and the trousers that were supposed to have an insulated lining, and his socks and his boots were still on his feet, and the woollen bobble hat was tucked down over his forehead and covered his ears and was almost at his eyebrows. He craved sleep and could not and, because he did not sleep, he felt the warmth close to him. She had not loosened anything or freed a buckle or opened a zip or unfastened a button, and her coat was round her and everything underneath was pulled down, and the trousers were rounded at the hips and shaped her waist, and her gloves – wet and mud-covered – smeared against him. All that was missing from her clothing was the one shoe, left in the mud. She did not sleep and her breathing quickened and her mouth was against his neck.

Merc entertained a kaleidoscope of thoughts. A few were memories: swerving between petrol drums at speed, the drabness of the emergency area and the familiar exhaustion of the surgical team, and of the bulk of the big man trying to get through the razor wire and into their trench. Brief memories and jolted movement between them. Nothing of the present, and the rest of the thoughts were the future: the width of a river, the prominence of the watch-towers, the flow of the current and the power of militia launches on full throttle and the distance to the centre point where, technically, jurisdiction changed, and the narrowness of the board and the weight that would be put on it, and going under . . . the worst of the thoughts. Drowning was the thing that frightened Merc more than capture. Sinking down and the clarity of a sky, day or night, disappearing into a vagueness, and grappling for any of those damn straws that might have been floating on the surface, whipped along and heading for the Baltic seas, feeling a soggy softness and trying to snatch for more of them, and sinking slowly – and her. Her pulling him down but him unable to loose her . . . Might stand a chance if he did, tear her hands off him, but could not. He would hold her closer and tighter, because a promise was given . . . and she shivered, was closer to him. Could not have answered the big question. Did he need her more than she needed him? Could barely see her face in his mind. Had almost forgotten her features. Could not picture the thrust of her nose, jut of the chin, whether the lips were thin, or full, whether they were hard or soft. He held her and would have near squeezed the breath out of her lungs and the warmth grew on his throat where her mouth rested, and he seemed to sink again and the water might have closed over him, and the board had slipped and was lost and would have been careering downstream and was beyond retrieval and there was no straw in his hand, only her. Asleep? He did not know, there, in the barn, how to sleep, nor did she.

Hands edging deeper.

His with a gentleness, hers with an urgency. Merc's softly as if not wanting to hurt. Kat's roughly as though not caring whether she did. Her gloves rested at his waist, then dragged up the sweater and the shirt and the T-shirt and her fingers searched out the scar where the skin had been folded over crudely, and rubbed along it, and tugged it, made patterns on it . . . A Czech field hospital, and a bored surgeon cleaning a wound, checking that it had an exit, after avoiding anything valuable, sewing him up, and two days of rest, and back in the truck cab. No big deal, not worth a Purple Heart, forgotten until she had found it.

Her hands now going down, and his. Movement growing and sounds as they shifted, and some animals had eased out of their sleep, and others who had maintained a watch on them were alerted. They came closer and nudged against her back and his, and the first slobbering tongues were on their heads and one would have had her hair caught in its mouth and she let slip a squeal and pulled her head clear and returned it to his throat, and kissed him there.

He pushed her jeans and pants down only as far as was needed, did not bare an inch of her, open it to the cold, that was not necessary. His fingers, in the crudeness of gloves, tangled in her hair, and she had a hold of him. She guided him, and he had a pig's nostrils in his ear and a heifer's mouth hissing hot breath at his forehead. He felt the heat of her, and she clung hard and if they had been going under, in the river depths, they would have floundered together. He called out. Did not know what he shouted. Broke near every rule taught him by the old guys, the veterans, and all the stuff that Rob or Brad would have lectured on . . . Some of the animals were startled and others more interested, and several of the fowls took flight.

*   *   *

'What?' Igor hissed in her ear.

'I don't know.' She spat back at him.

'What did he shout?'

'Not anything I know – could have been *Cinya* or *Cinar*. Don't know.'

'I'll catch my death.'

'You go in,' Marika told him. 'I am staying.'

They were at the barn door. The moon shone bright on them. Marika had prime position and a place on the plank doors where once a knot of wood had been, and it gave her a good peep-hole. He looked between planks but his sight was poor and he would see little. She did not have a fine vantage-point because of the press of the animals around that place on the spread of the straw five paces from her and Igor, but she could see movement in the barn, and the growing urgency and noises from both of them and from the beasts.

The old fool had tucked his hand under her arm, as if old instincts stirred.

A pause. Her freeing her hands from his back, then groping in an inner pocket of her anorak; having difficulty pulling back a zip fastener with her gloved fingers, then getting the sachet into her mouth and ripping the top from it. Then taking the contents and shaking the thing free, and spitting its wrapping clear, then sliding it on him, and a little giggle from her. Then burying him.

It could have been the cold, or the tiredness, or just that it was, Merc thought, so good. It lasted well. And he was slower, and thought the loving brilliant, and both worked hard and the animals around them pressed ever closer and seemed to share. There were no more shouts from him, but at the end of it he let loose a grunt, and she released at about the same moment a small squeal, and he held her as best he could: the moon had drifted, came down on to them.

Not about love, he thought, but about need. She rolled off him, and he helped to get her clothing back in place and he sensed the goose-pimples would have been forming on her skin as soon as he had shifted, and he took the thing off and buried it far down in the animals' bedding, and fastened his trousers and his zip and his belt, and he held her close to him. She was asleep before him.

The moon's light came down and through the roofing and it rested on her face and he saw her at peace. The giggle gone, and the fight, and the indifference at what her brother had done, and her head was on his chest, hair tucked under his chin, Merc thought she had no comprehension as to how it would be when they reached the river, retrieved the board, went into the water.

He'd try to sleep. What to assume? The same as any Gun for Hire would have. Opportunities came fast and went quickly, and with each hour the possibility of surprise and confusion ebbed. He had to rest, but with every hour gone, the chance of escape over the river diminished . . . which made sleep harder to find.

Where did it lead?

It would lead towards a summons, as dawn broke over the river and the street, and the first light fell on the Big House, to attend a suite of offices two floors above his box-room – where the three of them were crammed together – and he would be congratulated on the order he had brought to an investigation, praised for his diligence. It would lead to his removal from the inquiry, to his return to former duties. Also it would lead to a new team taking control of the conference room at the end of his corridor, and a security cordon would be placed round it, and the men and women staffing that inquiry would require his witness statements, his forensic results, then would close the door in his face. He might have been grateful . . . had already detected that few medals would be on offer if he followed his nose, went where it took him, drifted into places where he'd have to hold that nose because of the stench of corruption around him. He understood, now, what was the key, *who* it was. He could, with justification, have clapped his hands, marked an end point, stood at his desk and reached for his jacket, thanked both of them for their endeavour, called for a driver from the pool, gone home . . . Might have had four hours' sleep in his own bed before the order came for him to attend on General

Onishenko, then pass over the file. He put her on the screen, full facial frontal, and tried to read the mind of Yekaterina . . . who would lead him, and who he would follow . . . It would not be disobedience, merely the conscientious following of a previous line of inquiry in an older investigation.

He asked for more coffee, thanked both of them for their loyalty. He said quietly that nothing more should be committed to paper, and nothing more saved to an electronic file, said it casually and smiled at the raised eyebrows, and then repeated it with steel in his voice . . . and asked if a sandwich could be made.

Once the moon had shifted, and no longer threw light into the recesses of the barn, they slipped away. Hardened by the events of their lives, Marika and Igor left their vantage-point. Almost at their own door, the cough that had tickled in her throat had the better of her, and she doubled up in a coughing fit, and he croaked and spat phlegm.

He was disturbed and he thought she was. They reached the door, then began to bicker.

He rarely dared contradict her, but he had stood too long in the cold, had seen less than her. 'You are wrong, it is the left foot.'

'You see nothing. The left has the shoe on it. The right foot not.'

'The left foot has no shoe or no boot. I saw that.'

'It's her right foot that needs a shoe, a boot, whatever.'

'Wrong. You go, get a right foot shoe, or a boot, and take it to her. Perhaps they fuck again. Perhaps they are asleep . . . Whatever, you interrupt a fuck or a sleep, and you give them a right side shoe, boot, and you look with a flashlight and you will see you have brought the wrong one. Then, will you apologise?'

'I will not. And you, Igor, are an idiot.'

'An idiot? I know the difference between right and left.'

'You are an idiot because you do not know what I shall do.'

'What will you do, and not apologise?'

'I will take a right shoe or boot, and a left shoe or boot, and leave them by the door.'

Her laughter cackled. He had gone to the fire and kicked a smouldering log and sparks flew from it, and he swigged vodka from the bottle and any other time she would have yelled abuse at him.

'But we cannot help them,' Igor said.

'We cannot. We do not have that power.'

'And in the morning Pyotr will come.'

'He would shoot them. The drink will make you talk, talk too much.'

Igor said, grimly, 'Pyotr would kill them. Think no more of it than of them being a pig in the forest, or rats in his yard.'

The fire had lifted. He took Marika in his arms and shyly placed a kiss on her mouth and covered half of her face with his moustache and his beard, part white with age and part yellow from the smoke from his pipe. She pushed him away, but was slow to do it, then went to look for shoes and boots. Left him slumped in his chair. It had been a long night and their old lives would not be the same again because of what they had done and what they had seen.

Boot woke, a better sleep than before. He shook, wiped his eyes, and called to her.

'Anything?'

Daff answered him. 'Nothing.'

'We'd have heard?'

'We would.'

She gestured from his door and across the room and to the window. From his bed, Boot looked through the door and the window and saw the car and the cigarettes' glows inside.

'What's on the radio, from over there?'

'Not much. Suggestion of a gas leak leading to an explosion. Quite separate on the local police networks is an attempt by smugglers to break through a road-block, implication of drugs trafficking . . . Oh, and the Maid called on the secure line.'

'Wanting?'

'Big Boss under pressure. When was it different? Can I ask you a question, sort of personal?'

He seemed puzzled, squinted back at her. 'What do you need to know?'

'Just this . . . it's your job, and you are good at your job, better than good. You send people to bad places, where they endure seven shades of Hell, or worse. Play God with them, and sometimes you've volunteered them, and others have volunteered themselves. Could you do it, Boot, what you've asked of others – be silent in the cell, take the beatings in inter-rogation, what you ask of others? I couldn't, damn sure. What about you?'

'Don't think I heard that. Thanks for the rest – all right for me in the bathroom?'

She shrugged, seemed to say he could spend all day in there if that were his wish . . . *when was it different?* Never much different . . . older men stuck at the border and waiting for a sign that the agents would make it to sanctuary while all the time being nagged by the angels in the firmament. Would be good to shave carefully, wash comprehensively, and have a clean shirt for the day . . . All of them would have shaved that morning, both sides gathered on the twin flanks of the chosen battlefield, and cleaned themselves up even if only puddles of water from the overnight deluge were available. A bit later on, if events did not lurk on the horizon, he would carry his imagination down the track, on to the lane that led to the farm at Hougoumont. They would have washed, put on any fresh clothing they could find, and would have looked their best, and the young men around the Duke would have been in their finery. Damn cold out there and he'd be grateful, when the vigil resumed, for the waistcoat that went with his suit. He missed not having the Maid close to him, assumed she would soon be up and about, busy, would have cleaned around the outer office and his space, and wiped the picture of the 'great man', and likely given the Waterloo teeth a flick with a yellow duster. And he tried to picture the man he had sent, had plucked from one warm furnace and dumped in another, and who he had walked with by the Thames, and it troubled him that he could barely recall a word the man had said.

No hot water, when he went to the bathroom, just a tepid dribble, but he was pleased to have the chance to shave, would look presentable for the day – whatever it might bring.

Kat said, soft, 'I don't know who you are.'

He did not reply.

'You walk into my life, into my brother's . . . I am dependent on you. All of my future rests with you.'

She was above him, resting on one elbow, and some of her hair fell across her face and blurred the image of him but she did not bother to push it away.

'My life is carried by you. It might be long, and it might be years in a prison cell or in a box in a grave. Can I cross a river? I must because everything behind me is burned and I cannot return to what I had, a little but something. I put trust in you.'

Her fingers, in the gloves, slid across his face, found his ears, and the sockets of his closed eyes, and around his mouth where the stubble had grown and down the length of his nose, and into his short hair, and it was, for Kat, the best loving she had known.

'I did not have a string of men coming to the apartment, have to tell Nikki to stay outside because I am humping a man in my bed, and could be receiving presents. I do not do that. I was with you, went with you, and thought you shy, and led you, and I regret nothing . . . but it is, for me, not just like scratching an armpit, coughing and spitting, eating pizza because I like it . . . It was important, I wanted to – with you. I have to believe that you can cross the river – and afterwards? I think we will cross the river because that was a promise you gave. Then? Where do we go, what is our life? I have the right to know who you are.'

She thought that he heard her. Her voice was very quiet, and the animals around them seemed lost in sleep, and the cold was close. His eyes stayed shut but there had been moments when she had thought a slight smile drifted on his face: could not have been sure. A little of him, she believed, belonged to her, but she did not know who he was, and it would have to be prised out of him which

Gerald Seymour

would take time. They would have time, after they reached the far side of the river.

'I don't know who you are, what you love, hate, what is your ambition and what angers you, and what is a line you refuse to cross. I deserve to know because of now and because of what is ahead – and for us, what is the future: I have the right.'

Good questions, fair comment.

Merc was warm, was grateful for that. It was what the guys talked about, Baghdad and Kabul and Erbil and at any of the barracks where he had been with the Pioneers. Right place at the right time. Some of the guys would let it be known that they'd showed up lucky, then shrugged and then moved on, and others would have talked it through in detail, and a few might have had a bit of it stored on their phone memory. It was good to be warm.

Among the stink of the animals, in darkness with the moon long gone, Merc would have preferred the chance to think; one big river, one small board, one guy who had an idea of how to achieve it, and one girl who was a decent weight and would panic and would be a passenger. But the promise was the bigger burden . . . Some of the guys, not many, would have said they were going for a slash, given her a kiss, have crept out of the barn, would have done a runner. Probably the best strategy . . . he ditched it . . . him gone, her left and caught and interrogated and spilling it, and deniability lost . . . ditched it. Her voice had pattered in his ear, her fingers traced his face, and soon the cattle would grow restless – and soon they would move. The finger movements calmed him.

Merc was suspicious of calm. She assumed a future. What he stayed clear of was a hardening up of 'sometime'. Of course 'sometime' was up front, staring into his face. Sometime, Merc could go to the bank at Stoke Poges and tell the manager that he would be needing funds for the purchase of a property. He could get himself down to the dealership and admire the latest of the Mercedes Benz range. And, sometime soon might be right for a woman in his life. Because he thought about 'sometime', Merc lacked the concentration for what strategy was best, when they hit the river. And 'sometime' was when he came back into a world almost, 'normal' – and 'sometime' he would put all of this, and guns and road-blocks and man-hunts, and salients that had a Hill like 425 in their front line, behind him, walk away from it . . . if he had not drowned. He eased her back and belted the rump of a heifer, shifted it and stirred them all. Time to be awake, the resting finished. He slapped his body to liven it, then was statue-still. Merc could have sworn on a book that there was a footfall at the barn door, and the animals tensed, and he did too.

16

Merc strained to hear.

Picked up the sound of the footstep, imprecise, dragging. Then heard the rustle, slight but bold. And thought it was a rat in the straw.

It was a moment when he'd have picked up a weapon and swung to face the enemy and would have aimed at a shadow or a scrap of noise and been pinpoint accurate. He had no weapon. He identified in the faint light, the eyes, set close. And made out the shape of the creature. Excluding its tail, it might have been nine inches in length. He saw the whiskers and the yellowed teeth, two main incisors, a rough dark grey coat, and the tail seemed coated in a kind of snakeskin. It stared back at him . . . Merc knew rats from the bunkers under the parapet walls in the fire positions. A giant lived close to where he slept, recognised by a broken right tooth and fighting scars on its face. The second winter that he had been on that front line, with snow on the sandbags and the wire in front pretty with icicles, this one had come to sleep beside him – live and let live – and had been curled close, had never bitten him or threatened him. They had gone out of the line, and had been replaced, had come back a week later. His personal rat had been stiff and frozen, *rigor mortis*, and had been dumped in the wire, its head broken as if by a heavy blow or a kick. He wondered if, when they had loved, his gloved hands on her skin – and hers on his – there had been moments when they could have felt the caress of the rat's tail.

She screamed. A sound of anguish and horror the rat scurried to escape and he kicked out where he thought it fled and caught it, and the creature squealed, and he heard it fall. Merc thought they would have been around him, and Kat, all of the night, sleeping and loving.

A new noise: the scrape of the door hinges. A torch on his face. He could not see past it. Her scream continued and the animals in the barn were waking, stumbling and bellowing, and the chickens were coming down off the beam. He did not know whether – behind the torch – there were men with rifles, or . . . The light reversed. It shone on the old woman and the old man, and on two dogs, their hackles high. The scream died. The woman spoke to Kat. Kat answered her. The woman cackled. Kat grinned, stood, and tidied her clothing. The woman slapped a gnarled hand on her thigh, and the man grinned.

Kat said to Merc, 'They are surprised we saw only one. They have brought food . . .'

The tray was put on the ground, lit by the torch. They sat around it. The shotgun was propped against the wall. Two apples, a little rotten but mostly good. Bread. Slices of cold meat, tough and hard to chew, something in a bowl that seemed to Merc to be porridge, sweet with honey, and one spoon which they all shared, and cheese that was cut with a penknife from the man's pocket. Merc studied their faces . . . had seen them wherever he had travelled. They were lined, worn, weathered, and the flesh hung loose on the cheekbones, and the eyes were dulled and sunk far into sockets. She had loose strands of hair on her chin and he was sprouting stubble. Had seen them in Iraq, in Afghanistan and in the small villages outside Erbil. What was constant, Merc thought, was that they'd survived suffering, had learned to live beside it. They looked at him, as if interested in an alien creature, but he did not sense that they quizzed her. Who was he? Where did he come from? Why was he there? In near silence, they ate. At the end of the meal as the chickens scratched at the crumbs left where the straw was thinnest, a pair of boots was given to Kat. They were too large for her, but they were boots and boots could save her life. The woman peeled off her own faded socks, the pattern long washed out, and with holes in the heel. Kat wore them over her own, then dragged on the boots.

It was still dark when they left. A few words were exchanged with Kat. Merc saw them shrug, and the old man spat, a gesture of derision. They said goodbyes, he formally and she with a passion. His handshake and her kiss. Nearly dawn, and they walked away from the barn and towards a path that narrowed quickly, and the ground was harder from the cold, and their feet slithered on ice.

Merc asked her, 'Why did they help us?'

'Because we were fugitives.'

'That is a good enough reason?'

'Yes, good enough for many. They thought you would come back and did your clothes and left food. They assume you are opposing the "system" that looks to control them and do not think you a criminal, and the militiaman who came warned them of danger, which was an invitation for them, and . . .'

'And . . .?'

'Perhaps because we made a show for them. They did not have to go to a theatre or a circus. They watched us, outside in the cold. They saw the love we did . . . I think, watching us, gave them a happiness. I should trust you, they said. And . . . they say that to try to cross the river without a boat is not possible. That we will drown or be shot. They said that. But I should trust you, and they will remember a long time, all the rest of their lives, the joy we gave them, with our loving. And you, joy?'

He led, and she had her arm tucked into his, and he took the snap of the branches they bent back, and did the estimates of the direction needed. Slow-going, and the light had started to spread. He did not hear pursuit, but did not doubt that it would come.

Kat thought she walked well, did not slow him down. She hung on his arm and matched his stride.

In the city, she hardly ever walked. From the money Nikki gave her, she took trams and buses and the metro. She ate poorly, played no sport, but at the start of this day, and heading towards the river, she stepped out. She could walk well because of the

loving in the barn's straw. From the itching in the pit of her back
and down between her legs, Kat knew there was still straw pieces
and dust lodged there. And she knew she had entranced him
because he had called out, had broken a cardinal rule he had set
her, for silence, had broken it himself. She could not know what
he had shouted, something she had not understood. She was not
good, not practised, and she had thought him – a man with a
battle wound in his side and the scar tissue of a field hospital operation, done at speed – a novice. And knew nothing of him, except
that he had wanted her enough to lose control, cry out. A flat
stomach against hers, the two main bones fused, hair entangled,
and after the shout, a gasp . . . She would learn about him. She had
no doubt that she had entranced the stranger who had burst into
her life. She did not know where they were going, what schedule
he had set himself. Afterwards there would be time to learn, and
she would be a pianist at a school in London, perhaps the Royal
College which had been well spoken of at the Conservatory. No
complaint from her at the pace they went and sometimes the ice
screen broke under their feet and they slid down into mud pools
and their boots were covered, and sometimes they tripped on
exposed tree roots, and sometimes the whip of the branches
slashed and she'd tasted her own blood. She clung to him. She
realised, blundering through the forest, that she had only thought
once of her brother and the ball of flame rising above the flat roof,
the debris thrown up and the rumble of the detonation. Had not
prayed for him nor cried, nor understood why Nikki had extracted
the promise . . . He said they would stop and rest, but not yet.
Hardly needed to rest, felt strong.

Across the small hallway, the front door lay splintered, the hinges
ripped off. It had not been a strong door, and his sergeant had put
his shoulder into it twice, and the final entry had been achieved by
the young woman, done with relish, using her boot. They had
each taken a room.

The Major's hands were working methodically inside the
drawers of a chest. Small parts of his life were kept from his

wife. She'd have wrinkled her nose at the sight of him, in his work as an FSB investigator, trawling through a young woman's underwear. He would tell her – when he reached home – of the breaking down of a door, and tell her of body parts collected in a mortuary, and let her know of the fatal injuries suffered by the young people from the fire flash at the moment of detonation, what the glass had done in the blowback of the bomb, but would not tell her of his search among brassières and panties and vests and tights. He hunted for evidence. Where had little Yekaterina gone, with whom, what had she known, when would a truth drop into his hand? Everything was as if her departure had been fast, chaotic. Had rather liked her. She was more interesting than the exhibitionists who were obsessed with phallus shapes, and talked – their brains doped up – of revolution. He thought her musical talent was genuine, thought also she'd have performed well as an agent. Many, in his experience, first snorted refusal but then came to enjoy the clandestine power over others, enjoyed even more the rewards that came: food, cut-price travel tickets, help with accommodation bolt-holes, and the opportunity – in the far future – of embracing a new identity. He found nothing.

Nothing of herself, and nothing of her brother whose body parts were now as small as those on a butcher's slab. Her car was gone from the usual place she parked it, the neighbours said. The bank statements were trivial, the utilities bills were paid but on 'last reminders'. He searched in vain for papers that demonstrated her involvement with the activists, and found no trail that showed anything of the skills of her brother, nor what had happened to the monies he had been paid. One clue remained. She had left two drawers full of poorly folded underwear, and the contents of a plywood wardrobe – warm clothes for the winter and light dresses and blouses for the summer – and in a corner was a heap of foot-wear – boots, shoes, trainers. In the bathroom was her toothbrush, and his, and soap and a small bottle of cheap eau de toilette. He asked the young woman, the lieutenant, why she would leave these items behind.

He was answered, a voice without an opinion and not offering judgement. 'They are left, Major, because she does not rate what is here. It's low quality, she thinks. Where she is going she would not care to wear them. That is what she thinks. That is where she believes she is going – and will buy, or be given, new clothes.'

They left, did not attempt to secure the broken door. He thought the place would be looted by the middle of the day. He was due to see the general, and swayed from tiredness as he went down the flights of stairs, and understood more.

Pyotr saw the line.

It had been a night of savage cold, the worst of the winter so far, but dry. The ground in front of the farmhouse was covered in a fine frost, and the wheels of his vehicle had crunched on ice on the approach lane, and he saw what had been done to confuse. Efforts had been made to obliterate the tracks that led from the barn's door in a straight line. Where the footprints milled close to each other, made a mess of the ground, he thought there had been farewells and then the line had resumed. Two sets of tread marks on the stunted grass between the barn and the forest, not meandering but going directly. The attempt to hide them had been done by the animals. He assumed they had been driven back and forth across the trail that two persons had left. He was a hunter. Pyotr could track a boar or a deer, a rabbit, and thought that once he had even been close to a lynx when his rifle had been on his back and not ready to aim, and could easily follow a bear in winter. He had good eyes, and an instinct for a track left by fugitives. He did not say what he saw.

They were poor liars.

To Pyotr, they were as family. More important to him than any living relation, even his mother – and any of the women in Kingisepp with whom he enjoyed fragile relationships – were Igor and Marika. Where he stood would in the future belong to him, it was promised. The lie was obvious and denials had tripped off their tongues. He had warned that they should keep the barns locked, should be alert for strangers in flight, had told them his own life had been threatened at the road-block by desperate, dangerous men: they had lied. No one had come, they'd said in unison. They had heard nothing, nor had the dogs been alerted.

The cattle and the pigs and the sheep, Pyotr believed, had tramped over the line, then had been fed on it. Insufficient to fool him. One was a man with a heavier tread and one was a woman who had worn small boots. He could have gone to the barn and pushed past them, inspected the interior, and probably he would have found flattened straw where *they* had rested in the night. If Igor and Marika lied about them, it was near certain that *they* had also been fed . . . and his anger rose at a steady pace. He remembered the surge of the cars at the road-block, coming out of a wall of darkness, and the sparks of fire as they cannoned off the sides of the drums, and his own fear when the shadows, in silhouette against the street lamps, had hurtled towards him, and the crack of his bullets – and still had the bruising at his right shoulder from the recoil. He did not challenge Marika or Igor. He might have been dead, cold in a mortuary at the hospital up the St Petersburg road, and at the hand of people who had been given shelter, safe fucking haven, by the senile old pair that he helped. But Pyotr did not accuse them, and the property was promised him when they died.

They had brought him coffee. He stood on the grass and frozen mud and cupped the mug in his hands and did not try to search the barn but traced the route they had taken. He knew the forest well, and the few routes through it. The sun was up, low on the trees, and from the east and to the west was the Narva river. Old men in Kingisepp talked of the battle in the winter of 1944 when the Red Army had pushed across it, taken hideous casualties, to gain a foothold, and all spoke of the power of the current's flow which had driven the landing craft out of formation, left them as easy pickings for the Fascist forces. Too wide, too strong, and no boats there to be stolen, all cleared from the security zone which he patrolled.

He imagined the old couple, wrapped against the chill, watching two fugitives from justice leave – who could so easily have been his murderers – waving off their fucking guests. He made conversation. The animals were good? They had enough logs for a decent fire that day? Anything needed from the shop other than the milk and bread he had brought with him? He was given brief, evasive answers. He smiled, and urged them again to be careful of 'ruthless criminals'. He said he would be back, but not who he'd bring with him. In his vehicle, bumping away up the track towards the Ivangorod to Kingisepp road, he imagined who he'd report to, what he would say. He might have been dead, and hate fed him.

She talked, he hardly listened. What books did he read, what authors?

Merc had given up trying to quieten her. Other than her, and their footfall that broke twigs and scuffed pine needles and the snap of broken branches, he heard nothing. He was unaware of pursuit or radio static, and smelled no cigarettes and they were far from the farm chimney's smoke. He would grunt, monosyllabic, or cough, but not answer.

What music did he like? They had sat on a fallen trunk. Taken a short rest, drunk cold water, then he had pulled her up and pushed on and into deeper forest. He had not yet found the trail he had used from the river. Sometimes she held his hand and allowed it to be used as a prop, keeping her upright, other times she clung to the sleeve of his coat. Was always close to him. Where had he been, were there Russians there?

Enough rest . . . He led, and allowed memories to intrude . . . top of them was the big first contact, him and Rob and Brad. They were part of the Special Forces close protection unit assigned to the Green Zone. The ambassador could not do his usual helicopter ride to the airport because of low cloud, and they must have heard that he was a top man for the Route Irish run. Not the armoured Range Rover, but a battered Nissan, smoked privacy windows and a tuned-up engine under a bonnet where the paint was scraped and rust showed. It had gone without incident, His Excellency safely delivered, and they'd done the run back and an RPG had been launched and hit the car in front which had a Polish team in it, and Merc had swerved out of the way and then done an evasion routine, and the boys had let rip a couple of magazines, but it was the driving they had noted, not their own 'free fire' response. He had seen them around, and taken beers, and done kit talk, tactics chat, and they'd separated him from the military contractor mob. Then they'd gone, moved on . . .

Did he have a home in England – what sort of home did he have?

Fifteen months later, they'd met again. Was everywhere he went a war zone, were there beaches anywhere he went? A drawl. 'Hi, matey, how you doing?' Then a chuckle. 'Great place, isn't it? Told the property is cheap if you want to buy and settle.' He had been in the vehicle park at the Bagram base, thirty miles out of Kabul, had just brought in a convoy. They'd come to pick up some Special Forces kit that had been airlifted for collection, and had dropped off a prisoner at the interrogation block. He'd been asked if he knew the road they'd be taking to a forward base on the far side of Kabul. He had not done war stories, but had described a 'bad' road, and had yanked out a map and showed them where the 'worst of the bad' places were . . . forewarned, forearmed, that sort of stuff. Had seen them a week later at one of the NATO compounds. They had been hit where he said they might. They had come through it: his advice had been sound. They were thankful, and showed it: he had fresh medic packs slipped him, and he'd learned more from them about the tactics of close-quarters combat. Then they'd shifted out again, taken the big bird home, gone with a couple of boxes – had sent him a clip of the coffins being unloaded, and a caustic note of thanks, which meant they'd have driven through Wootton Bassett at speed in a Land Rover and not gone through slow in a hearse. It could have been because of the advice he'd offered. Had lost touch again . . .

At his home in England, was there, close by, a place where she could study?

Walking up a main drag in Erbil, on the edge of Shah Park and looking at the citadel, a piercing wolf-whistle, then, 'Look, Rob, a bad penny, what keeps turning up.' And a growl of laughter, 'Jeez, Brad, we got to teach him it all over again, everything?' And hugs and cheek brushings and later that evening some more kit coming his way, and the next day he'd done a drive along the front line for them, and in the evening he'd brought them to his people who were going forward late that night, and they'd taken a class in survival skills and evasion, then target recognition. Good boys . . . His people had loved them except for one haughty woman who hadn't the grace to smile, nor thank, because she did not do celebrity worship, but he thought she'd listened to every damn word. An old question: How do you know when you're in a minefield? An old answer: When the guy behind you is blown up. Rob and Brad had been with a gang of Kurd fighters and doing a reconnoitre and one had lost a leg to a long buried PROM-1, and Merc was near enough to monitor the radio and knew a rough outline of the place, and had gone in, had near shat himself, had brought the guy out – had drunk with Rob and Brad that night, had not crawled from his pit the next day until after dusk. That the air strikes had come in after his ultimatum would have been down to them, to Rob and Brad, whatever they'd reckoned in VBX. Good to think of them . . .

They went on through the forest and sometimes he was hunched double because of low branches . . . His home was an apartment or a house? In the country or the city?

He tripped. He sprawled across a tree trunk. His nose was into the concrete-hard ground. There were scuffs on the far side of the trunk and he felt an additional layer of cold on the back of his neck. He did not need to be told, but she did it.

'We did a circle. It is where we were a half hour ago. We've gone nowhere.'

His face flushed embarrassment. His head was turned away and hid it. A little laughter rippled in his ear. He stood, caught her hand, tugged her clear, and did not know how he had been capable of that degree of error . . . Time had been lost, could not be recovered, added to the danger facing him, and her . . . Did he never make a mistake? No answer offered.

Up and breakfasted, the apartment tidied, the washing up done and cutlery and crockery stowed in cupboards, and the bags packed. Daff went first out of the kitchen window, and Boot crawled up on to the draining board. The bags followed her. Time to resume the vigil. One leg went out through the open window and half of his body and most of his weight, and he realised he was toppling, and snatched at an arm – thicker than Daff's. The surveillance man was there to take his weight. He was, with scant dignity, lowered to the mud surrounding the building. The start to the day that might prove the most significant of his professional life. And his cover shredded, and he was so obvious to the big wide world, so blatant, that a man not supposed to be aware of his comings and goings had taken on the task of aiding his descent from the window. Preposterous, amusing. For Boot, there was a behavioural rule book . . . what would Ollie Compton have done? Would have smiled gratitude, then let the arm take the strain, would have relied on a safe landing . . . and Ollie Compton would have murmured 'Dear boy, what a champion you are', then would have led the way to the nearest bar, beaten on the door until it opened, would have started a tab. Only one Ollie Compton. He thanked him, straightened his tie, tugged down his waistcoat, allowed his bag to be carried to the car.

Boot said, conversationally, 'Don't suppose you know about Hougoumont, the farm at Hougoumont?'

A shaken head, a roll of the eyes, a snort of laughter from Daff.

A trifle of warmth from Boot. 'It was on the right side of Wellington's line, a bit forward and a bit detached, a vital obstruction to the French. You see, young man, they could not turn our flank while we held the farmhouse and its immediate grounds. Coming up this summer it will be two hundred and three years since the fight there. I think it was the critical point in a critical front, at a critical time in history. It has been said that Waterloo, in particular the defence of Hougoumont marked a "day that changed the tomorrows of years to come". Apt, I feel, as it says there, "there is a duty to remember those who made history". If I was not here it's where I would have wanted to be, am there in soul. I like to sit under a tree in summer and dream of it as it was, smoke and carnage and knapsacks of courage, and huddle in the chapel in winter. I'm there rain and shine most weekends. The Coldstream Guards held the position, grand men, but it was a desperate business. A French *sous-lieutenant*, Legros, broke through the north gate, smashed it down with a heavy forester's axe and for a minute or so the battle was in the balance, and so was the future of Europe, but the Guards closed the gate and trapped Legros and thirty others inside. All hinged on the gate being closed and the defence of Hougoumont continuing. This giant of a man was killed and all with him except for a drummer boy, aged thirteen, who they spared. Slaughtered the rest. A romantic colouring of a brutal day, and true. Wellington himself said that the closing of the gate turned the day. And a resupply. Running short of ammunition, and a regimental carter drove a load of bullets right through the French lines and into the defended perimeter. Cannot make them up, those brilliant stories. I always go there . . . You know, today, there are huge dead trees – great gaunt things where crows sit – that have perished because of the weight of lead shot they absorbed. Extraordinary. It's my obsession, you see, and in the next few hours the obsession and my professional career will come together, walk hand in hand. Rather important to me . . . Did you say you had heard of Hougoumont?'

They waved as they drove away.

'I suppose this will be the day,' Boot said.

'They make it, the boys and Merc, or they don't. It'll be the day, good or bad.'

'Never done it myself,' Boot said. 'In answer to your query, belated: been there, behind the lines, running or bluffing or doing the covert bit? Never done it, and never been anywhere like the farm at Hougoumont, anywhere that required undiluted courage.

At Hougoumont, the Duke needed those Coldstreams to make supreme sacrifices. They had to, and the same is as true today, and I'm suggesting the necessity of that damn word, *sacrifice*. Cannot win without it. Do I sound as if I am trying to reassure myself? Don't know where we get those people from . . . Still we can hope for the best, can't do more.'

An end of a shift. Firearms back in the armoury, paperwork completed, vest and kit hung in the locker, and no scares – not where the two guards had their watch. London livening up, and the traffic clogging, and a cold wind coming in from the east, replacements greeted, time for Roy and Arthur to scuttle for trains home from Vauxhall. A disappointing end to the duty.

Not a sniff of Boot, nor Daff, neither sight nor sound of the Director or the Maid.

'Do you reckon, Arthur, it's all gone down the plug, whatever it is and wherever?'

'For me, Roy, the glass is better for being half full. Has to be tonight, can't be longer, can't be.'

They went their separate ways, and would doze a bit at home, maybe fiddle in the greenhouse or rake leaves off the lawn. They'd be back in the hut beside the gate slap on the dot of their duty start up. Arthur would have said that he felt part of some distant drama, had a stake in it, and doubted Roy would have said different.

She had the teeth in her hand. The Maid would not normally have disturbed them. She lifted them, studied the dentures, and they might have been yanked from French dead or from Germans or from the British boys on the left flank or the right, from infantry or artillery or cavalry, and they were still perfect two centuries after extraction. She was alone but still flicked a glance over her shoulder to be certain she was not witnessed, then clattered them, let the rattle play through the room. Then replaced them on the shelf where they took pride of place. What was it all for? The Big Boss demanded clarification – or justification. Some might have considered it a bit bloody late in the day for posing the question . . . They'd need sandwiches in the Pimlico block, and the coffee machine filled. A diversion for her was a text from north London, her parrot was well, was fed, had had its cage cleaned. More immediate, had the silly man forgotten what he had signed off? A message had come down from on high. The Brains Trust was to be reconvened. To be done that morning, not tomorrow and not next week. She assumed the Big Boss suffered, and Boot's silence hurt him. Damn well hurt them all. Boot, of course, employed correct tradecraft . . . Was too close to the Russian border for extra messages to be sent to London, probably sent nothing because he'd little or no idea how his little army fared, hopefully trudging towards the frontier – hopefully. A good question for the clever young people to wrestle with. What was it all for?

The Brains Trust had set an agenda for dealing with Lack of Moral Fibre, Squeamish Syndrome, or Getting in a Funk. The top men wanted justification, like a priest handed down absolution. Not convenient to gather at that time, that location, but a whip was on their backs. For each of them a basic fact was available. Some thirty-six hours before, a building in the Kupchino district of St Petersburg had suffered severe damage in an explosion, with casualties . . . *What was it all for?*

Bob from Five: 'It was a convention for Black Hats, our view of them. We took down some of their best and brightest. Those people have been hitting our banks, our utilities, our research and development in engineering – military and civilian, and crossover. Just a matter of time before they hit us with a Category One assault. You could argue forcefully, that the hack-attacks are tantamount to an Act of War. Take that further . . . We are entitled to strike back, utilise a justifiable counter-measure. With an Act of War goes the right to an Act of Self-Defence. They hit us and we hit them. They slap our ear and we bloody their nose. We can argue that it was an Act of Self-Defence when the US and Mossad coalition dropped a memory stick in a car-park outside the nuclear centre where Iran spun centrifuges. Just dropped it. A guy picks it up, that guy plugs it in. That is Stuxnet. Might have pretty holiday snaps, might have a porn film, unimportant as long as it is interesting and then it gets passed on. The virus runs: acorn stuff, humble beginnings, and the bomb-building programme is delayed by many months. We are taking a hell of a beating from them in sophisticated cyber warfare and have not yet raised a fist, gloved or bare, as reprisal. NATO Article Five is about collective defence, but in cyber it is vague because of the problem of attribution. We had it, copper bottom. They are hurting us and costing us; they are bullying, and we are responding. Not before time. It was a good plan. Clear up whatever dirt our people have left behind and it will have been a brilliant plan. Create confusion and internal argument and it could be an exceptional plan. I rest.'

Harry was VBX, and did the coffee pouring and would write up their findings. 'The Kupchino meeting offered a unique opportunity. We had a date and a time and an insider. Not for me to say whether the force used was excessive. We had them in place and a chance to degrade their capability through confusion. Human intelligence will always beat – sorry, to all of you – electronic intelligence. We had a Jo in there, and he was calling it for us as state-sponsored. That is the highest organs of their security apparatus targeting the UK and affecting all our capabilities to protect national security – and the US and half the rest of the world – and it will have been sanctioned at the top of their tree because that is the society they have, top down. We are not dealing with the aims and ambitions of a gang of thugs who look to swallow money out of our banks, our credit unions, or rip off our blue chip companies. We are naming their government as an aggressor. Heavy talk. This is not some ancient Bear bomber lumbering down the east coast with a pair of Typhoons alongside. It is theft on an industrial scale and decided on by the administration. They go to the Black Hats and pull in a group of them who they rate, and they give them a shopping list. Confession time: I am not a Genghis Khan throat slitter, but I am not losing sleep on this . . . but we have to be off territory and evidence cleaned for us to feel satisfied.'

Digestive biscuits went round the table. Leanne from the 'private sector' spoke. 'I am the outsider, looking in on your world. What do I add? I can tell you about the frustration of an arm tied, strong knots, behind a back. The arm cannot counter the volume of traffic that is directed against our critical national infrastructure. They are walking through us, over us, confident of total safety. We don't understand them. We cannot talk to them, learn their mind-sets, get under the culture of those who deploy the hack teams. They are into our banks and utilities and military structures. On average, twice every day, we are defending against Category Two or Category Three attacks. Every day. Our experience is that they pull together tight teams, Russian people, pay them well, have them under close discipline. We are not supposed to display emotion towards our enemies, our adversaries. Many talk of the need for appeasement, not aggravating an already difficult scenario. I disagree. I want them hurt. They are groping inside our knickers for every facet of government policy – energy, diplomacy, intelligence gathering, anything. We should give them pain. Why? Because if they are hurt, after the pain I feel in my work, then I can go home, open a bottle and feel good. But if the confusion is to linger, and the back-biting in their ranks to continue and breed, the people on the ground have to make it home. Put another way, what would scalp the operation, destroy the mission's effectiveness, is for evidence of UK involvement to be in their hands. Worse, a prisoner in a courtroom and singing . . . But you know it and will have taken all necessary precautions. Yes?'

The turn of Dunc, off the dawn train from Cheltenham. 'All very simple, but first where we are. What we hear is that an explosion took place, and caused fatalities and injuries. An Organised Crime *autorite*, hurt, accused a rival group of causing the explosion. Accusations made inside FSB that two "roofs" fell to fist fighting inside the HQ building. A general has now taken charge of an investigation – named Onishenko – veteran of Chechnya and recently in Syria. This morning a team has come in from the capital and will take charge of the evidence-gathering procedure. At the moment the local news outlets are merely reporting an industrial accident. Currently, but about to be relieved of responsibilities, the man in charge is an FSB major, low-level and unimportant. So, these are critical hours, and we await with some anxiety the information that we have successfully retrieved our people. A trail of guilt would embarrass. What is simple? We are led in this aspect of warfare. We have fast jets, a few tanks, effective Special Forces, proven ground-to-ground, ground-to-air, air-to-ground missile systems, decent intelligence-gathering capabilities, but in this field we are not in the same game as them. They are ahead and drawing away. What use is our conventional weapons systems if our population has its savings stolen, its bank accounts emptied, cannot feed itself, cannot heat itself, wealth leaching and our primary economic assets stolen from under our noses? If we then seek to deploy what military we have we may discover, unpleasantly but not a surprise, that the logistics of defence have been sabotaged. A window opened. We climbed through it. Equally simple, we have to rely on the team having the ability to climb back through that bloody window before it slams shut. It was good to do, but it isn't finished. That's about where we are.'

The laptops were shut down, except for Harry's. He would write the report. What was it all for? It would be on a desk in the upper reaches of the building on the south side of the Thames within an hour. The others were heading for the door.

Leanne said, 'Will it be what is wanted by them up high who launched it?'

Dunc said, 'More important, will it do any good?'

Bob said, 'Rather me than them, those on the other side. Easy here, isn't it?'

Harry looked up from his screen. 'Have a party tonight, hardly in the mood. What old people say, *On a prayer and a wing.* See you guys, the next time – if we ever do this kind of caper again.'

*   *   *

Boot said, 'Might as well be here. Good vantage.'

Daff said, 'I'd hoped he'd be over by now, across.'

They sat on a bench, close to the wall of the bastion, and could see the river below them, and the bridge to their right, and noticed the increased number of guards milling at the far end, where the barrier was.

'Didn't come in darkness, cannot come in daylight. A day to kill, except for your boys, Daff.'

'It's where they have to do it, over the bridge. Don't have the training for anything else – drive or walk.'

Rare venom. 'Another of these bloody bridges. Watching for a man approaching a checkpoint, and having the glasses on him. He offers up his papers, usually forgeries, and he's hoping the blighters are half-asleep, or thinking of women, or of the next meal break, and we see them, and they start walking, start driving. Getting too damn old for it. Always the crucial bit, the approach to the centre span, where that white line is, and maybe they are playing games or maybe they have second thoughts on the validity of the papers they've been shown . . . The noises start. They shaft into your bones, the klaxon would wake the dead, the sirens, and up here, elevated, Daff, we'd hear the weapons cocking, one up the spout and ready. We have to wait for them, least we can do . . . Then go to look for our boy, and that bloody river . . . Be a good girl, Daff, find me a mug of tea.'

She grimaced, then headed for the café. The cold bit at him. Responsibility weighed, but excitement out-performed it. Too damned old, but addicted.

The Major said it like he thought it was.

The General did not take a note.

The Major tried to be coherent but accepted that extreme tiredness caused him to hesitate, to stammer over the more complicated arguments, and sentences went unfinished and conclusions left to hang. They were alone, no aide present; no record would exist. He had started to talk of a girl, and a cleared apartment and a meeting in the car-park of a supermarket, and of an incident at a road-block on a bridge at— The General lifted his finger, made a slight movement in front of his face, across his mouth, broke the Major's thread.

'Thank you, Danik. I appreciate your rigour. Your intellectual courage I knew of and the physical courage you demonstrated with the thugs close to the airport. You have done well. I believed you would, and your reputation travelled ahead of you, an independent thinker. If I surround myself with people who tell me only what they assume I want to hear, then I will not know when I am wrong. Sometimes there are occasions when I am in error, make substantial mistakes, but I never apologise for them.'

He did not speak directly to the Major but stood looking out of the window, and might have followed the craft on the river, some of the last sailings of the year before the ice came, and his voice was quiet but not conversational, and he'd not have tolerated interruption.

'I choose to disregard the conclusions you veer towards. Myself, I lean in two possible directions. Less credible is the opinion that, for reasons not yet established by forensic examination, there was a gas explosion in the building, maybe overloaded electricity circuits in conjunction with a supply pipe. More credible is the suggestion that two vile creatures, major crime players, fell out over the awarding of a contract by state security: hacking, stealing, but the interests of our country are involved. Intelligent young people, usually engaged in activities that are basically illegal but who are not prosecuted, were gathered together. Considerable funds would flow into the pockets of one *autorite* while another would feel cheated. That to me is the most likely eventuality. Jealousy, greed.'

Austere features marked him and because of the angle of his head, the Major could clearly see the scar that ran below the lobe of his left ear and down to his throat and disappeared under his collar: said to be from a combat injury.

'A fresh team has come from Moscow and will no doubt take stock of what evidence is available and I am confident they will follow the correct path … It should lead to the suspension, pending investigation, of two FSB colonels for systematic corruption. Also, two criminal figures will be arrested and will face the full severity of the law in regard to non-payment of taxes, money laundering, perhaps even charges of murder. The matter of the explosion will be kept close to the seat of the detonation, that building and the purpose of that building, where it belongs.'

The pitch of his voice did not change, nor did he look for a reaction from the Major. Subsequent disagreement would pit a general's word against a junior officer's, a man with a chest of decorations against a foreigner from Belarus. The Major stayed impassive.

'It was a position that you seemed to be going slowly towards, Danik, that a third party was involved. I reject that. I have little time for leisure, but when I find it and with my family, we watch American crime films, always fancifully enjoyable. There is a phrase common to many of them: the smoking gun. It is a grand moment when the smoking gun is discovered, confirmation of a theory that up to then seemed impossible to substantiate. You were interested in the location of the detonation and the belief it *might* have been close to where the hacker, Nikki, sat. You believed it significant, but I would imagine the table was littered with laptops and files and that these kids were constantly moving, coffees and to pee … Not conclusive of anything. Do you, Danik, in this matter, have a smoking gun?'

He had no evidence … only understanding. Said nothing.

'I think not. You needed one but have not produced one. Go back to your regular duties having handed to the Moscow team what information you have collected. You should hold up your head, feel pride in your work, especially the taking of control at the seat of the explosion, which impressed me. What would I have done had you produced that smoking gun, Danik? You are entitled to ask, but you will get no answer. You did not. Thank you for your time, and thank you for your work. Go home and sleep.'

The Major took the elevator down to his own floor. He ordered all the material collected for the investigation to be deleted from his computer. He said where they were headed and after the deleting was done he led out his sergeant and the young female officer, and they were bent under the weight of the combat vests and their side-arms. He locked the door behind him, and they went to the basement and signed for a jeep with good off-road capability.

He sat in the back, dripped confidence, told them their destination was Kingisepp, what sort of man he wished to meet there, and spoke of the scent of cordite from the barrel of a gun, the equivalent of 'smoke' . . . He would be asleep before they were clear of the city.

They left Toomas.

Had argued, spat over it. Hissed exchanges between Martin and Kristjan while Toomas's head rolled between them as they carried him, taken all his weight. As if he did not hear a word of what was said. Neither knew how much Toomas had bled internally from the wound. Nor how much longer he could live without emergency care. The decision for Martin and Kristjan, the biggest of either of their lives, was to deny Toomas the possibility of survival through the intervention, assuming it remotely feasible, of a trained team in an accident/emergency hospital: survival from a gunshot wound in the gut, and then . . . That side of the river or the far side? That side was identification, interrogation, perhaps the same drugs as used on Toomas's grandfather to keep him alive a few more hours and dumped in a basement cell.

Kristjan had said it. 'Honest, truthful, do you want him to live? Is he better dead?'

Martin had not answered.

They were on higher ground. Away to their right was the smoke pall above the chimneys of Ivangorod, and the upper turrets of the castle. And beyond, lit by an early sunshine, the façade of the fortress built by the Swedish monarchy as a protection for Narva. Shame would live with them, Kristjan said. Neither – if they survived the next few hours – would be free of it . . . No one would know beyond the two of them, it would be bottled guilt. They could not carry him any farther. A compromise was agreed.

'He has it, has the possibility to use it.'

Martin said, 'We put it in his hand, put his hand against his head.'

A big decision for Martin, since his return from the Kaliningrad assignment, and the leaking of the money he had been paid, was whether an interior wall was best in magnolia or avocado or brush-pink paint. Martin thought the big decision for Kristjan would have been how much of his wage to slot in his hip pocket on a Friday night when he hit Narva's casino.

They laid him down on the frosted ground. No grass, just a layer of needles shed by the trees. Martin said again, repeated it, that he could not manage to carry Toomas any farther, and Kristjan just shrugged, and stood above their friend – after a fashion a 'friend' but one linked to them by the catgut of history, not easily broken – and both gasped air into their lungs and hunger ravaged them, and thirst. Martin reckoned that Kristjan gave it grudgingly, put the Makarov into Toomas's fist, and curled the index finger around the trigger guard, and cocked it and freed the safety, and Kristjan raised one finger of his hand as confirmation that a single bullet was in the magazine. One shot left, and it would have seemed to both of them that the option left with Toomas mitigated what they did. Already the guy looked thin, no colour in his cheeks; he still breathed, but did not speak, and sometimes his lips bubbled.

Turning away, didn't wish him 'Good luck, friend', no mention of 'Back soon as we can with help for you', nothing of 'Don't feel good about this, but no other way'. They blundered clear . . . By the early afternoon, Martin said, they should be south of the town and then moving into the remote bog land of lakes and streams, and be within sight of the far bank and of refuge. Martin felt the cold on his face, worst where tears had run and turned near to ice. Neither looked back.

Merc caught her arm, held it tight enough to halt her.

Another pace forward and Kat would have been out of the darkness of the pines and among the birches, the edge of the forest. She gasped, seemed to go limp. Had reason to, would have realised the width of the river, might then have seen a tree trunk carried in the flow, their side of the imaginary centre line, moving fast and showing the current's strength. She would have seen, also, the barrier of densely packed reeds, as high as her head. He relaxed his hold but laid a finger on his lips. She looked to the right and saw a small boat in the far distance, downstream, two fishing rods poking over the side, and looked left and saw the patrol boat, the Russian flag on the back and an open wheelhouse where a uniformed guy was driving it and another was out behind him with binoculars and scanning their bank. And beyond the boat was a watch-tower. And she looked ahead, stood on tiptoe to see above the reeds, and seen the late morning sunlight on the far side where it bounced on car roofs. It looked pretty there, the far side, and would have made pictures for postcards. But was formidable, frightening, and Merc was taken on trust.

He had been in the barn with her, had made a desperate loving with her, had warmed her, and she was not certain what he felt for her ... a friend? Adored? A vehicle for releasing the pent-up tension? Merely needed? Reflected.

Should he judge her by her possible usefulness on Hill 425, and the speed with which she could reload an assault rifle's magazine? Was the 'sometime' any day soon? Well justified, in looking across the expanse of moving water, feeling the chill of the wind on her face, seeing patrols, estimating distance, and feeling fear. What to do with her? Could ask her to hide, stay quiet and calm, or take her when he went to find the board. He did not recognise where he was, did not see the marker he'd left. Had to have the board, had to watch for patrols. Had to hope the board was sufficiently buoyant. Too much to do and look for ... but a promise had been given, was not to be forgotten ... and he imagined a pack closing behind him. Rob was not there, not Brad; had no one to ask.

'Time to rest.'

Trying to be cocky, and not getting there. 'Then . . .?'

'Find what I hid on this side.'

Trying to be brave and failing. 'Then . . .?'

'Survive this time of maximum danger.'

Trying to cling to the boldness and falling short. 'Then . . .?'

Merc said, 'Then we go across.'

They were sitting on crisp grass and her shoulder nuzzled under his armpit, and the river, big and powerful, flowed clear towards the Baltic sea in front of them.

17

He didn't want her with him. Merc thought the board and suit were hidden away downstream but was not certain. He preferred to be alone when he looked for it, relying on scraps of memory, and would not accept quizzing. He murmured in Kat's ear what he intended. She thought at first that his lips on her ear were affection and was reaching up to loop an arm around his shoulder and his neck, but he blocked it. Her face clouded. They had been in the barn, the animals as voyeurs, and she had clung to him and his fingernails had ground through the thickness of his gloves to grip her. She had the right.

'I am going forward. I have to find the place where there is a board, how we cross.'

'What sort of board?'

'A swimmer's board, for surfing on waves, and—'

'I cannot swim.'

'It will float, and I will support you.'

'But if I lose the board, and cannot swim, and I go under and—'

Merc was brusque, not tender. 'That is how it will be, the way it will happen.'

'How long do I wait here?'

'Until I am back. Stay here. I come back when I am ready to, then we go across.'

He would have had the rasp of authority in his voice. Rarely used. He could be quiet with the guys and the girls on Hill 425, and he was seldom harsh; usually conversational, better for exercising control. They were crouched where the tree line thinned and the ground was raised a metre above the narrow open strip before the final dip into the reed beds. A beaten down path ran between the tree line, dense pine and the reeds, probably made by pigs or deer. Beyond the reeds was the Narva river . . . However long he lived, a few hours, the rest of that day, a long lifetime, he would not forget the sight of it. It carried debris as if it were light-weight flotsam, had white crests from the wind that funnelled from the north. A section of a dead tree's trunk came down the river, chased by a floating rubbish bin, then a tangle of withered, branches followed. The speed was awesome. She had full justifica-tion in feeling naked fear: she could not swim, she might believe he would save himself in the water, let her wrist slide from the grip . . . and she had loved him in the barn. Had the right to voice disappointment, puzzlement, and suspicion . . . Might disappear into the undergrowth, abandon her. But Merc did not play games of reassurance, was not gentle. He stared back into her face and her chin shook and her lips were narrow with cold, and she blinked, and she shivered.

He said, 'You wait here. I will take you across because that was my promise – for now you wait, and you do not move, and do not show yourself. I will come back for you, and you will wait. End of story.'

She seemed to crumple. Merc accepted she was not a fighting girl. They had a stereotype within the Fire Force Unit, those who peered over the parapet of a Forward Operating Base. They were tough, hardened, walked with a swagger, rejoiced in killing an enemy who was in terror of dying in combat at the hands of a woman, gave short shrift to delicacy, were confident and did not make a drama out of a crisis, could load a DShK machine gun and could strip a Kalashnikov's innards, could lob a grenade with accuracy . . . Could not play a piano, could not dream of an unfet-tered freedom, could not shed tears. Merc saw one of them in his mind and twin images clashed. The haughtiness in her eye with the blaze at her mouth when he slapped her arse and told her to duck and not make it simple for the sniper; it merged with the sight of her in the bed, and the tubes and the anaesthetised rhythm of breathing and the surgery team bending over her: he had been an unwanted intruder and unwelcome spectator. Kat, no muscle, no swing in her stride, no uniform, no weapon trailing from her hand, was not a fighting woman. He thought her a passenger, would never have categorised Cinar as a burden . . . but a promise had been given.

The light had dulled. The sun was buried in cloud, and spits of hail hit his cheeks and some rested in her hair, and the wind had not slackened. He did not know whether it would snow that day, or in the night, how soon it would come. Snow, sleet, hail, were all enemies because he would leave a trail of boot marks. He assumed that pursuit followed them . . . Wondered how the boys did, how near to the river they were, whether it went badly for them. He did not kiss her, did not squeeze her hand. He thought her exhausted, afraid, and incapable of contributing. He nodded to her. She seemed frail, small, desperate for a protector. Merc had known he must keep his promise to Nikki from the moment he had understood that the boy would stay with the bomb. He slipped away. Wondered for a moment whether he should again have emphasised the need for absolute quiet, minimum movement, what any man of experience in war would hammer at a novice recruit, a novice in survival. Did not, was gone. He went back into the trees, stayed in their cover, and went downstream and the branches closed behind him and the wind sang above him.

It was an open wound. Neither needed to speak of it, but the pain coddled them equally. Kristjan led and Martin followed.

And neither mentioned Toomas, who might as well have hovered over them, and both went quietly and strained to hear the sound of a single shot, and both would have wondered whether he still lived or whether he lay alone, or whether he had been taken and had not found strength to squeeze the trigger. Hunger took them worse, and thirst, and the cold chewed at them. Toomas was not spoken of. Nor what they would do with the wage promised them, the larger part to be paid on completion which was encouragement to get back across the river. The gap widened. Martin did not hurry to catch Kristjan. Kristjan did not slow his pace. They were no longer comrades. The bond had been broken when the Makarov pistol was placed in Toomas's fist, and the tip of his index finger laid inside the guard. It would not be spoken of if they succeeded in crossing, *if*, the Narva river and reached Estonian territory. If they met again, *if*, there would be a handshake and a hug and a kiss on the cheek and talk of how they did and the life they led after home decorating and shelf stacking, courtesy of the new monies paid them. What had happened in a forest on the eastern side of the town of Ivangorod would be buried deep in silence. Both would have reckoned their grandfathers – forever young and captured in sepia-tinted photographs and with an impertinence, a cheekiness that had bred courage – would have denounced them from unmarked graves. Sometimes they were in the depths of the forest and had to go on hands and knees under the bigger branches, and there were places where trees had been felled by loggers, and they had a view of the top towers of Ivangorod's fortress, and the great Russian flag that flew in the wind.

Each of them had probably made a plan of how they hoped to get back, and which of the bars in Narva would play host to them, what they would drink, eat, where they would sleep that night, but not discussed. Nor was the pain that would be inflicted on them if they were taken, *if*, talked of . . . and both had already, several times over, in their minds spent the money owed them. They pressed on, and the gap between them grew; one did not hurry and one did not slow, and neither spoke to the other.

Daff babbled.

'What is so bloody awful is not being able to do anything. That's it, isn't it, *anything*. Just consigned to standing, sitting, here, drinking coffee, chewing on bloody gum. Don't know what to do, what to say.'

He might have said that if she did not know what to say then to stay quiet could be helpful. But Boot did not, had never ditched tolerance of her. She kept going, as if it were her own therapy road.

'Wondering where he'll be, wondering that he thinks. Not proud of it, but I have put the three boys at the bottom of my priority list of concern. Don't give a shite about them. Only Merc that matters.'

And Daff was wrong not to carry in her backpack anxiety for the three men – middle-aged, paupers, snatching at the money she had offered – because any one of them could blow a hole below the waterline of the mission, of Copenhagen. Realised it now, had not before accepted how fragile were the chances of the three boys making the home run to Narva; had not comprehended how dangerous it would be to travel to St Petersburg, escort the courier, then run him and the passenger back to safety and success. Had not factored in the matter of events that turned up unannounced, unexpected, unpredicted, and that screwed the best-laid plans. They could, any one of the three of them, turn the business into headlong disaster . . . Probably why she had become a dripping tap of talk. She had recruited them, well inside budget, would be a prime target if it came to an internal inquest. They were on the bastion just downstream from the bridge and they watched the cars coming from the east, and saw the pedestrians, and waited.

'You don't have to answer me, Boot . . . I mean, is it always like this? I'm wondering how many poor bastards you've had under your wing, inspired by good words and talk of the flag and duty, and they've been on the wrong side of a fence, a wall, a river. Is it always so bloody hard? What I'm saying is – a cardinal law of the jungle that I'm breaking – I really like Merc, always have. Would have taken him to bed, too right, but I don't think he ever noticed me. God, it's cold. You good, Boot?'

She paced and would stop dead after a dozen strides and then slap her shoulders and her chest with her gloved hands, try to return circulation to her body. That high above the river there was no break on the wind. Boot wore his three-piece suit, had woollen socks under his brogues, and the tail of his coat flapped by his knees, and often he reached up to steady the trilby on his head. He was, certain of it, a damn great caricature of the old warrior deployed on Cold War duty – and revelling in the role. She would have had to carry him, kicking, back to the apartment and manacle him to a chair if she had wanted to preserve him from the chill; his face had a blue tint to it and his teeth were clamped on a small cigar.

'I'd be hung out for the crows if I lost you, Boot. Sure you're all right? He never saw me. I could have been in a swimsuit with the straps sagging and he would not have, could have kicked in the door to his hotel room and he'd have told me to leave ... It's because of the focus he carries. We see them come, Boot, don't we? They come and they go, but this is the boy that's remembered. I don't know why. If anyone can get out of that place, then it will be him. I said "anyone", Boot. Perhaps no one can. You thought of that, Boot? Something nags at me ... I'll try it on you.'

Boot had not turned. He might have assumed that the surveillance guy was in place, had an eye on them, assumed it and been correct. She supposed it the sort of weather when the elderly caught pneumonia or pleurisy. Where her childhood was, any man worth a groat would have settled early in front of a hissing log fire, nursed a Scotch, or three – or would have dressed in proper gear, gone out, climbed in bogs before dropping a stag that needed culling. Would not, absolutely not, have sat on a bench and stared down at a lone bridge and noted each lorry, van, car, bicycle coming from the other side, and each pedestrian. If one were captured, they were shafted. Deniability was built into the mission's fabric.

'How long do they keep going, men like Merc? That's what I'm floating by you. That pressure ... how long? What happens to those men? Do they wake up one day, and draw back the curtain, look out on the normal world, say that "There's where I want to be"? Check in the gun, send the camouflage gear down to the charity shop on the High Street, make a feature in the garden with the combat boots and plant pansies in them? What I am asking, Boot, is whether, on that supposed morning, they just kick it into touch, the old life. No one can do this day in and month out, year in and decade out. Has to be an end point. After this one, Boot – looking at the bright side – will he want to quit, hook up again with ordinary folk? What do you say, Boot?'

★　　★　　★

Boot said, 'When I was a child, my parents used to take me annu-
ally to the theatre in London. Same theatre, same show, and same
emotions aroused . . . God, this cold is brutal . . . so, because of
that play I can answer your statement, my dear. A man absorbs
pressure in the military or intelligence-gathering field. He is in
great danger, or directs others on to that road and must take
responsibility for their fate. Huge burdens are imposed. A man
begins to loathe the pressure exerted on him, and he dreams of
little more – once the flush of excitement has dripped off him –
than escape. The escape, in your view, will take him to some
humdrum, dreary life where nothing is on the line, and the tension
will only increase with a Friday night quiz in the pub. He won't
sign up for that . . . How do I know? The play I was taken to watch
each Christmas holiday gave me an insight into these useful men,
and women, because old truths hang around.'

Sitting on the bench, with the sleet settling on his shoulders and
on the brim of his trilby, and gathering on his knees, he felt shriv-
elled – as if weight and strength leaked from him. Always that
sensation when the matter had moved away from personal control.
His spectacles seemed to droop on the bridge of his nose and his
view of the bridge misted.

'And the play . . . a good rollicking story, and captivating. A
nursery full of children abandon their beds and fly off – yes, *fly* –
away into the night and are at the beck of Peter. Lovely lad. They
have all manner of adventures, pirates and crocodiles, but then the
children want to go home, be back with their dog. Not Peter . . .
He could have exchanged the thrills and the scrapes for a conventional upbringing. They return and offer Peter security and safety,
school and a haircut, learn a bit of Latin, but he balks at the chance.
He is afraid of conformity, leaves them, out through the window,
heads off for the stars – is off again to a sort of Never Land. Never
grows up. Never looks for the ordinary. Never abandons the
excitement bred from danger and comrades. You are wrong, Daff,
if you think that Merc is any different to Peter and his Never
Land . . . Not many of them about, but a few, and so useful that
we've come to depend on them.'

When he shifted on the bench, twisted to wrap his scarf tighter, he glimpsed the surveillance car and its exhaust fumes and the windows had steamed except where a crude square had been rubbed to enable the watch to be kept on them.

'They don't grow old. Merc and those like him. Don't hope to prove me wrong, Daff ... They always return to the "Never Land". Little else matters to them ... Enough of that. Outside your remit and mine. I don't expect we'll repeat this conversation, no point.'

He was so fond of Merc, and all of them like him. Was not supposed to be and hid it well.

Boot said, 'He'll come tonight. It's the boys now that we're looking for, waiting for.'

The Major settled in his seat, and the local man – called himself Pyotr – gave a casual salute, as if they were almost equals. They had met at the bridge at Kingisepp. A half-dozen local militia had queued to tell the Major of the breakthrough by two vehicles at the checkpoint. He could have called them incompetent, could have told them to their faces that they had failed in a simple task, but he had listened. The Major knew that more was learned by listening. Pyotr, in a rusted jeep because the wealth and power of the modern state had not reached the militia station at the town straddling the main road west from St Petersburg, had brought four others with him. The Major and the lieutenant, the young woman, and his sergeant followed. The sleet had intensified. Both vehicles went fast, ignored the ice on the road, and the traffic heading to and from the frontier point at Ivangorod, backed off the main highway and gave them a clear run.

He was taken, first, to see sunken tyre marks heading off the road and across the verge. He was led on a narrow track between the trees and followed the ruts. The burned-out vehicle still stank. Farther on was a second car's shell. There had been a broad description of a man and woman in the Polo ... Good enough. The Major straightened, stood at his full height, and sniffed at the air. He was told that men had gone with a dog in the direction south of the outskirts of Ivangorod but the weather made it difficult for the tracker. He was asked by Pyotr why more men, of status and rank like himself, had not come from the city and why there was no serious investigation with full resources. He ignored the question. He had seen enough, turned away. He appreciated the abilities of these local men.

To his wife, the Major would have described Pyotr, as gross, bovine, appearing stupid and simple, but showing obvious cunning, blessed with a natural intelligence, good hearing, fine eyesight, a knowledge of the countryside – where FSB officers seldom saw a need to visit. Pyotr blinked and concentrated. The Major assumed that he would have known where a deer or a pig had slept. Pyotr said that a woman had been in the second car, because the seat was far forward. That vehicle was better hidden, and if the rain had come on more heavily, or if the sleet had turned earlier to snow, then it would have remained hidden until the thaw, months away. Cleverly done, but not sufficiently clever. The driver's seat was forward. The Major pictured Yekaterina. The militiaman, Pyotr, showed him no deference. The Major was told where they would go, but received no explanation.

First down the road, then away on a track with a stone base and off into the forest. His sergeant drove, followed the militiaman. Darkness hemmed them in. The sleet could not penetrate the canopy of branches. Only a local man would have known this track and recognised its turning off the highway. There was an alien smell in the air, trapped between the trees, recognised it from the cabin by the river far out of Minsk where he went for New Year with his wife and his son. An open fire, damp wood, smoke spurting up from an unswept chimney. He heard the scrape of a weapon being armed and a barrel poked from the side of the lead jeep, then the men squatting in the back took their cue and loaded rounds into the breeches of their rifles, and the lieutenant behind him copied them. The Major dropped his hand on to the holster at his belt. They came into a clearing.

The Major saw the smoke from the chimney and saw animals dismal in the weather and chickens scattered and two sheep stampeding back towards a barn's open door. An old man, stooping, came out of the farmhouse and carried a vintage shotgun, then a woman emerged, frail but with bright and hostile eyes, the wind rippling her shawl. He slipped down from the jeep and walked to the militiaman's shoulder.

'It is where they might be, Major, or where they might have been.'

Twice Merc had been certain he had found the small area of open ground where the deer had been, where he had come ashore, where the board was hidden. Twice Merc had been wrong.

For a man who appeared to a stranger cold, emotionless, not victim to mood swings, there had, twice, been moments of relief because a hanging branch had seemed familiar, or a plastic bag had been tucked on the top of a rotted fencing pole which he had thought he remembered. The triumph, twice, had surged. He had gone forward each time, faster and with less care, had cursed his own impatience. He had stood in the centre of a small open space. The sleet had spat on him and the trees had been ruffled by the wind, and the reeds had danced, and there had been a distant rumble of the river's flow. He had looked around him and searched for the strip of cloth.

Each time the same. He did not find it, six inches long and half an inch wide and tied in a simple knot and on a sodden length of old branch that had been carried downstream, then come to rest when last year's flood subsided. Twice he had reckoned he had found the place, twice was mistaken. Time slid by. He recognised it; his performance had deteriorated. He should have found the marker by now, should have located the board and the suit. Should have retained his calm, but it slackened. Merc stared around him. At no time in his life had he felt such numbing cold and the wet was in his boots and his socks were sodden and his feet frozen. Bloody kit was failing him . . . all his clothing was wet. And frustration bit into him. He could see across.

Dulled lights, through the low waves of the sleet, showed the vehicles on the far side of the river. Could have been as much as quarter of a mile away from him, the distance increased by the depth of the reed banks on both sides and then the trees and scrub before the raised road. Two worlds, his and theirs, and without the ability to communicate. Still had the phone and would not have dared to switch it on and have his position located, monitored. Lorries, vans, cars edged along the road in difficult driving weather and kept a constant speed. He could focus on a lorry with a high cab and hold it in sight, then lose it. He wondered where Daff was and Boot. And wondered whether they were here, and had binoculars, and kept a watch, or whether they had a view of the bridge upstream, or whether they lounged in a café and had hot coffee and toast and . . .

Merc was a man who survived by the meld of instinct and confidence. One was dimmed and the other fractured. Needed to start again, and make another big decision. Had he come too far along the bank, gone past the clearing where he had left the marker? Had he not gone far enough? And a new worry . . . while he dithered in his search, was the girl still good? And what did he think of her, and was it merely because a promise had been given? He thought of her, alone and frightened – and cold. He thought she would start to shift, then move, then come from the hiding place, then stand and listen, try to hear his return. She might, a possibility, start to call out for him, her voice growing in pitch, becoming a scream, then a shriek and ending in choked tears. She might come in search of him. His thoughts cavorted . . . Yes, the board found, and the suit, and a place across the river where Boot and Daff waited, and him hurrying back to the point where he had left her – but no one there.

Had not wanted her trailing near him, had thought of her as a burden. Considered the days when he'd escorted principals, done close protection, and they were not expected to contribute to decisions on when they would go out of a door, cross a pavement, when to sit in the back of an armour-plated vehicle and hunker down.

Could have been right and might have been wrong. Realised his abilities had slipped. Seemed to Merc to be too difficult to get back into the protection of the tree line and have to push back damn near every low branch to make progress. He stayed on the animal track that was between the pines and the reeds. Then dropped to his knees. A patrol boat went by, going upstream and flying the Russian flag. And the opposite way, downstream, was a barge with timber props and he heard the greetings of the two crews as they passed.

Merc was hurrying which was poor practice, and he no longer looked for the lights on the faraway road that was the other side of the river. He searched for the board and the suit, and could not find the cloth strip he had left as a marker. It was a possibility she would call for him, a probability that she would come after him, and he thought of her as a cross that he carried. God alone knew why he had come, agreed to it. On the move, searching, not finding, and a stampede that stopped his heart when a heron escaped from the reeds, flapping its wings against the fronds and flew up and into the sleet and lowering cloud.

He heard the dog.

Between sleep and unconsciousness and being vaguely awake, Toomas heard a throaty howl from deep in its chest. When he had slept he had dreamed of the young man with the ambition to become an academic, to learn modern history, then teach it in the university of Tartu. When he had been unconscious, time had filtered away and he had not dreamed nor felt the pain. When he awoke he saw the movement of the branches above him and the and sleet drifting on to his face and had felt sleet weight of the pistol in his hand. He heard the dog again, louder and closer. It pleased Toomas that he had rested and was more alert than when the boys had carried him. He craved a whisky, a vodka, could even have sunk a plastic beaker full of water. His tongue smeared his lips.

He supposed that the final decision left in his life span – not where he would get Scotch whisky or Viru Valge vodka, or water – was when he would line up the barrel and press it as hard as he was able against the side of his scalp, then work the index finger

inside the trigger guard. Do it now, do it later? Toomas was a big
man, heavy and sporting a gut, and when he wore the suit of chain
metal, and the steel helmet with the eye slits, and wielded the
double-handed sword of the Teutonic knights, the tourists at the
castle were nervous of his size and strength. The fear was that,
now, he might not have the strength to pull the trigger. In the last
hours, he had thought of his grandfather in the basement cell of
the old KGB building on Pikk, and the pain meted out to him . . .
Nothing about loyalty to the woman who had pressed money into
his fist in the café at Narva, nothing about the cause of a strike
back against the Russian state. He thought of his grandfather and
the loneliness of his last hours. He could see the dog. It strained on
its leash, slobber at its mouth, and was on its back legs, a handler
struggling to control it. If he were caught he would be kept alive,
and he would be tortured. If he were tortured he would give the
names. He was pathetic, and wet himself and tears froze in his
eyes.

He felt the barrel and worked it toward his ear. Weapons were
trained on him. The leash went slack. The dog was loosed. He
struggled to find strength in his finger.

The Major gazed at the couple. Then he smacked his fist against
the cheek covered in a carpet of stubble. The blow was light but
might have dislodged the man's dentures. The militiaman, Pyotr,
had taken the shotgun from the old man, had called him Igor, had
declined coffee from the old woman, Marika. The Major slapped
again, his other fist. He rarely discussed his work in any detail with
his wife. His wife rarely described the difficulties of her day in the
consulting room. And he never talked of the times he went down
the steep steps to the holding block in the basement and wore thin
leather gloves and might alert a prisoner to the need for cooperation and 'rough' him. The husband, Igor, would have fallen but for
the woman, Marika, supporting him. There were times in his work
when the Major was not proud of what he did, but he would have
vigorously defended himself from any charge of employing 'gratu-
itous' violence. They had searched the farmhouse and had found

nothing of significance and he had realised the bond that existed between the militiaman, Pyotr, and the couple: there would have been tugged loyalties between a mellow and well-tested friendship and the desire to perform well in the presence of an FSB officer and be rewarded financially and with promotion opportunities. Personally, he had checked the crockery, old and chipped, its decoration faded, on the draining board and could not have sworn that extra mouths had been fed. Nor was there evidence that any bed had been used, other than that in which the couple slept. They had gone outside, entered inside the barn.

His reputation at the Big House was because of his results. He thought such a reputation justified his methods. The stench of animals hung heavy and the pigs rampaged around them and he had stepped on an egg and the lieutenant's boot slid in manure . . . He knew such places from his childhood. On the outskirts of the villages near where he had been reared and gone to school there had been remote farms with a handful of livestock, and a life that was primitive and hard. Thrown into that scene would have been the horrendous experiences of the Great Patriotic War; he had realised that this couple were old enough to have witnessed the advance of the Panzers, then their retreat three years later, and the arrival of the Red Army; and he expected that deeper in the trees around the clearing would be hidden graves identifiable by a squat cross or a heap of stones. He had noted that the old man, Igor, boasted a glass eye. They had found nothing in the barn. Back outside, Pyotr had shouted at them, in frustration: where their loyalties should lie, about saboteurs, about people who might have – but for God's blessing – have killed him, *him*, their friend, Pyotr, who helped them. But they had stayed silent.

The Major was uncertain. No evidence that fugitives had been here. Among a few of his contemporaries in the Big House there was a debate concerning methods of coercion that were appropriate for the extraction of truths. Beatings and kickings and the use of truncheons and electric shocks had all been used against suspects during the 'difficult' times of the Chechen wars: but there, the enemy were vermin. Anyone who captured a Black

Widow suicide team was justified in using 'harsh measures' to learn where a bomb would be detonated. The Major's dilemma was not based on principle but on effectiveness. Some doubted that torture, violence, physical abuse, extracted more than sleep deprivation or even friendly and personable conversation. Pyotr had tried the friendship line, and had been greeted with sullen and unresponsive silence. Another slap. He knew how far he would take it. A shove at the man, a gesture to him that he was held in contempt. He thought the woman stronger, and more likely to talk, if there was anything to speak of, in an effort to save her man.

The Major would say nothing of what he had done here in the forest to his wife; her eyes would glaze over and she would look away from him. Why? The couple, Igor and Marika, both at least eighty years old, were the mirror image of his own parents, and his wife's. Smallholders, hand-to-mouth farmers, survivors, owning little except each other. Neither his father and mother, or hers, would have betrayed a fugitive coming in the night and needing food, wanting shelter. Would never have done ... It was, to the Major, as if he struck his own father ... His phone rang, shrill.

He slapped a last time, without enthusiasm, then answered his phone. As he listened, they peered back at him, suffering and silent. He was told of a body's discovery. He could not match the militiaman's confidence that this place mattered above all else.

The question was asked behind him. 'If he is here, if I find him. Is he for dead or is he for alive?'

He answered brusquely, not looking back, 'Either way, if you find him. Alive is the better. Yes, alive is what I would want.'

It was his impression, as he strode away and left only Pyotr with them, that he heard phlegm spat on to the ground where he had stood – it was what his father would have done, or his mother, or his wife's father or her mother. He had the coordinates of where the body was and it was said there was hot pursuit of another man in flight. He had told Pyotr to call him with any developments, gave the number, saw the militiaman write it with a ball-point on the palm of his hand, then climbed into his jeep. There had been no evidence. He needed evidence, a prisoner, if he were to stride into the Big House, march with echoing boots down a long corridor, dragging a captive in his wake, and deliver him to a general as a 'smoking gun'. He was driven away.

The news was collected by the monitoring agencies based in Cheltenham, sucked down on to their saucer dishes. Two men arrested in the western outskirts of St Petersburg. A report on police radios said an *autorite* from the Kupchino district, a survivor of a bomb explosion, had been held. Also on the radios was the arrest operation for a gang leader close to the Pulkovo Airport cargo complex. Both men – it was said – were linked to corruption. And the news was circulated, disseminated, was of interest to a small section at Vauxhall Bridge Cross.

While the diesel cloud from the Major's jeep was still fog in the air, Pyotr headed in a different direction, along a track leading towards the river.

He left the couple behind him. No slaps and no kicks, and no betrayal asked of them. A flicker of a glance towards the track's opening in the trees had been sufficient for him. His speech had been quiet, without passion and had explained a truth to them. 'They were here, I know it. They are murderers, assassins. I believe you gave them food, drink, and I think they slept in the barn with the animals. You can indicate to me in which direction they went when they left. I presume it was at first light. If you do not show it me, the direction, then I will be patient until you do. During the patience I will shoot – one by one – the animals you have here: cows, pigs, sheep. And I will throttle the chickens, and kill your beloved dogs. I will not harm you, will not have to. With no animals and without me, you will starve. When you are starving – unless you commit murder-suicide with the shotgun – I will send the Social Care people from Ivangorod to collect you and you will go to different homes, for men and for women. You will not see each other again, or this place . . . That is if you do not tell me which path they took.' He had then unhooked the strap on the weapon from his shoulder and had seemed to look beyond them as if

evaluating which animal he would choose first. Could have been
the milking cow, and could have been the heifer that he had promised to take to market and sell for them in the spring, could have
been a pig that might have fed them for weeks after he had cleaned
it and hung it for them in a month or two, but all the time watching
them. He had seen the glance, then had hung the weapon again on
his shoulder. There were slow running tears on the face of Marika
and Igor bit at his lip and drew blood.

Would he have carried out the threat? He thought he would
have. He had made a decision. Pyotr, a militiaman from the town
of Kingisepp, believed the Major from FSB in St Petersburg
offered him a better route for the benefit and wealth of his future
than did the old couple with their forest smallholding and their
few animals. For many years he had been the couple's friend, and
he had known the Major only a handful of hours, but the decision
was good. The trees closed round him. It was ground he knew,
knew it as well as the deer and the pigs and the few bears who'd
made it their refuge. He believed he might have broken the old
couple, but the world moved on, and future advancement
beckoned.

He could not see boot prints on the ground, did not need to,
had already found a strand of bright wool snagged on a branch.

His face quivered, his eyes flashed, his feet stamped. Boot shook
himself. It was his method of regaining concentration. He wiped
sleet off his moustache and eyebrows.

Daff had spoken to London, to the Maid, the last throes of the
battle. The moments when the issue had teetered between failure,
and victory. Each time he visited the field, he exercised control
and moved with the itinerary of the day and those before, but
coming now to the crisis time. Probably raining there. Usually did
across those sloping fields at that time of year. Sometimes he
would have sheltered under an umbrella, one of those handed out
to Gloria by exhibitors at an antiques show, and squatted on a
collapsible stool. He had adequate rainwear, but felt more comfortable with the umbrella and the stool. He appreciated a time of

crisis, that gap between failure and victory. There was no shelter
where he'd have been. He lived for those moments, reckoned the
chasm between a good result and catastrophe was never wide. He
would have sat where the squares had formed: three ranks,
wounded and commanders in the middle, and a porcupine barrier
of fixed bayonets – the last resort to the volleys of rifle fire when
the cavalry came close. Noise, smoke, screams and shrieks and the
cries of crippled horses. Could always see it and sniff it, and the
squares had held, but if they had broken and the men of the
infantry battalions had fled, then the day was lost . . .

He gazed down at the bridge, saw the slow queues of cars and
vans and lorries pulling away from the checks on the Russian side,
and saw the foot passengers. Daff had reported that – at VBX –
the Big Boss had been down to the fourth floor requiring updates,
but the Maid had packed him off with a response of 'You'll be the
first to know'. Daff had said, rain or shine, they'd be home the
next day, and the Maid was checking flights. If it succeeded, and
was deniable, then celebrations would wait until a touchdown at
Heathrow, and if it failed it would be the local station in the UK's
embassy who had the job of sweeping the shit off the pavement.

. . . the final and crucial turning point of the day, when the nerve
of two adversaries was tested to breaking point. Boot, had he been
there and not above the bridge at Narva, would have eased off his
stool, folded it, tucked it under his arm, held the umbrella high
and would have gone to the rim where there was a view across the
fields. Ploughed, this week or next, in November. Full of unhar-
vested maize, not yet ripened, two centuries and more before. He
pictured the advance of the Guard, veterans of the Emperor's
wars and considered an *élite*, and heard the thunder of their drum-
mers coming through the crop. No reserves left, and standing
officers on both sides urging their men to stand firm. It had
seemed, to Wellington's surviving aides, that the next few minutes
would decide who carried the day. A hoarseness in Boot's voice,
under his umbrella and looking over the Belgian landscape, when
he would shout – did it every time – '*La garde recule*'. They had
turned, had fallen back in poor order when the German army, the

Duke's allies, had appeared on the eastern flank. He could see
sparse traffic on the narrow roads of Ivangorod and a few shop-
pers bent under the weight of their plastic bags; and beyond the
town and the riverside bungalows were the forests, where the last
act would be played out. Always had to clear his throat, hack a
cough, because it was raw when he shouted the cry that the guard
fell back . . .

Daff was in a litany of the events forecast for his diary, where
he was to be and when: a routine medical check, farewell drinks
for a colleague, a conversation with a Russia Desk specialist of the
Fivers across the Thames. He thought she talked for the sake of it,
which was a reflection of the tension she felt, and his. He hid it
better, but would not chide her.

. . . and he would be again on the move and drift on the path along
the ridge towards the farm at Hougoumont and pause at the small
memorial that marked where Captain Mercer had sited his battery
and had fired some 700 rounds of case-shot at close range, and
inflicted hideous casualties on French cavalry, and in the summer
visits he would hear skylarks over the farmland, and that day he
would have heard only the steady drip of rain from his umbrella.
And Boot would breathe in hard, accept the victory, and would
recite in a whisper – his shouting done – the words of the Duke: 'The
nearest run thing you ever saw in your life. By God! I don't think it
would have been done if I had not been there.' Not from any sense
of arrogance, but more from duty, Boot thought it better that he
should be there. He must not show anxiety, nor shiver from the cold.

Kat stood.

Too cold to sit any longer. And fearful because she had been
left, isolated, and tension had merged into fear. She heard the
wind in the trees, and the whines and groans and simpering as
branches rubbed each other, or smacked together.

With the fear came anger. She should not have been left. Her
loving had not been praised, nor her driving. He should have done
that, given praise. A first step. She moved. To go where? To go to
find him. Rational? Hardly. Disciplined? Not . . . The sleet was

heavier. She stood at full height and could see over the reed beds and on to the expanse of water, and the lights of cars on the far side. No praise for her driving through the road-block, and no praise for the gentleness of her loving, and for calming him; and after the fear and the anger came the thought that had driven her to her feet. She was ditched . . . All the talk was of a promise made to Nikki, who was dead, who would not call in the debt. Perhaps he had already gone into the water, left her.

Merc and the deer gazed at each other.

Neither moved, both barely breathed. Their eyes locked.

And beyond the deer was the piece of torn material on the branch where he had left it. Then it backed, little delicate hoofs moving together and with utmost caution, but stepping away from him, though the eyes – amber-coloured, bright and wide – held his. He stood his ground. The sleet pellets had become flakes of snow and blew up the river, funnelled from the Baltic, and came from behind the deer, covered his scent and the sounds of his approach. Then it was gone, crashing away through the under-growth. It had been a Christmas card scene: a deer with ears high and snow dusting its scalp where stunted horns grew. He skirted the open space where it had fed or come for water. The strip of cloth marked where the board would be and the suit. Merc thought the cloud had come down, nudged almost level to the water's surface, and grey merged with grey and the snow seemed heavier. He crouched, groped, and his gloved fingers found the hard shape of the board. He eased it out from under the brambles and scrub, and the suit. He did not often show emotion. Merc despised clenched fist salutes . . . permitted himself a short smile that cracked lines in his stubble-covered face . . . A different feeling of cold. Not from the damp or the wind, and not from the flakes blown into his nostrils and resting on his lips.

Where an animal had hackles, the cold on the back of his neck erupted.

Merc would not have noticed the anti-flash attachment at the end of the rifle barrel had it not been for the scrape in the paintwork and the dulled clean metal. He knelt beside the board, half exposed, and the suit. The barrel was aimed directly at him. No sudden movements from Merc. He bought time, a few seconds, and evaluated initial options available ... He looked above the attachment on the rifle barrel and fixed on the needle foresight, and blinked and changed focus, blinked again, and saw the sheen of an eye, further back and behind the V-sight. Silence clung in the air except for the roar of the river mocking his efforts to survive, and his promise seemed to have lost importance.

18

Merc moved first.

Might be shot, might be challenged, might face one weapon and might have half a dozen Kalashnikovs trained on him. He was kneeling and could not shift quickly if any sort of opportunity came; eased himself into a position where he was on the balls of his feet, hunched down and with an ache gripping his legs, but at least could now push himself upright. Knees stiff, hunger and thirst and cold taking turns to bite him, and his board half revealed, and the suit with it. Without either, the chance of getting across was fragile; with neither was negligible. He began to consider his options.

The assault rifle was pressed against a broad shoulder. The eye was over the sight. He did not see anything of weakness or indecision as the man came forward and cleared the cover. Uniform worn, good quality kit, and a balaclava hiding the face except for the mouth and eyes. Merc was usually able to form impressions of men, could read eyes and body movement and posture. Took no comfort from what he saw. He read him as a countryman, a hunter, a guy who did not panic: no overwhelming excitement would lead to stupid action . . . too calm. A forest man, and hard to deceive.

The rifle seemed small against his bulk, like a toy . . . There had been a young officer in the Pioneer Corps, pretty useless at where to site a field latrine but a stalker of deer in the remote north-west of Scotland and he liked to talk of 'grallocking' a stag on a hillside, cleaning out the intestines, leaving a banquet for the eagles. This man, the balaclava and the combat fatigues, would have done it fast and expertly. The rifle was aimed at Merc's chest, and the range between barrel tip and his body was five yards, six at most. This man would have been able to track down an injured, furious and suffering wild boar and shoot it dead when it abandoned any more attempt to hide and charged instead.

And worse, as the man came forward. Slotted on a strap across the chest pocket of his tunic was a mobile phone, in a leather case. It was what Merc knew about, calling up the cavalry. The man wore the same uniform camouflage patterns as the men at the road-block. He remembered a larger man at the tail of the block who had fired, then dived clear. Could have been a match. The snow came down between them. Merc lost sight of the river's far bank, the lights of vehicles . . . They would not have expected him yet. He believed that Boot and Daff would be in position near to the tank memorial, and they'd have image intensifiers to pick him up on the board, see him struggling to keep it steady.

They were now three or four yards apart. A gloved finger was inside the guard, rested on the trigger. Merc assumed the safety was off, one in the breach.

The hand that steadied the weapon came off the barrel and reached for the phone. The barrel did not waver, and the eyes held their line on Merc. He could lunge forward and might get a grip on the barrel and might have sufficient impact to break the aim and topple the man, but he was not hopeful. Reckoned it more likely that he would be shot through the chest. More fast thoughts . . . Had seen enough of them, in triage, having the clothes stripped off them on the gurney because it was important to get the scalpels and tweezers into a wound fast to extract detritus from clothing and dirt and the contamination of a fracturing bullet. Had been short sharp days before in the emergency area of the hospital as the clothing was stripped away from the girl's chest and stomach, and there would be flowers, the merlot shade of chrysanthemums, beside a bed. He'd not have that . . . Would be alive and treated as a hostile, or would be dead, no flowers. What the boys said, Rob and Brad – and anyone who had made a study of escape and evasion – was that the business had to be done fast. Had to be done quick – but had to be done with a chance of success. The fingers were on the buttons on the phone. They started to tap. What should he do? He did not know.

He kept his eyes locked on the chest of the bent figure low in front of a mess of bushes and reeds. He watched him over the top of the rifle, the V-sight and the needle. He thought he'd reason to be cautious.

It had been, at the road-block, the most unnerving experience of his life: the two cars belting toward him in the half light, full speed and front on, had been worse than anything before. Earlier danger moments were not in serious competition . . . a big boar, well-tusked and with a stomach wound from a cousin's bullet and making a last charge from close scrub, or the moment that a saw's chain snapped and flew back and might have taken off the front of his face . . .

Pyotr could have been blindfolded and led to a ground sheet on which the parts of a Kalashnikov rifle were laid out, but in no order or pattern, and could have reassembled the weapon within a minute, a minute and a half at most, and another half minute to slap on the magazine, take off the blindfold, fire at and hit a target at fifty metres. The fingers of one hand tapped out the number he had scrawled on the palm of his hand, but the barrel of his rifle never wavered.

He thought the man interesting . . . Did not seem to panic or hyper-ventilate. Did not speak. Pyotr, part-time militiaman, part-time forester, and part-time 'friend' of an old couple who would – one day – pass on their smallholding to him, had not been in the regular military. Of course, as did everyone who served in the militia, he devoured the magazines that told the stories of the exploits of the Special Forces units, Spetsnaz teams in Syria and especially of the death of a 'hero' officer who was surrounded by his enemy and called down an airstrike on himself, and many of 'them' went with him to their God. But he had not been in the army – too young for Chechnya and too old for Ukraine. The man did not seem to show fear and Pyotr thought he rated his chances as low.

He tapped out the numbers. Heard a connection made, heard it dial, and memorised what he would say, how he would tell the officer from St Petersburg of his success, his triumph, heard the female voice with a tinny pitch report that a call could not be taken but a message could be left. There were many places down the river, upstream and downstream of Ivangorod, where a mobile signal failed. He cursed out loud. Had had the words ready, cocky, confident. But not to be shared with a recording machine. He said he should be called back, soonest, and cut the link. He watched the man with care, and the man's stillness and silence told Pyotr of the danger he could bring to him. The snow fall slackened but the wind was stronger and the noise in the trees greater, and the water was rougher out in the river's main channel.

There was blood and exposed flesh from where skin had been torn back, and both were dead: the response of the pursuit team had been understandable but not clever. The Major did not criticise. The dog's handler, in hot pursuit and with his colleagues running behind him to keep up, had seen a figure on the ground, half covered in snow but with a service pistol, a Makarov, in his hand, and had released the dog. The dog had taken the man at the shoulder, as it was trained to do, and the arm had swung round and the man had convulsed and a shot had been fired. The dog had taken a fatal head wound. A barrage of shots from behind the handler, might have been twenty bullets striking the man.

A simple story and one with no clever ending because the fugitive had been killed. Might as well have hung from an abbatoir hook for all the evidence he would cough up. An older wound was hard to find under a drying blood pool, but the woman with him was not squeamish and had slipped on plastic gloves and found it. A wallet with little of interest, no address, an ID that he sensed immediately was bogus. He turned away.

The Major checked his mobile, had no signal, was called by one of the team who had been with the handler and had radio contact on their net from the Kingisepp barracks . . . They were to go south, fast, and coordinates were given.

He strode past the handler. The man wept openly at the loss of his dog. The Major did not criticise. He thought the snow had eased but the wind was savage and the cold brutal and conditions for fugitives were poor, which brought a slow and mirthless smile to his chafed lips. He and his escort hurried back to their jeep.

She blundered forward, a creature of the city.

Kat did not have him to support her, nor to deflect the whip of the branches off her body. As a student she had always pleaded sickness when the time came for the summer camps where the kids would be under canvas and savaged by mosquitoes, and nowhere to crap . . . The city was her home and where she found safety. She went slowly and quickly lost the little confidence she'd had when quitting where he'd left her. Close to the river the snow had covered any track he might have left . . . She could go back towards her starting point, and might find it and might not. She could go forward, in search of him and perhaps would be successful and perhaps not.

She recognised that many of her actions over the last several days had bordered on the idiotic. She went noisily, and did not possess those skills of moving in silence through a wilderness; would have screamed if she had startled a pig or a deer . . . She tripped on a root, fell, bruised an elbow, cut her lower lip and began to weep, soft, quiet tears, and saw him. Saw Nikki who was her brother. Saw him as he had walked away from her towards the security gate, carrying the bag with the laptop . . . saw him as he had gone through the doors . . saw the flash of light in the sky and the eruption of the roof . . . and saw what she imagined was the debris of a body that had been at close quarters to an explosion . . . Saw the peace on his face when he had last slept in the flat . . . saw Nikki and tried to cry out to him, and the face was gone.

Eyes watched her. They had a lustre, and seemed to reach out to her in the feeble light. She was about to shriek when a bird took off. It glided away from her. No clatter of impact against the low branches. She had seen a bird like it in the zoo in the city, the Great Grey Owl. It went in a ghost's silence, and though she strained to hear it there was no sound of a wing-beat. She pulled herself up.

Kat smeared her arm across her face and wiped away tears and spread some blood, and smeared mud over her cheeks. She had fallen, she had pitied herself, she had disturbed the creature in its own territory . . . and she despised herself. She set off, would find him. She could have justified what she had done by the loneliness of sitting in the shelter of trees, hour upon hour, and learning nothing, seeing less. She stayed at the edge of the tree line, and went along the bank of the river, downstream, and did not know how she would explain to him, when she found him, why she had disobeyed him . . . and did not know what she would do if she did not find him.

His eyes narrowed, the snow gathered on the lids and the upper skin of his cheeks. Boot saw the flash of the surveillance car's lights.

Daff reacted. She stood, leaned over him, handled him like he was a care-home patient. She cleaned the snow off his face, with a briskness, no trace of the sentimental, and she was off.

Boot looked away from the vigil. He saw her go to the surveillance vehicle, and a cigarette pack was passed out through a barely opened window. She helped herself and was passed a lighter, and its flame was brief, bright, and then her face clouded in the first exhalation of smoke. She bent, had her ear against the gap, listening. She straightened. The window was closed and she blew the two boys inside a cheery kiss, then returned to him. Boot, not often but occasionally, allowed himself a surge of temper. What he wanted most in the world, on that Saturday afternoon as the light began to fall, was the chance to shed his shoes, peel off his wet socks, replace them with a clean, dry and warm pair – and then see his men come home.

He would have sounded peevish. 'Am I entitled to ask, when did they sign up for our team? We are a covert operation, straining the tolerance of allies by our very presence, and should make a virtue of discretion. We are not working alongside them, and I would appreciate if we could, *please*, remain separate entities.'

'God, Boot, that is just so fucking pompous.'

And could not remember when she had ever before spoken to him in that tone, made more provocative by laughter that showed her good teeth and was wafted away on the wind.

'We are in control, it is our show . . .'

'In a hole, Boot, don't dig deeper.'

He stiffened. 'I think I am owed an explanation and . . .'

Dragging deep on her cigarette, like it was precious, she said, 'Say it how it is. We have no control. We do not influence events. The boys we sent over are on their own. We have no helicopter fleet on stand-by for an exfiltration flight, we have no boots on the ground to cover a landing zone. They are left to do the best they can and ringing in their ears will be our heartfelt plea – "Don't get caught, stay deniable". Oh, yes, what those intrusive beggars over there wanted me to know – all on a barter scene, mutual help and all that, doing it at low level so that we both get an easy life – would possibly be of interest to you, Boot – possibly.'

In the pit he had dug it might have been the last shovel of dirt he'd throw over his shoulder. 'I doubt, at that level, they'd have information that justified this collusion, and . . .'

She chucked her cigarette into the wind and allowed it to spiral away. His peevishness might be the indicator that his time as a frontier watcher, waiting, was playing out.

She bored back at him. 'Can we start with some basics? We have no protection here. To get their grubby fingers on you, *you*, Boot, would be a considerable coup for the other side. You and me, we wouldn't know what had hit us if they did. They have that history – snatching, fast and quick – then, Boot, you might learn first hand what you have been asking other men and women to risk. Now, moving on to what those guys behind us offer. Their people have picked up traffic from St Petersburg. Seems two FSB colonels have been suspended from duty, escorted from their offices, and the intelligence is that both men are linked to crime groups. You understand? They have bought into the legend. Nastiness inside the gang scene. Almost there, that's what I'm saying – there except for getting the boys home, Merc and the others.'

He watched the river, watched the bridge, thought himself bowed by responsibility. He was unfamiliar with the protocol of apologies.

The militiaman tried the phone. They watched each other.

Dialled the number and checked it with what was written on the palm of his hand, heard it ring out. Almost a game, but Merc did not yet know whether the game was his to win, his to lose. Would have heard it cut to an answering voice and the request that a message be left. It was the fourth time the man had failed to get through. But the eyes were never off him. A hiss of breath, and then an oath.

A brief message was snarled into the phone. Merc liked what he saw. Each time the call was made and not answered, he reckoned the anger of the militiaman grew. He had begun to hope . . . would Rob and Brad have hoped? Assumed that anyone with a fighting background always believed that something would turn up, a chance. But they would have been together, like two hunting dogs working in tandem, and one might feign sleep and one might plead stomach pain and . . . Merc was alone. Then the eye contact was broken. Quite sudden, no warning, and he sensed the skill of the man with the rifle and whose eyes penetrated but had a dull-ness. Merc might have exploited any of them – and Rob and Brad would have made an art-form of using them for advantage – but he saw no passion, no charity, no hate, nothing that would make the man's actions irrational. The contact was broken as the man moved to his left and away from the river towards the tree line, then followed the trees. Merc could no longer see him.

The moment he was shot? He did not think so. Bet his shirt on it? Could have. No need to shoot him in the back of the head when the front of his skull, between the eyes, was as available. He had thought he played a good game, had kept calm and watched the man's eyes half of the time and the barrel end of the rifle, where the attachment was that killed flash, the other half of the time. He realised the man would have gone behind him to check out what was hidden – the board and the suit. Not a killer moment. like air released from a tyre, Merc relaxed, and felt the numbing weight of the blow to the back of his head.

Had not anticipated it.

Merc slumped, was going down, was hit again. Darkness closed on him. His face was in the mud and snow. He could not have fought. Fast movements, and his arms were wrenched back and the wrists heaved together and lay in the pit of his back, then the restrainers were around them and tight, and it was done and he sensed the man had moved back, could now regard him. Game over . . . No contest . . . Match lost. He was tied, as helpless as the old Christmas goose who would have heard the blade on the grindstone. The chance was lost. Would not have been lost by either Rob or Brad. He had been hit, the rifle had been put down, two hands used to fasten his wrists. Out-thought, out-manoeu-vred, and not supposed to happen to him . . . not since his father's death such a sensation of despair.

His mind cleared . . . He seemed to see her face, the curl of the lip and the contempt at his failure and would not then have slapped her backside because her head was too high above the parapet, or was slow with the reload on the machine-gun's heavy belt. Would not have slapped it because she lay on it as they'd bared her chest and stomach to get at the entry wound. Merc heard the call made again, and another message left. A curt and pointed message of which he understood the meaning, not the language. It would be the militiaman's commander who was either out of a signal area, or had the phone switched off, did not check it, too busy.

Other than himself, he hadn't another target for blame. Had stayed around too long, and should have used his last visit back to UK better. Done it when he was on the trip to Stoke Poges and asked the bank manager how much he had in his account. After getting a property if there'd be sufficient for him to hustle down to the showroom and do the test drive. Had let the 'sometime' drift in front of him, had not snatched at it. Merc lay in the mud,

had let 'sometime' go past him and had not quit when ahead . . .
Was now at back-marker, far behind.

Kat went forward. A snail would have gone faster. In the wet
season before the real cold came, when the walls of the apartment
ran with damp, snails would emerge and they'd poke their noses
out of their shells and advance up the wall, between the fading
prints. Would go slowly, as she did.

She copied what she had seen on the TV, films of military exercises, what they did in the Caucasus region when they closed on a
target, stayed silent, disturbed nothing. So slow. The commentary
said it was a 'leopard crawl', and also on the TV were wildlife films
from Africa where the cheetah stalked prey, crept close . . . She
could not see the target, her prey, but had heard the voice. She
moved on her elbows and knees and stayed in the tree line and
under the lower branches of the pines. Periodically, the voice
guided her. Each time it was easier to hear: she was closer, and,
more important, the voice betrayed a greater irritation and was
louder.

She thought that the rats in the barn where she had loved him
could not have moved with more stealth. Long past, the moment
she had nakedly betrayed her country's régime. Easy to understand: '*Will you, sir, respond to my message, answer me. Call me
immediately. Just call me. It is where you should be . . . Call me, sir.
(Pause) For fuck's sake, just do it.*' Kat believed herself intelligent
and gifted, enough to succeed as a concert pianist wherever she
found herself, sharp enough to know the meaning of impatience,
spoken in a peasant's dialect, a coarse accent. She went nearer.
Much of her life was not sensible, nor Nikki's, but she thought of
the man she had loved, who had loved her. Would not lose him.
She slid forward on her stomach.

He ran towards the dinghy. He had the chance to be ahead of his
pursuers.

The water sloshed in Martin's shoes. Two men were yelling at
him. They had their rods in the dinghy, but had brought the

outboard motor to the picnic table outside a wood cabin. They would have been friends, enjoying their pensions, and the fishing would have been, sunshine or snow, their valued recreation. They shouted abuse at him; they realised he would outstrip them to the dinghy, loosely tied against a willow sapling, and in shallow water. Behind him were militiamen, half a dozen of them, and some were fitter and faster than others and the nearest were now within a hundred metres. They had been after him for more than half an hour, almost from the time that he and Kristjan had split.

He had seen the dinghy but the anglers had seen him. He'd thought he was close to losing his followers but the two old bastards had spotted him, yelled in anger, and now guided the men who'd tracked him when he had left the forest . . . No hug with Kristjan, or talk of which bar it would be near the square in Narva where the taxis parked. He heard the piercing sound of a siren. It slowed him to look back but he did. The snow had stopped, replaced by light rain that slanted on to him, and it was easy to see the brilliance of the blue lights through the trees and closing, and he could make out the camouflage uniforms of the militiamen following him . . . It was a small dinghy, big enough, just, for the two men to sit in, not more than two metres in length, and not much more than a metre in width. To get to the dinghy he had to wade the width of a small bay, and the water was nearly up to his waist, and the shock to his body was horrific.

Kristjan had gone his own way. What would happen to Kristjan, where would he go, and how would he attempt to get across? Martin neither knew nor cared. He splashed towards the dinghy and the shouting was muffled and the siren incoherent, and he was the man who was trapped in the past by the death of a grandfather. He had wanted to be an accountant, and respected, and had failed, and had wanted to be loved by women and was not, and had succeeded only in a trade of painting and decorating in the town of Haapsalu where, somewhere and without a marker stone, his grandfather was buried. He thrashed in the water. The cloud was breaking and the rain slackening but the wind stayed constant and beyond the narrow bay, where there was a gap in the reeds, he could see rough water.

Martin reached the side of the dinghy and struggled to get a leg up and over the inflated side, and fell back and fought for a better grip – then was into it and sprawled over the wooden slats on its floor. He fumbled for the rope and its loose knot. How long did he have? Might have half a minute. The rope went slack, and the dinghy started to drift, and the wind caught it and started to push it out of the bay between the reeds. No paddle, but the wind was his friend. He put his hand into the chillingly cold water at the side and levered it and might have achieved some traction, but the wind did more.

The river, here, was wider than at the bridge linking Ivangorod to the Estonian town of Narva, and the waves were high as they often were on the Baltic beach of his home. The tourist strands of Haapsalu, where the Finns came in droves for the summer, would be empty now, been beaten by surging waves. He realised that he went faster, because of the wind, than he could have paddled. Martin could see across the water, and there were small lights, pinpricks, in the streets, and cars went slowly far in front of him. No one stopped. No one stood on the far shore and watched for him. He heard a shout but could not make it out. Not the yelling of the anglers, nor the bellowing commands of the militiamen who had followed him. The shout had authority, but he could not make out the words. Very soon he would be halfway across.

'Shoot.'

'You are sure, Major?' From the sergeant who held the rifle at his shoulder.

'An order. Shoot.'

'Him or the boat, Major?'

'The boat. Put him in the water.'

'He will drown, Major, if he goes into the water.' From the lieutenant who stood beside him, gazed at him and clutched a handkerchief in her fist.

'Shoot. Now.'

The Major watched the dinghy heading towards the main flow

of the river and the navigation buoys that designated the frontier. He had no doubt in the justification of the order he had given. A quiet fell. The anglers no longer yelled and the militiamen who had tracked the man on foot stood, gasping for breath. The Major had never seen a man who chased after freedom and was stopped only by a rifle bullet. A faint whistle of air between the teeth of the lieutenant, who would have been on many FSB firing ranges but would not have seen it done for real. He saw that the man in the dinghy, at the last edges of his strength, making frantic attempts with his hands to paddle. In a handful of seconds the dinghy would have passed the buoys. The Major could see, nudging away from the far side, off a wooden quay, what he assumed was a patrol boat. What distance? Could have been a hundred metres . . . The Major was not a good shot, not on field exercises and not on a practice range. He preferred to fish. He thought he could have managed a hit and . . . The quiet was broken. The shot fired. It belted in his ears. He watched, did not flinch from the noise of it.

The dinghy bucked, seemed to rise clear of the water and then toppled, and the man was thrown clear from it. The dinghy lost shape and he imagined that the rubber side had been ripped by the bullet's impact and that the air fled it. He did not know if the man had the ability to swim; there was splashing in the water and his view was of the head and upper body only and a single arm gripped the side of the craft but it seemed to sink under his weight. For a few seconds he could see the bobbing head then it went under, came up again. On the far side, beyond the markers, a launch pulled away from the quay but he knew it would not cross the line that separated two power blocks, two cultures, divided by a sporadic line of orange buoys. Waves were whipped higher and debris from the anglers' boat rose and fell, and the Major realised he could no longer see the head.

He queried with a local man, from the militia, where would a body come ashore. Was told it might fetch up on the grille protecting the inflow to the hydro electricity plant downstream, or might take the secondary channel and go under the railway bridge, then the second one that was called the Friendship Bridge. The

Major was about to look at his phone, turn away from the water, when more news was fed him . . . A man had gone into the casino, was reported by management. He was described . . . What should be done? He answered.

The sergeant drove him. The lieutenant had once, only once, wiped her cheek. They went towards Ivangorod and headed for the garish lighting of the casino.

He was alone except for the croupier girl. Kristjan played. He'd be at the table until the euros in his hip pocket were exhausted.

The minders watched him from behind. No other players joined him as the wheel turned and the ball bounced . . . He had come out of the forest, had split from Martin, and had walked down the hill and into the town, then had crossed the main road in sight of the bridge, but had ducked away and had pushed the doors aside and gone in. And the ball settled, and the slot was wrong and the colour was wrong, and he was brought – not requested – another big measure of Scotch whisky, no ice and no water, and did not realise the staff were at pains to keep him there. His fingers trembled and his hand shook from the cold, and the heat inside could not thaw him. Rock music played loud. His clothing hung sodden on him, his hair was plastered down and stuck sweetly on his scalp and he had left a wet trail across the deep carpet and some drips still fell from him as he perched precariously on a stool. The bank notes flickered in his hand. He put more money down, and the number chosen was nineteen because that was the age of his grandfather, and the colour was black. The girl in front of him wore a scarlet dress that was low on her chest and was slit at the sides almost to her hip, and her hair was wedged in place with lacquer and her face was expressionless. He thought she read him as doomed, and would have read him well. One more throw after this . . . Irrelevant if he won or if he lost again, more irrelevant if he broke the bank . . . There were mirrors inside, set in a wall behind the girl who was spinning the wheel and then let the ball go. He raised his glass and drank and felt the burn of the alcohol in his throat and lifted his head and tilted the glass so that he would drain it, and he saw the reflection of blue lights mounted on two jeeps, and the lights were cut and a gaggle of men stepped clear of them. He saw it, then watched the number he had chosen and the ball started to dance.

On duty at the gate, or on 'stag' as they liked to call it, they'd had the briefing from the pair they relieved. Dennie had been sent home so the Big Boss was again on the couch. No sniff of Boot, and his office woman had been out with a carrier bag and had come back with another microwave supper, and a wrapped picture safe in a sheath of protective plastic.

Arthur murmured. 'Has to be tonight, doesn't it? I mean it has to be.'

Roy said 'Should have been wrapped by now, Arthur, and isn't.'

Arthur said, and scratched his backside, behind where his Glock was holstered. 'I feel good, as if I'm supporting them. A comic, a Yank said, "We can't all be heroes because someone has to stand on the kerb and clap as they go by." Reckon he was talking about us.'

They stood at the main gate, well wrapped against the cold, and dry and well armed in case of threat, and would have revelled at what they believed to be their insights.

The paper from the Brains Trust, all five pages of it, dropped from his fingers. The Big Boss, master of all he surveyed, had called three floors below and demanded that a junior employee, the Maid from Boot's office, attend him. He was in need of an audience, of company, a presence with whom to share the isolation of a decision-taker. He had read her much of the paper in a detached and hesitant way, now addressed her.

'Can't tell it to the Young Turks that bustle round me, would not have a clue what I'm yammering about . . . You lose sight of what it was for. Now, at this moment, all we can think about is whether that team is coming home, together, or is going to fall at the final fence. One prisoner, and we will regard that as abject failure. The whole gang rounded up and paraded for the flashlights and I'm spending

time snipping roses. Easy to lose sight of the goal. Why I had the
Brains Trust knock me up another paper. It was about hackers,
sending them a discreet message to stop fucking in our backyard, to
knock them off balance, done with discretion, but make it as if they
feel they've a boil between their collective cheeks. It's the new
warfare. Not aircraft carriers and tank divisions, even chemical-
tipped artillery shells, or dogfights between fighters and interceptors
that each cost, excess of, a hundred and twenty million smackers,
and I fancy all those expensive toys will prove obsolete, ready for
the knacker's yard because of the pimply-faced kids and the
keyboards. That is the big picture, not some damn frontier and poor
devils running for their lives. We are into retaliation, strike back –
totally illegal in the eyes of our courts, judges, that apparatus
– against an enemy's war machine that threatens to overwhelm us.
It's not tanks on our lawns or bombs raining down on our cities, but
in terms of destabilising our nation then the threat is every bit as
great . . . I regret nothing, nothing. Let me show you this, this
picture. It is their command bunker for planning future attacks, not
buried under a nuclear bomb-proof layer of reinforced concrete,
but a building in a dreary suburb of their second city – and we hit
it. They had funerals today of the kids we took down, each as important as a Special Forces company. There have been arrests and I
venture to say our mischief-making has worked well – so far. Thank
you for giving me a shoulder and an ear . . . That is all.'

    He turned away from her. She had sat primly in front of him,
now stood and ducked her head, stole a final glance at the satellite
image of a building with the roof blown clear, and a montage of
photographs of funerals – all poorly attended – in a cemetery
crowded with tall memorials. She thought she understood him
and the loneliness he carried in his knapsack, and went out of the
suite. His regular staff, all half her age and half Boot's, barely
noticed her. She walked briskly to the elevator that would take her
back to her own bunker where she minded the phones and the
screens, and would wait, and might take time to admire the picture
she had purchased.

                    *   *   *

The lights had flashed again. Daff had reacted. Boot watched her keenly. The surveillance boy was out of his car and pointed past Boot and past the bastion wall and across the river. Boot saw what they saw. The light had dropped but where the man pointed was a mess of gaudy lights that lit up the dank mist over the water. She came back to him, pulled a face.

'Spit it.'

'Doubt you'll enjoy it, but it's not Merc. No sight or sound of him. The others . . .'

'Try me.'

'Here goes. The local net for the militia across there is giving us this. One unidentified male shot dead in the woods east of the town. Another unidentified male believed drowned in the river upstream, had stolen an inflatable and was trying to drift across. They fired on his craft, sank it.'

'Does it get worse?'

'In bucketfuls. That building there, all lit up and waiting for a party is where a third male – so far unidentified – is playing roulette. It is suicidal . . . I read it somewhere on the file, an addiction to gambling. Kristjan. He will play, we assume, until his money is finished. He is soaked, filthy, exhausted, and he is drunk, pretty much broken up. There is an FSB Major in charge and he has the building staked and presumably is waiting until the show becomes boring, then picks him up.'

'I suppose we asked too much.'

Daff said, 'They're what was available. Which is getting us nowhere that we want to be. We are – were – close, Boot, to a triumph if . . .'

'Yes, if, always that bloody *if*. Always.'

Boot thought himself within reach of touching it, success, and close enough for failure to grab him by the throat. The great Duke had known of the tiny gap between the two. Often, when he was there, on his stool or of a summer's evening sitting under a tree and in the shade of the day's last sunshine, he had spoken aloud the quote, *Believe me, nothing except a battle lost can be half as melancholy as a battle won.* When it was over, he would go back to London and have the Maid take down his dictation of the events as best he knew them, and he would be, fast as his scrawny legs could take him, off to the train terminal and return there and find some solace on that field. When it was over.

He was a big man and he paced. Not hard for Kat to see him.

The light was falling and the low cloud blocked the last of any sunshine; he smoked incessantly. She saw small eyes and big lips behind the slashes in the balaclava. The last time that he had barked out a message on his mobile phone then snapped off the connection, he had sworn with crude filth. Easy to see him and the glow of his cigarette marked him as he paced, like a bear in a zoo. Harder to see the one who called himself Merc – who had loved her. Kat went closer She had slipped off her gloves and used cold, narrow-boned fingers to ease apart fronds of crisp frozen grass and brambles that would have caught at her coat or snagged her face. He was face down. His breath came back off the mud, made little clouds. His arms were fastened behind him. And closer, a cigarette was chucked away and burned its last.

She would have said she was too talented, too exceptional, to resort to anything as vulgar as violence, would have said it before she had seen the roof lifted high off the building, would have said it before she had seen this boy, her lover, helpless. She could make out the shape of the board and beyond it was the river, almost in spate and high, and the wind clipped. And she went closer, took the greater risk.

Another try by Pyotr. Another failure to connect. Another message left. Another oath.

Merc would be cursed. They would stand in an orderly line to have the chance to hurl shit at him, those who deigned to acknowledge in public that they had ever had dealings with him. The cold was in his body and he'd been on the ground too long to keep the circulation moving in his legs, arms, through his body. Stiffness enveloped him and the warmth beneath his clothing, against his skin, had gone, but he felt too tired to shiver.

That night, when he did not come over, Daff would drive Boot, fast, to the airport and she'd have selected a passport for each of them from the stack available, and they'd be gone on the dawn flight to pretty much anywhere, and she'd say, 'Sorry and all that, but I really thought he was made of better stuff. Let me down, and I shouted his praises too high. I can only repeat it, sorry and all that. Always such a bloody killer when you talk up a guy's qualities too high.' And Boot would be hunched in the seat beside her and would be planning a strategy of evasion for when he returned to the building on the south side of the Thames, his voice dry and devoid of humour and, with anger suppressed, he'd condemn. 'Too often we ask too much of people who are really rather ordinary, but – sad thing – in this world you get what you pay for, and he came cheap. We should have bust the bank and done it with better men.' Merc would not have disagreed if that had been the conclusion: too high, too cheap.

There might have been – all the hindsight joys – a chance to break away at the very start. The rifle had been aimed at him, but the man might have bottled it, could have frozen, at the moment it mattered. It took courage to tense up, then charge, leave your back exposed to close-range gunfire. He had not seen an opportunity that had convinced him, then had been clubbed, disabled with restraints The pile of cigarette ends grew. They said it was good to get some bonding going, not overdone, and he had looked up from the discarded fag end, each time it was offloaded, then had caught the militiaman's eye, and had won neither a blink nor a fraction of a smile. If there had been an opportunity he had not realised it.

In the building on the Thames, senior men and high-ranked women would gather round a table for an inquest, and a brief would be agreed that covered their backs. A big man, good suit and decent cuff-links, a fine tie and well-groomed hair, would say, 'We gave it a fair crack, and the man we sent would probably have been able to do the business and get clear had he not delayed. We had been told, very clearly, that "passengers" would not be tolerated on the run for home. They should have been down that road from the moment the asset walked into the building. He had a good background, the individual we sent, but fell short and the consequences are grievous. With what's coming to him, he'll have no sympathy from me, and less than none if he spills all he knows to his interrogators. The blame is there, not with us.' And there would be a drumbeat of agreement.

He thought the militiaman grew steadily more angered that his call was not picked up. Had his hands been free, Merc did not think he'd the strength left to run; a volley of assault rifle shots would come at him. The despair was justified. The procedure was predictable. When the cavalry came, he would be marched to a vehicle, tossed into the back, kicked enough to humour his captors, and driven to the nearest garrison camp. He would be stripped bare in a cell, left with a rug across his shoulders, no other heat, and he would hear phone calls and radio messages shouted from Control. They would not question him at that time but would wait for the big cats to show. And in the queue now would be the Station Chief from Moscow, briefed on a secure line, and he'd be saying, 'Not much I can do, sunshine. Tell you the truth, if I had been inside the loop on this ludicrous manoeuvre, I would have hit it on the head with a lump hammer. The concept was doomed to fail, and that you sent this incompetent is beyond belief. Don't expect me to get involved.' They would drive him to St Petersburg, over the bridge where he had crashed the block, past the supermarket where he had met the girl and loitered too long. Down a street beside an industrial and housing complex with a building short of a roof. Into the centre and down a slipway to an underground garage with access to the cell corridor. There it would have gotten unpleasant.

Unable to shift the restraints on his wrists. Heard his stomach growl. Wondered how much longer he would last before wetting himself. Sometimes, above the river roar, was the faint sound of a lorry's klaxon or a car's horn, and once there was a gust of a sharper wind on which was carried the roar of a motorcycle. The man had tried his phone again and had snapped another message for the recording, but had the patience of a hunter, for whom time was not important, only the result.

He would appear in court. A junior from the embassy consular staff would be allowed to meet him in the cells before they brought him into the cage. He'd be wearing fatigues, not so different from the gear given out by the 'bad boys' for the next in line for a decapitation. It would likely be a young woman, a severe black suit, and she'd say under her breath but expecting them to have microphones that could pick up dust falling, 'The trouble is, Mr Hawkins, we don't really know who you are, why you were in the situation in which you find yourself. No office in Whitehall is claiming you, and the suggestion remains that you are a freelance operative and therefore without governmental protection. I do have to say that the opinion in my office is that the whole mission, whoever financed it, was cack-handed in the extreme ... That's not a personal opinion, but the gist of the telegrams I've seen. The less you say, of course, the better: there will be a day when government looks to weigh in on your side but for reasons of humanity, not obligation. I was asked to emphasise that point. Keep your chin up if you can, and good luck.' If he was lumped with the boys he'd not recognise them, and if they walked the girl in front of him he'd ignore her.

News of his capture would reach Erbil. Always did, bad news. The opportunity to chew on it would not be until the evening and a beer in the bar of the hotel where they lodged. Brad would say the most, and Rob would nod agreement. 'You'd have thought he'd have had more sense than get involved in something like that. Obviously concocted by an arsehole who's never been away from a desk. "Oh, yes, Merc, my old darling, just take yourself up to St Petersburg, blow a building up, waste a few kids, give a hack-fest a headache, no problem. Always remember, we're right behind you, Merc, and our word is our bond, and we've done all the risk assessments and it looks good." God, how did he fall for that one ... Tell you what. How did *we* fall for it? Should have had him nailed down to the floor of his room, should not have let him go on that saucy little plane they sent for him. A good boy but not bright enough. He'll grow old there. They'll throw the bloody key away.' And they'd have another beer, and another, and pretty soon, Merc would be history.

He saw movement. It was near to where the last spent cigarette had been flicked, at the edge of the clear space. Could have been a leaf dislodged by the wind and fluttering down, could have been where a low branch offloaded snow or sleet, could have been where a rat scurried away from the water line. He saw movement, then nothing, then saw it again and knew what he saw.

From the angle where he lay, Merc saw only a part of her face, close to the ground. He looked away, not daring to attract attention to her.

He started to think about what to do and the wind was bitter on his face and the pain was sharp in his wrists, and his stomach ached and the back of his head was bad where he had been clubbed. Thinking did not come easy, but he had seen her and she had come for him.

19

His mind had cleared. He looked anywhere but at her. Merc saw the sky and the leaden cloud ceiling, and the branches of leaf-stripped trees, and saw the movement of the reeds where the wind tickled their tips, and the great highway of the river, and the occasional lights on the far side.

His mind ditched the images of the trench on 425, and the shiny gloss of the bodywork of a new Mercedes, and the austere interior of the bank in Stoke Poges, and the yard behind the terraced house where the chaffinches and sparrows fed, and a girl on a gurney who needed life-saving surgery. All erased. Boot was forgotten, and Daff. Gone were Rob and Brad. Out of mind were three men, with an unfulfilled dream, who had come for a ride and had gone their own way. He thought of himself and thought of the girl, and of the big man who paced around him, smoking cigarettes, and keeping the rifle barrel aimed at him.

He looked for a pattern. How many paces forward, and how many pauses to cock a head and listen for the wind and the heave of the water going past. How long he took to make each circuit around Merc . . . No rhythm to it. If the concentration of the man had lapsed then there could have been opportunity for Merc to move, as clumsy as a beached seal, and hack at him with his legs, flail below the knee, and hope . . . Hope that at such a moment, and without coordination, Kat would lunge towards him and kick him or bite him or scratch him, any damn thing. The militiaman would sometimes take twenty paces and sometimes ten, and sometimes would move only a couple before stopping in his tracks . . .

An old dodge, a driver on the Kabul to Jalalabad run had voiced.

The driver had smacked a fist into the palm of his hand and had mouthed what was obvious to all of them who did that run: 'I mean, like, anything is better, you know, than those fuckers getting their hands on you. Might just try it if they were all around, and had to divert them, make them switch attention.' They'd all talked, even Merc, about the final scenario.

Merc was not certain how to do it . . . He wanted to give the girl the chance to get closer and have an opportunity to intervene. Merc did not know how, or with what weapon, did not know even if she would. He had no better chance than to try it. The militiaman was between himself and where he had last seen Kat. He thought she was ten yards from him, and thought the man was four yards away, not more.

He twisted on to his back. Went rigid. Opened his eyes as wide as the frost caking them allowed, let the whites show. Tried to get some spittle in his dried mouth. Rolled and convulsed, and moaned like a hurt animal. The weapon was aimed at him, and the eyes beaded on him from the slits in the balaclava, and he stopped. Merc lay back, play-acted exhaustion.

The man stood taut and gazed down on him. Sympathy? Merc doubted it. No more charity would be shown him than to a deer that needed a final blow to the skull or a slit across the throat to end pain and shock, no more than a bullock was given at the entrance to an abbatoir. But he had gained attention, and it seemed important. When the militiaman resumed his pacing, Merc looked for the girl and did not see her. He was treated with greater suspicion, as if the man was uncertain whether a trick was being played on him. On his back, Merc simulated fierce panting. He could not see her.

She might have used the distraction as an opportunity to ease herself back. Did she have a loyalty to him? Might have . . . And Merc, did he have a loyalty to her? Might have . . . Like two kids in a station waiting-room, late evening, alone and not knowing whether to talk and share, whether to ignore and stay quiet. Trust? Not sure he could have coughed up a reason why she'd trust him. She had found him, had witnessed the failure. Wondered if she had turned away from him . . . started the long walk to Kingisepp for a bus going up the highway, east, to St Petersburg. Merc quit the panting, lay still.

The militiaman tried his phone again, failed and spat. Then held the rifle one-handed and gouged into a pocket. A quarter of a chocolate bar emerged in his glove. No hesitation, no glance at his prisoner; the wrapping was unpeeled and dropped, and the chocolate was wolfed down. The chocolate was not used to taunt him. 'Just doing my job, mate, nothing personal and all that.' The chocolate was finished, and the wrapping was bright on the ground, and the man kicked it away and it lifted sluggishly in the wind and landed near to where Merc had seen the girl's face. Did not see it now, had no sight of her. The militiaman paced again. Merc recognised his patience. He would have the signal in a quarter of an hour or half an hour or an hour. Merc assumed the calls were to one man in particular, or one control centre, and that a moment of raw triumph awaited the militiaman when his success was recognised.

The wind had come on harder and the clouds had begun to break and a milky lance of moonlight edged down on him. Merc realised how much he had been lifted when he had seen the girl and how far he had gone down now that he had lost her. Despair was contagious, so hard to fight.

No money left, all the chips gone. The croupier girl, bored and with her nose curled in disgust at the smell and the mess he left, turned away from Kristjan. He lifted his glass, held it above his mouth, and the smallest drip materialised. He would barely have tasted it. It took a big effort but he came off the stool and straightened and looked around him and started to walk. Not a bad stride, took a reasonably straight line across the thick carpet. He did not go for the big glass doors beyond which the jeeps were parked, but headed instead for the toilet sign. Those who watched him, big men, would have grinned and reckoned it appropriate that a guy going to the cells would not want to piss himself before he reached them, and been so wrong. The door slammed shut behind him.

Kristjan stacked shelves in the Fama supermarket in the town across the river. He had wanted to be a professional boxer, had seen himself with bloodied eyes standing in a ring as the guy in the white shirt and black tie lifted his hand . . . If he went now, he would be back and across the bridge and have a chance to put on dry clothes and be in the aisles by the time his shift started, and he'd need the money because the bitch in charge of the wheel had taken all he'd had. Past the Female door, past the Male door, and a fire escape exit at the end of the corridor, and it had been on the local radio in Narva that the casino had passed all the safety tests from the Russian administration: the door would not be padlocked – it would be alarmed. A sucked-in breath was followed by fists clenching and muscles stiffening. Kristjan caught the bar of the door, wrenched it, and reeled back as it opened. His ears rang with the alarm's scream. The cold slapped his face. He started to run.

All downhill to the bridge. The afternoon had dulled into evening. The lights were bright ahead of him on the far side. He was in a side street flanked with small homes, wood planks nailed to the concrete for walls, and all spitting out smoke from their chimneys, and the road had ruts and holes and some were repaired and some not, and barking dogs hurled themselves at the garden gates. He fell, foot twisting in a pit gouged by last year's weather, and the impetus threw him forward and he rolled over twice, and the breath was belted from his body . . . He would not be late for the shift in the Fama supermarket. Most evenings, at the start of his work, he filled the shelves that carried chilled groceries and afterwards he would turn to . . . And Martin would not be doing a shift of painting or decorating, and Toomas would never again shrug into the chain-mail tunic. Too tired and too battered, too drunk and too emotionally drained to consider realities . . . He ran, and ahead of him were the brightly illuminated huts, the guards, and the barrier at the start of the bridge.

Men running and men shouting, and he ran faster than he had known it possible, and raised his knees and swung his arms and sucked at the chill air and heaved it down into his lungs and nearly fell again but kept himself upright. Horns chorused behind him. The guards ahead were wrapped against the snow, sleet, wind, whatever the weather threw at them. They wore balaclavas and fur caps, and some had lifted the thick hoods from the collars of their uniforms. They might not have heard the sounds of the chase.

Kristjan, grandson of a patriot who had no known grave, sodden with alcohol, famished and on the last leg of a tilt at survival, ran towards the barrier.

Kat, at the extremity of her reach, had her hand on it.

It might have lain there, unseen, undisturbed, for more than seven decades. She thought it a metre long and a coil of wire was wrapped on it. Kat held the rusted length and began to tug. She needed a weapon. No stones at the edge of the river where the ground flooded some of the year, and no half-rotten fence posts. This bar would have been dumped there, or fallen, or been dropped in one of the attempted river crossings by the Red Army in the winter or spring of 1944. She knew the stories of the battle for Narva and for the slopes on the far side, at Siivertsi, and on the hillside at Sinimae to the north, then all supplies had to be ferried to the bridgehead across the river, and in winter, and in the cold, and the water high and the current powerful. It had been in the history curriculum at school . . . and she knew of the casualties because the school kids were lined up in front of the memorials on the various anniversaries of the stages of the battle to take Narva town and bypass it. She had a hand on the bar.

But it was snagged. Kat imagined that the post had been left, then would have been covered in fine silt when the next flood came, then that covering would have flaked off in hot weather and the bar exposed, then covered, then revealed, repeating the pattern for more than seventy years. She had seen him play at being an epileptic, and had seen the broad back of the man who covered him with the rifle, had seen the gloved finger inserted inside the trigger guard, and she had realised what he did when he thrashed, panted, had the froth on his lips. She had moved to her right, behind thicker scrub and tired yellow grass, and the tip of the iron bar had gouged into her face . . . She had never, in her life, used violence. She pulled on it, as hard as she dared.

Violence had never in serious degree been inflicted on her. She might have sat with the group seeking to reach a pinnacle of opposition by painting a penis on the bridge in front of the Big House, or going topless to a demonstration. Might have talked it through with them – and gone to the Leader for endorsement. Might have argued the case for more posters on a police barracks wall where there was no camera cover to breach their anonymity. They could talk about it for an hour, a day, or a week, and huddle close to the radiators in the café, and might send a new kid out to buy pizza, and take the tops off beer bottles. Talk about it.

She had her hand on the iron bar, attempted to free it. It was stubbornly held. She had loosened it but the lower part remained in the fine sandy soil, frozen, below the grass and the roots of bushes. Her brother, Nikki, drunk and lounging on the sofa, talking through the alcohol fumes about what he did – hacking for anyone who would pay best – would use the word *maskirovka*, would boast of the success of the tactics of 'deception'. The man on the ground, wrists tied, watched by the rifle barrel, had tried to deceive and had won her the opportunity to move to the right, unseen, silent, and then the spike of rust-caked iron had struck her face, fucking nearly taken her eye out. She did not think the group would sanction such a use of force, not without discussion, argument, a weighing of consequences. He, the man who had loved her, had attracted attention to himself in order that she could move, search for the weapon . . . They were together, bonded.

The debate for Kat: what effort could she use to free the bar? The militiaman – a peasant, stupid, a servant of the régime but cunning and in line for a reward – had left messages on the phone, most of them with respect but also with added impatience, and he waited. The opportunity could not last hours longer, maybe only minutes. The militiaman had resumed his pacing. His back was to her.

Kat took the chance, dragged on it, used two fists. It came clear. Dirt rose into her face, her shoulders pushed back small branches.

She did not know if she was hidden, or whether a part of her body showed. He knew, her man did. He rolled. On his back and then on his front, and again, and a little sobbing cry in his throat, and a choke. The militiaman gazed down on his prisoner. The bar had come free.

A skeleton hand gripped it. The hand was taken off at the wrist. It would have been the wrist of a Red Army soldier. Blown up by a mortar shell, cut down by machine-gun fire, hidden from sight and clutching at an iron bar as if it might give him help. On a finger of the hand, loose on a bone but not dislodged, was a ring of dulled yellow metal. What her mother still wore, what her father had worn until it was taken off his finger in the mortuary. A soldier who had died in combat, for the Russia he might have loved, might have hated, and with NKVD machine-gunners behind him to make sure that he went forward and then clambered into the barges that were taking them across, under fire. But had been felled in the moments before and had clung in desperation, last moments of his life, to an iron post on which barbed wire had been hung. She was fascinated by it, and the chink of light it made. The hand of mud-smeared bones slid from the bar, lost its grip, and the ring with it – and the ground closing over them.

She had an iron bar, and a target. The militiaman loomed over her, sometimes moving and sometimes still, oozing power, and had a rifle and a finger inside the trigger guard . . . He would have to tell her, show her the moment: if he called the wrong moment then they were gone, both, as useless as if buried in the silt soil of the river.

Confusion delayed them. All of the Major's training in intelligence and the military had been directed at removing chaos from an equation, replacing it with fast analysis and action.

The alarm had sounded. Shrill bells ringing at the back of the building. From the doorway, with amusement, he had watched the slouched figure bent low on the roulette table, the languid moving arms of the girl as she scraped away his chips. He would come out of the same doorway, fall into their arms, offer up his wrists for the

manacles to snap on to . . . His sergeant had been nearly certain,
almost certain, that this man had been in the supermarket car-
park. Same time as Nikki had come there, in the hours before the
bomb had taken the roof off the building, had taken many lives of
the best, brightest, of their trade: only *nearly* and only *almost*
certain . . . and the sergeant had been almost certain that a
foreigner had been in an adjacent car to that used by Nikki and his
sister. He had been considering – when the alarm had sparked –
what degree of 'persuasion' would yield fast results from an
inebriated idiot. Might be a slap and a kick, might be the dropping
of his trousers and his underpants and a gloved hand squeezing,
might be the sight of the pliers from the repair box at the back of
the jeep, and their proximity to his fingernails. Might be the
sergeant lighting a cigarette and handing it to the lieutenant and
the glowing tip coming close to his testicles, his face, cheeks . . .
And they had all started to run, a gaggle of pursuit, towards the
back, then had seen him already well down the sloping road that
ran alongside the main route to the bridge, and the frontier
crossing point. The Major had screamed for his own people to
stop. Could not have abandoned them and gone back, alone, to
the jeep – did not have the fucking keys. Had grabbed the sergeant
by the collar, had halted him, had turned him.

That was the delay . . . They went down the main drag to the
bridge. He had a good view of it.

Arms out, rifles still slung on the guards' shoulders. Men,
grotesque in size because of their heavy clothing, lumbered into
place to intercept a lone runner who weaved in and out of the
vehicles going down the hill, coming up it. The Major did not
know what orders they had on relevant force to be used: not East
Germany and the fence of a quarter of a century before, not the
border troops on the Berlin Wall. The Major doubted they would
shoot. The target was past the guards but the rhythm of his
running was broken and he started to shamble forward crazily as
if the alcohol had kicked in. There would be a halfway point on the
bridge, there always was. Any bridge that divided them, the
Federation and the NATO, had a line to mark the halfway point.

The sergeant drove, hit the horn. The barrier was raised. They veered between oncoming lorries and those waiting to go west, they saw pedestrians freeze on the footpath section. They closed on the man . . . In the Major's mind were old films of long-distance runners, grained and in monochrome, collapsing within sight of a finishing line, might stagger over it and might fall short. They would not catch him.

He told his sergeant what he should do. The Major had looped his arm on to the sergeant's shoulders and squeezed hard with his fingers at the man's neck so that his order would not be ignored. The lieutenant screamed, like a young deer trapped in a snare, and twisted and looked away, frightened to witness it. . . . Or they let him go, allowed him free passage across the line.

The Major reached inside his unbuttoned tunic for the pistol in the shoulder holster, and then felt the vibration. The nuisance wobble of his phone that had been buried far down in his clothing, moving and irritating. He had the pistol and started to aim and was pitched forward as the sergeant braked, stamped on it, as he had been told. Aimed again. A half dozen paces from where the line would be the man rocked in the road.

The Major had a steady arm.

Boot, with a clear view of him, showed no hint of emotion. Might as well have watched a feisty sports competition. He stood forward of the bench, his feet a little apart, and swayed gently on the balls of his feet. His suit, decent tweed, was darkened by the damp on the legs but his overcoat was open and showed the cut of his jacket and waistcoat. The street light above illuminated him. As a seeming afterthought he had straightened his tie in the moment before he had left the bench, and he had the trilby pulled well down over his forehead. His hands in the leather gloves, Gloria's present at Christmas the year before last, were clasped together in front of his stomach.

He'd a good sight of the officer.

The one in front, staggering the last few steps towards the bridge's centre was – Daff's voice in his ear – Kristjan. She might, a sign of her stressed nerves, have then embarked on a biography, salient points and irrelevancies, but he waved her to silence. Not interested ... He reckoned the officer a dozen steps behind the man, aiming.

What was salient in Boot's mind was early experiences with Ollie Compton on the Inner German Border, a happy hunting ground of minefields and wire fencing and famished dogs on running wires and watch-towers with machine-guns mounted, and useful cash bonuses paid by the bankrupt régime of the DDR to border troops who successfully brought down a would-be escaper. Boot had seen it once, a wretch on the wire and left hanging upside down for the rest of the day after being shot, and had heard the detonations of the automatic guns triggered by trip-wires that could dismember a man's body ... Had also seen at the Berlin crossing point the apprehension of an agent who had so nearly reached freedom. The klaxon still sounded at the far check-point. Militiamen were gathered at the barrier. Traffic had stopped. Pedestrians on the walkway had either sprinted for the Estonian end or had turned back and had run towards the Russian side. None stayed to watch, or crouched or lay prone. Boot saw the officer with the raised pistol, and the figure in front of him had now fallen and was on his hands and knees, like a toddler, unable to walk, crawling towards an imaginary line ... Might have already crossed, might have straddled it, might not yet be there. He reached for Daff's binoculars, took them, focused them. Handed them back to her. Allowed her to use them.

Boot murmured, 'Come on, my boy – your eyes are better than mine, Daff, but I think those are major's insignia on his shoulder, an FSB major. Get it done with, Don't piss about now. Shoot. That's the right thing to do, my boy, best foot forward and shoot.'

He did as Boot wanted. Even against the cacophony of the klaxon, the shot was loud, clear in the evening air. One shot only and the back of the head seemed to disintegrate. A good shot, Boot would have said, because he knew it was not easy to fire with accuracy with a hand gun at that range and in a state of tension ... Perhaps he watched an officer who could keep his calm, hold and cosset it.

Daff swore. 'Murderer, cold fucking murderer.'

Not on Boot's reckoning. 'A very much better outcome than being grabbed by the ankle and hauled back into their jurisdiction – much better.'

Daff had her hand on his arm. He remembered her peevish remark earlier, parading her concerns about 'responsibility', that sort of irrelevance, but harboured no ill towards her. A useful result because it was now evident that all of the Estonian recruits – 'pay peanuts and you get monkeys' – were removed from predatory investigators, as good as if they had all escaped. Probably, as the light faded evening, time to go downstream and wait, watch, for Merc. He was about to turn when he noticed that the Major, in front of his jeep, looked up from the level of the bridge where the life had bled from a fugitive, and his eye would have tracked up the height of the centuries-old bastion, and had alighted on him. Eye contact? Nothing as precise at 200 yards, give or take, but the gaze was held. The officer pulled open his tunic, returned his pistol to the holster and then his fingers flicked quickly at another pocket and a phone was taken out. The officer glanced at it, and Boot no longer figured in his attention. The phone was in the Major's face, as if he was reading messages, then he was running. He sprinted to the jeep, slapped his man's back for encouragement, and the young woman, might have been a lieutenant, jumped athletically into the open back seat. The jeep spun, left the body for others to retrieve.

'I think we should be on our way,' Boot said. 'God keep you safe, young fellow – do that, God, there's a good fellow, please.'

Merc saw it. The militiaman had grabbed at his phone when it rang. At last, a response to his many messages.

Silly, small things noticed, and they helped form the mosaic of what would play out. An officer called. The militiaman stiffened his spine and stood tall and barked words that Merc did not understand. He assumed there would be coordinates, the fastest route from whatever was the officer's starting point. Also there would be back-up, a posse of troops called in. He sensed the pride of the man whose rifle watched over him. Merc knew those bumlickers who would only share news when it would benefit them and would scramble to be noticed. Among the contractors there had been enough who only wanted proximity to a diplomat or a chief executive officer. Bigger matters . . . He did not know where she was.

Not where, nor her intention, nor her capability. Could not search for her, peer into the fading light, nor could he lift his head, draw back his ears and strain to hear, and identify where she was – if still on her stomach and close. Time running out on them, like the bloody sand in an hourglass and starting to fall slowly and then gathering pace, tumbling down and unstoppable.

If she were there, he had no way to warn her. The militiaman stared at him. Could not, because of the balaclava, read the mood but the eyes of the man seemed to feast on him, and there was a glance at his wrist as if checking for how much longer he needed to wait. He heard nothing but the wind and surge of the water, and a call from an owl. He steeled himself.

One chance . . .

Kat could not see his face, but was aware of a shadow shape on the ground.

The militiaman waited, restless.

They might have been ice statues.

Men made them from floes taken out of the river running through St Petersburg in winter, did the same with frozen bergs on the Svislach river that split Minsk where he had worked before his transfer. The lights of the Major's jeep lit them. They were two white figures and the snow had layered over their clothing, had settled on their faces and rested on the little hair left exposed. The broken shotgun crooked in the man's arm was like a theatrical prop. Behind them, to the left, was the farmhouse. No fire pushed smoke up from the chimney and no lights were lit inside. He thought they had been there all day, from the time he had left them after what he considered to be mild roughing. They would not have eaten and not have sheltered from the snow or the sleet or the wind. Behind them, to the right was the barn door, opened. The jeep's lights threw shadows inside the barn. A dog was curled beside the door, half in and half out, as if loyalty to the old couple had done a deal with the need for self-preservation: it had a look of sheer misery, its head down between its front paws. He thought the dog cowed by what had happened to the pair of them. The Major understood. They were defeated by betrayal. He would not know, did not need to know, what threat or compulsion had exercised on them by the militia sergeant, but it should have been obvious to him that the fugitives had sheltered here, had been protected by the couple; a natural instinct but stupid. A feeble gesture and one likely to bring down retribution. Inside the barn, the animals were huddled, pigs and sheep and cattle, and their arrival would have disturbed the vigil of the stock as they waited to be fed, but nothing had been brought, and the couple had stood together. Shamed, coated in snow, close, he assumed, to hypothermia. He approached.

The Major said softly, 'You need warmth, you need hot drinks, you need to eat, and your animals have to be looked after . . . Which direction do I go in?'

He waved forward his lieutenant. The couple were similar to his own parents who had eked out an existence in a smallholding to the east of Minsk, and it was likely the lieutenant had grandparents from the country who had experienced hardship, suffering, persecution . . . all the things anyone of age in these parts had endured. He told her to clean the pair of them, then take them inside, light the fire and stoke up the cooker and do the necessary with the feed for the animals in the barn. He saw the distaste at her mouth: she would have been from an élite entry into FSB and might have believed she could break through the ceilings that existed in the organisation, and was not to be used as a housekeeper for old people. Should have been front line, and had witnessed two killings, and was in shock, and . . . The Major told the couple what would be done for them but asked for help. The threat would have been implicit, but it was a request. He could hand down mild torture, could shoot to kill, could speak with gentleness. The old man gestured with his thumb and the head-lights – at the edge of their cone – showed the track and its slit entry into the forest.

He asked, 'Why did you help them? What were they to you?'

It seemed important, used up precious moments. He thought he needed to know.

The old woman said, a cackling voice, and defiant as the lieu-tenant wiped snow from her face, cleared her mouth and cheeks and the bridge of her nose, 'We have no beauty in our lives. We have never known beauty. They were here, in the barn, with our animals, and they loved. And . . . and he is a fighter, and brave. We know what a fighter is, but can only imagine beauty. They showed us. Is that enough?'

He nodded. The lieutenant was ushering them towards the house and the dog slunk on its stomach to join them. His sergeant revved the engine and they bounced away and on to the track and dark closed around the beams of their headlights. It would be that moment of triumph, a vindication, evidence that could not be denied . . . He would not tell his wife about the bridge, nor about the holing of a dinghy, but he would tell her of a couple and their loyalty to a stranger, and their image of beauty. They went towards the river and branches scraped against them and the wheels strug-gled for traction . . . It would be a fine moment for him when he had them, and his pistol had the scent of cordite, and would seem to be smoking. A very fine moment.

The sound, distant, at first confused Merc. Then was clear to him.

A jeep straining in mud or ruts or climbing over exposed roots to go forward, was in a low gear, its engine racing.

No more delay, Merc accepted it. The militiaman was now on his last cigarette and the carton had been tossed towards the reeds, and he still paced and still looked towards the narrow track leading into the forest, but might not yet have heard the approach of the vehicle. Now, or the jump suit and the appearance in court, and the flashing of photographers' bulbs, and the bruises still on his face from the beatings, and . . . It was now. *Now*, Merc would learn what the girl, Kat, could do – if she were there.

He rolled on his back. He kicked out with his legs, haphazard and confused, and seemed to writhe on his spine, and let out low grunts. He did what he could . . . Merc had no comprehension whether or not the act was convincing. The darkness was thick around him and the moon feeble, and the wind gathered force noisily, but he had heard the vehicle. He thrashed with his legs.

The militiaman watched him, had stopped pacing, dragged on the cigarette but had the barrel aimed and the finger, Merc thought, still lodged inside the guard. There were shadows behind him: the trunks of trees, and the ill-defined shape of bushes, and they were a tight clump of birches, and one moved.

Merc saw the outline of a branch or a fencing post raised high, and she was another shadow. It would have been good, then, if he could have talked her through it – the usual shit that fighting men did for each other about 'decisiveness of movement' and the 'thrust of action' which meant that an attack must be forced through, 'body to body' and coming from an 'inexhaustible well of willpower'. And it was instructor language . . . She was Kat, a small-time girl with a dream of protest and perhaps a talent for playing the bloody piano, and she was there. Might be better value to him than any of the guys, Martin and Toomas and Kristjan, that Daff had hired. Might be able to drive a car fast from a major crime scene, might not be able to disable an armed man. The big figure loomed close to him. How would he have done it himself? Two paces forward, at least, and a heavily swung blow landing on the back of the neck where it joined the shoulder. Not a slap, not a tap, but a blow that used every last semblance of strength, all he possessed – except that it was not him, was her.

Merc thought the militiaman had heard the vehicle for the first time, or was aware of the movement behind him. His head had gone high, he seemed to snort at the air, and there was the start of an oath, but the breath and the noise of it were strangled in his throat. The militiaman seemed to buckle, and he staggered and she had the weapon raised again and his arms were outstretched as if his first reaction were to fend off a subsequent blow. One second, or two, not more than three, and she either put him down or he would have the weapon swivelled and aimed and would fire at close range. It was the second blow, less effective, had hurt him but not dropped him. She had lost surprise. Merc moved, went like a snake but on his backside, and kicked out with his feet. He took the man's ankles away from under him. The bulk of the militiaman collapsed across Merc, squeezed the breath from him, and the rifle dropped from his grip. Merc, under him, could not move. He looked up. She stood tall and raised her weapon again. She brought it down, used it with the ferocity of a woodcutter who brought an axe to split rings of firewood. Again and again, blow upon blow. She sobbed as she did it.

The blood of the man on top of him ran on to his face and his neck. Wet and warming, and the voice above him gasped and tried to speak but the words could not escape and were only muffled. Another blow . . . and Merc shouted out. It was 'enough', it was done. She seemed reluctant to stop. A further blow and each time when the impact shuddered through her target it was a shock wave into Merc. He was wriggling, yelling for her to help him . . . and he realised, crystal sharp, what he had done to her.

There was a bayonet on the underside of the rifle barrel. Standard issue. The militiaman was rolled off him and Merc twisted and presented the bound wrists to her. She was rigid, upright, and clutched her weapon and her breath came in great pants . . . He might have made a monster of her. He supposed that an instructor, at that moment, would have slapped her face sharply, right cheek, left cheek, then given an order again. It was about the buying of time, and the vehicle came closer and he heard its engine and the wind and the sounds of the river's progress and heard her staccato breathing, and unless she had the bayonet from its clip the two of them, him and Kat, went nowhere, and fast – other than into the arms of more men, who'd have handcuffs and loaded magazines. It was said among the convoy drivers that they needed luck, but that luck did not come cheap, must be earned. It was luck that he lived, but luck would be snatched back if she did not get the bayonet. She made no move, and he kicked her. His right foot hit her left shin, halfway up and she squealed and he thought that she was about to strike him, hammer him with the weapon, then she dropped it. She was shivering, and slight whimpers had started in her throat, because of what he had brought to her life. He told her to get the bayonet. It came slowly, the retention of discipline. It was dark and her fingers were clumsy on the rifle and he could not help her.

Merc had taught the girl to fight. He had shown her that the reason for fighting was to remove an enemy from the field. Easy for the girls who were in the trenches outside Erbil because theirs was a culture of war and defence against a merciless enemy – not Kat. He thought, as long as she lived, she would harbour the experience of killing a man. It was what he had done . . . he would have wanted no responsibility for the contamination of another. And apart from her, he was part of the plan that had taken the roof off the building in the industrial estate, and he had seen the scale of the explosion and had heard the screaming cries of the ambulances racing to get there . . . She had the bayonet free. He rolled on to his stomach and presented his wrists. She started to saw through the plastic of the restraints. His arms were freed.

She wanted love and opened her arms to him. They knelt, facing each other. Her arms were around his neck and he massaged hard at his own wrists, then pushed her away. He might have destroyed her, might have changed her beyond recognition. He used his sleeve to wipe the militiaman's blood off him, and lost its heat and the sweet cloying scent of it. She refused to free him, and he pushed harder.

'Did I not do well? Was that not what I had to do?'

'Did well, did it good.'

Said without praise. Would not have been different if it had been any of the girls who were in the Fire Force Unit in a Forward Operating Base and had just taken down their first 'bad boy' fighter and left him on the wire. Would not have gone round and handed out Horlicks and boiled sweets and told them they were their God's gift, so precious, to the world of combat survival. He was free, and stood. She scratched his face. She came after him, went for his face, and for his eyes, and he deflected her.

Merc picked up the rifle. No argument in his mind. He had no more use for it. He lifted it by the barrel and swung back his arm. Had never handled a loaded weapon in that way before. He threw it, saw it for a moment against the softer grey of the sky, and close to where the moon came up, lost sight of it, and heard a dull splash.

He had made a promise. It might cost him his life, and might cost her life. He pulled the suit out from under the board. It was there because of vanity. Merc understood . . . The militiaman had wanted to present whatever officer hurried to the scene with the evidence of what he had found, how it was hidden, demonstrate his cleverness, had not dragged the suit clear of the board and punctured it – nor had he damaged the board. Merc was grateful for the conceit. He lifted the suit, tossed it towards her. He told her that without it she was dead, told her to get into it. Merc did not know how, without a suit, he'd survive in the water.

Told her to hurry – heard the vehicle's engine – and lifted up the body of the militiaman, life gone and the blood flow slowing, struggled with it, and waded into the river to where the ground started to shelve steeply, and eased the body off his shoulder. He saw it float, sink a bit, then start to move in the eddy of the backwater towards the reeds, and hopefully would clear them. He watched her fight to get into the suit and heard her cry out in frustration, but did not help her. He looked across, and upstream from where they were, and saw some car headlights on the road.

'About right?'

'As good as anywhere.' Boot stood on the bank and gazed out into the darkness beyond the flow of the river, and saw nothing.

'It's downstream of where he landed, so that's where he will have left his board, and then he'll be pushed farther down when he's launched. I think this is about right.'

'Where we are and where we stay.'

He had no wish to talk . . . upstream from them was a watch-tower and occasional bursts of light came from it, but he thought it nearly a quarter of a mile from them, and the next one, down-stream, was close to a mile away. Voices carried over water deceptively. About the worst thing they could do for the boy, for Merc, was chatter away, do a fish wives' convention, and alert whatever patrols, static or mobile, were deployed on the far side. He was unwilling to snap at Daff, a good girl, that she should shut her mouth, tie a knot in her tongue . . . Ollie Compton would have done. She'd have felt the thick edge of his language for chatter. Stressed people always wanted to talk as if inanities gave comfort. The surveillance team were behind them, on the road, lights doused. She left him, went to them, would gossip and smoke with them. A whistle would bring her if she were needed. He saw the lights, flickering and interrupted.

The vehicle was among the trees and its engine revved and dawdled, then stopped. The headlights speared out – broken in zebra lines by the tree trunks and their branches – but reaching out over the river and would have illuminated the water close to halfway across, and the lights made little diamonds of the crests left by waves breaking with the wind. Always good to see an oppo-nent, Boot thought . . . The Duke had never fought Napoleon before that June day, had never seen him before a telescope view of the Emperor outside Ligny on the eve of Quatre Bras. But had studied him and understood his method of battle. Would have been in similar darkness, with only pinpricks of little fires to guide him, and moving almost alone across the battlefield. Boot usually went out after his supper in the farmhouse to sit in the fields, under a tree or an umbrella, and consider the cost of it . . . One surgeon alone had done more than 300 amputations in the after-math of the battle, all had worked until exhaustion rocked them, then had gone on. That same night women had come out from the nearby villages and with crude pliers taken out the teeth from the young men's gums and they'd be – the proof was in his office by the Thames – used in the best dentures of western Europe and across the Atlantic in Canada. The defeated army, those who had not fled fast enough, would have been hard at work digging pits for the dead. The same pits were later excavated and the bones of the fallen brought back to Hull and sold on for grinding to agricultural fertiliser. Boot liked those stories. He stood and watched the lights that fell far short of him, then saw a man, uniformed, cross close to them. Same build, same sort of uniform. It was always helpful to see an opponent – not meet, but glimpse . . . The following evening, God willing, he would be on that battlefield in the Belgian countryside, with this bloody place and this bloody river, and this bloody matter, all behind him.

A car pulled in behind him. He turned. The lights dazzled him. The interior lights of the surveillance car flashed on. A small saloon car and a boy barely old enough to shave and a girl whose face was screwed up in shock, and they'd have been looking for a quiet spot by the river to do some lusting, around the gear handle, and had blundered across them. A snarled word, some expletives and the surveillance lights were killed, and the intruder backed away, spun his car around and returned to the road, and quiet fell.

Fast as lightning strikes, flashes of memory. The Major remembered.

Papers that had sifted across his desk, or been on his screen, logged in his mind but the detail of them, not considered important at the time, were now clear. An old pen-pusher, a functionary probably employed to count paper clips in whatever building KGB used in the city of Tallin in 'former times'. Left behind. The pension he would have been assured of had gone down the pan, and he needed to work to put bread on his table. Work was menial cleaning in the new ferry terminal . . . And a man had come past him off the overnight boat from Stockholm, and had triggered recall. A veteran professional and therefore inculcated with the need to provide detail. The recall was of a British spy who had been at a conference in the immediate months after the 'collapse', when the fate of the Soviet Union's nuclear arsenal was discussed with the patronising attention of the NATO *apparatchiks*, and there had been a conversation, brief, about the outcome of the battle at Borodino. All listed in the report, and the appearance . . . good detail supplied. The style of hat, the clothing and the coat that matched the stereotype of the English 'gentleman', and the

spectacles, and . . . enough in the report passed on down the train
of bureaucracy, enough in the headlights across the river.

He had seen the brown tweed and the dark outline of the trilby
hat, and the heavy-rimmed spectacles were prominent. Clear
enough across the river's width when the man was lit by a turning
car, full headlights, only for a few seconds. Proof of a sort for what
he believed. And good to have a rival of style and ambition, so
much better than going to war against the gangland thugs, or the
kids who bought paint for daubing slogans. The briefest of sight-
ings and then the car had turned away and darkness cloaked the
far side. He thought they were close to where the man, Pyotr,
would be. The sight of an opponent, across the width of the river,
had deflected his attention.

The focus of it, the attention? His failure to monitor his phone,
buried under layers of clothing, during the heat of a chase. The
failure of the militiaman to explain why eight increasingly impatient messages had been left on his phone, and the ultimate coy
refusal to explain the urgency . . . The man wanted a grand
moment, the pulling back of a curtain, the exposure of either a
body or a prisoner, gold-plated evidence and with the whiff of
smoke . . . The man over the water, the Major reckoned, was an
old soldier of the Cold War, would have known success and failure,
would accept it . . . But the phone in his hand, did not make the
connection. He did not know where the militiaman was, and time
dripped away from him. Sudden annoyance and then anger:
where was the fucking man, and where was his triumph? His
sergeant shouted.

A clear voice, but with a quaver in it, as if shock lodged in his
throat. And the shout came again, greater urgency. His sergeant
was farther along the bank and his shadow marked the extreme
edge of the lights from the jeep. Not the cold from the wind, or the
chill sitting on the water surface, but the moment when it was
apparent to him that the success had been snatched, that failure
was offered.

Obviously a body. Face down. Uniformed. A washed head
wound visible. Its weight, in the current, bent a branch against

which it had lodged, debris from an earlier storm, and caught in the reeds. An unequal struggle, and about to be freed. The Major did not need to see the features. He felt an absence of any sympathy for the militiaman who might have been bludgeoned to death before going into the water, or might have drowned when helpless, incapacitated by injury. Felt very little. There had been a dream moment of marching a prisoner, or dragging him by the ankle down a third floor corridor in the Big House and going to the door of General Onishenko's office suite, and dumping the man there, or even doing it with a body bag and leaving them to unfasten the zip. He had lost the dream moment, accepted it. The branch had bent to breaking point, then sprang back and the body progressed out and into the flow of the current. He saw it for only a few seconds, then lost sight of it.

The Major stood with his sergeant gazing out on to the water, was minded to see how it finished: whether they survived, Yekaterina and the man who tried to take her out.

They were in the flow. He had taken her into the water upstream from where the vehicle lights now lit a strip of the river.

She was on the board, clinging to it, and the wetsuit enveloped her, too large and flapping loosely. She clung, both hands, to the board's sides. He had a strap to hold on to. The strap was attached to the back end of the board and he needed to cling to it with both hands, and propel himself forward by kicking with his feet, sort of paddling, the way dogs did. He had no protection against the cold of the water and his body seemed already frozen and clumsy when he had launched. He had said to her that they needed quiet and would be taken into the light but must not splash or shout. There was no other way, and no other place. He had put her on to the board and she had squealed at him that she could not swim.

Merc had said, a whisper but forceful, 'You go on the board or you turn round and start walking back. There is a man you have battered to death, and he will buy you a little time, but only a little. His body will appear somewhere between here and the sea and will be fished out and his injuries evaluated. On your clothes, now, is his blood. They will have the technical knowledge, bet your life on it, to match the blood, or to do DNA from his home. You turn back and that is what you will face . . . All of the rest of your life in a cage. It is that or you go on the board.'

He did not plead with her, nor promise she would not drown. It was the equivalent of what he would have said to the kids on the Hill, belting their backsides for exposing themselves to a sniper round, or for being too slow on the reloading of the DsHK machine-gun. She had gone down on the board and he had kept a good hold on it and floated it off in the bay and waded after it . . . had twice caught her ankle when she had almost slid off the board, and that was when his feet touched the bottom and before the foothold was lost, and the undertow snatched at him. He had clung to her ankle when she had seemed likely to fall off the board and had dragged her back and snapped at her.

'You do it for yourself, hold on to it. If you lose the board and me, then you drown. It is not a funny place to be, the last moments before drowning. You cling to it or you are gone. It is the only chance you have – believe it.'

The cold of the water had gone from his feet to his knees and into his groin, shrivelling him, and up over his belly and around his chest, numbing him, and he had lost the feeling of every limb, and the river water and its residue of mud was in his mouth and his nose and sloshed in his ears. They were out of the lea of the bank and into the main current, and wind had made waves and they splashed over him. Every few moments he lost sight of what was ahead and had his eyes clamped shut, and his nose and his mouth, as water broke over him. He thought he could guide the general direction of the board, and make slight progress with it. Merc could not have said whether he would have done better had he been alone . . . could have said that the presence of the girl, squirming, terrified – gave him a degree of 'additional determina-tion': what a unit psychiatrist would have called it. Himself, he had no need to articulate, and had kicked into a survival cocoon . . . The boys driving the convoys or going down Route Irish always claimed on the bad days that no guy ever looked at the worst outcome, stayed with 'Something'll turn up, always does', clung on it. She seemed to have a better hold, but the board had begun to shake and pitch. Waves came across it, as if they were on the open sea, and lifted it, let it fall and battered it. Sometimes it seemed inevitable that it would capsize, turn over and throw her off and nearly break his wrists as he tried to hold it stable. And sometimes, more often as they went farther out, he heard little shrieks from her. He thought only of the grip that she had on the board, and how long she could hold it, and for how much longer he could balance the board and kick enough to push it, farther into the river and towards the centre.

They lost the darkness. The lights caught them. No way to lose them. He had to hope that the wind disturbed the waves, made white caps and masked them, gave them cover. Had to hope it. The current would take them out of the lit area and it was a chance they would not be seen, and she screamed.

It was a howl of sheer terror. It was a cry that would carry over the noise of the wind and the breaking crests and the slap of the reeds behind them, and over the noise of a rifle being cocked, the grate of the metal parts. It rang in his ears, and he could not have silenced it, and sometimes they were lifted and sometimes they fell, but her scream stayed constant and might kill them, and he had heard the rifle armed, and he could not go quicker, and knew no place to hide.

20

Merc waited for the shot. It might be single and aimed, and might be the start of a burst of automatic, spraying them.

He could not silence her, nor give comfort. She would be exhausted, near to the simple desire to end the hell of slipping and bouncing on the board, as it was when people – grievously hurt – wanted only the peace to sleep. He saw her brother, gauntly thin, pale face, old acne traces, concave shoulders, and whose clothes hung loose on him, and who was a genius on a keyboard. Who had ended his own life in order to inflict an act of vengeance on those around him. He had no idea what they, those who he mixed with, had done to Nikki, bred his hatred. Merc had understood so little but had given his pledge. Amongst those he fought alongside there was no more powerful motive for going forward than a given promise. It was the bedrock guarantee the drivers and escorts and the mercenaries all believed in. A promise given was a banknote, had purity. They were still held in the light. Merc imagined that a marksman had a needle wavering in a V sight and tracked them, would have had a view of them when they rode a wave and then lost them when they went into the trough, shallow but sufficient to hide them, and her scream was strangled.

It pierced his ears, then gurgled, then there was emptiness and silence.

He had hold of her ankle. His grip was above the level of her boot and below the sealing join of the wetsuit, and when the boot came off and his grip slackened, Merc thought the river would take her. All other thoughts were obliterated, only the concentration of keeping a hold on any part of her foot and lower leg. Right down to the toes as the board heaved and bucked her and he felt her go sideways and away from it. One hand clamped on the holding strap and one squeezing the life from her toes and looking for a grip, and then seeing her face as it emerged from the water, lit by the vehicle on the shore, and seeing only the fear and the gaping mouth that took in water and knowing that she, who had been the fighter and who was now a killer, had thrown in the towel.

He waited for the first shot.

It was likely, Merc reckoned, that it would cause her to struggle and he would lose her. He held her toes, might have been hard enough to break her bones, and he trod water and the board was on its side and wrenched on his fist, and he thought she'd scream again . . . A monstrous wave hit them. She was spluttering and choking, and her arms cartwheeled and there would have been air inside the suit, giving her buoyancy. Merc pressed the board down, used his stomach to do it and was contorted because he must hold the strap, never let go of it. He pulled her back. When part of her body was on the board he took the chance and loosened his grip on her ankle, and she would have convulsed in the moments between him freeing her and then having a hold of her again, close to the waist. She slipped again, her grip failing – almost – then retrieved it. An arm on each side and a leg hanging loose on each side and his fist held the strap and held a leg below the knee, and they went out of the cone of light.

There were moments when they rose that he saw the moving vehicles on the road at the edge of his horizon. A terrible loneliness gripped Merc. No searchlights from the far side played over the water and looked for him. None to locate him, guide him home, be his angel escort; were no navigation lights from small craft, with the throb of outboards, coming out from the shore to corral and then lift him from the water. No flares fired so that he could see how close he was and how much farther he needed to go. She was quiet.

He wondered if she were quiet because she had lost consciousness and only luck and her body weight kept her astride the board. Maybe, later, he would start to sing – not yet. She might have lost consciousness and he might drift to sleep and be held to the board by the strap looped over his wrist. The determination, what he had believed in, part of the religious core to the life of Merc, began to desert him.

He no longer felt the cold and the water no longer chilled his body. He struggled to see her face. He tried to keep kicking and drive the board across the current towards that far shore where the road was and the traffic, and sometimes he heard the thud of a deep bass beat and music from a car radio. A bus went along the road and headed away from Narva and nobody came off at the stop. There were no fishermen's hurricane lamps, and no craft on the river, not even the guys who ferried over cheap vodka and cigarettes and perhaps a decent supply of fresh heroin that transited Russia from the Caucuses . . . Delirious? Not quite but would be soon – and her, unable and unwilling to survive? Perhaps not yet, perhaps soon. A larger wave came, a rogue.

Merc was lifted and seemed to get a better view of the moon and – almost – could detect its contours, and looked around, in front of him and behind him, and realised that the vehicle's headlights were switched off and nothing showed ahead. He could not kick, wanted to but could not, nor could the girl. The current took them and they drifted and he couldn't say if either had the strength to hold on, and he waited for the shots to be fired.

He might have ordered the sergeant to do it. The Major might have demanded it. Or might have held out his hand and snapped the instruction, been given the rifle, then have cocked it, moved a bullet to the breach. He'd have had the rifle snug at his shoulder and made a line with the sights, and waited for the moon to come to a gap between scudding clouds. He would have been able to shoot, would have backed himself for a hit, perhaps by a deflection off the water, but when they rose high on a wave then he would have seen sufficient of them for clear aim, and he would also have backed the sergeant to have had hits, with a burst or with single shots. But the order was not given.

The sergeant stood half a pace behind him, had been there since switching off the headlights. No reason to keep them on

when the fugitives were beyond the reach of the headlights unless
the jeep was manoeuvred. The sergeant had the rifle and leaned it
against his shoulder, as a hunter would when expecting game to
be flushed through by dogs and beaters. The Major was not as
qualified a marksman as his father who had hunted all his life and
who excelled at a killing shot that despatched boar or deer; had
even shot, at long range, a bear that ravished a neighbour's honey
hives. It was the girl that he saw most often, on top of the board,
and he thought of those kids who rode waves off the west of
America or Australia that he had seen on the television. He saw
her most often, and had heard her.

A defining moment in his life had reached him, and he thought
he recognised its significance. Along the corridor where he worked
in the Big House, he could have rapped on any door, given a brief
history of where he was and why, asked whether he should shoot.
He'd have been half deafened in response. 'Why not? Of course.
Nail the bastard and drop the bitch. Shoot.' He kept his own counsel.
He might have used the phone, had the number loaded in it, of
General Onishenko. Would have done a brief résumé, would have
requested guidance, would have been told to shoot to kill if capture
were not possible. He did not make the call, and did not ask for
advice from his sergeant . . . had needed neither authorisation nor
that advice when he had fired on a fugitive on the bridge or when
the dinghy had been holed and a man abandoned to drowning.

And, each time they were lifted – still not at a halfway point in
his estimation – he saw the head, pale against the darkness of the
water, of little Yekaterina. Could picture her across the table from
him, having taken no care of her appearance and fit only for fast
sex with the Leader of their small, misfit group. She would have
walked down a street and not been spared a glance, would have
entered a crowded room and not turned a head, and he thought
her defiance was something to be treasured. What made her
different? He saw so many of them. He could write, without
opening an individual file, a biography of each of them shep-
herded into the interrogation room . . . those who revelled in
impertinence which they mistook for intellect, and those who

parroted slogans learned in their seminars; those who gloried in the freedom to smoke the stuff that was available or popped the pills that lifted their conceit. The Major would have said, of Yekaterina, that she possessed a degree of pure naivety that had a charm, and it made her contrariness, obstinacy interesting to him. He did not want to sleep with her, even less did he wish to debate with her, did not regard her as particularly interesting nor as a target worthy of his attention . . . It was the simplicity that appealed. A refusal to compromise, turn a cheek, had put her here.

He would not shoot. If she went into the water, she would not survive . . . He doubted it had been the intention of the veteran on the far bank, splendid in his tweed suit and trilby hat and overcoat, to have her delivered into his lap. He supposed it a trade-off. The phone he had not looked at carried a stack of witness statements given after the explosion. He knew of the jealousies and hatreds of young Nikki and of the ones who went in near anonymity by the names of Gorilla and HookNose and the Roofer . . . all so clear to him. But he had no evidence and his General would not wish to hear him out if he did not bring the bomb's courier to heel.

And he would not ask for the rifle. He was a man renowned for his diligence, and thought that his dedication had become boring . . . His career would end, here on the banks of a dirty, deep, dark river. But he would see it played out, as if he owed it her. She no longer shrieked, but the man with her shouted and sometimes sang.

Half of the way: might have been.

His feet flapped but had no feeling.

It was a waste of breath to call out but a sort of deliriousness gripped him. The conversation, not with her but with himself, at the full croaked pitch of his voice, was about – at first – Mercedes cars. He went through the models, and the performance histories, and what the prices should be, and then he could drift towards the manager of the bank in Stoke Poges and what sum of money could be withdrawn in twenty four hours, and how the showroom would be paid, if the Mercedes were purchased. Not concerned

with who heard him or whether the darkness held an audience. He
yelled about the joy of polishing the wax on the bodywork, of
loading the liquids for windscreen cleaning, and buffing the
leather work – of course, leather. He did not think they had been
fired at, but might have missed the impact of gunfire with the
wind on the water and the splash of waves breaking around them,
and the noise of his own voice. She did not contribute, nor was
she in the passenger seat of the Mercedes coupé, it was not her
hair that flowed in the slipstream behind her and around the head-
rest. And he yelled directions as if to a driver, as to what turning
they should take if they were to use the lanes linking Flackwell and
Burnham and Hedgerley and Middle Green, and what pubs there
were on the way . . . Then the hallucination caught him. He saw
the vehicle parked, outside a small house on a small estate, and the
front door was open. Inside, a young man in a grey suit shook his
hand and gave him a set of keys and smirked and his view was the
same as when the Special Forces boys put a small drone inside a
building and did the virtual tour: there was nothing inside that he
knew, and the rooms were empty and the walls bare, nobody there
whom he knew and nothing that was familiar . . . He was running
away and through the hall and into a patch of a front garden and
throwing the set of keys at the young man, and sprinting past the
Mercedes car, and running and running and was nowhere that he
knew.

He was at the edge, or beyond it, of survival, and his voice had
almost died. Might have reached the halfway point and might
have crossed it, and might still be short of it. The Mercedes was a
broken dream, and so was the cottage that he had promised
himself he would reach out for and buy 'sometime'. He tried to
kick harder.

And remembered her, and called to her, and was not answered.
Merc clung to Kat's leg and tried to bury his numbed fingers on
the wetsuit surface – and again found his voice, sang. From his
childhood, hymns and scout songs. From the cub camps his father
had taken him to, and the hymns from a chapel near his grandmother's home, and some had been heard at his father's funeral,

and some were from the Sunday morning services that the new proxy parents insisted he attend . . . and there were more hymns from the brief and self-conscious gatherings of the contractors when one of the guys, dosed up on steroid pills, and with a load of cannabis in him, had not played sensible on Route Irish or the convoy runs out of Kabul and been zapped. They could get a padre out and do something in a secure lorry park, and then get the bag, often not a proper coffin, taken by helicopter to the airport, but after growling and tuneless voices had done a hymn . . . The best was 'I vow to thee my country all earthly things above' and it would end up, flat as tarmacadam with ' . . . and her ways are ways of gentleness and all her paths are peace' which was bloody rubbish because the guys there were draped in weapons, might kill that night or kill the next day. He sang that and he sang others. And felt so tired. And wanted to sleep. And needed to close his eyes and cuddle and be warm.

A voice yelled at him, her voice. 'Don't you give up on me. You shout rubbish, you sing worse than a sick cat. You should keep strong. We can do this, can get there. You and me, as it is meant to be. Your future, and mine, is there . . . There is a road behind the shore. There are cars on the road. I saw the road from headlights, they showed a tank beside the road, an old Soviet one, it is where we are on course for. While you talk like an idiot, sing nonsense, I am steering us. I direct us. The tank is my target. It is a Soviet tank, I recognise it . . . Our future, our lives together, is about reaching the tank. You've done so much, come so far. For our love, keep strong. Please, for the future and for love.'

He tried to kick. Had heard her, each word. Tried to kick and could not.

'Do we have this sort of kit available?'

Back from the surveillance car, Daff showed off the new toy she'd been loaned. She passed Boot a pair of binoculars, bulky and heavy and with image intensifier capability. He did not answer, thought petulance was bred by extreme tiredness, excessive stress.

She said, 'They have good kit and are good people, and they seem interested in taking good care of us – but within limits.'

'Have they, are they, do they – and the limits?'

'There are no patrol boats so they will not be picked up out in the river, no collusion can be shown. That I suppose is good. Given no help and . . .'

A soft-spoken query. 'They . . . You said *they*, and intentionally?'

'It is Merc, and he is in the water. On the board and in Merc's suit is a young woman. I seem to remember, we said passengers were not an option, inked it pretty hard. The glasses showed her clearly. She came up on a wave. It is a young woman.'

'We did, insisted and emphasised.'

'Which puts his own safety in jeopardy.'

'Indeed it does.'

'God knows who she is. If she hazards Merc I'll bloody strangle her.'

He detected the emotion, her feeling of proprietary rights over any late-comers who might be floating down some awful torrent river on the fringes of Europe. Ridiculous, went without needing to be said, because if Merc were hazarded and seriously, like a case of drowning, any bit of a girl would go with him, and Daff would need to strip to a bikini and go into the water and fish her out before getting those powerful hands round the necessary windpipe. Emotion, and he could thank the blessed Lord that he was seldom troubled with it. He thought he had seen the second head when the board had crossed the cone of light thrown out by the vehicle's headlights on the far side, but he had said nothing. He reckoned that too few of the younger generation of recruits coming into the Service had learned the glories of silence. He remembered the callow youth in the hotel room and brief talk of a family that consisted only of a sister who wanted to be a concert pianist and of course had the talent but . . . A shrug had been given as a reason why a career was off the tracks. He imagined the barter done on the hoof. Taking the bomb into the building, staying there and not running out, being certain that it detonated with maximum efficiency. He knew that Nikki, manipulated like a marionette puppet in a Stockholm hotel room, some carrot and an amount of stick, had not survived. Had he lived, then the radios the Estonians monitored would have broadcast Wanted warnings and named him. Like a street-market trade, and the sister balanced the scales . . . And his mind moved on and he began to consider ways in which 'disinformation' could be scattered round, grains to fall on fertile soil.

She had not finished. 'Boot, what I don't understand . . .'

'What do you not understand?'

'This, Boot . . . There was an officer at the bridge, and he fired. He prevented an escape from their territory. Earlier, a dinghy was holed, and one of the other boys drowned. Before that, the third of them was killed in the forest. Hardly squeamish . . . We think that same officer is across there, and they had the chance. Could have shot. Had them in the headlights. Could have, did not. Boot, why?'

He did not think she would have understood. He was a public servant. He lived with his wife in a semi-detached house in a conventional street, and shared train carriages and buses with 'ordinary' people when he went to and from work, and his wife was knowledgeable in antiques and his expertise was in the safety of the realm and its citizens. He did his best and pushed legal matters to their limits and sometimes strayed well beyond, and did the Almighty well when called to act that role. If the men and women who followed his instructions died or were mentally destroyed then he could always fall back on the hackneyed line that all good outcomes carry a cost. There would be a time, might be close, when he decided that enough was enough, that the price of it was just too bloody extortionate – that the burden of the state should be borne by someone else, hunger satiated. And just a few days ago it had seemed run of the mill, and quite interesting, a matter with promise. His man was out on a swollen river, and half frozen to death, and with a young woman with whom he had no obligation nor argument. He mouthed, silently, what the great Duke had said on that evening after riding the length of the battle-field, Copenhagen stepping over the dead and the wounded and the shattered equipment of war. Said to himself, not to Daff, 'It has been a damned serious business'. A good turn of phrase, and appropriate. *It has been a damned serious business … it has been a damned nice thing, the nearest run thing you ever saw in your life.* And Boot thought he had run his time. Thought also, that an officer on the far side of the river, probably middle-aged, a careerist, had grown equally weary of interrogation rooms and dawn raids and the sight of quivering broken idiots opposite him, and had not bothered to shoot. Might just have experienced tedium, lost the stomach for it after his afternoon's hard work.

Boot said, 'Why he didn't shoot? I've not the faintest idea.'

Merc no longer sang the old chapel hymns, and had lost sight of a Mercedes car, and it was the water of the Narva river in his mouth and throat, not the taste of English beer, and the sound of waves in his ears, not conversation or laughter.

He had been about to drift. She would only have known if she had twisted her whole body, risked coming off the board and slithered half round on her stomach and had little grip in the suit. If she had not done that, she would not have known that the drift had begun. She had kicked him. Hard in the face and might have bent his nose and had cut his lip. That sort of kick. He had not the energy to wring her leg or pinch it, nor to bang it down on the board. He took the kick, and thought she yelled at him, but he could not make out her words. It would have taken more than a kick to provoke him. She had to go back to her former position, arms either side, legs apart and trailing. He had one hand on the strap and one hand on her leg and his nose hurt but it seemed a small matter.

Merc saw lights away to his left and they were confused and went by him and it was beyond him to figure their importance. They grew closer, but it meant little to him. He heard a shout, a woman's abuse, and did not place it. Merc slept.

Did not dream and saw no one that he knew. He went to no place that he had been to before. Was not on the Oxford Road and not in the lanes around Stoke Poges, and was not on Route Irish or the highway between Kabul and Jalalabad, and was not under the walls of the citadel in Erbil, and he had no sense of time. Nor any sense of discomfort. Water came over him and he swallowed some of it and coughed it clear. More shouting but he did not recognise the voices. A little moonlight shafted down, a prettiness to it. And he was grabbed. Fists clutched at him and he woke, and did not know who held him, where he was, and he fought them, and he was punched in the face, and quietened.

He heard, 'Steady down, Merc. It's all right, it's good. You made it, bloody brilliant, star boy, what we always knew . . .'

'. . . God, it's bloody cold in here.' Daff hung on to him.

She had a hold of Merc's collar and then worked an arm under his elbow and had better leverage. She was up to her waist and the bank was shelving steeply, and he had gone limp after that first thrashing of arms and legs, and the attempt to break free. There was no light on them. She understood that the surveillance guys behind would not draw attention to their presence, nor intervene. Low key, which was the way of most things that the Service did. Under-resourced and under-staffed, which was the reason that she was in the water and bloody near to being swept off her feet, and why only Boot was with her – and why they had brought the freelancer, Merc, to do a job with a gang of local misfits. It was where they were, unlikely to change. She was shouldered aside . . . had just realised that Merc's hand was locked on the girl's leg and had seen her face as the moon passed a cloud gap, recognising a mix of triumph and shock, of elation and exhaustion . . . and real-ised that Boot had come into the water and was beside her, and had forced her to back away from Merc and now supported him. Boot had waded into the water which broke in wavelets above his knees, and the suit was his pride and joy, and he was inseparable from those brogues, and for once his trilby was tilted.

Daff accepted, took the girl. No kid gloves as Daff handled her. She accepted that the girl had the waterproof gear and had been on the board, and Merc had been in the water and had supported her, and Daff reckoned the girl had damn near killed him. She pulled the girl ashore, dumped her, and was turning to go back in and take her turn with Merc. Boot struggled under his weight. She was turning when the girl reached up and clawed at Daff's sleeve, and coughed hard, spat water, then found her voice.

'It is because of me that we are here, him and me. He was their prisoner. I killed his guard. I did . . . I would have given my life for him, because we are together, will be, always together, him and me.'

Boot splashed up the bank, sodden shoes spitting sand, and let Merc subside. He said to Daff, crisp and authoritative. 'I doubt violins will play, and diamonds sparkle. What we said, Do it. Get him out and away.'

She did. Left Boot behind her and doubted he'd be sympathetic to a kid who might have defected with high hopes of the future or might have simply been swept up in the tide of events swirling around her. Daff thought Boot's conversation skills would be a rude awakening. She hooked Merc up, had one of his arms over her shoulder and hissed for him to make a last effort and they went up the slope and were close to the tank on its plinth. They were passing the surveillance car and a window came down and a half bottle was hold out. She took it, poured a slug down Merc's throat, and one for herself, and handed it back. She saw the boys inside look at her, like she was an entrant in a wet T-shirt competition, gave them a finger and a grin, and lugged him to the car.

He could of course refuse what she and Boot had planned as the aftermath – assuming he made it out, *if* he came through – but she did not expect him to. Into the passenger seat, doors slammed, engine engaged, a spinning turn and the tyres kicked mud and the last of the snow, and ice crystals were lit ahead of them. The head-lights gave a final glimpse of the churning river, showing no sign of interest in them as it powered towards the Baltic, and she hit the road.

'You all right, Merc?'

'What else? I'm all right.'

The Major had waited.

He saw the first car pull away and, as it turned, it lit the old man, the one who wore the tweed suit and whose glasses were askew and his hat about to topple and who dragged the girl up the beach and towards the silhouette of the raised tank on its plinth. He had been correct in his analysis of the cause of the explosion, and did not have evidence to support his argument. His sergeant did not intervene, stayed correctly silent. The Major would face no Inquiry Board, would not have to justify his actions: it would be reported that a gang of smugglers, probably trafficking in Class A or amphetamines, had been pursued towards the Friendship Bridge, and one had shot himself in the forest as the hunters closed on him, and one had stolen a small dinghy which had capsized upstream from the bridge, and one had attempted to run across the bridge and had been shot after repeatedly refusing to surrender . . . And a missing girl, the sister of one of those killed in the Kupchino district explosion? He knew nothing of her, had no knowledge of her since releasing her from custody in the Big House. Nor could the Major have justified, with coherence, what he had done and why. He would remember her face.

Walking back from the river bank to the vehicle, the Major told his sergeant that they would return to the farmhouse, collect the lieutenant, would pay them generously, and get coffee or sweet tea, or a bowl of broth to warm them . . . He had forgotten a body in the water, would not retrieve it in his memory. He could not have explained himself, and did not wish to.

In the morning, after a few hours' deep sleep, he would be back at his desk.

Dawn broke, a fair start to a new day with a bright chill in the air as the streets and bridges over the Thames awoke to the bustle of a fresh commuter rush.

The bed folded and stowed, and the duvet tightly rolled and consigned to a cupboard, the Maid had been out into the corridor and had borrowed a carpet cleaner from the early shift and had tidied her own, and Daff's, area, and had run the machine purposefully across Boot's room. She had telephoned upstairs, to the quarters of the Big Boss, and given a cursory résumé and had heard a heaved sigh of relief. She had called a number in the

Pimlico district north of the river where a small department handled 'safe houses', the accommodation bureau for defectors, and employed discreet minders. 'I gather she's just a bit of a girl who was slip-streamed into an exfiltration from Russia. Arrival time? Mid-morning, I think. Has very little importance except for what she witnessed in the last forty-eight hours, just needs a little husbandry . . . Oh, yes – if a piano was available that would be good. Thanks, more later.' The Maid was a woman who could put her hand on any small item that might – one day, sometime – be of use. At the back of a drawer in her desk, after some rummaging, she put her finger on a picture hook and nail.

It was a print, sadly, not an original. But good enough and what was possible. Inside Boot's room she looked for a decent sighting and fastened on a stretch of bare wall to the left of the reproduction of the Wellington Boot. She unwrapped the frame, binned the protective packaging, estimated the right height then slipped off a shoe and used its heel as a hammer to bang in the nail, and hung it. The mission, seemingly completed with success, had been Copenhagen, Boot's name for it. The image was of Copenhagen, the horse that had carried the Duke throughout the day at Waterloo, 'steady and calm' under fire, and which had been buried – 182 years ago – under a large tree on his estate. It was a bronze fashioned from a death-mask and located in the quad area of the school bearing the victor's name. A proud head, some said, with irresistible traits of stubborn superiority. She dusted the glass, admired it, and thought it fitting . . . Much to chat about with her parrot that evening.

She had the cars booked, Daff coming in first, and Boot later and he was bringing the girl . . . A triumph. Of course. She would have expected nothing less.

It was Arthur who spotted her first.

'Look here, Roy, look at her, see what she's carrying.'

'Arthur, no lie, they cracked it.'

'Must have been a big one, and those are a decent pair – of bottles.'

Both could chuckle without moving their mouths. They saw the blonde pay off her taxi, pause for a moment and look up at the great building which was her second – or first – home. She carried two bottles in a transparent plastic airport bag. Might have picked them up wherever she'd boarded the first flight of the day. Both Roy and Arthur, staple to their trade as marksmen, had decent vision, could see the bottles wore the Bollinger label.

'I'd wager, Roy, we're the first to know that a good one has done the business.'

'Like the old days, turning back the clock.'

Not that either of them spoke to her as she came to the checkpoint, and as she juggled with her backpack sliding on one shoulder. And had the bottles' bag in one hand, and needed to ferret in her shoulder-bag for the ID card, and a wintry smile, not returned by either of them, and both were trained for observation of detail. She was gone, a haughty swing of the hips which might have been for them and might not.

'You see her legs, Roy, her feet?'

'What I saw, Arthur, was that they were still soaking wet, and the jeans were all damp right up to you know where. She'll have come through on the red-eye flight from some place where she had to do some paddling. You think it was rough, where she was?'

'And she smelled, like it was ditch-water, horrid and stale . . . Walked across a river? Don't know . . . Main thing, it all went well, or there'd not be bottles for breaking open.'

'Spot on, went well. No argument.'

The stool supported Boot.

The darkness was around him and the nearest lights were through the trees circling the Hougoumont farm down the winding track, and then more were across the shallow valley and up by the buildings of La Belle Alliance where Napoleon himself had been during the battle, now a night-club and noisy. But close to him was the quiet and the peace and the misery that followed combat. That night, when one army had fled the field and another was in pursuit, only the dead and wounded 50,000, estimated, would have been among the crushed maize fields, but coming towards them would have been village women with bags in which to drop booty, and some military wives would have been out and abroad with hurricane lamps to search for their men . . . There was light rain, not incessant but he had his umbrella opened.

He had been home, taken there by the car that the office had organised.

'Hello, go all right?' His wife had greeted him.

'Went all right, yes, all things considered.'

'Don't mind me saying it, but you look a bit of a mess.'

'Suppose I do . . . took a bit of a soaking.'

'Just off to open the shop. If you get out of those things, I'll drop them off at the cleaners.'

'That would be grand, thank you.'

He had stood in the hall and had taken off his coat and his suit jacket and waistcoat, and she had emptied the pockets, and then he had dropped his trousers and underwear, and peeled off the sodden socks and the Narva's water was still in his shoes. Gloria would not quiz him, but stuffed yesterday's newspaper in the shoes and bundled the suit into a plastic bag. Did he want some breakfast? No, was going to VBX. And then? Well, he had rather missed the battlefield, but he'd be home the next evening. She'd gone to work, via the dry cleaner, and he had put on fresh clothing and dry shoes, and had hurried out, locked the door behind him, gone briskly to the waiting car. A pretty average English morning, not too cold, a damn sight warmer than beside that wretched and unforgiving river.

There was traffic on the main road that ran north to Brussels. He loved to be there . . . Some in the office tittered behind their hands at his obsession with the history of this place. He thought he benefited as a protagonist in the intelligence war from what he saw and learned – probably from the stoicism of the fighting man, his nobility. Sometimes he imagined he heard the voices of commanders, and more often and after the darkness had come, he heard the soft cries of the injured. He thought it a good place to be.

The car had dropped him at the building's entrance and he would have sworn that the armed men at the gate had given him 'the eye', as if they had known something. He had nodded curtly to them and might have heard a faint growl of congratulation. A very satisfactory picture was on the wall of his office, and he had kissed the Maid's cheeks in gratitude, and Daff was already there still damp from a shower, fresh clothes, and a half of the first bottle already lowered between the women, and the Big Boss had come in, and the second bottle had been started.

'It was first class, Boot, and I think it worked really rather well.' The Big Boss had raised a glass to him.

'He's a good man that we sent, and I venture that I'd use him again. No hostage to fortune left behind to face interrogation. Sad about the local increments, but they played a part. I never met them ... What we do now is drop a few words to selected bloggers. One in Lisbon and one in Chennai, and there's a useful outlet in Vientiane, and we feed reports of gang warfare among the hacker groups, jealousies, corruption inside FSB. It's the virus we can shift into their system and it should lead to an uncertainty among their prime players, a slow-down in offensive operations. Not easy to quantify, but as a strike back it will have been effective.'

'At what sort of cost? Their side?'

'Hard to estimate, inexact areas. We took down some leading Black Hats, can't say for sure how many. Had a good bang for the buck. I don't have a figure for their wastage. But, enough, and I very much believe we'll see vacancies in their recruitment prospects.'

'Cost to us? How do we come out of it?'

'Well, I think ... the increments were the only downside. Financially, it was excellent value. The explosive we use does not come cheap, but everything else was well within budget ... I believe they'll squirm ... Look, we wanted to send a message, indirect and obtuse, and we did. There was an opportunity, it was taken advantage of.'

'And the man we sent, where does he put his feet up?'

'Where he's comfortable . . .'

'I'd like to have met him, Boot . . . Why didn't you bring him up?'

'He wanted to move on. The way he is, has his own agenda.' Boot had done his little smile, and the conversation was closed. They finished the bottle, but even the good stuff could not, quite, get the taste of the river out of his mouth. He'd gone, a little wave at the door to the Maid and Daff, had hurried away.

At the farmhouse they would have left a plate of cold meats and a salad for him, and a beer, and he'd stay longer on the stool and listen to the patter of rain falling on the umbrella. He wondered how many of the men who had come through the day on the fields around him, ploughed and muddy, would have said to themselves, in the privacy of their thoughts, that enough was enough, time was called. Perhaps the majority, but a few would not have escaped from the addiction, the narcotic, of it . . . He remembered as he had told it to Daff, of a child who would not come in through the open window of the nursery . . . Thank God for it, because when there was business about, *damned serious business* in the Duke's words, there was always need of such men.

The cross-winds at Erbil International were fierce, and Merc was jolted hard in his seat when the flight out of Istanbul touched down. He barely noticed the juddering landing and his hands were loose on the arm rest.

Had planned it. Merc knew what he would say. Not a good man with words and he had worked on the few that he reckoned would be necessary, and had included two short sentences in her language, had tried them out – with shyness – to an elderly woman in the adjacent seat and she had chirruped in laughter and then had squeezed his hand, had congratulated him. There was sunshine and the apron glistened with its warmth after overnight rain. He felt as if he had come home, was where he wanted to be . . .

Daff had driven him to an apartment near to the big church in Narva, had chucked clean clothing at him, had allowed him the luxury of a shower in tepid water, had knelt beside him and had massaged – fierce, strong hands – over his legs and stomach, then his chest and arms, had worked hard enough at it to warm his body, had let him dress, then had pushed him towards the car. 'Was the girl anything special, Merc?' He'd shaken his head, then had said, 'The device worked because the kid stayed with it. Where I work that's called martyrdom. I said I'd take her out. It was the deal. Go carefully with her, please.' Daff had shrugged. 'Carefully, yes.' A flight into Frankfurt from Tallinn, another down to Istanbul, and now the last leg into Erbil International. He remembered her, that damned haughty, obstinate face and had expensive chocolates from the German duty free that might soften it, and said again the two sentences in her language, and grinned, and felt like a kid, and grinned some more. He came off the aircraft.

Merc had a spring in his step.

They were inside the terminal, before he had cleared anything. He nodded. Two impassive faces. He hugged Brad first, then Rob. There was a local behind them and the guy led them away. Never did get to show his passport and never did get to declare his chocolates to the Customs people. They walked out into the sunlight, crisp shirt-sleeve weather, and when they reached the jeep, Rob dropped his hands into his backpack and retrieved a Glock in a holster and a couple of magazines.

Merc put the holster on, a shoulder job, and felt a bit naked because they were in uniform and he was in the civilians that Daff had given him. Brad drove, and Rob had an Armalite across his lap, and Merc was in the back and the wind blustered him. Rob asked him if it had been 'good', and Merc said it had been 'all right'. Then Rob asked him if he'd achieved what he went away for, and Merc said that the people in charge seemed content.

'Anything fruity?' Rob asked him.

'Nothing as you'd have noticed,' Merc answered.

Brad turned, eyes off the road and punched his arm lightly, and there should have been happiness there, a mucker come back home but there was cold in his eyes, and that might have been when Merc knew.

And knew more when they came to one of the roundabouts on the way towards the city, and it was about which turning they took and which side of the citadel they'd be going. It was bad traffic and the usual mixture of horns and shouting, and the stall-holders going at full volume, and a bit more of the confirmation came when they drove by a flower stall, one that had a sea of buckets of big bright blooms and they had not slowed and he hadn't requested they stop. Merc scratched his head.

Didn't feel like saying anything and let them drive, and the silence had sunk over them as if talk was inappropriate.

It was a big cemetery. There was a sector, over on the west side, that was reserved for casualties from the defence forces. They took that way.

Out of the jeep and they all walked, and Merc brought his box of Swiss chocolates. The first part of the sector had stones set above flat graves. Farther on there were wooden posts and the earth mounds had sunk. Merc kept on walking. It was at the end of the line in the farthest row and they had not yet got round to putting a post in at the head, and the earth was fresh and recently turned and still high because it had not yet had time to settle. Rob and Brad dropped back.

He went on walking and the tiredness seemed to gather again, and the pleasures of his return were draining, and he saw the lively colour of the flowers. They were what he had asked for, what Daff would have sent, and he imagined that Brad and Rob might just have taken a day off soldiering, fighting the war, to scour the florists of Erbil for a bunch of chrysanthemums that had the 'merlot' colour. He thought she might have died two days ago or three, and thought she might have been buried yesterday or the day before. Where might he have been, when she'd died in the hospital, presumably rampant infection and sepsis? Might have been in a car-park, waiting for a roof to lift off and a young man to kill himself which would serve the government that paid into Merc's account in Stoke Poges, and she might have been buried as he had settled down on the hay and fodder in a barn with a girl clinging to him and both fumbling at their clothing. Merc could not remember when the drivers and escorts riding shotgun duty on Route Irish or the Jalalabad highway had done a good and reverential send-off for a friend. Useless at hymns and useless at prayers, but sometimes – not often – wet faces. He remembered her, and the shape of her, and the spirit of her glowering face, and her ability to change a belt for a DsHK .50 calibre, and remembered how he had cursed her for exposing herself at the parapet. He crouched down and laid the chocolate box, coated in cellophane, in front of the flowers, paused there, felt the stiffness in his joints, said something but was not sure what, then stood, paused again, turned, and walked. He reached the boys.

A query in the glance Brad gave him and Merc said where he'd like to be taken.

He thought they had an idea of the schedule back at the barracks. A new section had been put together in the Fire Force Unit, and they had left for the Forward Operating Base around a quarter of an hour earlier. Nothing said, nothing needing to be said. At the armoury Merc drew weapons, grenades, medical stuff, and a protective vest, and a uniform . . . Might have been the same as he had handed in just a week earlier that would have been put aside for him by the quartermaster.

They went fast out of the city and swung to the west and the desert opened up, and he could hear the distant sounds of war, artillery and mortar explosions, and a long way off was an airstrike with high smoke plumes and the rumble of fast jets. He knew the road well, and welcomed the thought of a return to Hill 425, and might have said to a friend – if he could have named one – that it was the best home he had. Brad said that the sector had been quiet. Rob said that the opposition were thought to have regrouped and would be back and hitting. They waved to him, drove off, went with a spit of dirt. The section seemed to be waiting for him, were parked up in a forward revetment and it was as far as vehicles went.

Merc saw their faces. Maybe they had not been told he was coming, perhaps it had not been certain that he would return to fight with them. They were all new, none of them had been brought back by him after holding the position. Huge smiles and a resurgence of confidence and a glow in the eyes as if he offered inspiration. Eight guys and four girls and all young and all raw and all exchanging nerves for courage because he would be with them. He could have said, 'Steady, friends, I am nothing special, and all I can offer you is a bit of organisation and basic discipline, and you will have my best effort, only that.' He said nothing. They lined up. He inspected the kit, made some modifications, gave them all a cuff on the shoulders – the guys and the girls. Their trust would be the burden he carried.

He led them up the communications trench, towards the flag that flew over Hill 425, where he knew and reckoned he belonged.